D1488362

NIGHT CHILL

A NOVEL

By

Jeff Gunhus

SEVEN GUNS PRESS

Printed in the United States of America

Cover design by Eric Gunhus
Edited by Sheryl Hart

Library of Congress Cataloging-in-Publication Data
Gunhus, Jeff
Night Chill / Jeff Gunhus
ISBN-13: 978-0615828381
ISBN-10: 0615828388

ALSO BY JEFF GUNHUS

ADULT FICTION

Night Chill

YA FICTION

Jack Templar Monster Hunter
Jack Templar and the Monster Hunter Academy
Jack Templar and the Lord of the Vampires

NON-FICTION

Wake Up Call
Choose The Right Career
The Little Book Of Secrets
No Parachute Required
Reaching Your Reluctant Reader

For Nicole

I love you

He who fears death dies every time he thinks of it.

-Stanislas

I said to Life, I would hear Death speak. And Life raised her voice a little higher and said, you hear him now.

-Kahlil Gibran

Never open the door to a lesser evil, for other and greater ones invariably slink in after it.

-Balthasar Gracian

ONE

Nate Huckley leaned forward against the steering wheel, eyes searching the colorless brick buildings that slid by on either side of the street. He glanced at his watch and shook his head. He couldn't believe he was spending valuable time, time he didn't have, looking for a hardware store in this backwoods, one-factory, Pennsylvania town.

Huckley spotted the store. The boy back at the gas station had stuttered like a moron, but his directions had been good enough. Huckley pulled into the small gravel parking lot next to the concrete tilt-up building on which the last remnants of the word "Hardware" clung in tall, flaking letters. The lot was empty except for a beat-up VW Bug, more rust than metal, squatting in the far corner. Huckley checked his time and felt the anger churn harder in his stomach.

Grabbing the roll of tape, he marched through the parking lot, the hard soles on his leather boots crunching the small rocks into the dirt. *Like stepping on bugs,* he thought. He smiled and started to twist his foot on each step and stomp down a little harder. By the time he reached the double-wide glass doors that faced the street he felt a little better. Until he saw the sign.

CLOSED.

Bullshit. Huckley pounded on the glass door with the tape. He leaned down, opened the mail slot with his forefinger and shouted, "Hey! Get out here. I know you're still there, Godammit! I can see your car."

He stood up and kept beating the door until he saw a light go on in the back room. A smile spread across his face. He always got his way. Always.

The door in the back opened, and Huckley saw the outline of a person walk down the aisle. Huckley grinned a little wider. He'd expected an old man, but it was a young girl who came to the door. She squinted at him through the glass, twisted the locks, and stuck her head out toward him.

"We're closed," the girl said. She rolled her eyes in case her tone hadn't made her annoyance perfectly clear.

Huckley looked the girl over. Dark circles ringed her eyes as if old layers of eyeliner had melted into her skin. Her cheekbones stuck out like there wasn't enough skin on her face to go around, giving her an emaciated, hungry look, like a stray dog who thinks a wrapper with grease on it is a meal. Black roots a few inches long told the world her bleached-blonde hair was more bleach than blonde. The girl was a mess. Huckley couldn't believe his luck.

"Well, hello, sweetie. When'd you start working here?"

The girl ignored the question. "Mr. Cooper left me to close today. Told me not to let anyone in."

"That's what Mr. Cooper said, huh? Well, I'm sure he didn't mean me."

The girl looked up and down the street. Huckley already knew there wasn't anyone there. He had checked when he first saw that it was a young girl coming toward the door.

"Look, I'm new to this town, mister. I don't know who you are. So I think you'd better go now. Come back tomorrow."

"C'mon now, it wouldn't hurt to talk to me a little." Huckley smiled as he concentrated. The girl's mind was an open book. He pushed a little and the pages tumbled open, images dancing free form, garbled and non-linear. Hers was the kind of mind that used to confuse him, but that was a long time ago. Now it was easy. With a little concentration he could find out everything he needed to know. Like how the girl was a druggie, a loner, picking up a few bucks before moving on.

How she was frustrated the owner hadn't trusted her with the cash register yet. How the first time he did, she'd take the money and be gone. And there, amid all the adolescent self-consciousness and emotionalism, was a burst of sexual images. Many partners. Some for money. Some for drugs. And blazing out in front was an evolving fantasy with Huckley himself.

Ahh, young hormones, he thought. Little teenage girls could never resist his looks – white skin unmarked by any blemish, blonde hair combed back flat against his scalp, lips dark red as if he had spent the day sipping wine, eyes squinted half shut as if he held a secret too valuable to share. Although he appeared to be in his thirties, it was always the young ones who found him most attractive. And they were always so eager to prove they were women by following him to whatever bed, car seat, or back alley he chose.

He left the girl's sexual images behind and sifted through her thoughts until he found the right information.

"Your name's Doreen, right?"

"Yeah, how'd you know?"

He smiled at the girl. "I just guessed. You look like a Doreen."

"Is that a good thing?" she asked, tugging on a few strands of her blonde hair and twirling it over her ear.

"Sure, pretty name for a pretty girl." God, it was so easy. Huckley moved a step closer to the girl and inhaled through flared nostrils. Cheap high school perfume mixed with cheap high school marijuana. He smiled. *That's my girl.*

"So Mr. Cooper left you all alone, huh? Surprised your father let you work a job like this. What are you, seventeen?"

"I'm eighteen," she lied. "Don't know who my daddy is. Even if I did, I wouldn't let him tell me what to do."

"I see. But you let this Mr. Cooper tell you, huh?" Doreen shrugged. Huckley held up the roll of tape, "Listen, I really need some duct tape. This stuff doesn't work for what I'm using it for."

"I'd like to help, mister. I really would. But the register's closed and emptied out for the day so…" Doreen started to smack the chewing gum she'd been hiding in her mouth.

"No problem. I'll just leave some money and you can put it in the register tomorrow. I'll be in and out of here. Let you get back to your own business – if you know what I mean." Huckley raised a hand to his lips and took a drag off an imaginary joint. Doreen broke eye contact and stared at the floor. Huckley smirked. "Hey, there's nothing wrong with it. Lord knows I've smoked my share of weed."

Doreen smiled self-consciously. "You smoke?"

"Are you kidding? My generation invented the stuff." He leaned in and whispered in her ear, "In fact, I wouldn't mind a hit if you have any left. I'll pay you a little extra for it."

She hesitated, looking up and down the street again. "I don't think that'd be a good idea."

"All right. I understand. Maybe you're too young for me to be talking like that anyway. I'm sorry." Huckley turned to leave.

"I'm not too young. I told you I was eighteen."

"Yeah, that's what you told me."

Doreen bit her lower lip, then moved to the side to let him in. "I don't believe I'm doing this."

"That's a good girl. You know, I was really lucky you were here." Huckley smiled. "You have no idea how much time you've saved me."

He leaned in to her as he passed. An electric jolt moved through him as his arm rubbed against her breasts. Huckley curled his hands into fists and rubbed them up and down his thighs. He knew he had to wait until she closed the door behind them, but this was his favorite part. He could hardly contain himself. He smiled at his good fortune. He was back on schedule.

TWO

Jack Tremont was late. That he would be running so far behind schedule was unthinkable, especially since the two clients waiting for him were his most important. The traffic light ahead of him turned yellow. He thought about running it until he saw a stop sign thrust into the air behind the row of cars to his right.

His Jeep Cherokee, a far cry from the BMW 750 he had driven just a few years ago, braked easily before the intersection. Still, the school crossing guard shot him a withering look for stopping a foot into the crosswalk. He returned her scowl with a smile, but it was wasted. With a look of disgust, the guard held up her stop sign in front of his bumper. She stared Jack down as she waved the mass of school kids across the street.

Jack knew the woman, Mrs. Hilder. She was no-nonsense New England, and she had little tolerance for the relaxed southern attitude abundant here in western Maryland. All of the kids and half of the adults in Prescott City were scared of her. The parents remembered her as the crossing guard when they were in school and they carried the same fearful awe as their kids did now. One of the parents had admitted to Jack that she still stood up a little straighter each time she saw Mrs. Hilder coming down the street. Tough as woodpecker lips, the parent had whispered, laughing but glancing around as if the crossing guard would come charging

5

at them any minute. Mrs. Hilder's stare was enough to convince Jack of the truth of it. He tried to ignore her and watch instead the stream of colorful jackets, cartoon lunch pails, and action hero backpacks parade in front of him, all headed toward a carefree afternoon. No stress. No worries.

Jack took a deep breath and felt the tension drain from his shoulders. He couldn't help but laugh at himself. When would he learn to relax? He and Lauren had moved to Prescott City a year ago for exactly this reason, to undo the mess they had created trying unsuccessfully to balance two high-paced careers while starting a family. To be fair, it had been more his mess than hers. She was an overachiever but always seemed to keep things in balance. He was the workaholic to whom family had become something squeezed into planned increments in a schedule.

The outrageous materialism of living in Orange County, California hadn't helped matters either. They had chased success so hard that they hardly noticed they were failing every day.

Then the accident happened.

As horrible as it was, in some strange way, Jack realized the accident had probably saved his marriage. Almost two years later, he was still paying for this marital help with nightmares and a constant black guilt that clawed in his stomach like a living creature. He bore the suffering without complaint. For what he had done, he knew he deserved worse.

The last of the kids skipped across the street and, with one last glare, Mrs. Hilder returned to the sidewalk to let Jack pass. He smiled and gave a little wave.

"C'mon, Mrs. Hilder. Give me some love," he murmured. Nothing doing. The crossing guard's stern mouth grew more wrinkled as she scowled. Jack shook his head and laughed. "Playing hard to get, huh? Maybe next time."

A few minutes later, he pulled into the pickup area and saw his important clients hanging out on the swing set next to the head office. They saw him and squealed in delight. Grabbing their matching purple Groovy Girls backpacks, his daughters ran over to him and gave him a huge hug.

"Sorry I'm late, girls."

"Are you late?" Becky asked.

"Yeah, a little," he smiled. Every day he was away from the business world, he was reminded that life didn't have to be so difficult. In the real world, being five minutes late wasn't such a big deal. He looked back at his girls piling into the Jeep. "You girls know what today is, don't you?"

"My birthday. I'm gonna be seven!" Sarah shouted.

"Your birthday's not for months, silly. And you're only six," Becky said, poking her sister in the arm.

Jack twisted around in the front seat and said in a serious voice, "I can't believe you don't know what day this is. How could you possibly, possibly forget that today is…" – he paused for added drama – "ice cream day!"

The girls screamed and then giggled at their dad. Soon they were lost in an important discussion about the relative coolness of different flavors of ice cream. As Jack edged into the after-school traffic, he thought that moving to Prescott City was the best thing he had ever done. He actually knew his kids now. He and Lauren were even starting to feel normal again, as if the worst was finally behind them. Lauren had started to talk about plans years from now, not just weeks and months. It was a subtle change, but its significance wasn't lost on him.

Prescott City had been good for the Tremonts. In California, they had sped through life, racking up wealth and accomplishments instead of memories and relationships. Here, they were all taking notice of life and enjoying it. Besides some periodic consulting work, he'd even taken the time to dabble in writing mysteries. Sure, life was simple here, but he was learning that simple wasn't the epithet he'd thought it was. Simple was good, and he hoped things stayed that way.

THREE

Doreen couldn't breathe. She pressed her tongue between her lips and pushed against the gag over her mouth. Nothing. She couldn't move it. Mucous blocked her nasal passages and they wouldn't clear no matter how hard she tried.

Tears flowed down her face, and she whimpered from the effort. Her lungs burned from lack of oxygen. On reflex, she bit down and her mouth filled with blood. Then, with a violent snort, she cleared the blockage in her nostrils, and she was able to inhale.

A few breaths and her head cleared enough to allow a different kind of panic to take hold. Her hands were bound behind her back, her legs bent back at an awkward angle in the confined space. Her first thought was that she was in a coffin. Just like in the horror movies. Buried alive. Then she noticed the smells around her. The air reeked of oil and dirt.

Where am I? Oh God, what's happening to me?

Her head ached. Thoughts churned too fast for her to hold on to anything coherent. She closed her eyes and tried to focus, but the world spun around her. She opened her eyes wide, swallowing hard to fight down the urge to vomit. Even in her confusion, she understood the danger. If she threw up while the gag was over her mouth, she would choke and die.

Then the earthquake hit. Everything shook, and her body slammed into the metal walls surrounding her. Something dug into her back, sending a sharp pain through her body. She tried to twist to the side, but it was too tight to move. The walls closed in on all sides, the ceiling only inches from her face. She flexed her arms and legs, but the more she strained the more the bindings cut into her skin. Finally, the pain was too much to bear, and she stopped struggling. The world wasn't shaking any more.

Maybe it wasn't an earthquake after all.

She lay there in the dark, trying to slow her breathing, trying to understand what had happened to her.

Then she felt it.

Tha-thump...tha-thump...tha-thump.

She recognized the rhythm from a different time. A better time. Lying in the back seat, wrapped up in a blanket, listening to soft country music on the radio as her momma drove home.

Tha-thump...tha-thump...tha--thump.

Tires going down the highway.

Then it all crashed over her. The blond-haired man at the hardware store. Being grabbed from behind. Strong hands pressed against her mouth. A bad smell. Like chlorine. Then everything went black.

The seconds it took for the scene to replay in her mind were long enough for her to organize her thoughts. Everything fit together. The sound beneath her. The sudden, jolting movement. The cramped space. The smell. She understood what had happened.

Kidnapped – I'm in the trunk of a car.

Panic followed close behind realization. She screamed through the duct tape covering her mouth. She kicked and thrashed her body against the walls of the trunk but accomplished nothing except to inflict more pain on herself. Finally, her body went limp again from exhaustion and frustration, the only movement coming from the sobs that shook her small frame.

Doreen Johnston hadn't whispered a prayer since she was a little girl in Sunday school, but she closed her eyes and had no problem recalling how it was done. *Sweet, merciful Jesus, please let me get out of this alive.* Over and over, she recited the same words, trying to find strength in them, trying to find hope. But she knew she was in real trouble. The kind of trouble where no amount of praying was going to help her. Tremors shook her limbs, and she squeezed her eyes tight – as if it could block out what was happening to her. *Sweet, merciful Jesus, please let me get out of this alive.*

FOUR

Ice cream was a hit. The girls settled easily on a flavor, pink bubble gum. Sarah waited until Becky made up her mind and then copied her. Jack was happy that the girls enjoyed being around each other. Becky and Sarah fought every now and then, but they generally got along. He just hoped it lasted. The thought of having two teenage girls in the house at each other's throats over boys and clothes made him cringe.

After ice cream and the ritual cleaning of faces and hands, he herded the girls back into the car and headed to the Dahl's house. Kristi and Max Dahl had two girls the same age as Becky and Sarah, and they took turns having play dates. The girls had been confused the first time they arrived for a visit. "This is just a regular house. I thought we were going to a doll's house," Becky complained. It was one of those moments now firmly fixed in Tremont family lore, trotted out and retold at family functions.

Kristi Dahl must have seen them drive down the tree-lined driveway that led up to their property because she was already waiting for them at the base of the stairs when Jack rolled the car to a stop. As he threw the Jeep into park, Kristi walked to the passenger door, her arms hugged across her chest. Jack rolled down the power window as the girls unbuckled themselves from their car seats and climbed out.

"Hi, girls. Julie and Jesse are waiting for you." Kristi Dahl pointed to the side of the house. "Go on back."

The girls slammed their doors shut and took off running without saying goodbye. Jack, still in the car, hung out of the window and called out to them, "I'll pick you up in a couple of hours." Becky waved a hand but didn't turn back.

Kristi smiled. "So independent."

"Yeah, they're growing up fast." Jack turned his attention to Kristi. Usually the type of woman who wore make-up and designer clothes for even a trip to the grocery store, Kristi's appearance took Jack by surprise. Her hair was pulled back tightly, revealing a pale, splotchy complexion, her cheeks burning red as if from a fever or from walking outside on a brisk day. The skin beneath her eyes tinted an inky purple; the edges of her eyelids looked raw, like they'd been scrubbed with a wire brush. Worn out from crying, he guessed. Her arms were back across her chest, hands clutching her sides for added security. Jack wanted to ask how she was doing, but it felt too awkward, too much like an intrusion. And, in truth, he was afraid he already knew the answer.

"Is Max around?" he asked.

"Are you kidding? You know where he's at."

"Piper's?"

"Where else would he be? I swear to God they're going to hang a picture on the wall to honor his perfect attendance record."

Kristi looked down, and an uncomfortable silence hung in the air between them. Finally, Jack decided he had to ask, should ask, the question. "How're you doing, Kristi? You hanging in there?"

Kristi nodded and forced a brave smile. Her eyes welled with tears. "It's hard but..." She shrugged and looked away. "No, I'm good. Really, I am. Think everything's going to be all right, you know?"

Jack pretended not to notice her wipe a tear away with an angry flick of her finger. He and Max had become close friends in the short time they had known each other, but the tragedy the Dahls were living through was nothing friendship of any length could prepare someone to handle. "Lauren told me to say hi. Told me that if you need anything to call her. No matter what time it is."

"Yeah, she called earlier today. It helped to talk."

"Hey, what do you say I hang out and watch the kids? Give you some time to yourself, you know?"

Kristi smiled, a hand patting her hair as if checking the position of a stylish curl. "I look that bad, huh?"

"No, it's not that—"

Kristi cleared her throat and rapped her knuckles on the side of the car. "Go on. Get out of here. I appreciate the offer, but I'm fine. It'll do Max good to see you."

Jack hesitated but finally nodded.

Kristi smiled, fingering her necklace and pulling together the sides of her blouse. "It's supposed to storm tonight," she said, looking up at the sky.

Jack was about to answer, but he realized she wasn't really talking to him. Her mind was far away, drifting among the dark clouds gathered above the tree line, lost to her own thoughts, her own problems. He waited a few beats, not sure what to say. "Right, then. I'll be back soon."

Kristi snapped her head toward him as if he'd snuck up on her. The flash of anger in her eyes was quickly replaced by a self-conscious smile. "Sorry, I guess I was drifting."

"You sure you're all right?"

"Yeah, don't worry. I'm looking forward to seeing the girls have some fun. I'll see you soon."

Jack shifted the car into drive, mumbled a quick goodbye, and headed back toward the main road. When he glanced in the rearview mirror, he saw Kristi standing in the same spot, her arms across her chest, staring up into the sky. Jack wondered if he ought to turn around and stay with her, maybe watch the kids and force her to take some time to herself. He hesitated at the end of the Dahl's long driveway and watched as Kristi turned and walked around the side of the house to where the girls were playing.

He didn't like seeing her that way, but what did he expect? He wondered if he would be able to hold it together if the roles were reversed. Kristi was actually holding up well considering the circumstances. Besides, Jack thought, the kids were old enough now not to be much of a bother.

He thought of Max, likely well into his bar tab by now. He would need someone to talk to, maybe someone to drive him home. Mind made up, Jack accelerated down the driveway, took a right turn on the main road, and headed toward Piper's.

FIVE

Prescott City sat in a shallow valley surrounded by two mountain ranges: to the north and west, the rolling hills of the Allegheny Mountains, to the south and east, the Appalachians ancient mountains that stuck out of the earth like worn-down nubs of once sharp teeth. The mountains created a false sunset a full half hour before the sun reached the true horizon. The long twilights gave evenings a stretched feeling, as if night were something to be put off, as if Nature herself feared the dark and held on to the day as long as she could.

Jack arrived at Piper's just when the rain started. He glanced up at the sky and headed toward the front door. The ambient light that filled the sky was a peculiar yellow hue, like tornado weather he'd been in once during a trip through the Midwest. He could make out the storm front coming in, a low wall of dark clouds tumbling down the mountains toward them. *A wick'd blow cummin' on* would have been his grandmother's proclamation. The old lady never had use for weather stations, but relied on her internal barometer, which never seemed to be wrong. Until her dying day, neighbors checked with her first before they made plans. Jack preferred science to Grandma's old country intuition and wished he had watched the weather report that morning to see what was in store for the area.

There was a body propped against the crumbling concrete slab next to the bar's front door. Albert James was the man's name. Jack had seen him around before, usually passed out at a booth in Piper's or sometimes in the park downtown, shouting at the trees, or sitting on a bench, rocking in place and mumbling to himself. Guys like that were everywhere in L.A., but Albert James had the stage to himself in Prescott City.

He had on his usual costume, dirty camouflage overalls, a black t-shirt, and work boots caked with mud. He had thin hair through which his scalp, all spots and flakes of dry skin, was clearly visible. Albert's hair had grown to his shoulders, and it hung heavy with oil and dirt. He somehow managed to shave often enough that he never grew a full beard, but patches of grey whiskers stuck out at odd angles. The whiskers did little to hide burst blood vessels that spread out across his cheeks like spider webs. Albert James never made any attempt to clean himself up. He was the town drunk, a position he held with an improbable pride.

"Hey, Albert," Jack said. In L.A. you didn't talk to folks like Albert James – you just walked and ignored them the way you ignored an unsightly crack in the sidewalk. Around here, people recognized that, as screwed up as he was, he was still a man. "How're you doing today?"

"Dying," Albert said, his voice a distracted murmur.

"Yeah, I guess we all are." Jack went to open the door to Piper's.

"Some soonah than others."

Jack paused. Something in Albert's voice had changed, as if he were suddenly more alert. He looked down at the man, but Albert's head still hung limp against his chest. "Yeah, you take care now. Stay out of the rain."

"Like lil' Saaarrraahhh." Albert breathed out the words as if his lungs were deflating.

Jack stepped back and looked down at the man. "What'd you say?"

Albert turned away like he was going to be hit. He buried his head in his chest, moaning.

Jack crouched down, shaking his head. Must have been his imagination, but he could have sworn–

Albert's body convulsed violently, his legs spasmed out in front of him, and his head banged back against the brick wall. He twisted in place as if jerked forward on invisible ropes tied to his joints, his contorted face pushed even with Jack's own. "Yor lil' gurl, Saaarrraahhh. She's in troubl'. She'll be dyin' sooner than you think, I reckon."

Jack's stomach tightened, and the ground seemed to sway beneath his feet. He blinked hard. He reached out and toward Albert, who turned away and covered the sides of his head with his arms.

"How do you know my daughter's name? Why did you say that, Albert?" The man flinched like a dog used to being kicked just for being around. Jack knew he was scaring Albert but didn't care. He raised his voice, "You tell me. Why would you say something like that?"

Jack reached out and seized Albert by the shoulder, meaning to pull him to his feet. But as soon as Jack made contact, Albert snarled and lunged at him. He grabbed Jack's hand and yanked hard and brought him to the ground. Arm cranked behind his back, his face flat to the concrete parking lot, Albert forced him down.

Hot, boozy breath huffed in Jack's ear.

"You listen good now, Jack. There's bad weather comin', see? I mean real bad. You get your family outta here. They're gonna get lil' Sarah, I know it. I jus' know it. They'll kill her, see? And you cain't stop 'em, Jack. You cain't stop the devil himself."

Jack froze with the words. His logic disappeared and animal instinct took over. A chill passed through his body and every hair stood on end. There was something in the voice. Deep and resonant. Jack didn't hear the words – he felt them.

"You hear me, Jack? You cain't stop the devil himself. So don't you try." Then soft, no more than a whisper, a child's voice, *"Run while you can. Take her away from here before it can happen. RUN!"*

Jack pushed violently off the ground, and Albert fell off him. Jack crawled away, unable to breath. He knew that voice, but it was impossible. She was dead. If there was any truth he knew, it was that the girl was dead. Jack had killed her himself.

"What the hell is going on?" Jack whispered.

Albert, curled in a ball on the ground, looked up, and Jack saw a flash of someone else behind the man's eyes. Then, just as fast, it was gone.

Albert rocked back and forth, singing off-key,
Swing low, sweet chariot.
Comin' fo' tah carry me home.

Jack stood up and backed away from the man, his hands shaking.

The door opened behind him, and Jack jumped. Two men exited the bar, giving him a sidelong look as they noticed Albert cowering on the ground.

"Everything okay here?" asked the older of the two men.

Jack steadied himself. "Yeah, everything's fine. This guy here might need a ride home, though."

"Ol' Albert?" the younger one jumped in. "Hell, I think he is home. This is the only place I've ever seen him."

Albert clutched his legs to his chest. Rocking. Rocking.

"What's wrong? Did you do something to him?" the first man asked, taking notice of the dirt on Jack's clothes. They both looked at him suspiciously.

Jack brushed off his clothes. "He was all sprawled out, and I tripped on him. I feel awful."

The two men seemed to accept the story. They bent down, grabbed Albert under the arms, and stood him up.

"Albert, did you trip this guy?"

"Let's just leave him alone," Jack said.

The older man said, "Don't worry. We'll take care of him. Why don't you go on in?"

Jack gave them a nod and, with one last look at Albert, ducked through the door and into the bar, heading toward a much needed drink.

Piper's was a dive. The ceiling was worn decorative metal tinted a coppery orange by decades of tobacco smoke. A battle-scarred oak bar covered by a half-inch of lacquer extended along one wall, fitted with brass railings and draft beer pulls. Bottles of booze lined the counter behind the bartender, but nothing fancy. The patrons at Piper's weren't picky about brands, and if they were, Jim Butcher, the big German who owned the place, had no problem jabbing the stump of his amputated right arm at the door and telling them to get the hell out.

Round tables and booths of dark wood surrounded the two pool tables near the wall opposite the bar. One pool table tilted to the left and the other to the right. The only fight in the bar in years had happened when an out-of-towner insisted on trying to level the tables only to find out that the local crowd liked their pool just the way it was. Piper's wasn't for sad drunks trying to lose themselves – it was for good people meeting friends and having a good time. People threw their peanut shells on the ground, cheap beer flowed until the owner decided it was time to close, and everyone knew pretty much everyone else. It was pure small town, and that was just fine by the people who went there.

Jack spotted Max Dahl sitting at the end of the bar and headed over toward him. Jack knew most of the regulars in the place. When he'd first moved here, people had raised a wary eye when he mentioned he was from California, as if that was all they had to know about him to know he was nothing more than a flake and a liberal weirdo. Jack hadn't realized the disdain most people had for Californians before he'd moved. But it wasn't long until he was one of the guys, thanks in a large part to his early friendship with Max, who seemed to know everyone, and his assurances that while Jack was from California, he was born and raised in Iowa. His Midwestern credentials helped offset most of the skepticism about his character. Jack wasn't quite a local yet, but he felt welcome and figured it would take a few more years until people stopped introducing him as the guy from California. He shook a few hands as he crossed the bar and finally made it over to Max.

"Maxi-million, what's the score, my friend?"

Max raised his beer and said, "Max Dahl three. Jack Tremont zero. Dahl wins."

"No fair. You always win this game," Jack said with a smile as he ordered a beer.

"I see it doesn't keep you from playing. Besides," – Max eased back from the bar and rubbed his bulging stomach – "I have a weight handicap to make up for."

Jack played along. He knew the serious talk would come later. For a while at least, Max wanted to pretend all was right with the world. Jack understood the need and was happy to oblige. "Drinking beer is where that thing came from. You should take better care of yourself. Can they bar you from practicing law in Maryland if you get too fat?" Jack said, nodding toward his friend's gut.

Max called out to Jim Butcher, who was standing at the cash register at the other end of the bar, "Dammit Jim, I thought I told you not to let my wife in here anymore." Butcher looked up as if he was ready to take a swing at whoever had the bad taste to yell at him in his own bar. Seeing that it was Max, he grunted and waved him off like he was swatting away a mosquito. "I think his sense of humor was in that arm he lost," Max mumbled.

Jack held his hands up. "All right. All right. I'll back off."

"Good, let's shoot some pool."

"Which table? Left or right?"

Max dusted off his beer. "You pick. I'll kick your ass either way."

SIX

Huckley hadn't expected the storm to be this bad. The wipers were barely able to keep up with the rain that battered the windshield. He checked his watch. He was still making good time. The Boss didn't expect him for a few more hours. He decided to play it safe and took the next exit off the highway into a rest area.

The place was deserted. Still, he chose a parking spot far away from the restrooms in case another car pulled off the highway to wait out the storm. It seemed unlikely that anyone who entered the parking lot would walk by his car, but he wanted to be careful. That was always his weakness, the thing the Boss had been working with him on, being careful. He was used to taking risks, living on the adrenaline rush of playing right on the edge. But the Boss was right. There was too much at stake now. They were so close to their goal.

Tree branches thrashed in the gusting wind as if angry giants shook the trees by their trunks. The air was filled with early autumn leaves and small limbs that had been torn off and sent spinning. Sheet lightning turned the world into pulsating bursts of photographic negative, black trees set against searing white light. Even before each flash of lightning dimmed, thunder blasted the atmosphere and shook the ground.

Huckley reached in the back seat and grabbed his umbrella. Sticking it out of the door first, he opened it up over him and stood outside the car. He moved around to the trunk, fumbled the keys, but finally inserted the right one into the lock.

"Aww, what have you done to yourself?" Huckley moaned when he saw his prize. Blood and mucous ran from her nose down over her mouth and spread out over her neck and chest. Seeing him, the girl started to kick at her bindings. More blood snorted out of her nose from the effort.

"Shhhh, now. Shhhh," Huckley said. "You're not going anywhere, so just stop that."

The girl stopped kicking and stared at him. Huckley reached toward her with one long finger extended. Her eyes tracked his hand as it moved toward her face. A low whimper came from deep in her throat. Anticipating his touch, she closed her eyes. Huckley scraped a fingernail across her cheek, digging in hard when it came up against the duct tape that stretched across the girl's mouth. He pressed the tape between his thumb and forefinger and tugged. The girl's cheek lifted with each pull, but the tape held in place. He smiled, happy with the result.

Huckley leaned in toward the girl until his face was inches from hers. He sniffed, taking in the saltiness of her sweat, the sweetness of her blood. She smelled of fear. He closed his eyes and allowed himself to see the images in her mind, savoring the horrific scenarios she conjured for her death. He lingered in her mind, relishing the acts of rape and creative violations of her body the girl imagined. Huckley laughed. She wasn't even close.

Huckley slammed the trunk shut and contented himself by listening to the girl struggle inside. This wasn't his favorite part of the process, but he certainly didn't mind it. He wondered if he would ever get tired of it like some of the others had. God, he hoped not. Even if the Boss figured out the Source, Huckley knew he'd never give it up. For him, death was the only thing that really mattered.

SEVEN

Max slid his beer down the side rail to get a better shot at the eight ball sitting next to the corner pocket on the opposite side of the table. "Get out your money, hot shot," he said through the cigarette clenched in his mouth. In a smooth motion, he tapped the cue ball just enough to send it on a slow roll. The shot would have been off on most tables, but Max was on his home turf. The ball made a slow arc to the right as it rolled, ending in a gentle kiss on the eight ball and dropping it in for the win.

"I knew we should have played the left table," Jack laughed, throwing a wadded up five-dollar bill on the table.

"Who are you kidding? You've had one beer to my four and you still couldn't beat me. You're a disgrace."

They walked over to a booth and sat. Max lit a new cigarette. "So what's bothering you, sport? You're not quite right with yourself tonight."

Jack leaned back and rubbed the back of his neck. He hadn't mentioned Albert James. Max didn't need anything else on his mind right now. But Jack couldn't shake the churning that'd been in the cold pit of his stomach since his run-in. He heard Albert James in his head still. *They're gonna get lil' Sarah, I know it. I jus' know it.* The warning about Sarah spooked him, but it was even more of a reason not to mention it to Max. It hit a little too close to home. So he made up an excuse. "Yeah, I know. I'm driving myself crazy with this writing thing."

"I thought that was what you wanted to do. I mean all that Father-of-the-Year bullshit comes first, but I thought writing was your thing."

Jack smiled. He wasn't fooled by Max's bravado. His friend was crazy about his own kids and would do anything for them. That was the problem. The reason Piper's had become his second home.

"Let's just say it's harder than I thought it'd be."

"When do I get to read something? Is it any good?"

"I'm not quitting my day job, that's for sure. I'm still doing some consulting."

"Yeah." Max blew out a stream of smoke. "Like you need the money."

Jack smiled. Max was always giving him a tough time about money even though Max was one of the wealthiest men in the area. Jack lowered his voice and leaned across the table. "Hey, have you heard anything new?"

Max looked down at his pint of beer rather than make eye contact. He slid his glass side-to-side in the small puddle of condensation that had collected on the table. "Yeah, we heard back from the specialist."

Jack didn't need to wait for his friend to compose himself. Max's body language told him the story. The specialist had been the end of the road, the last Court of Appeals. Jack reached out and grabbed his friend's forearm. "I'm sorry, Max." He left his hand there for a few moments before pulling it back. "Is there a next step? Something else they can do?"

Max shook his head. "Nothing except wait for a donor. But they said…well, there's this list." He took a long pull from his beer and cleared his throat. "They said it didn't look good. Not to get our hopes up, you know?"

They sat in silence. The background noise of Piper's, a country western song on the jukebox, the jingle of the old-fashioned cash register behind the bar, the grunting laughter of men from the corner, all seemed disconnected, somehow gaudy instead of the comfortable familiarity the same noises had held only minutes earlier.

"You know if there is anything I can do for you. Anything."

"Got a spare heart sitting around? Size extra small?" Max smiled but kept looking down at the table. When he did look up, his eyes were red and swollen. "My little girl's going to die, Jack. I'd do anything…. Anything."

"You've done everything you could, Max. The best doctors. The best medical care," Jack said.

Max downed the last of his beer. "Yeah. But, it's just not enough, is it? No matter what I do, she's still going to die." He leaned forward and whispered, "You know, sometimes I think I could go out and get them what they needed. I swear to God, if I thought they'd use it, I could go out and get them a heart. Just the right size too."

"Easy, Max," Jack whispered. "Easy."

"I'd go to jail, but Jesse would be alive, you know? I swear, if I thought they'd use it."

The lights in Piper's flickered and then came back on. Thunder exploded outside so loud that it felt like it was in the room. Grown men straightened in their chairs. It was a few seconds before nervous laughter around the bar broke the tension as the fight-or-flight impulse buried in each man's psyche gave way to rational thought. Everyone went back to their drinking.

"Blowing hard," Max said, looking a little guilty for his outburst and sounding eager to change the subject. "We better head back to the house." Max looked out of the window. Without warning, he shouted, "JESUS CHRIST. Someone call a doctor!"

Max pushed himself out of the booth, his beer mug crashing to the floor. Jack twisted his head to look out the window. His stomach turned. Right in front of him, not more than ten yards away in the parking lot, was Albert James. Or what was left of him.

Jack turned away from the window. "Call a doctor!"

"I'm doing it," Jim Butcher yelled back. "What's going on out there?"

People were scrambling to the windows by now. Others were heading out the door to follow Max outside. Jack ran to the door with them and raced to where Max was huddled on the ground.

Albert James was more in need of a hearse than an ambulance. That much seemed certain. A six-inch crater was dug out of the man's head right above his eyebrows, charred black by the heat of the lightning. The hole marked the entry point for the million volts of electricity that reached out from the black clouds to run the length of the Albert's body. As it passed through the soft flesh, it blew ragged holes through the skin, holes that now leaked thick, viscous blood on the black asphalt. The blood poured out fast enough that even the driving rain couldn't wash it away fast enough.

"Jesus, I think he's still alive," someone said.

"Shee-it. That boy's dead as they get."

Jack got down on his knees next to Max. This close, he could smell the burned flesh and see into the head wound. It was deep, probably three or four inches. The intense heat of the lightning had cauterized the wound. Jack realized he was looking at a perfect cross-section of Albert's brain. It was too much for him. He was going to be sick. He turned to vomit but something grabbed at his leg. He looked down and saw the hand on his knee. It was a bloody pulp, each fingertip blown out where the lightning had left the body. Still, it flexed into a fist, digging into his muscle. The men around the body saw the movement and staggered backward.

"Oh shit, Goddamn som-bitch is still alive."

"Shut up. He's tryin' to say somethin'."

Jack shook his head. It was impossible. He was looking right at the man's exposed brain. There was no way he could be alive. The hand could be nerves, like a frog leg twitching after it'd been cut off. But alive? Couldn't be. Still, sounds were coming out of Albert's throat. More than that. His lips were moving as if trying to form words. Reluctantly, Jack leaned in and put his ear next to the dying man's mouth. The stench of the burnt skin was almost unbearable. Next to him, Max whispered, "What is it Albert? What are you trying to say?"

Jack was soaked to his skin. The storm raged around him. But for a few seconds, all that disappeared. The world faded away, and it was him and the man dying on the asphalt underneath him. The words came out slow but clear. They were exactly what Jack feared they'd be. *"You cain't stop the devil, Jack.*

You jus' gotta run from 'im. Gotta run. Gotta…" Albert James's hand went limp. A slow exhalation of breath and then he was gone. Jack looked up at Max.

"Did you hear that?" Jack asked

Max shook his head. "I didn't hear anything."

Jack stood to the side as they dragged Albert James out of the rain and waited for the ambulance to come take him away. Everyone wanted to know what Albert had whispered in Jack's ear, but for some reason he didn't feel like telling anyone. Somehow, he felt that he wasn't supposed to, that the message had been meant for him alone. He stood in the rain and wiped blood off his clothes, repeating the warning over and over in his mind. Finally, Max convinced him to go inside and have a quick drink before they went home. It was already eight o'clock. For the second time that day, he was late.

EIGHT

Max took clean, dry clothes out to the garage for Jack to change into so the girls didn't have to see blood on their dad. Putting on a pair of Max's pants gave Jack another chance to make a smartass comment about Max's gut, which gave them both a much-needed light moment. Inside the house, the kids gave Jack hello hugs, not even noticing he was wearing different clothes. They said their goodbyes to the Dahls, ran out to the car, and buckled themselves in.

Jack was thankful the girls had played hard and tanked up on pizza. It made them too sleepy to notice the crazy weather they were driving through. Of course, Max and Kristi had insisted that he stay and wait for the weather to calm down, especially after what they'd seen at Piper's. But Jack not only wanted to get home, he also didn't want to intrude.

Little Jesse Dahl was worn out from the visit and had developed a bad nosebleed, a regular side effect from the blood-thinning medication she took. Jack couldn't help staring at the little girl. Outwardly, she looked healthy. Knowing that her heart was a ball of diseased tissue was almost too much too bear. He didn't know how any parent could manage it and still remain sane. Not for the first time, he reminded himself that such a thing could happen to one of his little girls. Death kept his own schedule and didn't discriminate. Just like Albert James. A bolt of lightning and it was over. A visit to the pediatrician and turns out your daughter has degenerative heart failure. He tried to force the thought from his mind, but it lingered like a bad headache.

Despite Max and Kristi's pleas, Jack decided to head home. One look at his tired kids was all it took. But now he wondered how smart his decision had been.

Trees lining the highway snapped back and forth in the wind; leaves and twigs flew through the air and bounced off the Jeep's windshield. The wipers were on the highest speed, but they still had trouble keeping up with the driving rain. The right lane of the highway was a murky pool of water. Jack switched lanes after a few tense seconds of hydroplaning, but even there the water couldn't run off fast enough to keep from pooling. Every couple of minutes he'd hit a deep patch, and the Jeep would lose traction with the asphalt. He drove at half the speed limit but still gripped the steering wheel with white knuckles and sweaty palms.

"Thank God," he mumbled on seeing the rest area sign. He slowed down even farther and moved over to the right hand lane. The flooding was worse here, and he felt the water pound the undercarriage of the SUV. He leaned forward over the steering wheel and squinted to try and make out shapes in the night. "Come on. Come on." A crash of thunder tore through the sky, sounding like someone tearing the roof of the car with a fire ax. Jack glanced in the rearview mirror, expecting to see some shocked faces. He couldn't believe it. The girls were sound asleep. "Ah, here we go." Jack took the off ramp and drove into the rest area to wait out the storm.

NINE

Nate Huckley watched with only casual interest as a pair of headlights appeared at the far end of the parking lot. As he predicted, the car turned and parked in the spot nearest the rest rooms, in an area that was better lit than where he'd parked. With the weather, he doubted the people in the Jeep could even see him.

He leaned his head back and was about to shut his eyes to nap when it hit him.

Like always, it started in his gut, like nausea. Then it burned and spread out from his stomach, hot pain racing up his body. Into his chest and throat, the pain was a claw scratching its way up his windpipe. A gurgling sound escaped from his mouth as his larynx convulsed.

Then it was in his head, a hailstorm of nails driven into his skull. A roar hammered against his eardrums. His hands squeezed the sides of his head to block it out, but it wouldn't go away. The roar became a voice. The voice telling him what to do. How do to it. His eyes bulged outward from the agony inflicted on every part of his body.

But something was wrong. It never lasted this long. The pain was too intense. He clawed at his ears, willing to tear them from his head if it would just stop the voice. He screamed from the pain.

His body twitched in his seat. Huckley knew he would go insane if it didn't stop.

Then it was gone.

No pain. No roar. No voice. Just the incessant beat of rain punctuated by the random bass of the thunder. Nothing of the visitation remained.

Nothing except a new interest in the contents of the vehicle across the lot. And a word. Two syllables that repeated over and over in his brain. He drew in a deep breath to bring the word to life. Exhaling slowly, he hissed the first syllable through clenched teeth, enjoying the way he could undulate the sound. Then, with a burst of air, he let the word out.

Ssaaa - rah.

Huckley knew what he had to do.

TEN

"*All circuits are busy. Please—*"

Jack snapped his cell phone shut and tossed it on the dash. He knew Lauren would be nervous when they didn't get home on time, but phone coverage was horrible in their area on a good day. Tonight, he'd have a better chance sending her a homing pigeon than getting through on the cell. Still, he felt awful about making her worry. He should have thought to call her before leaving the Dahls.

Straight ahead of him, next to the restrooms and a boarded up concession stand, was a pay phone. He twisted around to look at the girls. Sound asleep. He looked out each of the windows, even stretching over to the passenger side to get a better angle. There wasn't another car in the lot. He figured there wouldn't be any harm in leaving the girls in the car for a couple of minutes, especially since they'd be in full view the entire time.

He popped open the door and raised his jacket over his head to block out as much of the rain as possible. Hoping not to wake the girls, he didn't shut his door all the way, but let it rest against the latch so it closed just enough to keep out the rain. He took off on a sprint to the pay phone, splashing through puddles that came up over his ankles.

The pay phones were under a short overhang, but the wind was so strong that it provided little protection. Jack fished around in his pocket for change but came up with only pennies. He dialed "0" for the operator and waited as the phone went through a series of clicks. A computerized voice said, "A,T and T," and then a tone and more silence.

"Jesus Christ. Come on!" Jack started to glance over his shoulder at the Jeep, but the operator finally came on and Jack turned back toward the phone. He was halfway through giving his credit card number when he heard the blast of a car horn behind him. It was followed by the same sound again. And again. Even in the rain, it was loud and urgent. The Jeep's panic alarm.

Jack was always hitting the panic button on the remote by accident. He dug for the keys in his pocket. God, the girls were probably scared to death. He found the keys and pressed the button as he turned around to point the device at the car.

There was a man.

Standing next to his car.

The driver's door was open.

Jack dropped the phone and ran back to the car. "HEY! HEY YOU!"

The man didn't acknowledge Jack but just stood and kept staring into the open door. Even over the noise of the rain, Jack heard the girls screaming as he got closer to the car.

How long was I turned away from the car? One minute? Two? He couldn't have hurt them in that time. Could he?

"Get back from the car. RIGHT NOW!"

The man finally turned. He raised his hands in the air and stepped back. Jack slowed down a few paces from him. He wanted to check on the girls, but he wasn't about to turn his back on this stranger. Jack sized the man up. Late thirties, decent build, average sized frame, nothing too intimidating. Then again, the man could have a gun in his pocket, and then none of his physical characteristics would make a difference.

"What are you doing?" The adrenaline tearing through Jack's system made it come out more a threat than a question.

"Hi. Sorry about that. I was just making sure everyone was okay. Bad weather and all."

Jack moved to the open car door, putting his body between the man and the door. Standing closer, he could make out the details of the stranger. Even in the poor light, the man's pale face stood out from the night – like a glowing mask. He might have been an albino except for the black pits for eyes. Jack didn't like the look of the man's thin, colorless lips that twisted into a forced smile as they stared each other down.

Something about the man didn't seem right. Maybe it was the storm. Or the scare he got from turning and seeing the man unexpectedly appear at the car. Maybe it was that an hour earlier a man had died in his arms talking about the devil. Whatever it was, Jack's instinct warned him of danger.

He was reluctant to let the stranger out of his sight, but the girls screams were too much to bear. Quickly, he turned his head to make sure they were just scared and not hurt somehow. "You girls all right?" he called out. Becky and Sarah looked terrified but unharmed. Jack relaxed a little. Maybe he was over-reacting. Chances were the stranger was just trying to help. This wasn't California. It wasn't so odd that someone would go out of their way to help out on a stormy night. And he knew Albert James had put him in a weird place emotionally. Satisfied the girls were fine, he turned back to face the man, ready to apologize. "Listen, thanks but—"

The man was gone.

Jack spun around. He didn't see him anywhere. Then a voice came from the other side of the car, across the hood on the passenger's side. "Pretty girls you have there. Very pretty."

Soaking wet, Jack still felt the hair rise up on the back of his neck. All the tension returned. "Listen buddy. I think it's best if you get out of here. Maybe you're trying to help out, but you're scaring my kids."

The stranger leaned back to look through the Jeep's rear window, then back at Jack. "Scaring them? Or scaring you?"

"Look, just get out of here. All right?"

"These girls don't have anything to worry about from me." The man rubbed the hood of the car with the palms of his hands. "I want to be their friend. Especially the little one. She's very special. Sarah. That's it, isn't it? Little sweet Sarah?"

"Get the hell out of here, right now," Jack yelled over a thunderclap. He had only been in one fight as an adult, but if the car hadn't separated them, he would have taken a swing at the bastard in front of him.

The man slapped the hood of the car in a slow beat. "Bam, bam, badda, bam, bam," he murmured as he thumped out a rhythm, his eyes locked with Jack's, a grin spread across his lips. "Feel helpless, Jack? You don't mind if I call you Jack, do you?"

"How the hell do you know our names? Who are you?"

"Oh, I know more than that about you. I know what you dream about at night. I know the secret you keep from California. That dark detail about yourself you don't want anyone else to know."

"I don't know what—"

"Jack, you don't really think you can stop the devil, do you?"

Jack froze. "What did you say?"

But the man wasn't listening. He continued to beat out a rhythm on the hood, striking the car harder with each beat. *Badda, bam, bam.* He paused and held both fists out toward Jack. "Let's find out, shall we?" His fists crashed into the hood. *BADDA, BAM, BAM.*

On the last beat, he ducked down behind the car and was gone.

"Shit." Jack scrambled into the car and shut the door. He dug at the controls on the armrest to make sure the doors were locked. They were. He looked across to the passenger side. The door shook from the man tugging on it. The girls screamed. Jack dug his hand into his pocket, desperate for his keys. Nothing. He looked on the floor, on the seat. He pressed his face against the window and looked on the ground outside. They weren't there. When did he have them last?

Dreading what he would see, he raised his head to look through the windshield at the building in front of him. There, on the ground next to the payphone, were the keys to the car.

ELEVEN

Jack beat his fists into the steering wheel. He had searched everywhere in the car he could think of for the spare key. Nothing. He looked back up at the keys on the concrete not more than thirty feet from him. He must have dropped them when he first saw the man next to the car. The girls choked back their sobs, more scared by their dad's outburst than anything. He noticed the silence in the back seat and turned around in his seat to face the girls. "Hey, easy now. I didn't mean to scare you. Everything's okay."

Becky spoke first. "Who is that man?"

"Listen, that man was probably someone who doesn't have a home, and he was caught in the rainstorm. He doesn't want to hurt anyone."

Sarah whispered something. Jack leaned toward her. "What did you say, sweetie?"

She didn't answer him but just stared out of the window, shaking her head slowly.

"Sarah, honey. It's okay. Talk to me."

The little girl kept looking out the window. She whispered, "No, I don't want to."

Jack was confused. "You don't want to talk to me?"

Sarah turned away from the window. "Not you, Daddy. I wasn't talking to you."

Jack leaned into the back seat to look out of her window. There was nothing there. "What do you mean, sweetie? Who were you talking to?"

"The man. I was talking to the bad man." Before Jack could say anything, she turned to him and whispered. "And you're wrong, Daddy. He does want to hurt us. Especially you."

"Sarah, honey, that's not true. Why would you say that?"

"But it is true, Daddy." Her eyes welled up with tears as she pointed out the window. "The bad man just told me so. He said he's gonna take me with him. Is it true, Daddy? Is he going to take me?"

"No honey. It's not true."

"He said I should open the door, or I'd end up like Melissa. Who's that, Daddy? Who's Melissa?"

For a few seconds all other noise faded from the world. The only sounds Jack heard were his own breath and the blood pounding in his temples. He stared at Sarah, trying to understand how those words could have come from her mouth. Becky stared at her little sister and then back at her dad, her eyes wide. Thunder tore through the sky above them, so close that it felt like an earthquake. The girls squealed, and Jack jumped in his seat.

"All right, we're getting out of here. Girls, listen. I left the keys by the pay phone over there. I have to go get them."

"Noooo. Don't leave us here."

"I'll be right back. I promise. The car will be locked. No one can get in."

"I want to stay with you," Becky pleaded.

"Don't leave us here."

Jack looked at his terrified girls and then back to the pay phone. He could be there and back in half a minute. If he took the kids with him, it would take a lot more time and leave them all exposed.

He hadn't seen the stranger since he tried to force the passenger door open more than five minutes ago. Maybe he realized there was a problem when Jack didn't start the car right away. He felt a surge of panic. What if the man saw the car keys on the ground by the payphone? He'd be able to open any door. Jack wasn't worried about fighting the man, but if the stranger had a gun, or even a knife, there would be no contest. The man could shoot him through the window if he had a gun.

If he kills me, what will he do to the girls?

Jack knew he had to get them out of there. Waiting in the car was not an option.

"I'll be right back, girls." He checked to make sure the man wasn't crouching outside. Nothing. Blocking out his daughters' screams, he threw open the door and burst out into the storm.

TWELVE

The parking lot was an ominous landscape of hiding places and unknown dangers. The storm-wracked trees next to the streetlights cast erratic shadows like dark birds flying on damaged wings. Jack sprinted toward the pay phone. He slowed only to glance over his shoulder to look for the man. Nothing. Only shadows.

Jack reached the phone and snatched the keys off the ground. He was about to turn back to the car when he saw the phone hanging off the hook. He froze. The new option dangled there in front of him. He looked back to the car, then to the phone. He didn't want to run away from this man, he wanted him caught. Besides, the call would only take a second.

Jack lunged forward, grabbed the phone, and slammed it back into place. He lifted it up and jabbed his finger into the keypad. 9-1-1. The dial tone disappeared and the phone clicked through the relays. "C'mon. C'mon."

He switched the receiver to his other ear so he could twist around to look back at the car. The dome light was on, and he saw the blurry outline of the girls sitting in the back.

No sign of the stranger.

Where is the Goddamn operator?

The phone continued to click.

His eyes shifted to the far corner of the parking lot. A dim light twinkled through the rain. He hadn't noticed it before. Then headlights came on and started to move toward the rest area exit. Jack breathed easier. The car must belong to the stranger. He was leaving. It was over.

Then the car stopped. The rain slowed for a moment, and Jack could hear the car's motor across the parking lot. The driver was revving it hard, over and over.

"Oh, God." As the words stumbled out of Jack's mouth, the driver engaged the clutch and the car's wheels spun on the wet asphalt. Once the tires found traction, the car bore down on the Jeep, engine whining.

Jack tore off across the lot, screaming at his daughters. "Get out. Get out of the car!"

The car closed the space. It was going too fast. He would never make it in time.

"Becky. Sarah. Get out of the car!"

The rear side door opened on the opposite side from the approaching car. Through the windshield, he saw Becky pulling her sister by her jacket. Finally, they tumbled out of the car and started to run.

As the girls cleared the door, the incoming car turned hard to the left, its rear tires losing traction. The car's back bumper crashed into the rear panel of the Jeep in a grinding screech of metal on metal. Sparks flashed, then disappeared in the rain. The stranger kept the accelerator down and the wheels spun again. In the seconds it took before the tires found purchase on the asphalt, the car trunk popped open.

Jack wiped the rain away from his eyes. He could have sworn he saw a face staring at him from the trunk of the car, and thought his mind was playing tricks on him in the stress of the moment.

He staggered forward a few steps and stopped.

Jesus, it was a face.

The face of a girl tied up in the back of the stranger's car. A young girl, not more than a teenager, with duct tape stretched across her mouth, blood covering her shirt, her body twisted into a grotesque fetal position. The image lasted only a couple of seconds. The tires grabbed, the stranger's car surged forward, and inertia forced the trunk closed.

Jack stood frozen in place and watched as the car sped out of the parking lot and disappeared into the storm. He had to do something. It had happened so fast he couldn't tell if the girl had moved. Still, somehow he was sure she was alive. Her eyes had begged him for help. And people didn't look scared when they were dead.

He cried out as something ran into him from behind and wrapped itself around his leg. He reached down to defend himself and felt something soft and smooth. It took a second to register – the texture of children's jackets. Becky and Sarah. They were hugging his legs and crying.

He knelt down, scooped the girls into his arms, and held them. Their hug lasted only a few moments while the image of the girl in the trunk forced its way back into Jack's brain. "All right, girls. Back in the car. Quick now." They obeyed him without hesitation, needing no urging to get away from the parking lot as fast as possible.

A minute later, they were on the road. The girls were silent in the back seat, strapped into their car seats, too afraid to do anything but whimper. Jack looked in the rearview mirror and watched Becky reach across to her sister and run her fingers through her hair. He smiled. It was what their mother did to comfort them when they were sick or scared.

Taillights appeared on the road ahead, one red, one white, where the rear bumper was smashed. The stranger's car.

Jack flipped open the cell phone and dialed out. Seconds later, it beeped and an error message appeared on the LCD panel – "Signal Faded."

What now, Jack? What the hell are you going to do now?

When he looked up from the phone, the taillights were gone. Jack didn't remember a curve in the road here, and there were no off-ramps either. Still, the road ahead of him was pitch black, as if the stranger's car had disappeared into a tunnel. Jack slowed to a crawl and squinted through the rain-spattered windshield. There were steep ditches on either side of the highway, so the man couldn't have turned. The windows started to fog up, and he realized that his breathing was too quick and shallow. He needed to calm down. He reached up with the sleeve of his shirt to wipe off the fog on the window in front of him.

As he wiped the condensation away, he saw the car out of the corner of his eye, sitting on the side of the road, its lights turned off.

As soon as Jack was past, the headlights came on, and the car swerved onto the road behind him. In a matter of seconds, Jack had gone from being the hunter to the hunted.

He gripped the wheel and accelerated. The Jeep reacted and surged forward, but the stranger's car already had momentum and bore down on them. The rearview mirror blazed with the approaching headlights. It was right on his bumper.

The girls screamed with the first hit from the car. Jack steered to the right, careful not to overcorrect on the slippery road.

The stranger pulled alongside and swerved into them.

Jack felt the blow on the door next to him.

Sparks flew as the cars ground into each other, speeding down the road side by side.

Jack stepped on the brakes, the ABS system controlling the deceleration on the wet highway.

The stranger didn't react fast enough, and his car continued down the highway.

Once Jack was clear of the car, he accelerated again to stay behind the stranger's car.

He wasn't going to let him out of his sight again.

The stranger's car lurched to the right once the Jeep decelerated, but soon corrected itself. A second later, red light filled the Jeep's windshield.

The car had locked up its brakes.

Jack didn't have time to react.

The Jeep smashed into the car's back fender.

Screams erupted again from the back seat.

The force from the collision ripped open the car's trunk. Jack lost sight of the road as something landed on his windshield with enough force to shatter the safety glass into a spiraling web of cracks.

Oh, Jesus, not again. Not like before.

Jack tried to turn, but the cars' bumpers were caught together. Then he saw it. In the lower corner of the window, where the windshield was still intact, was a face.

The girl from the trunk.

Her body, thrown from the trunk by the impact, was draped across the windshield.

And she was alive.

Her eyes stared at him through the glass.

Full of pain.

Full of terror.

Jack cried out.

Then the face was gone.

The world turned on its end and gravity ceased to exist. His girl's screams mixed with the whine of metal twisting in on itself. Jack heard a muted explosion and felt pressure over his chest and face. And then darkness.

THIRTEEN

Jack slowly opened his eyes, wincing at the room's raw light. Lauren sat on the edge of the bed, holding his hand. Jack figured she hadn't slept all night, but God, she still looked fantastic. A youthful thirty-nine, not even the hint of a wrinkle appeared around her blue eyes. Her physique had survived two pregnancies thanks to a rigorous running and regular yoga schedule. She could put most men to shame on any endurance course.

This afternoon, though, she looked like she had endured her limit. She let go of Jack's hand, walked down to the end of his bed and pulled his chart. As she studied it, a nurse walked in pushing a food tray. When she saw Lauren, she shook her head impatiently. "I told you to stop messin' with that chart."

Lauren didn't look up. She just kept reading.

The nurse stood beside her and held out her hand.

Lauren looked up at the nurse. "Just checking. You know…," her voice trailed off.

"He's fine. Just look at him. A little cut on the head won't hurt his pretty little face." The nurse gave Jack an appraising look and turned on her sassy voice, "I'm telling you suga', he's *fine.*"

Jack clapped his hands. "You tell her, Janice. I'm ready to get out of here."

The light above the phone on the wall lit up. Lauren pointed to Jack. "You behave." Then she turned to Janice and handed her the chart. "And you. Don't let me walk in here and find you giving him a sponge bath." She smiled. "He's a smooth talker, so watch out."

Lauren picked up the phone. "Yes, this is Doctor Tremont." She paused. "All right, I'll be right down." She turned to Jack. "It seems that our daughters are fighting over what cartoon to watch. Becky thinks she's in control because she has the cast on her arm, but Sarah doesn't seem to agree."

Jack grinned. "It's amazing how fast everything gets back to normal."

"Thank God for air bags and safety seats."

Jack noticed the catch in her voice and knew his wife had just pictured what might have happened if they hadn't been so lucky in the crash. He had done it a thousand times over the past twelve hours. "Hey, Lauren." She looked up and he saw tears in her eyes. "We're all okay."

She came over and hugged him. Janice turned away to give them privacy, but she snuck a look with a smile. Lauren let go and headed out of the room. "Now I'm off to make peace with the sisters. And I thought being a doctor was hard. Remember, Janice, no sponge bath. No matter what he tells you."

As Lauren left the room, Jack heard men's voices in the hallway. They were arguing about something, but he couldn't make out the words. Lauren walked back in the room followed by Hugh Janney, Prescott City's sheriff, and one of his deputies. They stood at the foot of his bed in an uncomfortable silence.

"So," Jack said, leaning forward. "Was she dead?"

Sheriff Janney cleared his throat. "No, Mr. Tremont, she wasn't dead."

"Thank God." Jack lay back in the bed. "Is she here? In this hospital?"

Janney looked down at the floor and then over to the deputy. "Mr. Tremont, I'm not sure how to tell you this." The sheriff ran a hand across his chin and then rubbed the back of his neck. Finally, he looked up and met Jack eye to eye. "We looked everywhere you told us. As far as we can tell, this girl you told us about doesn't exist."

FOURTEEN

Even after hearing the details of the search, Jack couldn't manage much better than a dumbfounded stare at the sheriff. How was it possible that the body was gone? He had seen her. She was right there on the hood of his car. There was no way the body could just disappear.

As Jack processed the information, a pit carved out a space in his stomach. The three other people in the room waited for an explanation. He suddenly realized they didn't believe him.

"I saw her. I swear it. Did you look in the woods? She probably crawled into the woods."

The sheriff held up his hands. "Now look here. I've had men out there since last night, and we've been looking all day. Deputy Sorenson here and myself did most of the search ourselves. We even brought the dogs out."

"And?"

"Nothing. Not a thing."

"She couldn't have gone far. She was all tied up."

"Yeah, you told us that." Janney opened up the notebook where he scribbled his notes from the morning. "You said she was bound and gagged with duct tape. That she rolled off the hood of your car right before you rolled into that ditch." He closed up the notebook. "That's what you said this morning."

"That's what happened."

"Yeah, so you say," the deputy said.

Jack ignored him. "How about in the man's car? What's his name…Huckley? You had to find evidence in the trunk of his car."

Sheriff shook his head. "Looked myself."

"And?"

"Nothing. Not a thing."

"Impossible. I just don't – I mean, how could…"

"Mr. Tremont, I'm gonna need to ask you a few more questions, all right?"

Lauren reached down and took Jack's hand. He appreciated her gesture of support, but he wondered if it made him look guilty, like he needed the support because he had something to hide. He wondered if they knew about the last time the police questioned him.

"Were you over at Piper's last night?"

Jack felt the muscles in his stomach tighten. "Yes, I was at Piper's last night from about four to seven."

"Have a couple of drinks?"

"Yeah. No…just one drink actually."

"You had one drink in three hours?"

Jack remembered the shot of whiskey he and Max had after watching Albert James die. "No, I guess it was two drinks."

"Uh-huh, now it's two drinks. You want to think on it a little longer?"

Jack didn't care for the sheriff's tone. "Wait a minute. What're you thinking? I got blitzed, picked up my kids drunk and hallucinated that a psychopath tried to kill me? Jesus." Jack raised himself up in the bed. He was yelling now. "What the hell's wrong with you?"

Janney was a big man and not intimidated by Jack's outburst. He pointed a finger at Jack's chest. "You *will* calm down. And I mean, right now." He took a deep breath. "I'm just trying to figure all this out. All I know is that I have two smashed up cars on my highway and a crazy story with no proof. I have no victim, no blood in the trunk of the other car."

"I didn't make this up," Jack insisted.

"You were at Piper's when Albert James took a lightning bolt to the head, right?"

Jack nodded.

"Shook you up pretty bad, huh?"

"The man died in my arms. Yeah, it shook me up. But I—"

"Then there's this business in California a few years back."

Jack felt Lauren's hand tighten in his.

"The little girl. What was her name?" Janney flipped through his notebook.

Not until that moment did Jack realize how much he had let himself believe no one would ever find his secret in his new life, that at least the public side of it was behind him. He knew the private torture would never end. But he thought he might at least spare his family from living through it again. Jack's voice had a catch in it when he answered. "Melissa Gonzales."

"That's right. Melissa Gonzales. Damn shame about that."

"Damn shame," the deputy said.

Lauren squeezed Jack's hand. "That was an accident," she said.

Jack closed his eyes and tried to put his mind somewhere else. Of course, he'd seen the similarities. Of course, he knew it was a bizarre coincidence. He'd been working it through his brain all morning. But it didn't change what he'd seen last night.

Janney puckered his lips. "Yeah, got the whole report sent right over to me. Says here, little Melissa hit the windshield just like—"

"Their tire blew out. He ran right into me," Jack whispered.

"And the girl went through the windshield of her daddy's pickup and landed on the hood of your car. Just like this girl last night? The girl you were trying to save?"

Jack turned away. A shiver started at the base of his spine and worked its way up his back. He closed his eyes, but the girl's face was there to look back at him. Not the girl from

49

last night, but Melissa Gonzales. Ten years old. Honor student. Played softball and liked blues music and horses. Wanted to be a doctor or a vet, her grandma had told him at the hospital. Right before she spat in his face and called him a murderer. The official report said the deaths weren't his fault. It wasn't anyone's fault. Accidents happen. It was what his friends told him too. Still, he caught the looks they gave him. Something had changed. He'd killed someone, and that was part of who he was now.

Their reaction was bad enough when they thought he was innocent.

It would have been much worse if they had known the truth.

The sheriff was right. Melissa Gonzales had smashed into his windshield just like the girl last night. He could still see her face when the air bag deflated – wide, unblinking eyes that stared at him while a flood of red spread out of her hair like a halo. That's where the image was different. The girl last night had been alive. He was sure of it.

"I know how it looks. But you have to believe me, I didn't imagine this."

"I'm just sayin' I can't find a body or evidence of one. I'm just sayin' that it doesn't take a shrink doctor to wonder if something's not going on in there." Janney tapped the side of his head.

"Did you question the guy in the car yet?" The deputy grunted and turned away. Jack turned his attention to him. The man looked to be in his mid-twenties, clean-shaven with a crew cut. His uniform was starched with the pleats of his pants pointing down to polished black boots. Everything he carried seemed to shine. Jack imagined the kid sitting in his living room at night intensely cleaning his gun, millimeter by millimeter, praying for the day he'd have a chance to blow someone away. He probably polished his handcuffs too. Jack just hoped that Sheriff Janney had been smart enough not to give the kid any bullets. Jack decided he'd had enough of the deputy's attitude. "Excuse me. Do you have a problem?"

The deputy glared back but held his tongue.

Janney jumped in and broke the staring contest. "Jack, the man you hit—"

"That I hit! You mean the man who attacked me."

"Yeah, okay. Like I told you, his name's Nate Huckley. It's not like he's some drifter. He's pretty well known around here. He's a little on the strange side, sure, but nothing like this. You gotta understand it makes your story that much harder to believe."

"Okay. So what does Nate Huckley say about all this?"

Lauren answered before the sheriff. "He's in a coma. There's not so much as a scratch on him, but he's not reviving. We have to do more tests."

"Will he come out of it?"

"Hard to say. He could wake up an hour from now, a week from now…"

"Or never," Janney said.

"Or never," Lauren agreed

The deputy mumbled something.

"What'd you say?" Jack said.

The deputy fixed him with a hard look. "I said, 'Another notch in the belt'."

"You son-of-a-bitch."

Janney grabbed his deputy by the arm and pulled him toward the door. "All right, that's enough of that. You wait outside." He waited until the deputy was gone. "Sorry about that. He's a damn fool sometimes. Don't let him get to you. Listen, I'm gonna keep looking into this and try everything I can to figure it out. A lot of folks are gonna wonder if Nate Huckley is getting a fair shake here."

"What are you saying?"

"I'm just saying I've got to look into the possibility that Huckley is the victim in this mess."

"I don't understand," Jack said.

"You're driving home, had a few drinks—"

"I wasn't drunk."

Janney started to say something but seemed to think better of it. He tucked his hat under his arm and headed for the door. He paused, a little too dramatically, Jack thought, and stared at Lauren. "See, funny thing is, when you were brought in they didn't check your blood for alcohol. That's standard policy, isn't it, Dr. Tremont?"

Lauren was tight lipped. "It should have been done. I'll check into it."

Janney smiled. "Oh, I checked. Wasn't done. Nurses say you treated him when he came in and said it wasn't necessary."

"It wasn't. I could tell if he was intoxicated or not."

"I'm sure you could," Janney said. "Just looks a little funny, you know? Anyway, I know this sounds like some bad cop line, but don't be leaving town for a while, okay? It might take a little time to figure this out, and I'd like to have you both around to answer questions."

"We'll be here," Lauren said.

"All right, then. I'll be getting along now." Janney nodded to Jack as if he'd just stopped by to wish him a speedy recovery. Jack and Lauren watched the sheriff leave, and Jack silently wished he'd never come at all.

FIFTEEN

Jack changed into the fresh clothes Lauren had brought from the house. As he sat on the edge of the bed to button his shirt, Lauren slid behind him and rubbed his shoulders.

"I know what I saw, Lauren."

"I believe you. Focus on the fact that you and the kids are safe. Focus on that."

Lauren, the calm. Lauren, the wise. How many times had she filled that need for him? A hundred times? A thousand? He still couldn't believe he had almost lost her. He leaned back into her and she wrapped her arms around him. "You should have seen the girl's eyes. She was so scared."

She held him tight and then kissed him on the cheek. "I have about an hour of stuff to do around here and then we can all go home. Why don't you go down and hang out with the kids?"

Lauren started to pull away from him, but Jack pulled her back close. He still hadn't told her about Sarah's strange behavior in the car. That their daughter somehow seemed to know about Melissa Gonzales. The words had been replaying in his head all day.

He said I should open the door, or I'd end up like Melissa. Who's Melissa, Daddy?

Then there was Albert James' bizarre warning about Sarah being in danger, a warning that turned out to be right only hours later.

Jack wanted to tell Lauren, have her rationalize it all so he could put it aside, but he didn't know where to start. Besides, he knew how it would sound. Especially now with everyone doubting there was a body in the back of Huckley's car. He couldn't afford to look like he was losing it.

He kissed her hand and let go. But as she started to get up, he said, "Why didn't you let them do a blood alcohol test when I came in?"

Lauren hesitated. "When they told me you and the kids were on the way in to emergency from a crash scene, I ran down to be there. It was horrible to wait there, not knowing what was going on. Testing you for alcohol was the last thing on my mind."

"It wasn't because you smelled alcohol on my breath." Lauren didn't answer. "I wasn't drunk. I had one beer and a shot over a four-hour time frame. I would never put the kids in danger, you know that."

"Yeah, I know. Listen, I've got to run. I'll see you in an hour."

Jack could tell he'd rubbed her the wrong way. With everything going on, the last thing they needed was a fight. He called after her, "Hey, sorry. I'm a little on edge. It's just..."

"It's just what?"

"I love you."

She flashed him the same smile that had made him fall for her ten years earlier. "You're just kissing up. Angling for that sponge bath when we get home," she said with enough playfulness to let him know everything was all right between them.

He reached up and rubbed his neck. "I am a little sore."

"If you're a good boy. Maybe." She gave him a wink. "See you in an hour or so."

Jack spent most of the next hour in the room with Becky and Sarah watching TV and brushing their hair. They amazed him. The whole ordeal was like a movie to them, something scary while they watched it happen, but quickly forgotten once it was over. Signatures from the nursing staff already covered the cast on Becky's right arm, and she brandished it about with pride. She only had a hairline fracture, so the cast wouldn't be on for long, but she was making the most of it. Jack couldn't help laughing when Sarah asked if she could get one too.

At a quarter to five, Jack got up from the bed and told the girls he'd be right back. A Disney cartoon about little round robots was on TV, and his daughters didn't even look up as he left the room. Jack walked down the hospital corridor toward the elevator. The hospital had three stories, and he had visited Lauren here enough times to know the layout pretty well. Although she ran a small family practice in Prescott City, once word of her credentials got out, the doctors at the Midland General often called her to consult on cases. With a medical degree from Stanford and post-doctorate research at Johns Hopkins and UCLA, she was a medical celebrity in the mountain towns of Western Maryland. Midland was only a half hour from Prescott City, so Lauren didn't mind making the drive. Jack guessed it also helped keep her sane to treat more than just swollen tonsils and bee stings day in and day out.

He got off the elevator on the top floor where the long-term inpatients were kept. The floor was a reverent quiet, partially because Midland wasn't a very busy hospital and most of the rooms were empty, but also because the patients here tended to be old and very near their natural ends. The corridor was like a library at two in the morning – the kind of place where you just knew to be quiet.

A nurse sat behind the oval desk across from the elevator. She made no effort to hide the book she was reading. He couldn't see the title but saw the distinctive mark on the cover designating it as an *Oprah's Book Selection*.

"Can I help you?"

"Hi, my name is Jack Tremont–"

"Oh, you must be looking for Dr. Tremont. Let me page her." She started to pick up the yellow phone on her desk.

"No, I know where she is. I'm actually looking for a patient. Huckley. Nate Huckley."

The nurse pursed her lips together and shook her head. "Terrible what happened to him, isn't it? Drunk driver, I heard."

Jack felt an ice ball in his stomach. He fought back the urge to correct her. It would only make it harder for him to accomplish his mission. "Yeah, it's terrible. I wanted to check in on him. Dr. Tremont asked me to."

She arched her eyebrows at him. "She asked you to check on a patient for her?"

"Yeah. Just wanted me to pop my head in and make sure everything was fine. You know how she is."

The nurse hesitated, then pointed down the hallway to the right. "Room 320. You know not to touch the equipment, right? Maybe I should come with you."

"No need. I'll only be a second." He pointed at her book. "Looks like a good one."

The nurse smiled. "Oprah never lets me down." She lowered her voice and glanced up and down the halls. "This one has sex scenes."

Jack grinned and pretended to look at the page she was reading. The nurse shooed him away with a giggle. Jack whispered, "I'll let you get back to it then. I won't be long."

He strode down the hall without waiting for an answer. A quick glance over his shoulder confirmed that the nurse was settling back into her chair, book in hand. Good. He wanted to do this alone. Jack walked until he came to room 320. He rested his hands against the heavy wood door of Nate Huckley's room and turned his head to listen for any sounds coming from inside. He heard nothing, so, with a deep breath, he pushed on the door.

SIXTEEN

"Hola, Felicia. Que Pasa?" Lauren said, pulling back the curtain from the bed.

The little girl gave her a weak smile. "Your accent is getting a little better. Could still use some work though."

"Oh, I don't know. I think it's pretty good," Lauren said. "So tell me, how are you feeling?"

"Sore. I'm sore everywhere," Felicia said.

Lauren leaned forward and smoothed back a few strands of loose hair on the girl's forehead. She was a pretty thing, ten years old, with dark skin and long black hair. Over the last week, Lauren had grown attached to the girl. Even though Lauren wasn't a pediatric specialist, Felicia's condition had immediately attracted her attention. "I'll get you something to make you more comfy, all right?"

Felicia nodded and watched Lauren write in her file. "Dr. Tremont?"

"Yes?"

"I'm gonna die."

The little girl's matter-of-fact tone caught Lauren off-guard. It was as if she had read Lauren's mind. Lauren stared down at her notebook while she thought of the best way to answer. She had never lied to a patient before, but she couldn't bring herself to tell the girl the truth. Before she could say anything, Felicia reached out and touched her forearm.

"It's okay, Dr. Tremont. You don't have to lie to me. I mean, I'm scared a little, but I don't...I don't want to feel this way anymore."

Lauren swallowed hard and put her notebook on the bed. "You listen here, young lady. There will be no more talk like that. We're going to find a way to beat this thing, all right? But I need your help. I need you to fight."

Felicia smiled but looked away toward the window. "Mom told me I would see my Nana in heaven. That'll be nice." She closed her eyes as she spoke, her voice winding down like a toy that needed a new battery. "She was always so nice to me." Seconds later, Felicia was back asleep.

Lauren sat on the edge of the bed and rested her hand on the little girl's shoulder. She had grown close to Felicia. Her clinical detachment was gone, replaced by a maternal need to protect the sick child however she could. It was impossible for her to look at the little girl and not see her own daughter in the bed, her own daughter sick with some mysterious disease that Lauren, despite all her education and skill, could not stop. This was no longer medicine. It was personal.

Lauren circled the tests she wanted done on Felicia Rodriguez's blood work. The symptoms read like a med school multiple-choice test. Open sores on the skin, hair loss, abdominal cramps, weight loss, heart arrhythmia, erratic pulse, fever, and so it went. It was like her body was giving up on her. The young doctor who first admitted the patient had worked hard to fit the symptoms into anything in the literature but had come up empty. Lauren worried that she would come up against the same brick wall.

When she was first told of the case, the litany of past terrors ticked off in her head: Ebola, cerebral encephalitis, anthrax, hemorrhagic fever. The sores, especially, raised a concern. They were dark purple, like bruises, and drained yellow pus when ruptured. But the interview with Felicia's father reduced Lauren's initial fear that some strange contagion was at work. None of the high-risk behavior was present in the patient or her family. No travel out of the country. No interaction with livestock. No intravenous drug use. The backwoods of western Maryland hardly seemed a likely site for a terrorist attack. The only high-value target was the presidential retreat of Camp David, but that was more than fifty miles away.

Lauren knew these factors only reduced and didn't eliminate the possibility of a highly contagious virus. Her work at Johns Hopkins on West Nile Virus taught her that mosquitoes were nature's most efficient disease transmitters, better than any manmade device for germ warfare. As were ticks, fruit flies, bad water, mold, and tainted meat. The list was endless and frightening in its banality. The most important fact she'd learned from the interview was that the Rodriguez family had six other children, and all had had close contact with Felicia since she became sick. None of them showed any symptoms.

Her father, Raoul, lowered his head in shame when Lauren asked how long Felicia had been ill.

"Three weeks. She sick bad for three weeks."

Frustrated, Lauren asked why it had taken him so long to bring her to the hospital.

He turned red and stammered, "I bring in. Downstairs give me pills. Tell me make her sleep and give water. No money, you know?"

Lauren patted him on the arm and assured him that she would take care of his little girl and that "no money" wasn't a problem. Downstairs meant that he had brought the girl to the emergency room. Lauren had seen it a hundred times, especially in California. Migrant workers with no insurance using the emergency room for general care and getting the blow-off by overworked doctors.

She'd argued the case on more than one blue-ribbon panel of medical experts, for all the good it did. The system was broken. The best care went to the highest bidder, to those who could afford a lawyer if something went wrong. The directors of the hospital could afford benefit dinners at the Ritz Carlton, but pro bono services to the neediest were targeted for cuts at every budget review. She knew that emergency room doctors were good, and they did their best, but limited time, resources, and sleep made for snap judgments, and snap judgments led to mistakes. Someone made a mistake with Felicia Rodriguez and hadn't taken the time to properly diagnose her. Now the little girl sleeping in front of her was paying the price.

"What do you think?"

She jumped from the edge of the bed with a start, holding the chart against her chest like a shield.

Dr. Stanley Mansfield stood in front of her. He was the chief of staff at Midland General and had been so for as long as anyone could remember. Tall and lean, with salt and pepper hair, he didn't look older than his mid-fifties, though the older nurses assured Lauren that he had to be well into his sixties by now, maybe even early seventies. The doctor knew the staff liked to speculate about his age, so he kept it a closely guarded secret, saying that it would be revealed only at his funeral. His way of making sure people showed up, he liked to joke.

"Stanley, you scared me to death." Lauren laughed. She had not only learned to respect Dr. Mansfield's judgment in the short time they'd been colleagues, but they'd developed a friendship as well. He ran a tight ship at the hospital, but the medicine always came first, and he supported his doctors no matter what happened. When nurses and patients weren't around, he and Lauren felt comfortable enough to call each other by their first names.

"It's okay to be a little jumpy after the day you've had. In fact, I can't believe you're still here."

"We're taking the kids home in a little bit. I just wanted to check on Felicia first."

"And?"

"And I'm stumped. I'm not sure what to think. I want to send some blood to Atlanta. What do *you* think?" Atlanta was home to the CDC, the Center for Disease Control. Between the facilities there and its military counterpart at Fort Dietrich, every virus capable of destroying the world population was stored and experimented on. The best testing technology coupled with the brightest medical minds protected the public from devastating outbreaks and helped doctors around the world understand the illnesses they were fighting in the field. Lauren didn't know where else to turn.

Stanley made a soft humming sound behind pursed lips. Lauren smiled since she knew this was the doctor's habit whenever he was thinking something through.

"Yes, let's send blood to the CDC and see what they come up with."

"The CDC tests should help the determination. This might be something no one has ever seen before."

The older doctor turned to Lauren and said seriously, "You know what I've never seen before?"

"What?"

"You getting out of here when you're supposed to." Lauren started to protest, but he raised his hand to stop her. "Listen, I'm working tonight. I'll spend some time with Felicia here. I'll take the samples myself and make sure they are expedited to Atlanta. You need to take your family home and spend some time with them."

Lauren looked at her watch and shook her head. "I am running late. You don't mind?"

"Get out of here. I'll take care of everything."

Lauren handed him the chart. "Call me if anything changes," she said over her shoulder. Stanley didn't acknowledge her. He was standing over the bed, humming as he flipped through the chart. Lauren headed out to gather her things. She just needed to track down Jack and the kids, and they'd be ready to go.

SEVENTEEN

The door creaked as Jack applied just enough pressure to make it move. Inch by careful inch, he opened the door, ready to let go on the first indication that anyone was inside. A faint *thunk-thunk* of a respirator and the electric buzz of monitors were the only sounds in the room. Dim lights cast a pale orange hue over everything. From the door, the room opened up to the left after a short hall with a doorway for a toilet. For someone standing at the door, the angle cut most of the room from sight. Designed to provide patients with a higher degree of privacy, it also hid Huckley's face from view.

Jack stayed close to the wall as he slid further into the room. He could see the lower half of the hospital bed extending from the left side of the room. Huckley's legs were a hump under the grey hospital blanket. Two more steps into the room and Jack would be able to see his face.

He stopped and steadied himself against the wall. His heart pounded in his chest and he was suddenly short of breath. What was he doing here? What was he trying to prove? He knew what happened last night, and seeing the man wouldn't change anything.

But Jack had to see him. He lived by confronting the challenges that stood in his way – the physical ones anyway. He purposely pursued his fears in order to overcome them. He feared heights, so he'd taken up skydiving. He feared public speaking, so he spoke at college campuses and to business groups. Most of all, he feared failure, so he forced himself to pursue the most difficult challenges and take the greatest risks.

Something had happened inside of him last night, something he didn't like. In a few seconds, a maniac had nearly blown his entire world apart, and he had been powerless to stop him. All the security he spent a lifetime building for his family was laid bare at that moment, and an awful truth forced itself onto him, the same truth that haunted him from the day of the car crash in California, the day Melissa Gonzales died on the hood of his car. The unsavory truth that everything he loved could disappear in a heartbeat.

There were no rules, no fairness, and no breaks for good conduct. Life could turn to death in a matter of seconds and you never knew when something could lash out and strike you down. Like the bolt that had burned a hole through Albert James' head. Acts of nature. Freak accidents. Wasn't that enough to deal with without having to add a deranged psychopath to the list?

Jack believed that through sheer diligence he could somehow protect his family from the bad things of the world. Deep down he knew it was naïve, but he allowed himself the fantasy. He didn't know how else to deal with a world where everything could be taken away without warning. But Huckley had pulled the sheet back and exposed the fragility of his fantasy. The encounter kept replaying in his head; each time Huckley became less of a man and more of a monster, unstoppable, uncontrollable. It felt as if his run-in with Huckley had immersed him in cold water, shocking him awake to his own vulnerability. And now, as Jack stood just out of sight from Huckley's body, the chill of that immersion made his hands tremble.

Jack detested the way he felt, the weakness, the lack of control. The only way he knew how to deal with a challenge was confrontation. In his mind, Huckley was a pale, ghoulish mask in a thunderstorm, a twisted smile, a dark dream more nightmare than real. Jack needed him to be just a man again. Something natural. Something normal.

He stepped into the room.

Relief was his first emotion. Huckley lay prone in the hospital bed, the covers pulled up to his chest. His arms were on top of the blanket and fitted with an IV and sensors. Other wires and tubes ran from Huckley's disabled body to the monitoring equipment arrayed next to the bed. An oxygen mask and nose tube covered his face and measured out his breathing. Jack wasn't sure what he expected, but the person lying on the bed in front of him was definitely not the monster he had built up in his mind. Relief at Huckley's utter plainness soon gave way to confusion. This was the face of a murderer? He looked more like someone's favorite uncle than a killer. *No wonder no one believes my story.*

Jack checked the corners of the ceiling to make sure there were no cameras. Seeing none, he stepped farther in to the room to get a closer look.

As he approached the bed, he noticed the bland smell of antiseptic mixed with the vaguely acrid smell of iodine. Jack stood next to the bed and looked down on the man who had terrorized him the night before.

The pale skin was even paler, but it no longer made him look menacing, just sickly. The man's features didn't gel with the sinister image burned into his mind from the night before. An angular bone structure and a rounded chin made Huckley more pleasant looking than handsome. He had pale blonde hair, so pale that his face seemed to lack eyebrows. Jack had been hoping to find some sign of evil, something to point to, for his own piece of mind. A tattooed swastika on his forehead like Manson would have been great. Anything to prove that the night before had not been his imagination and that this man was evil. But there was nothing and that disturbed him. For the first time, Jack wondered if he could have misinterpreted what had happened last night. He leaned against the bed, both of his hands on the blanket, even with Huckley's chest. He closed his eyes and tried to clear his head.

He thought he felt movement in the bed, and his eyes snapped open. Nothing. Huckley remained motionless.

Jack shook his head and laughed nervously about being so jumpy. Lauren was likely done and looking for him by now. He knew she would be upset if she found out what he'd been up to, especially if she discovered that he had told the on-duty nurse that Lauren had asked him to check on Huckley. Sheriff Janney would have field a day with his clandestine visit. Jack could hear him now, spouting something about returning to the scene of the crime.

Again, Jack thought he felt movement on the bed. He looked down. Still nothing.

He had risked coming to the room for no good reason, he thought angrily. What the hell did he hope to accomplish here anyway? What was done was done. It was only a matter of time before they found the woman's body. Then everyone would believe him. Sneaking into this crazy man's room accomplished nothing.

This guy was just some nutcake. End of story. The girls were fine. Just like Lauren told him, he had to focus on that. They were all fine. Life went on.

Turning towards the door, he caught a blur of motion as something seized his wrist. It felt like metal bindings digging into his skin. But it wasn't metal. Just human fingers clenched like an animal's claws.

It was Huckley.

Sitting up in bed, grabbing at Jack.

Jack cried out. He pulled back, prying the fingers back with his free hand. Huckley lurched upright in the bed. His other hand ripped off the tubes attached to his body. He yanked on Jack's arm and pulled him to the side of the bed so they were face to face.

Huckley's mouth parted in a smile, and yellow teeth poked through dry, cracked lips. His nostrils flared as if he were an animal smelling its prey. Jack struggled against the man's grip, but it was impossible to break away. Huckley licked the air with lewd flicks of his tongue.

With his free hand, Jack swung a wild punch and landed it against Huckley's jaw. A gash opened across Huckley's face like a crack in dried ground. The wound was deep but no blood poured from it. Huckley's mouth hung down at an impossible angle, his jaw broken.

Huckley shoved Jack away with both hands. Jack flew back from the bed and crashed into the far wall, barely staying on his feet. His instinct was to run to the door, but he couldn't move. He could only stare at what was happening in front of him.

Huckley stood on the bed, his clawed hands holding the sheet to his body. With a flick of his hand, he threw the sheet down and exposed his naked torso. Dark sores covered his skin, circular purple splotches with black centers. A foul smell like rancid meat filled the room. Jack gagged at the stench.

Huckley laughed, thick guttural noises that gurgled with phlegm. He pointed at Jack and laughed louder; a mix of spittle and dark blood bubbled out of his mouth and dripped down his chin.

With his other hand, he stuck his finger into the black center of a sore, pushing it in one knuckle at a time until the entire finger had disappeared. Huckley worked the finger around in a circle with a wet, sucking sound.

Jack pushed his back against the wall behind him, as if he might push hard enough and climb into the wall and away from the monster in front of him. He wanted to close his eyes but could not. He raised his arms to cover his face and gave into his horror. He filled his lungs and screamed.

"What the hell is going on in here?"

Strong hands were on his shoulders. Jack felt hot breath against his skin. He lowered his arms. Sheriff Janney's face was inches from his own.

"What the hell are you doing here?"

"It was Huckley. He…" Jack looked over the sheriff's shoulder at the hospital bed. Nate Huckley lay there hooked up to the *thunk-thunking* respirator and quietly humming monitors. The bed sheet was tucked in around him, smooth enough to roll a quarter across.

"He was what?"

Jack rubbed the side of his head and closed his eyes. In his mind, he could still see the open sores. He heard the laughter. But it wasn't real. Just his imagination. He had to get a grip on himself. He opened his eyes and smiled. "Sorry. It's been a tough one. Lack of sleep's making me see things."

"Let's see you get on out of here," Janney said. "What the hell were you thinking?"

Jack didn't try to answer. He just nodded his head and went for the door. The nurse from the front desk stood in the hall, clutching her book to her chest. Jack nodded in her direction as he walked out of the room, but the nurse stared down at the floor.

Served him right, he thought. After all, he had lied to her to get into Huckley's room. He turned to say something, an apology, anything, but she looked horrified. That's when it hit him. The nurse wasn't mad – she was scared of him.

Jack wanted to say something to make it better, make her understand that he wasn't the dangerous one. It was her patient in room 320 that she had to worry about. But everything he thought to say sounded crazy, so he gave up and let Janney escort him to the elevator. The doors closed, and he and Janney rode down in silence. Jack winced as he thought of explaining his little adventure to Lauren.

EIGHTEEN

The girls ran down the hall toward the exit to the parking lot. They had already said their good-byes to the nurses, and now they were ready to go home. Lauren walked quietly next to him. And she wasn't happy. Jack was trying to explain why he had come into Huckley's room in the first place, but he couldn't find the right words. And the more he tried, the more irrational the whole thing sounded.

"Look, I'm sorry. I know I shouldn't have gone up there," he finally said.

"You're right about that," she snapped. "You told the nurse that I asked you to go there. It's so unprofessional."

"I know. It was stupid. I'm sorry."

She shook her head, still angry, but reached out and took his hand as they walked. "You've been through a lot. Maybe this thing shook you up more than you thought. You know, dragged out some old demons." Jack didn't meet her eyes. "They said you were screaming?"

"I wasn't screaming."

"They said–"

"I told you. When I saw him, it just brought the experience back. It was like a hallucination. I panicked. Now it's over."

"Okay." She squeezed his hand. "We are going to talk more about this, but it can wait. Let's just get home."

Together, they walked out of the hospital and hurried to catch up with the girls already climbing into Lauren's Volvo station wagon. Jack remembered with a groan that he had to get a rental car the next day and call the insurance company about getting his car repaired. As he went over the mental list of the next couple of days of errands ahead of him, thoughts of Nate Huckley, car accidents, and kidnapped women faded into the background. And that was exactly where he wanted those thoughts to stay.

"I'll drive," he said. He appreciated that Lauren didn't hesitate but tossed him the keys without comment. After making sure the kids were buckled up, he started the car, shifted the automatic transmission into drive and wound his way through the parking lot.

"Lights," Lauren reminded him.

Jack grinned at her. "Got it under control." He flipped on the lights. "Let's go home," he called out.

The man watched closely as the Tremonts left the hospital. They'd left later than he planned, but he wasn't worried about the delay's impact on his schedule. Everything was still a go.

It was an interesting turn of events, the involvement of this Jack Tremont character. He hadn't been on any of his lists until the accident, but Tremont had the man's interest now. It was still too early to tell, but finding Tremont might turn out to be stroke of luck. And it was about time he caught a break. After months of reconnaissance, he was getting impatient for action.

The man exited his car. The dome light, of course, had been disconnected so as not to draw attention to his vehicle. He zipped up his black windbreaker and jogged across the parking lot. On the slim chance the security guard had deviated from his usual schedule and was walking the perimeter, the man had chosen his wardrobe to make sure he fit the part of a casual jogger. Right down to the armband iPod and worn black sneakers. But there was no guard in sight so the man turned and sprinted across the hospital lawn.

He made it across the wide lawn and leaned up against the hospital's brick exterior. Even after the sprint, his breathing was calm and measured. He worked his way along the side of the building, using the bushes for cover. There were some exterior lights but no cameras that he could see. He was reasonably sure he had not been detected. Reasonably sure was as good as it got in his profession.

He turned the corner of the building and came to the old fire escape on the north side of the building. The metal walkways and ladders were part of the original hospital construction back in the 1920s, and the man wondered if the hospital kept them in working order. He knew that instead of paying for the rusting structures to be removed, some owners of old buildings just welded the ladders together once modern fire-suppression systems were installed. He spotted the drop ladder suspended high above the ground but could not tell if it was functional.

Three quick steps and the man launched himself into the air. He planted his right foot on the wall, then pushed off hard, arching his back and fully extending his arms over his head.

The man easily reached the end of the ladder and grabbed it with both hands. Even with his weight, the ladder held in place. Welded shut. That alone did not present a problem as the man easily pulled himself up onto the first platform, but he worried that if the ladder was welded shut then the entrances to the floor might be obstructed as well.

The man checked the window that opened to the second floor. With a little pressure, it started to open. He closed it back tight and filed it away as an escape option. The man checked for movement in the parking lot down below. Seeing none, he grabbed the ladder and started toward his objective.

The third floor window was also unlocked. He checked the hallway, then slid the window open and crawled through. It took him three tries before he found the right room. Lucky for him, the first two were empty, although he moved quietly enough that he doubted he would have disturbed anyone. The man didn't have the abilities of his brother, but when he opened the door to room 320, he *felt* Nate Huckley in the room.

He strode into the room and leaned over the prone body, peering into the face partially covered by air tubes. Huckley's pale flesh took on a ghoulish cast in the yellow hospital lights and his usually immaculate hair was greasy and pasted flat to his scalp. The man placed a hand on the blanket over Huckley's chest, careful not have any skin-on-skin contact.

"Don't die on me now."

The man crossed the room and returned to the door. No lock. He dragged the cushioned visitor's chair from the side of the bed and braced it against the handle. Satisfied he would not be disturbed, at least not without warning, he pulled off his thick black sweater and threw it on the floor. He wore no shirt, and the cool air in the room gave him a chill as a thin sheen of sweat evaporated from his skin.

The man reached back and untied the string that held back his hair. Once he worked it loose, a great mound of black hair fell down across his shoulders and upper back, laying on thick muscles that twitched in expectation. He left his faded blue jeans on but removed his shoes and socks. From his back pocket, he removed a small black pouch and a length of braided leather rolled into a ball.

The man's rib cage heaved as he forced air into his lungs. Pressing his forearms against his diaphragm and bending at his midsection, he exhaled the air completely. Slowly straightening, he refilled his lungs to their capacity. Like a free diver preparing for a challenging depth, the man repeated this exercise for several minutes.

Finally, the man felt he was prepared. On the last great inhalation of breath, he held his lungs full and let only a small amount of air escape his lips in a steady stream. His lips began to move and form words. Then a sound rose from deep in his throat, a bass tone that fluctuated in a steady rhythm.

He tugged on the strings of the black pouch and poured the contents out into his right hand. Once the pouch was empty, he closed his right hand into a fist and with the other hand, replaced the pouch into his front pocket.

The chant became louder as the man moved to the corner of the room and kneeled down on the floor. Holding out his fist, he relaxed the bottom two fingers and allowed a tiny flow of black sand to trickle onto the floor. Clenching his hand back into a fist, he stopped the flow and moved to the next corner where he repeated the action.

Only once all four corners were complete did the man move to the bed. He unrolled the leather braid and placed it on Huckley's torso, one end just below the neckline and the other ending at his waist. The man looked to the first corner and saw a barely perceptible line of rising smoke. The powder was working.

Soon, smoke columns filled each of the four corners of the room and gathered on the ceiling as a gray odorless haze. The man raised his hands over Huckley's body and started his incantation. He tried to focus on the ritual, but he found it hard to block out the nagging voice in his subconscious, the voice that wondered if what he was doing was crazy. Part of him thought so. Part of him hoped so. But deep inside he knew he was fooling himself. The nightmare was real and it was just getting started.

NINETEEN

Fire everywhere. The forest around the Tremont's house was blazing. Tongues of red and orange shot out toward the sky, spun into desperate pirouettes by the gusting wind. Bright swaths of yellow stuck out among the dark blotches where the fire had already devoured this year's fuel. The crackle of dry leaves being crushed under four pairs of hiking boots provided the soundtrack to the inferno.

The kids ran ahead through the fall foliage, somehow running full speed and still managing to kick every pile of leaves in their path. Days like this were the reason they had bought the house. Their real estate agent knew how to do her job. She'd asked them to postpone their house-hunting trip by two weeks so they would hit the peak fall foliage. They hadn't stood a chance. Autumn in western Maryland, as far as Jack and Lauren were concerned, was one of the miracles of nature.

The first time they drove down the long, winding driveway through the property's fifteen wooded acres, a family of deer wandered into the road in front of them. Unafraid, the deer took their time to move to the other side, even waiting at the edge of the woods as the car passed to check out the passengers inside the car. By that time, the house on the property could have been a two-bedroom shack instead of the five thousand square foot custom home listed in the ad, and they wouldn't have cared. It was a perfect place to start their new life. A perfect place to heal. They made an offer that day.

A few of their Orange County friends had come to visit, each one commenting on the beauty of the place and how much they envied having the luxury to move somewhere so secluded. Jack took it all in with a smile. His friends all had money to move out of Orange County, but they never would. He knew full well they thought he and Lauren were crazy for living out in the sticks and that it would only be a matter of time before they would be tired of it all. His old business partner Jason Reid had said, "Jack, it's like going camping. All the back to nature crap is fun for a while, but pretty soon you'll need a rubdown at the Pacific Club and a nice restaurant where the menus aren't made out of plastic."

But the move was good for them. He and Lauren needed time to work things out, time to take care of old wounds inflicted during years when professional pursuits were put above family needs. And it was working. Jack had never felt more connected to his family than he did now. And Lauren admitted it was the same for her. Thanks to technology, she was able to stay involved with her research life and run a small practice in town, mostly doing *pro bono* work for the area's poorer families. It'd been just over a year since they'd moved, and he and Lauren were better than ever. Taking long walks through the forest around their property was one of their favorite things to do, and it had never felt more needed than the morning after returning from the hospital.

"Becky. Sarah. Don't get too far ahead," Lauren called.

"They're getting so big," Jack said.

"Before we know it, there'll be boys over here. Can you imagine them dating?"

"Sure. I won't have a problem with that."

"Really?"

"Sure. I figure when they're twenty-five, they'll have the right to do whatever they want."

"Twenty-five!" Lauren laughed. "In your dreams."

"It'd be nice though, wouldn't it? Be nice to keep them this age for a while."

"This is a great age. It's funny but—"

"Shhh. Did you hear that?" Jack cocked his head to the right side of the path. The rustling of leaves. A sharp *crunch*. Then sticks breaking.

"What is it?" Lauren whispered.

The noise stopped for a few seconds, then started again, louder this time. It sounded like a rock rolling through the trees. The thick undergrowth slowed down whatever was coming toward them, but it didn't stop it. The bushes and small trees nearest to them shook. Jack felt Lauren's hand tighten around his. The noise stopped, and the forest was an eerie quiet. Jack felt as if something was staring him down, something hidden by the mesh of vines and bushes.

He put his fingers to his mouth and let out a loud whistle. Lauren jumped. The thrashing in the woods started again with even more energy than before. With a final lunge, a yellow beast cleared the tree line and ran at Jack and Lauren, its tail wagging.

"Buddy, what are you doing? Did you get stuck?" Jack bent down and picked off the leaves and thorny twigs snagged in the yellow Lab's thick coat. Buddy seemed to smile as he panted with his mouth open and sat patiently while they cleaned him off. He licked their hands whenever they came close enough to his face.

"You're supposed to be watching the girls," Lauren chided him as she rubbed his ears. "Go get 'em. Go on."

Buddy remained sitting and looked over to Jack for permission. Jack waited to make sure Buddy stayed until he gave the signal. Then with a slight nod up the trail, he whispered, "Go." Buddy tore off up the path, his wagging tail raised in the air like a periscope on a cartoon submarine.

Lauren and Jack laughed at the dog. Of all of them, Buddy seemed to enjoy the change from the concrete and asphalt of California to the forests and streams of Maryland most. Jack had always believed dogs were meant to be in the outdoors, chasing squirrels and digging holes, not confined to living rooms and small patches of grass. The move had been good for all the Tremonts, both two legged and four.

"Did you ever get a hold of Stanley?" Jack asked after they walked for a while.

"Yeah, finally."

"How's the girl doing?" Jack knew his wife was worried about this new patient of hers, Felicia Rodriguez. Spending the morning at home with him and the kids had been hard for her to do. If anyone other than Dr. Stanley Mansfield were watching over her, he guessed she would have been tempted to drive to Midland hospital to check on her patient.

"Fine. Stanley sent blood down to the CDC. They told him it could be a week, maybe even longer, before they get back."

"So long?"

"They're overloaded. Felicia's stable, and there's no sign that whatever she has is infectious so..."

"For once, you're low man on the totem pole."

"Pretty much."

They walked along in silence. Ahead, they heard Buddy bark. The girls screamed and then laughed as the big dog raced through the leaves.

"How are you doing?" Lauren asked. Her tone made Jack understand it wasn't a casual question. A simple *fine* wasn't going to cut it. As if by some unspoken rule, neither of them had discussed Nate Huckley since they'd been home.

"The way he came after us, it was crazy. Like he hated us or something. But what's bothering me is how fast it all happened. I mean, one minute everything is great, the next there's a maniac trying to kill the kids. I guess stuff like this happens, it's just..."

"It's not supposed to happen to us."

"Something like that."

"No one ever thinks things will happen to them. I've been around enough trauma rooms to know that. I've seen the look on people's faces when they come in. It's not pain or fear. Usually it's disbelief. Shock that something that bad could actually happen to them."

They crunched through the pile of leaves in their path. Lauren leaned in to him and took his arm. "Is there any way you could have misinterpreted what happened?"

"What do you mean?"

"I mean, maybe Huckley was trying to help. He got offended when you told him to get away. Maybe he was drunk. I don't know."

Jack stopped walking. "Lauren, the man tried to break into the car while I was in it. He tried to run down our kids." His voice was rising. "There was a kidnapped woman in the trunk of his car for Christ's sake. What else do you need?"

"Don't get mad at me. I'm just trying to figure this all out. I believe you, Jack. I do. But I just don't understand how the girl's body could disappear."

Jack turned away and laced his fingers together behind his neck. He took a few deep breaths to calm down.

"Could it have been the shadows?" Lauren asked carefully. "Something that looked like a face?"

Jack didn't turn around. "She was right in front of me. There was no mistake."

Lauren looked up the trail. "Did the girls see her?"

Jack turned around and shook his head. "I don't know. It was so dark."

"We've got to encourage them to talk about it."

"I thought they told you about it in the hospital. What'd they say?

"They asked me about the bad man."

"What'd you tell them?" Jack asked.

"That he couldn't hurt them anymore. And that he was very sick and in the hospital."

"They didn't mention the girl before but maybe if we talk to them again. We just have to be careful. Kids can have false memories if something is heavily suggested to them."

"You're the doc. It's just that they act like nothing happened. I hate to drag them back through it."

"They may act like nothing happened, but something did happen. We need to make sure they deal with it and not internalize it."

"I guess you're right. When should we do it?"

"Sooner the better."

"All right. Let's head back. Let's find out what they saw."

TWENTY

"Pancakes are served," Lauren said as she carried the steaming plate of hot cakes from the kitchen to the breakfast table.

The girls scrambled to their chairs, hungry from their morning walk. The pancakes disappeared quickly, chased down by frothy glasses of chocolate milk. Becky burped after gulping the last half of her milk, and Sarah laughed until tears ran down her cheeks. Jack, not wanting to encourage the behavior, tried to contain himself, but he found the girls' laughter too infectious. He and Lauren were soon laughing along with them. When the girls slowed down a little, Jack added a burp of his own, and they all busted up again.

After the plates were cleared, they sat at the table together. "Girls, we want to talk to you about two nights ago." Jack said.

"About the crash?" Becky asked.

"Yes, about the crash. Your mom and I want to make sure you girls know that it's okay to talk about it."

"If you feel scared or anything, you can talk to us," Lauren added.

Both of the girls looked down at the table. Lauren and Jack exchanged looks. Jack spoke up. "I've got to tell you, I was scared."

"You were scared, Daddy?" Becky said.

"Sure. Getting in a car accident is scary. And there was all that thunder and stuff."

"And that man," Becky joined in. "He was really scary."

Jack noticed Lauren rub her hands together. He knew how she felt. It physically hurt to hear about his little girl being scared by someone. "Yeah, I guess that man was kind of scary," Jack said.

"Why did he do that stuff? Was he mad at us?" Becky said.

"No, honey, he wasn't mad at you. It had nothing to do with you or with me or with your sister. He was just confused and angry for no good reason. But he can't hurt you anymore."

"Why not?" Sarah said, speaking for the first time.

"He was injured in the accident, and he's in the hospital. You'll never have to see him again," Jack said.

Sarah eyed him suspiciously, as if she wasn't sure she believed him. "And what about the girl?"

Lauren cleared her throat. "What girl, Sarah? You mean the girl in the hospital I told you about? The one that Mommy's trying to help?"

Sarah shook her head. "Not that one. The other girl."

Jack spoke carefully. "Becky, do you know what she's talking about?"

Becky shook her head, a little wrinkle appearing between her eyebrows. "Nuh-uh."

"Sarah, honey. Did you see a girl last night?" Jack asked.

She shook her head no.

"Then what girl are you talking about?"

Sarah looked at each one in them in turn, as if they were playing some joke on her. Tears welled up in her eyes. When she finally answered, the words caught in her throat. "The bad man told me I had to get in the trunk of his car. He said he had another girl in there. But I told him no. I didn't want to go with him." Tears ran down her cheeks.

Lauren tried to get up out of her chair, but Jack held her back. "Did he say anything else?" Jack asked. He wanted to see if she would remember asking him about Melissa.

Sarah nodded as she wiped her nose with the back of her sleeve. "H-he said if I didn't open the door and get in the car, t-th-that he was gonna kill you and Becky and the girl in his car." Her words came out in a blubbering stream of tears and snot. "H-h-he said it'd be my fault. When I wouldn't open the door, he started yelling bad words at me and told me I couldn't hide from him. Not ever. Is he gonna come here, Daddy? Is he gonna kill us?"

Lauren pushed her chair back and ran over to Sarah. Sarah clung to her and cried into her shoulder. Lauren patted her back and rocked her, whispering in her ear, telling her it was all just a bad dream. It wasn't real. Not any of it.

Jack stared at his youngest daughter. He remembered her in the back seat of the Jeep, just before he made the dash for the keys. He had asked who she was talking to. *I was talking to the bad man*, she had said. But it was impossible. The windows were shut, the doors locked. Becky would have heard anything Huckley said when he stood at the open door when Jack first saw him. But somehow, Sarah knew about the girl in the trunk. And, unless he had imagined it, she knew about Melissa too. His head spun and his chest tightened. Nothing was making any sense.

"Daddy." Becky whispered, breaking the silence. "I'm scared."

TWENTY-ONE

Sheriff Janney pulled into the gravel parking lot next to Piper's. Even at two in the afternoon, the lot was full, mostly with cars he recognized. The day had been frustrating and he was glad Piper's was his last stop of the day. No harm in throwing back a few drinks before returning to the office.

The weather was unusually clear and bright for this time of year. He'd left his favorite pair of aviator sunglasses at the station and had been squinting all day long. The result was a headache that started behind each eye, radiated through his skull, and came to rest in a knot of muscles at the base of his neck.

He thought about heading up the road to Midland. He'd heard from one of the police guys up there that there was a motel by the truck stop on Interstate 70 that housed some pretty good massage services. Supposedly, there was even a special law enforcement discount. But the thought of driving up there made the tension in his neck even worse. No, he needed to ask Jim Butcher a few questions about two different Jacks. Jack Tremont, whom he didn't care for, and Jack Daniels, a man he liked just fine.

The sheriff walked into Piper's, drawing in the smell of the place. Stale beer, sawdust, grease from the kitchen. His eyes adjusted slowly from the bright day outside to the cave inside. A little moan of satisfaction escaped his lips. This was exactly what he needed. If it weren't for the owner, this would have been Janney's version of paradise.

He picked out Jim Butcher through the smoky room, standing at his usual station at the end of the bar where the wood curved ninety degrees, forming a small side bar perpendicular to the main stretch. Jim Butcher's prodigious stomach fit almost perfectly into the curve. So perfectly, in fact, that the phenomenon had become a topic of debate over the years. There were three theories. One camp thought the shape was just a fortunate coincidence. The second was that Jim had the bar custom built that way so he'd be comfortable. The third and most popular theory was that he had stood in the same spot for so many years he had simply worn away the curve until it fit his bulging gut. Given his poor disposition and huge size, no one had ever asked him his opinion on the subject.

"What d'ya want, Janney? Nothin' goin' on 'round here," Butcher snapped, making a circular motion with the stump of his left arm.

The sheriff frowned. The man's backwoods accent grated on Janney's ears. He knew Jim Butcher didn't like him. That was fine in his book since the feeling was mutual. But it drove him crazy that the man felt no need to keep up appearances. He was so damn disrespectful. "Good to see you too, Jim. Always a pleasure."

Butcher turned to the side, rotating his gut in the curve of the bar until he had a straight line of fire down to the floor behind the bar. A gob of spit ejected from his mouth and hit the floor with a *splat*. The bar owner swiveled back around to face Janney, a thin line of spittle hanging from his chin. Janney's lips lifted up into an involuntary sneer. Jim Butcher had gotten worse with time. Still the same backwoods hick, he'd added a cocky arrogance to what had already been a distasteful personality. Janney glanced along the bar at the man sitting on the stool down the way. He turned back to Butcher and said, "Look here, I've got to talk to you about Jack Tremont."

"Whut 'bout 'im?"

"He was here two nights ago."

"Lemme think."

82

Janney had meant it as a statement, not a question. Butcher obviously wasn't going to make things easy. Janney licked his lips and looked down the bar again. "I know he was here, Jim. I know you remember. I just need you to remember how much he drank, if you get my meaning."

Butcher shrugged his shoulders.

A muscle twitched on the side of Janney's mouth. He lowered his voice. "C'mon Jim."

Butcher smirked and said nothing. He looked over Janney's shoulder and focused on the TV playing on the far side of the room.

Janney stretched across the bar, the veins in his neck sticking out like braided rope, his lips curled back over his teeth. His words came out harsh and slow, just loud enough for Butcher to hear. "You better help out with this, Butcher. If you know what's good for you."

Butcher didn't move. Not so much as a muscle twitched on his face. Janney didn't back down either. His body was taut, stretched across the bar. The two men stared down each other.

Finally, Butcher's lips moved. "Next time yah go threatenin' me, someone's bound t'get hurt."

Janney winced from a sharp pain in his abdomen. He didn't look down. He didn't need to. Carefully, he slid back and stood upright at the bar. As he moved, he saw a flash of motion as Butcher returned the hunting knife under the counter. Janney reached down and felt where the pain had been. The skin itched. He reached in between the buttons of his uniform shirt and scratched it. When he removed his fingers, he held them up to the light and rubbed them together. Blood.

He slammed his fist on the bar. Aware that the man down from him was now craning his neck to listen, Janney whispered, "You idiot. You only had to do one thing. There's a lot at stake here."

Butcher ejected another gob of spit on the floor and turned back to the TV.

Janney clenched his jaw hard. God, he wanted to pull out his gun and teach Butcher a lesson. It would feel so good squeezing the trigger, burying five or six slugs into the man's gut. That would show the smug bastard once and for all where he stood in the hierarchy of things. But he knew he couldn't. Self-control won the battle and he reined himself in. He reminded himself that lack of self-control had created the current situation to begin with.

Deciding against the drink he'd craved minutes before, Janney marched across the bar and exited without a look back. He climbed into the squad car and flipped on the two-way. "Sorenson, are you there?"

The response came back with a little static, "Yeah, right here."

Janney tapped the mouthpiece on the dash. Thinking. Thinking.

"Sheriff?" Deputy Sorenson asked.

Janney pressed the button to speak. "Forget it. I changed my mind."

"All right. I'm out here watching the Tremont house. Nothing going on."

"Roger that. I'm out for the night. Call me if something happens, right?"

"Roger. Over and out."

Janney hung the mouthpiece back on its handle and started up the car. He rolled out of the parking lot without knowing exactly where he was going, just a vague notion that he ought to do something.

He still didn't know where the girl's body was. He had no leads. Nothing. Without the body, the situation was still dangerous for them.

Janney looked down at the cell phone in the seat next to him. Sooner or later it would ring, and he would have no choice but to answer and give the caller the bad news. Janney shuddered at the thought of having to deliver the message.

The Boss wasn't going to like it.

TWENTY-TWO

The alarm went off for the fourth time. Cathy Moran stretched out an unsteady hand and slapped at the blaring black box until she hit the snooze button. Burying her face back into her warm pillows, she lay there waiting for sleep to take hold of her again.

She didn't care if she was late for school. First period was Mr. Detrich for chemistry, and she could flirt her way out of anything with him. Just arch her back and show a little cleavage and he forgave all her trespasses. How could she think about chemistry this early in the morning anyway? Then again, Bobby Mazingo was in that class and he'd sat next to her last week during an experiment. Maybe she should...

"Hey! Time to get up. Let's go."

She groaned at the voice; she forgot her dad was home today. Worse than any alarm clock. He banged on the door, but it sounded more like he was kicking her in the head. "I'm up! I'm up!" she cried.

She rolled over, swung her legs off the side of the bed, and yawned. Gathering enough will power, she pushed off the bed and dragged herself to the bathroom. At least her new so-called brothers were with their other parents for the week. A bathroom she didn't have to share was one of the few benefits of divorce, and there weren't many. Her dad's new Barbie-doll wife was nice enough even though she was half her mom's age.

Or at least half the age her mom would have been if she were still alive.

The shower usually woke her up. She cranked up the heat until it stung the skin on her back. Then she shampooed twice just like she'd learned by reading *Young Ms. Magazine*. The magazine was the discovery of the year. Everything from healthy roots to getting rid of pimples to being sexy enough to get any man she wanted. She felt a little weird reading some of the more graphic articles. Of course, those were the ones she read twice. The writers at *Young Ms.* knew their stuff.

Even though she was already running late, she stayed in the shower longer than normal. She couldn't shake how tired she'd felt over the last couple of weeks. Sleep wasn't the problem. She was actually getting more sleep than normal, napping throughout the day and crashing early at night. Still, her body ached for more.

She hoped she wasn't coming down with something. The weekend was coming up and her friend Gertie's parents were out of town, the perfect opportunity to invite some boys over. Maybe even Bobby Mazingo. The thought put a smile on her face and was enough motivation to get her going. She turned off the water and toweled dry before climbing out of the shower.

Steam covered the bathroom mirror. When she wiped away the condensation, she gasped at the image of herself. There was something strange on her chest and shoulders. The image disappeared in an instant as the steamy room fogged up the mirror again. She reached out and wiped it away with her towel.

Faint purple botches covered her skin. They were around her breasts, up to her chest and throat and down her shoulders. It looked like someone had beaten the hell out of her the night before.

She turned to run out of the bathroom and to go show her dad. This was exactly the kind of thing he'd told her to look out for since the therapy started. But she stopped herself. He'd overreact like always and they'd be off to the hospital for more tests. She had better things to do. Cathy stepped closer to the mirror to examine the spots. The blotches looked like bruises, but when she pressed on them, they weren't sore at all. She inspected the rest of her body put found no other sign of the marks anywhere else. That made her feel better. The blotches were probably just a reaction to something she wore.

Still, it was weird. And being so tired all the time made it worse. She worried that maybe the medicine wasn't working and the sickness was back. She didn't have a checkup until next week, but her last visit hadn't shown anything. Her dad had told her the therapy was a sure thing, that she was lucky to get it because not many people did. That was why she wasn't supposed to tell anyone about it. Her dad said if she told anyone, then the medicine would be taken away. And people died from what she had.

Now, looking in the mirror at the purple splotches, she couldn't decide what to do. It was times like this when she missed her mom the most. She was past feeling angry that she was gone and just felt miserable and lonely instead. But Cathy couldn't ask her mom, the cancer had taken care of that, so she decided to keep it to herself. There was no way she'd ever ask her dad's new wife. Barbie was the last person Cathy would trust with a secret.

She pushed the whole thing out of her mind. If she wore a high collar, no one would know. She'd just take it easy for the next couple of days and the marks would go away. She cursed under her breath when she remembered it was Wednesday. She had to work after school. Working had been a battle with her dad, and she knew he was waiting for her to give up on it just to say he told her so. She could call in sick, but if word got back to her dad that she hadn't shown up for work then the party at Gertie's this weekend would be off for sure. She couldn't let that happen.

Cathy Moran threw on her clothes, double-checked the mirror to make sure none of the purple blotches showed, grabbed her book bag, and headed downstairs. She had a long day ahead of her and all she could think about as she walked down the stairs was how soon she could get back to sleep.

TWENTY-THREE

Max Dahl brought a six-pack of Heineken with him. He and Jack sat out on the back porch enjoying the rare warm afternoon. Usually this time of year, the temperature was down in the forties during the day, so sixty degrees in the early evening was something to celebrate.

Jack knew why Max was there. Prescott City was a small town and he was sure rumors were flying. At least Max was up front about it. "Man, you screwed up big time," was his greeting when he first pulled in the driveway. Now that Jack had given him the whole story, Max leaned back in the teak patio chair and shook his head.

"Jack," he finally said, reaching for another beer, "that is one hell of a story." He popped the top and drained half the bottle. "You are either into some strange stuff or..."

"Or what?"

"Or you are completely full of shit."

"C'mon! I can understand that pompous ass Janney giving me grief, but you?"

"Hey, I didn't say I don't believe you. It's just that it's, I don't know, so weird."

Jack rolled his eyes. "Oh, much better. Jesus, why would I make something like this up?"

"See, that's the thing. I don't think you would. I know you weren't drunk since I was with you. I figure you have insurance. Even if you didn't, you have more money than God, so you wouldn't fake it to get out of paying the guy's medical bill."

"Okay, so what's left?"

"I'm your friend, so I can tell you this." Max leaned over and lowered his voice to a whisper. "Know what I think? Under this good guy exterior lurks a psychopath hell bent on ridding the world of cheap domestic cars."

Jack stood up. "Come on, this is serious."

The glass slider opened and Sarah walked out carrying construction paper and a box of crayons. She walked over to her dad and tugged on the bottom of his sweater. "Will you color with me?"

Jack reached down and rubbed the top of her head. "In a little bit, Bud. Why don't you sit at the table and start?" he said, nodding toward the patio table. Sarah stuck out her bottom lip and stared up at him. Jack laughed, "Go on, I'll be over in a little bit. We'll work on your numbers."

Sarah smiled. She looked over at Max and piped, "Hi, Uncle Max," and then headed off to the patio table.

"Smart like her mom, huh?" Max said. "Jesse's the same age as Sarah, and we're nowhere close to worrying about numbers yet."

"Don't let Jesse's enthusiasm fool you. You'd be hard pressed to understand anything she writes down. A bunch of well-meaning squiggly lines. She'll get it eventually though. She just needs time." No sooner were the words out then he regretted them. Max winced, but didn't say anything. A black shadow drifted over the two men even though the sun still shone in the cloudless sky.

"Max...I'm sorry...I..."

Max held up his hand. "Don't worry about it. I find myself saying stuff like that all the time."

She just needs time. Jesse Dahl didn't have time. Sarah would go to school, grow older, have a life. Jesse was going to die. Realizing that Max's little girl would never learn to write made it all the more real.

Max spoke first. "Enough of that. Let's talk about how you're a big screw-up."

Jack accepted the unspoken ground rule. No talk of disease today. "So, do you think I have anything to worry about from Janney?"

Max thought it over. "Folks around here trust Janney. Shit, he's been sheriff around here for almost twenty years. They think he's an egotistical prick, but they trust him. But you have me as your alibi that you were drinking like a little girl before you left Piper's. The only risk is that someone at Piper's wasn't paying attention and decides they saw you drinking the whole time you were there."

"But I wasn't."

"Yeah, but someone could have been confused. They see a bunch of empty bottles at our table, they see us having a good time, shooting pool and shooting the shit. Pretty soon, they *see* you drinking beer after beer. After that nightmare with Albert James and that shot of whiskey we had? Maybe people think you needed more than one. They assume it, they think it makes sense, hell, they know they had more than one shot of whiskey after that mess. Soon enough, they see you taking shots."

"What are you talking about? I had one beer the whole time I was there. Then that one shot with you."

Max shrugged. "Sometimes people see things that aren't real. I see it in court all the time. Two witnesses at the same event swear up and down that they saw different things. It's not that they're lying either. They believe what they saw. It's just sometimes the mind makes jumps all on its own, plays connect the dots."

"That's not what happened."

Max reached out and grabbed Jack's forearm. "Your mind can play tricks on you, Jack. Make you think you saw something that really wasn't there. And, sometimes, if you're not careful, people get hurt because of it."

Jack looked down at Max's hand then back up at his friend. "Are we still talking about people in the bar or something else?"

Max's stare lasted a few beats too long. Finally, he broke his grip on Jack's arm and gave him a wide smile. "I'm just saying you never know about those hillbillies at Piper's.

Hell, they might say you beat me at pool and we all know that's a damn lie."

Jack smiled uncomfortably. They sat in silence, drinking the rest of their Heinekens. The forest was alive with the rustling of squirrels and birds foraging for winter stores. A gentle breeze was enough to stir the dry leaves on the trees. A slow motion shower of color floated through the air as leaves twirled in a death dance on the way to the ground. Sarah's little voice came from the table behind them, serenading them with the theme song from one of her cartoon shows.

Max put down his beer. "I'd better get going. Kristi will think I'm out chasing another woman." He waved through the window to say goodbye to Lauren, and he and Jack headed down the path that led around the house.

"Daddy, you said you'd do numbers with me!" Sarah called out.

"I'm telling Uncle Max goodbye. I'll be right there."

Max shook his head. "And the Father of the Year award goes to..."

"I'm making up for lost time," Jack said. Again he cringed. Everything seemed somehow to tie into Jesse's imminent death. They continued around the house in silence.

Max hesitated in front of his car. "Listen, why don't you cool it a little about this girl in the trunk? At least until they find a body or something. I'll try to calm Janney down. I know him pretty well. We can just make this whole thing go away."

"My mind wasn't playing tricks on me. There was a girl, and I'm going to find out what happened to her."

Max locked eyes with Jack. For a second, Jack thought he saw a flash of anger in his friend's eyes. But just as quickly, it passed. Max hit him on the shoulder. "You are a stubborn S.O.B., aren't you? At least think about what I said. Okay?"

Jack told him he would and then watched his friend go up the driveway and disappear through the trees. He walked back down the path to the rear of the house and climbed up on to the deck.

Sarah called out when she saw him, "Look at what I did, Daddy. Look!"

Jack smiled and prepared himself to *ohh* and *ahh* at her most recent set of scribbles. His smile disappeared when he saw the papers scattered in front of her.

There were over a dozen sheets spread out on the table. The crayons were dumped out of the box into a pile in front of her.

Every sheet was covered with numbers.

Written in different sizes.

Different colors.

Jack picked up some of the papers and turned them over. The backs were just as full. Perfectly formed numbers covered every blank space.

It was the same number.

Over and over.

320.

Nate Huckley's hospital room.

And in the center of every page, written in large, block letters, was a single word.

RUN

TWENTY-FOUR

Perched in a tree stand, the man adjusted his scope to focus on the figure on the deck. The target was agitated about something, holding pieces of paper up in the air. The man knew the little girl was Sarah Tremont. The records he'd copied at Midland Hospital said the older sister Becky had been treated for a broken arm. The 3X9 Bushnell scope clearly showed the girl on the deck did not have a cast.

The target picked up the girl and went inside. The man did not have interior surveillance, so he climbed out on the thick branch below him and wrenched the tree stand away from the main trunk. Moving slowly in case anyone was looking out of the house windows in his direction, he climbed down the tree until he was ten feet from the ground. He threw the tree stand and his black duffel bag into a thick bush that absorbed the equipment with minimum noise. A soft push off the trunk and the man dropped from the tree, rolling on impact and ending in a crouched position.

The man shook his head. Too much noise. He was getting sloppy.

He grabbed his things from the bush and started the trek back to his car. The hike gave him time to consider his next move. He had so little information to go on. Nothing more than instinct. But time meant everything right now. If he was going to make a difference, he had to move quickly.

The visit from Max Dahl had been a surprise. He'd have to do some research to find out how close he and Jack Tremont were. The man didn't have audio, but the conversation had looked tense at times as he followed it through the scope.

Then there was the little girl, Sarah. He was angry at himself for not watching her at all while the men spoke. Tremont's reaction when he'd returned to the deck made him wonder what was on those papers. If he had only paid attention, then he might have known for sure instead of trying to make decisions with inadequate information.

Just like old times, he thought. His entire career had been one situation after another that demanded he make life and death decisions with limited knowledge. He was trained not to think of it as guessing, but rather as interpreting ground truth. The same training taught him the semantics of his profession. He didn't kill men, but eliminated his targets. He never hurt innocent bystanders; he incurred collateral damage. But the wordplay never changed the reality of the missions he was ordered to carry out. Death was still death, no matter what label it wore.

He thought he would be glad to be done with the military, but in some ways, he longed for it. A world of absolutes. Clear objectives. Orders that came without the need for interpretation or the inconvenience of exercising moral judgment. Now everything seemed grey and the confidence he usually felt on a mission was gone, replaced with almost paralyzing uncertainty. The superstitions he had run away from his entire life were coming back. The walls of denial, painstakingly built up since childhood, were crashing down around him. He faced a new enemy and it was one he did not understand, one he did not want to believe existed. All he knew was that this new enemy created in him an emotion he thought he had killed off long ago.

Fear.

Enough fear to catch him up for a lifetime.

The more he learned about his enemy, the more he wondered if he was up to the task. He did not fear death – that emotion had long been torn from him – but he feared failure.

He worried that his enemy was too powerful for him, too smart, had too many advantages. He worried that revenge was clouding his judgment.

Despite all this, the man was committed to going through with his mission. He had gathered enough intelligence. It was time to act. And time to decide if killing Jack Tremont was part of the solution.

TWENTY-FIVE

Sarah sat at the kitchen table. Her mom and dad sat side by side, the sheets of construction paper spread out in front of them. The number 320 streamed off the sheets, written in multiple sizes and styles. Sarah wrapped a lock of hair around her little finger, waiting for her parents to talk.

"Sarah, honey," her mom said softly. "These numbers look really great."

Sarah smiled at the compliment. The way her folks were acting, she thought she was in trouble for something. She reached out to pick up one of the sheets of paper.

Her mom came out of her chair and blocked her hand. "No! Don't touch it."

Sarah froze. She's never seen her mom looked scared before. She looked at her dad, hoping to find some comfort there. Only he looked scared too. "What's going on? Did I do something wrong?"

"Nothing, sweetie." Her mom motioned for her to come sit on her lap. Sarah slid off her chair and walked over to nestle into her arms. Mom rocked her back and forth. "I'm sorry I snapped at you, sweetie. Do you forgive me?" Sarah nodded.

"Sarah, where did you learn how to write your numbers so well?" Dad asked.

Sarah looked at him and then over at the papers on the table. She cocked her head to the side, realizing for the first time that it was strange that the numbers looked so much better than anything she'd ever done before. They looked like an adult's writing. She turned back to her dad and shrugged.

He mom leaned her back and looked at her face. "Why did you choose those numbers? Are those just the ones you know?"

Sarah looked down at her hands and mumbled, "I dunno." She said that whenever she was nervous, but it was the truth this time.

Dad cleared his throat. "Sweetie, you're not in trouble. We're really proud of you."

Sarah shrugged and burrowed deeper into her mom's arms. Her parents looked at each other. They sat in silence, staring at the pages sitting on the table. The faint sound of a sitcom laugh track filtered down from Becky's room upstairs.

Sarah looked around the room. The sales lady had called it a great-great room. It was huge, with ceilings two stories high, one side covered with layered river rock and another all windows looking over the forest. She knew the room was her dad's favorite. He always talked about how he loved the openness, the giant fireplace, the feeling of being outdoors. But Sarah shivered as she saw his eyes checking around. Maybe he felt as nervous as she did. Maybe he felt like someone was watching them.

Bam. Bam. Bam.

Everyone jumped at the sound. Her mom even let out a small cry as the knocking on the front door crashed through the house. But her dad laughed. "Wow, I guess we're a little tense, huh?"

"Are you expecting someone?" Mom asked.

"No. You?" Dad said. But Mom shook her head, that weird look coming across her face again. Sarah didn't like what was going on. Her parents were never supposed to be scared. They were supposed to be brave and in control. Being scared was supposed to be left to the kids.

Sarah watched them, rubbing her arms to make the chill go away.

Her dad leaned down toward her and said, "Probably Uncle Max, huh? He's always getting lost." He rubbed the top of her head, messing up her hair until she smiled. He walked toward the door. "You guys wait here. I'll see who it is."

Sarah reached for her mom's hand and found it. It was hot and sweaty, but Sarah didn't mind. She gripped it tight. For the first time in her young life, she felt like she was doing it to make her mom feel safe instead of the other way around.

TWENTY-SIX

Jack gave a low whistle, and Buddy fell in behind him as he walked to the door. As he got closer, he noticed the door wasn't locked. In fact, he couldn't remember the last time they'd bothered.

Buddy started to whine, his tail dropping between his legs.

"What's wrong?" Jack asked, rubbing Buddy's head.

He looked up and noticed a person standing with his back to the door just off the entryway. Even in the gathering late afternoon shadows, Jack could tell it was a man's frame, well over six feet, lean but broad shouldered. The man's hair was pulled back and tied into a ponytail. Jack opened the door, and the man turned around and stepped toward him.

"I think we need to talk," the man said.

Jack studied the man's face. A dark complexion hid any sign of age and provided only ambiguous hints at the man's ethnicity. He had dark eyes that were focused and intelligent, darting back and forth in constant surveillance. He had a wide, irregular nose, as if it had been broken and left to mend on its own. White scar tissue wrapped its way up from the man's throat over his jawline until it disappeared into his hair. Jack had hoped that it would be a door-to-door salesman. But something about the look of the man told him it wasn't the case.

"Listen, whatever this is about, you've caught me at a bad time. Could you–"

"Nate Huckley's coming after your daughter."

Jack stiffened. "What did you say?"

"I said Nate Huckley's coming after your daughter The young one. Sarah. And he's not working alone. I think we should talk."

Jack stepped out of the house and closed the door behind him. A couple of days ago, he would have told the man to get the hell off his property. But too many strange things had happened, all of them about Sarah. "What do you know?"

"I know you're involved in something you don't understand. I know Huckley tried to take your daughter away from you at that rest area. I know if he'd succeeded, she'd be dead right now. I know that if he wants her that badly then there must be a good reason. Once the rest of them figure out what that reason is, they'll be after her too. How's that for starters?"

"Rest of them? What do you mean?"

"Huckley isn't alone. He stumbled across your little girl, but believe me, his friends are taking notice of the risk he took. They're trying to understand right now what he found. They have their suspicions, but once they know for sure they'll stop at nothing until they get her."

"This is crazy. Who are you? How are you involved in all this?"

"I've told you more than you knew. Now I need a few answers from you."

"Like what?"

"What did your little girl write on those pages? Is Huckley trying to contact her?"

Jack was confused for a moment but then felt a surge of heat rush to his face as he realized the implications. The man had been spying on them. Watching from the woods. Jack didn't care what this stranger knew. The invasion was too much. Who knew how long he had watched from the trees. He could even be with Huckley. Jack took a step forward and jabbed a finger at the man's chest.

"You get the hell out of here, understand? If I catch you spying on my family again, I'll come after you. I swear to God."

The man wrinkled his brow as if amused by Jack's attempt to look threatening. He pointed at Jack's finger still waving at him. "You'll want to put that away. I'm not here to cause trouble. I came because I think we might be on the same side in this mess."

Buddy, fidgeting uncomfortably next to his master, snarled when the man pointed. Jack reached down without taking his eyes off the man and took hold of the dog's collar. "Like I said, I think it's time you leave."

The man looked down at the snarling dog and back to Jack. Finally, he shrugged. He reached into his jacket pocket.

"Hey, hey," Jack called out, almost releasing his grip on Buddy.

The man pulled out a small piece of paper and a pen. Jack steadied his breath. The man wrote something on the paper and held it out. "When something else happens, and something will happen, you'll want to talk. Name's Joseph Lonetree. That's my number. "

Jack took the paper and stuffed it in his pocket without looking at it. He nodded toward the driveway. The man smiled, turned, and headed back to his car. Jack watched until he made sure the car was far up the driveway. He walked back inside and told Buddy to stay on guard by the front door. One phrase from the exchange kept repeating in his head as he walked back to the kitchen. *When something else happens, and something will happen, you'll want to talk.* He had a bad feeling that the mysterious Mr. Lonetree was going to be right. And worse, he felt powerless to stop it.

TWENTY-SEVEN

Jack returned from the entryway and, without saying anything, went through the house and checked that every window and door was locked. Not many of them were. Then he pulled closed the few curtains they had, muttering to himself how easy it was for someone to see into the house. Lauren didn't ask who had been at the door. She would know by his silence that he didn't want to talk about in front of Sarah. They tried to stick to their normal routine, but Jack found himself too distracted. Lauren's manner showed she was still unsettled too.

Becky came downstairs to see what was going on. She sat at the table and looked over the sheets of construction paper with Sarah's writing on them and then at her dad rushing around the house. She must sense that something was going on. She called out for Buddy, and the dog happily jogged into the room and sat by her to get his ears rubbed.

Seeing this, Jack strode over and kneeled next to his daughter. "Becky, Buddy needs to stay by the front door for a while, all right?"

She nodded and gave the dog one last pat on the head. Jack whistled and walked back to the front door. Buddy followed with his head held low to the ground as if ashamed he had left his post so easily. He retook his spot next to the door and peered out of the window, his ears cocked upright to pick up the slightest sound. Jack leaned down and scratched the back of the big dog's neck. "You're in charge here, Buddy. You see as much as a rabbit hop across the driveway, you let me know."

Buddy turned his head just long enough to land a wet tongue on his master's hand, as if to assure him that he understood, and then turned back to resume his vigil at the front window. "That's my good boy," Jack said.

When he returned, only Lauren was at the table.

"Where are the girls?"

"Upstairs, brushing their teeth. Scared because their dad's been running around, locking up the house. Tell me what happened."

Jack sat down with her and recounted his conversation with Lonetree. He noticed her glance up at the windows when he told her about the man spying on them from the woods.

"If he saw her writing, then he was watching her while she was alone. You were in the front on the house with Max. He could have…"

"I know. I know."

"What's all this about Huckley wanting Sarah? About other people coming after her? It's crazy."

"It's completely crazy. But isn't that how these things happen? Sane people don't kidnap little kids, right?" Jack got up and crossed over to the kitchen.

"What are you doing?" Lauren said

Jack grabbed the cordless phone. "I'm going to call our friend Sheriff Janney and tell him about this guy." He punched in the number for information and had the operator connect him to the Allegheny County sheriff's office. "Then tomorrow I think it's a good idea if you take the kids away for a few days. Just until I can figure out what the hell is going on around here." Before Lauren could object, an annoyed woman with a smoker's hack answered the phone. "Sheriff's office."

"Hi there. This is Jack Tremont out on Forest Drive. I just had a suspicious man come to my house and threaten my family. Can I make a report or something? Have someone check it out?"

"That was Freemont, you say?"

"No, Tremont. Jack Tremont, out on Forest Drive in Prescott City."

"Was the trespasser a relative of yours?" the woman asked in a bored voice, obviously unimpressed. Jack figured by the question that the sheriff's office fielded a lot of domestic disturbance calls.

"No. I don't know the man. He gave me his name though. Joseph Lonetree."

"All right. Hold please."

The line clicked. Music piped through the phone, a country station playing old time Johnny Cash. Half a song later, the line clicked and the music disappeared.

"Deputy Sorenson here. You want to report a suspicious person?"

Jack's throat went dry. He recognized the voice. It was the deputy Janney had brought with him to the hospital room. Jack cursed himself for not realizing there was a chance he would answer the phone. "Yeah, someone showed up at my door tonight. He let it slip that he'd been watching the house during the day. And he threatened my family."

"Just a sec." There was a rustling of paper. The deputy came back on the line and asked in a bored voice, "Name?"

He cleared his throat. "Jack Tremont." As he expected, there was a long silence on the other line.

"Mr. Tremont," the deputy said. "This is Deputy Sorenson. I met you yesterday at Midland hospital."

"Yes, I recognized your voice."

"Sir, I'd like to apologize if I was rude to you at the hospital. My nerves were a little frayed. I'm sorry for my lack of professionalism."

Jack was stunned by the young man's change of attitude. Maybe Janney had straightened the kid out. He felt himself relax. "Don't worry about it. It was a long night for everyone."

"Thank you, sir. Now, please tell me about the intruder you'd like to report."

After Jack went through the details, Deputy Sorenson read back the report to check it for accuracy. "Is there anything else you'd like to add?" the deputy asked.

"Yeah, he told me to contact him if anything else happened."

"What did he mean by anything else?"

Jack did a quick calculation about whether to tell the deputy about Sarah's number writing. It took him about two seconds to realize the story would sound crazy to anyone who hadn't seen it in person. It seemed crazy to him, and he had been there. "I don't know what he meant," Jack lied. "The whole thing was strange."

"Did he tell you how to contact him?"

"Yeah, he gave me a phone number. He said it was a cell phone."

"I'll need that number."

Jack dug through his pocket to find the piece of paper the man gave him. He pulled it out and started to read off the numbers. Halfway through, he felt a sense of dread, like he was making a huge mistake giving the number away. Lonetree was the only person so far who believed his story about Huckley. He might have known more about the night at the rest area. Somehow he felt like he was betraying a possible ally. Before he could think it through, he reacted to his gut feeling and scrambled the last four digits of the phone number. The deputy repeated the number to make sure he had it right. With a deep breath, Jack passed on the opportunity to correct him.

"All right, I think I have everything I need. Is there anything else you want to add?"

"Not that I can think of. Do you have any idea who this man is?"

"No, sir. I'll check the computer, but the description and the name don't ring any bells. I'll let you know if anything turns up. And I'll send a deputy to check out the road by your house."

"Thanks. I'd appreciate that," Jack said.

"No problem. I wouldn't worry too much about this, Mr. Tremont. Usually these things are one-time deals. Drifters, you know."

"I hope so. Thanks for your help."

"No problem. Once again, Mr. Tremont, sorry about last night in the hospital. It was very unprofessional."

Jack smiled. "Forgotten. Really, don't worry about it."

The deputy promised to have a patrol car drive by shortly, said goodnight, and hung up the phone. Jack was glad he had called in, but he couldn't shake the feeling that he'd missed an opportunity to get more information out of Lonetree. He fingered the piece of paper with the phone number and considered making the call. He hesitated, then stuck the paper back into his jeans pocket. Maybe later, once Lauren and the kids were out of town.

When he walked out into the great room, Lauren was gone. Upstairs to tuck the girls in, he assumed. He was by himself, the large vacant windows staring down at him, the trees outside casting shadows into the room. He noticed little noises throughout the house. The hum of the refrigerator. The click of the furnace turning on. He guessed they were the same noises that rattled through the house every night, but now they took on new meaning. Every creak of a floorboard was a foot being put down as someone crept up the stairs. Every draft caused by a window being opened by a kidnapper. The openness of the great room gave him chills. He wondered when he'd be able to sit in the room again and think of it as a great view rather than a transparent cage for intruders to spy on his family. He wondered if maybe Lonetree was watching him at that moment, suspended high over the ground in a tall pine. He flipped the bird to the wall of windows and trudged off to the hallway closet.

After rummaging through two years' accumulation of coats, gloves, backpacks, and shoes, he found what he was looking for. He pulled out the Louisville Slugger aluminum baseball bat and shoved everything else back deep into the closet. He gripped the bat with both hands and took a few slow motion swings wondering how much damage a full swing would do to a human body. He didn't want to kill anyone, just stop them in their tracks. A long, painful recovery time would be good too. He used the tip of the bat to push the closet door shut.

As it closed, it revealed a body in the hallway, right behind where the door had been.

Jack gasped and raised the bat to his shoulder.

"Jesus, Jack. It's just me," Lauren said.

"God, you scared me. What are you doing creeping around?"

"I wasn't creeping around. I just came down to see what you were doing." She nodded to the bat. "Is that the secret weapon?"

Jack shrugged. "Can't hurt."

"Come on. The kids are all tucked in. Let's try to get some sleep."

"I'm a little wired for sleep."

"Yeah, me too. I just want to be upstairs. Close to the girls, you know?"

Jack put his arm around her and kissed her forehead. "Did they go down all right? I thought maybe we'd have them sleep with us tonight."

"If they asked, I would have let them, but they were okay staying in their own rooms. They're on the second floor and their windows are locked. I figured if they're not freaked out, let it alone."

"Fair enough." They walked into the family room. "Now that we're alone, what do you think about the numbers Sarah wrote?"

"There's got to be a simple explanation. Maybe she heard the room number at the hospital."

"But the way she wrote them. She's not capable of that."

"I don't know. The stress of the accident–"

"Made her smarter? C'mon, Lauren. Something weird is going on here."

"Okay. So what do you think?"

Jack rubbed his chin with the palm of his hand. He knew he had to be careful. After his scene at the hospital, he'd noticed Lauren watching him closely, almost clinically. "I'm not sure. But something unusual is going on. And it's not just from the stress of the crash. I think it's more than that. There's something I haven't told you about that night. Something about Sarah. When Huckley was outside, trying to get into the Jeep, I looked in the back seat and saw Sarah talking. I couldn't hear her, so I told her to speak up. But she kept talking to the window. Finally, she stopped and said she wasn't talking to me.

She was talking to the bad man outside. It was what she told us about today."

"She was scared. She's a little girl. It was just her way of telling us what she was scared of. You can't take it literally."

"You weren't there. She was having a conversation. Answering questions. Shaking her head yes and no to questions I couldn't hear."

"Maybe she could hear him through the window?"

"No way. With the rain and thunder, Huckley could have been screaming right at the window, and she couldn't have heard it. It was like she heard a voice that Becky and I couldn't hear."

"You think she heard voices in her head? Like she's some kind of psychic? Give me a break."

"I don't know what it is, but something is happening, something very strange. I haven't told you everything about Albert James either." He made her sit down at the table and went through everything Albert James said, both before he went into the bar and as he lay dying in his arms.

When he was done, the color had drained out of Lauren's face.

"Why didn't you tell me any of this before?"

"Because it sounds nuts. I can't explain how Albert James knew someone was after Sarah. I can't explain how Sarah was talking to Huckley that night. I didn't say anything because there is no explanation for it."

"Of course there is. There has to be," Lauren said, her voice less sure than her words.

"There's another thing too. That night, when I asked her what the man had said, she asked me who Melissa was. She told me Huckley said she would end up like Melissa if she didn't open the door."

Lauren's shoulders caved forward. Just the mention of the name was like a weight on both of them. "But she didn't mention it tonight. Are you sure–"

"Jesus, will you stop asking that?" Jack said, his voice rising. "I'm not making this stuff up. You heard her today. She told us what he said. He said he was going to kill us. Do you think Sarah would just come up with that herself? Somehow, she wrote those numbers down. Don't forget that."

"Settle down. I'm sure there's a rational explanation for everything."

"You think so? You want to know what I think?" He jabbed his finger into the table. "Something's happening. Something bad. Whatever it is, we have to figure it out before they come after Sarah. For whatever fucked up reason, I really believe someone is trying to get her. And I think they want to hurt her, maybe even kill her."

"Mommy?" The soft voice came from the top of the stairs.

Jack looked up to see Sarah standing on the landing above them, clutching a stuffed elephant against her chest. He forced a smile as if that would make her forget everything he'd just said. It didn't work. Sarah spun around and ran back to her room.

"Great. Just great." Lauren ran up the stairs after her daughter.

Jack was about to follow her up but decided against it. Better to let Lauren calm her down; then he'd go and make his peace. He only hoped she hadn't heard much of their conversation. He made sure Buddy was on guard at the front door, did another check of the windows, then headed upstairs, dragging his baseball bat with him.

TWENTY-EIGHT

The stretch of I-70 between Prescott City and Midland was empty. Sheriff Janney always found the drive peaceful at night. He drove with the radio off and the car windows lowered a few inches. It was a cold night, but that didn't stop him from enjoying it. The car heater was on high and pumped out air hot enough that he felt it through his thick leather boots. He stuck a hand out the window and diverted a burst of wind toward his face. It felt good and calmed his nerves. It was exactly what he needed.

Janney had avoided this meeting all day, hoping for some late breakthrough to save his skin, but it hadn't come. Now it was time to face the Boss. Face him with nothing but a shitpile of excuses for why he couldn't tie up Huckley's loose ends. And if there was one thing that put the Boss in a bad mood, it was excuses for not getting a job done.

Janney had cleaned up Huckley's messes before, but this one was different. Tremont was more credible than the usual backcountry folks he dealt with. A few tough words and most people backtracked whatever story they were spilling. But Jack Tremont was going to be more of a challenge.

At first, it had seemed all the breaks were going Janney's way. His wife waving off the blood alcohol test helped fuel the booze rumors. Tremont's past was a dream come true. The little girl's death in the crash back in California had made Janney giggle whenever he thought about it. It was just perfect.

Deputy Sorenson had played it perfect during their visit, goading Jack just like he'd instructed. That crash combined with Tremont's episode in Huckley's hospital room was making it easy for Janney to chip away Tremont's credibility. But there was one important piece of the puzzle missing, and it was driving him crazy.

He opened the glove compartment and pulled out a single page fax. It was the latest missing persons database. None of the new entries on the Internet matched Tremont's description of the girl. At least Huckley had always done his hunting out of state like they had all agreed, tracking down runaways, girls already reported missing years ago by parents who hardly cared. Huckley was a pain in the ass, but he wasn't sloppy when it came to the abductions. Not usually anyway. Trying for the Tremont girl wasn't like him at all. Taking such a risk didn't make any sense.

Still, without a body, Tremont couldn't prove what he saw. There was no evidence on the cars – Janney had seen to that himself. But without a body, Janney couldn't be sure this situation was contained either. The girl had to be somewhere. Had someone found her body before he got there? If so, why would they have taken it and not told anyone? Could it be the girl was still alive?

The cell phone lying on the dash rang. Only a few people had the number, and none of them would use it unless it was important. He checked the caller ID. It was blocked, as it was supposed to be. "This better be good," he answered, unhappy with the interruption.

"This is Sorenson. I just took a call from Jack Tremont."

Janney rolled up his window. "What did he want?"

"He had a visitor tonight. A man who told him Nate Huckley was after his youngest daughter."

"Really, who might this be? Don't tell me Max Dahl was over there again," Janney said.

"No. It was a Joseph Lonetree. Mean anything to you?"

Janney flexed his grip on the steering wheel. The name meant plenty to him.

Sorenson filled in the dead air. "I got the name from Tremont. I kissed his ass to make him trust me. Being nice to that puke made my stomach turn. Sheriff? You still there?"

"Does anyone else know Tremont called in?"

"Yeah, Bernice took the call. She got his name. Is that a problem?"

"No, Bernice is fine. She'll keep her mouth shut if I ask her to." Janney rapped his knuckles against the window as he thought. "Is Morales still out at Tremont's?"

"Yeah."

"Right. Let him know about Lonetree. Tell him he's a stalker so the story checks out if Tremont spots him."

"Roger."

"And Sorenson?"

"Yeah?"

"Lonetree is armed and dangerous. He's to be shot on sight if he's spotted on the Tremont property."

The deputy's voice came back serious but eager. A little too eager, Janney thought. "I completely understand, Sheriff. You can count on me."

"That's exactly what I'm doing, Sorenson. Just remember what's at stake here for you. There's no second chance." He pressed the end button and terminated the call.

So there was a Lonetree back in town. If it was true, the game was suddenly more interesting. Deputy Sorenson was no match for the man, but that was all right. Janney was starting to think his overeager deputy was too emotional and took too many risks. Of course, the deputy had no idea what he was really involved in. He thought they were just doing drug protection and that his fortune would be made if he did his job right. He was a recent recruit, and Janney already thought of the deputy as more a liability than an asset. If Lonetree killed him, it might be a favor.

Lonetree's return wasn't the only disturbing news. The message he'd delivered to Tremont was that Huckley was after his daughter. Janney had learned better than to place limits on what was possible and impossible in the world. Every limit he had once believed in had since been broken by the strange path on which he now found himself. Nothing was off-limits. What was Huckley up to? There had to be something about the Tremont girl. But what?

He rolled down the windows the entire way, and the car filled with cold air. The hairs on his exposed skin stood on end. His cheeks stung from the chill. Still, Janney felt sweat form in his armpits. He couldn't decide if the complication was an opportunity or a threat. This kept churning through his head until he came to his exit and forced himself to focus on the meeting coming up.

The Boss wasn't going to be happy about Lonetree being in town. Janney considered not telling him, but discounted the idea. The Boss had his own sources, and nothing was kept a secret from him for long. Hell, Janney wouldn't have been surprised to find out Sorenson was a plant, put there by the Boss to spy on him. Janney had always been a little suspicious of the way Sorenson appeared so conveniently after he got rid of the moralistic son-of-a-bitch who used to "help" him. The new deputy had been perfect for the job, but something still rubbed Janney wrong. Maybe there was—

He made a fist and punched himself in the thigh. *Shit, Sorenson's not the problem. Where's your concentration tonight?*

Janney considered that hearing about Lonetree might be enough to set the Boss over the edge. Janney slowed the car to a crawl. He needed more time to think. Maybe there was a chance for him to spin the events in his favor. Maybe it was the chance he'd been waiting for. A chance for him to take over Huckley's position, maybe even get rid of the bastard completely. Janney put his fear of the Boss to the side and focused on how he could use what had happened to his advantage. He felt the possibility floating in the air, not the way that freak Huckley felt things with his voodoo hocus-pocus bullshit, but more in his gut. Good old fashioned instinct. It was out there, he just couldn't put a finger on it.

He was out of time. He pulled into the usual parking lot and spotted the dark shadow of the Boss's car on the other side of the lot and rolled toward it, disgusted at himself for the way his sweaty palms slipped on the steering wheel. The same nervous sweat dripped from his armpits, dribbled over his rib cage, and left a cold, moist trail. The physical reaction to the

Boss's presence only reminded Janney of the man he was instead of the man he imagined himself to be. The face in the rearview mirror was not a leader of men, but a mere child afraid of an angry and unpredictable parent. A parent to whom he had to deliver bad news.

He pulled the Crown Vic even with the driver's door of the Boss's black sedan and rolled down his window. The Boss's window was already down, but the inside of the car was too dark for Janney to make out his face. Not that he needed to. He could feel the Boss in the car next to him, could feel the frustration and the anger pulsing through his bloodstream. The sensation was all the more horrible because he couldn't see the man's face, leaving the expression that accompanied the trembling fury up to his imagination. Janney wondered if the Boss had intentionally positioned his car in a deep shadow for this exact effect. Or maybe the Boss consumed light, like a black hole, and that was why the inside of the car was impossibly dark. The only illumination was a glowing tip of a lit cigarette.

"And?"

Janney cleared his throat. "I'm handling the situation. It will all be taken care of by tomorrow."

"I don't believe you."

Janney swallowed hard. "It's complicated. Huckley went too far this time. I mean, the Tremonts are too high profile. Too local. What about the rules?"

"I've spoken with Huckley. He came to me," the Boss said, sounding as if he were talking about a mutual friend who had stopped by for drinks.

Janney didn't buy it. If Huckley had found a way to communicate with the Boss while he was in the coma, it was new ground for all of them. Even the phrase the Boss used, *He came to me*, sounded uncomfortable coming from his mouth. "Is he out of his coma?" Janney asked just to be sure he wasn't reading too much into things.

"No, he's still unconscious. But he found a way to — communicate." The Boss paused, and the cigarette tip turned a brighter orange as he drew the smoke into his lungs.

In better times, Janney might have asked more questions, but it didn't take much to know this wasn't a time for casual conversation. If the Boss said Huckley had communicated with him, Janney would leave it at that.

"Huckley was a fool, but he had his reasons. Good reasons. The Tremont girl was worth the risk. *Is* worth the risk," the Boss corrected himself.

"You can't mean we're still going after her."

"Yes. Huckley has convinced me it's essential for the project."

"It's too dangerous. There are already too many loose ends. Jack Tremont saw Huckley. The girl from his car is still missing. And you'll never guess who just showed up at Tremont's house tonight."

"Joseph Lonetree, I expect."

Son-of-a-bitch. How did he know? Maybe Sorenson is sneaking around behind my back. "Yes, Lonetree. So going after Sarah Tremont is out of the question."

"Out-of-the-question?" the Boss said. The words were mouthed in ice-cold syllables that hit Janney like hailstones. "I will decide what is and is not out of the question."

"Yes. I just meant—"

"Sarah Tremont is a requirement, not an option. She may very well be what we've been waiting for. But Huckley and I will take care of her. You need to control the situation with the father and the accident. Now, if you can't make it happen," the Boss sucked back another lungful of smoke, held it, and then exhaled slowly. Janney wondered which the Boss savored more, the drag on the cigarette or the waves of fear streaming toward him. "You just let me know and I'll have someone else do it."

"I didn't mean that. Of course I'll—"

But the Boss's car was already moving forward. The meeting was over. Janney let his head fall to his chest and took several deep breaths. He recognized the ultimatum the Boss had given him and understood all too well the consequences of another failure.

The relief that his reprimand with the Boss was over and the stress of the problems he faced were overridden by his

115

all-consuming hatred of Nate Huckley. This whole situation was that freak's fault to begin with, and now he was the one taking the fall for it. He pulled up various fantasy killings that he had concocted over the years, all the painful ways to get rid of Nate Huckley forever, and let the best replay in his mind as he put the car into gear and looped around to exit the parking lot.

He would do as the Boss asked – there was no question about that. But he couldn't shake the feeling that opportunity was not only knocking on his door, but beating on the damn thing. He felt like a foot soldier with a grudge against an officer, suddenly in a battlefield, armed, and with no one else looking. All he needed was the guts to act.

Had he stopped to think clearly for a second, he might have wondered if this was exactly what the Boss had meant to achieve by the meeting, wondered if his sudden urge to stand up to Huckley wasn't just another form of manipulation. But he didn't stop to think. He *felt* it was time to act. And that was enough for him.

TWENTY-NINE

The world glowed under the three-quarters moon. Frozen air arrived without the fanfare of wind or storm, only a continual sigh as if in satisfaction for completing its long migration from the far northern reaches of Canada, content to settle into the shallow Appalachian valleys before continuing the journey on to the wide expanse of the Atlantic. The trees, attuned to the faded morning and evening light and aware that the Change was coming, communally bowed to the cold night with lowered branches and directed more of their lifesaving resources away from their leaves. The night's chill signaled the end of a season and the beginning of the next. The season of survival had begun.

The occupants at the end of Forest Glen Drive were finally asleep, warm under thick blankets and blissfully unaware of the dropping temperatures in the world outside. The house was quiet but not silent. No house is ever silent. Sharp creaks as wood adjusted to new temperatures and pressures. The hum of the refrigerator and the clunky tumble of newly made ice. The click of the thermostat sparking the heater, beating back the stealthy outside air, the seeping icy intruder. A house comes alive at night with its own pace and rhythm; its own breath.

Listening to the inhale and exhale of the dark structure was the one member of the Tremont family not able to sleep. Buddy remained by the front door as he had promised his master. He was not certain what was going on, but he had sensed fear in the people he wanted to protect from harm. The floor was not as comfortable as his usual cushioned bed in the corner of the room upstairs, but the discomfort helped him stay alert. Whatever threat was out there, whatever danger, he wanted to be ready to warn his master.

The clock in the living room struck three muted tones, simultaneously marking the depth of the night and assuring that morning was close by. Buddy lifted his head at the sound. He was used to this noise and most nights it didn't bother him. But this night was different. He didn't understand why, but something was bothering the family, something that came from outside. So tonight the sound snapped him to full attention. He sniffed the air, testing for any unknown scent that might give away a potential threat in the dark. Nothing.

Buddy turned to the front door and peered out of the windows. Even this late at night he could see the forest in great detail. The keen eyesight of his pedigree and the bright cast of moonlight brought the images of dark trees into sharp relief. Fingers of dark shadow extended from the tree line, across the driveway toward the front porch. The gentle wind rocked the smaller limbs back and forth, turning the shadows into flexing hands, creeping closer to the house as the moon descended.

A small whine escaped from the dog's throat. He felt the hackles rise on his neck. His nails clicked on the hardwood floor as he shifted weight from one paw to the other. He whined again, each breath ending with a low growl.

Buddy looked over his shoulder up the stairs and considered barking. He stared back out of the window. There was nothing out there. Nothing he could see anyway. But his instincts told him a different story. His instincts told him something was there. Something dangerous. Something bad. And it was heading his way.

THIRTY

Sleep came in pitiful increments. It plagued Jack with short bursts of dark dreams before stealing away back into the night, leaving him to stare at the ceiling above his bed and wonder what the hell was going on with his family.

Lauren twisted in the sheets next to him, fighting her own demons as she tried to get some rest. Jack reached out and placed his hand in the middle of her back, taking comfort in the gentle rise and fall of her body with each breath. Counting each inhalation, he closed his eyes and lured sleep back from its hiding place, welcoming the smooth comfort of drifting away from the world, away from his problems.

He was back in the dark hallway; a place he recognized. It wasn't a real place, just something from his dreams. And, like always, he held no misconceptions about the false reality. He knew he was asleep.

It was dark, always dark. He thought of it as a hallway, but it could have been anything. A tunnel. An open field. There were no walls that he could see, just a blurred edge of darkness, like a thousand layers of black veils, each one so shear that it would no more than tint the world grey on its own. But together, in so many layers, they created a shifting black barrier, impenetrable, but with enough depth that one believed that intense concentration was all that was needed to see beyond the screen and view the truth. But that kind of focus required curiosity about what lay in the periphery, and Jack lacked any such desire; the object in front of him, as always, consumed every bit of his attention.

The thing at the end of the hallway was the only light in this nighttime world. It glowed and this luminescence filled out an evolving, indecipherable shape. Like a human, but not. Like an animal, but not. Its indistinguishable nature was what made it impossible for Jack to tear his eyes away, fearing the second he did, the thing would reveal its true nature and he would miss it. Without anything to provide perspective, Jack could not tell if it was massive in size and a great distance away, or a thing in such miniature that a single step would put him in danger of crashing into it, perhaps making it spin out into the darkness to be lost forever. Not knowing filled him with trepidation. Like in every dream for the last two years, he stood paralyzed with fear.

It was the same image as always, but this time the object moved. Or he did. He couldn't be sure. The thing grew brighter and larger. A soft breeze crossed his face, giving him the sense of great speed.

Then the voice. Coming from everywhere. And nowhere. Coming from inside his chest. Like wind transformed into speech. Whistling. Harsh.

He's here. He's come for your daughter.

"Who?" Jack cried out. "Who's here?"

You can't beat the devil, Jack. You have to run!

Jack turned around and saw his bedroom far behind him, like a photograph hung on the opposite side of the room. He turned back toward the glowing object. "Who are you?"

RUN!

Jack bolted up in bed. His shirt clung to his torso with cold sweat. There was a noise from downstairs. He threw off the covers and swung his legs around to the side of the bed. The burst of adrenaline in his system shocked him awake before his feet touched the ground. He pushed the dream aside, grabbed the Louisville Slugger, and ran to the door. Downstairs, Buddy barked and snarled like a junkyard dog clawing at a chain fence. There was the noise again. A deep, bass sound beneath the dog's high-pitched yelp.

Thump-thump. Thump-thump.

Buddy's snarls broke into a new level of frenzy. Jack paused at the top of the stairs. The cold metal weight of the Louisville Slugger in his hands felt suddenly inadequate. As much as he was against guns, he cursed himself for not having a real weapon in the house.

He looked to his left down the hall toward the girls' rooms. He shook his head and tried to think through the options. The noise was downstairs. Buddy was downstairs. The threat had to be down there, probably still outside. And there was only one way up from the lower level. So whatever Buddy saw had to come through him first to get to the girls.

Armed only with his home run swing, Jack stepped down the stairs.

Halfway down, he could see into the great room. Though the lower windows of the room were curtained, the windows on the second story were uncovered. Enough moonlight filtered in so that he could make out the broad outlines of the room's furnishings.

Jack crouched on the steps and peered through the spindles of the stair rail. He mentally cataloged every dark shape, sure that one of them would move and charge toward him or rise up just as a telltale flash of light signaled a bullet was on its way. But all the shadows stayed in place. Nothing was out of the ordinary.

Except Buddy's relentless barking and snarling, almost insane now, like an animal caught in a trap.

Jack wiped the sweat from his hands and gripped the bat. Buddy was by the front door. Whatever was going on had to be there. Jack didn't like leaving the stairway unguarded. If someone was in the house, the stairway was the only way to get at his family. As long as he stayed there no one could get by. But he had to find out what was going on at the front door.

He moved off the stairs and crept through the hall leading to the entryway. Buddy raged at the front door, his barking echoing off the walls.

Outside. It has to be outside.

The entryway was dark, but Jack could make out Buddy's hulking shadow at the far end of the entryway. The dog was right next to the door, his tail tucked between his legs.

Jack walked forward on the balls of his feet, the bat held in front of him. As he came closer to the door, the other sound he'd heard became clearer.

Thump-thump. Thump-thump.

The front door. Someone was outside trying to break it open. It sounded like a battering ram against the thick wood door. More than a fist. Or even a foot. Whoever was on the other side had to be throwing their whole body at the door to make it shake so hard. And they didn't give a damn about the dog on the other side.

Buddy leapt at the door, clawed at it, his paws churning the air.

Again and again, the heavy wood door banged and shook in its frame.

Jack reached out and flipped a switch. The entryway flooded with light, forcing him to cover his eyes until they corrected themselves. When he lowered his hand, he saw Buddy also frozen in place by the sudden swath of light. Dog and master met eye to eye. The communication was clear. Something was wrong. Very wrong. The door had stopped shaking.

Buddy snarled and leapt toward Jack. With a jolt, the dog was choked back and the door behind him shook from the force.

Thump-thump. Thump-thump.

Jack stared at the door. One end of a thick leather leash was tied to the door handle, the other end wrapped around the dog's neck. The door had shaken because Buddy was tied to it. There wasn't someone trying to break down the door. Someone was already in the house.

THIRTY-ONE

Jack turned and sprinted back through the hall. He took the stairs three at a time.

"SARAH! BECKY!"

The girl's rooms were at the end, one next to the other. Becky's room was first. He flung the door open.

A little voice came out of the dark. "Da-Daddy?"

Jack flipped on the light switch. The room's bright primary color scheme jumped out at him. Clown faces painted on the walls stared at him with dead expressions. Meant as happy decorations, they were sinister now, their mouths bent into strange sarcastic smiles, eyes too narrow and intense. Jack half-expected one of them to peel itself off the wall and race him to Becky's bed.

Becky clutched a pillow to her chest, looking up at him with wide eyes. "You okay?" Becky nodded. "All right. Stay right here. Stay in bed. I'm going to check on your sister."

Jack locked the bedroom door with himself inside. The girls' rooms were connected by a shared bathroom. He decided to go through the bathroom instead of going back into the hallway. For all he knew, the intruder could be out in the hall right now, right behind the door he'd just locked.

He clambered across the room, toys skittering across the floor as he kicked them out of the way. The bathroom nightlight was enough to see by. He ran through the room and threw open the door. Even before he could reach the light switch, he knew something was wrong. The room was freezing cold. Like walking into a meat locker.

He flipped the switch. Sarah's room was a calm pink, a princess motif she'd picked out herself. Her bedclothes were frilly, white and pink. Under the pink blanket lay his baby girl, shivering in the cold, blue lips pressed tight against chattering teeth. Her window was wide open. Jack looked around the room. Nothing else seemed out of place. He ran to his little girl and put his warm hands against her cheeks.

"Sarah. Are you all right, sweetie?" She didn't answer. "C'mon. Let's get you out of here." He pushed back the covers and picked her up in his arms. With his one free hand, he grabbed the baseball bat. Together, they went back through the bathroom to get Becky.

The door to Becky's room was open.

Becky was gone.

Jack lunged into the hallway. Nothing there. Still clinging on to Sarah, he rushed down the hall. "Becky! BECKY!" he shouted. "Lauren! I need your help. Where's Becky?"

He ran into the master suite but stopped as soon as he was through the door. Lauren was asleep in their bed with Becky nestled against her. It didn't seem possible. How could they be sleeping as if nothing was going on?

Sarah slipped from his grasp as he lowered her to the floor. Too scared to complain, she curled up against the wall, shivering.

The still figures of his wife and daughter huddled on the far side of the bed, both facing away from him.

On the side of the mattress closest to him, a large lump twitched violently under the covers. With each spasm, the shape crept closer to Lauren and Becky.

With a cry, Jack leapt across the room and tore back the sheets.

There, under the covers, was Buddy, or what was left of him.

The dog's rear legs were mangled and useless, almost impossible to recognize as part of his body. A gashing wound was open across his side, deep enough to expose bits of bone.

The blankets were drenched with blood. The dog's head hung at a strange angle, the jaw shifted ninety degrees to the side.

Buddy turned toward his master, a single wild eye able to function. A gurgling noise came from the dog's throat as he tried to whine for help.

Jack's eyes moved over to Lauren and his little girl. Everything was in slow motion. A strobe-light world of sequential snapshots.

He walked around to the other side of the bed so he could see their faces. They stared back at him, wide eyed, mouths open.

Jack dropped to his knees and covered his mouth to block his screaming. The bodies were covered with black, oozing sores. Every one ringed by purple flesh. Dead. His baby. His wife. Dead.

There was movement on the other side of the bodies. Buddy was still alive.

Got to put the poor animal out of its misery.

Jack stood, nodding at the thought. His body was numb, feeling as dead as the corpses on the bed in front of him. He crossed back to the other side of the bed, back to the bleeding, whining lump that twitched on the bed. He raised the bat over his head.

Got to put the poor animal out of its misery.

The thought sounded strange to him. The voice was wrong.

The dog is suffering. You have to do it. End its suffering. Then the same for Lauren and Becky. Just in case they are in pain too. You have to end their suffering.

It wasn't his voice, but it didn't matter. The voice was right. He had to put the dog out of its misery. Then take care of Lauren and Becky. Bury their poor bodies. It was all clear to him. He knew what he had to do. Then, afterward, after he'd done it all, he'd get Sarah out of there. Take her far away.

Yes, take Sarah away. You know where.

Jack twisted his hands on the bat to get a better grip, flexed his arms to prepare for the downward swing.

Then a different voice roared up from deep within his mind.

"Stop, Jack! Don't listen to him. Wake up!"

Jack rocked back at the sound. He fought to make sense of it all. No, he knew what he had to do. He took a step forward, the bat poised to strike.

"Daddy, no!"

"Jack. JACK! WHAT ARE YOU DOING?"

He froze. The voices. It was Lauren and Becky. Not dead, but alive. It didn't make sense. He'd *seen* their bodies. How was it possible?

The bedroom lights flashed on. Lauren sat upright in bed. Becky was beside her, pressed up against her mom for protection. Jack looked down on the bed where he had aimed the bat. Buddy was there. Rolled over on his back in submission. There was no injury. There was no blood.

Jack dropped the bat on the floor and staggered away from the bed. He collapsed on the floor and sat with his back against the wall.

The voice rose up in his mind, like a wave crashing over him, pounding at him. It was in his head, it was everywhere, shouting at him, laughing at him. Jack recognized the voice.

Nate Huckley.

The words came across as clear as if Huckley were crouched next to him, whispering in his ear.

I'll be back for you, Jack. You can count on it.

Then the crash and roar of the wave disappeared, and the voice was gone. The only sounds left were Becky crying and Lauren's voice saying that everything was all right. Jack heard the voice like it was coming from an echo-chamber. "Daddy's okay now. Daddy's okay."

Jack turned to look at Sarah, still crouched against the wall on the opposite side of the room from him. He didn't know what to say, so he said nothing. He stared and tried to force a reassuring smile. Sarah leaned forward and whispered just loud enough for him to hear, "That voice. It was the bad man again, wasn't it?"

Jack crawled over to his little girl and wrapped his arms around her. It was her next words that sent shivers through his body.

"Is he really going to come back like he said, Daddy? Is he really?"

Jack squeezed his eyes shut. It was too much. He didn't understand what was going on. He just wanted it all to stop. As he sat there and rocked Sarah in his arms, the same thought ran over and over in his mind – like an old scratched 45 record stuck on the same lyric, *"What if I hadn't snapped out of it? What would I have done next?"*

One look at Lauren, and Jack knew he wasn't the only one trying to deal with that thought.

THIRTY-TWO

The party was tomorrow night. Cathy Moran couldn't think of anything worse than if she couldn't go. Well maybe. If she went and somehow everyone saw the dark spots covering her chest and shoulders it would be *catastrophically* uncool.

She could go and just wear a turtleneck. It was cold enough. But if she went, she risked an even worse scenario. Bobby Mazingo might be there. Then, if Bobby did try something, which Cathy hoped he would, she would have to say no. While this turn of events would make her dad the happiest man in Prescott City, "no" was not the word Cathy wanted to use. And she felt pretty certain that if it came to that, then she could kiss Bobby Mazingo goodbye, and not in the sense she was hoping to.

Cathy stood in front of her bathroom mirror and tenderly rubbed the discolored skin, probing with her fingers for any sore spots. That was the strangest thing about it, nothing hurt. The whole area around her breasts, neck and shoulders looked like she'd been used as a punching bag. The skin between these freakish oversized pox marks was a dead gray, flaking with dry skin. *Like freezer burn on meat.* The unexpected thought made a chill pass through Cathy's body.

She opened the cabinet under the sink. Neat piles of fresh towels filled the space, folded to exacting Martha Stewart standards. At least her dad's new trophy wife was a good housekeeper, although Cathy would never give her that compliment to her face. Barbara, or Barbie as Cathy preferred to call her, was a regular Martha friggin' Stewart. But with a great rack, courtesy of the best boob surgeon her dad could find.

The day of the wedding had set the tone for the relationship with her new mom. The ceremony was an hour late getting started since the maid-of-honor, a position grudgingly offered to Cathy to begin with, showed up an hour late with a surprise for everyone. Little sixteen-year old Cathy Moran staggered down the aisle drunk as a factory worker on payday, waving happily at the assembled guests with a silly grin pasted on her face. Adding to the spectacle, her dad got to see her new jewelry for the first time as she drew nearer. A thick band of silver hung from her nose, still swollen from the piercing only hours before.

The more witty guests would later comment at the reception that the wedding was a success because it had ensured job security for the groom. His daughter alone could keep Scott Moran's psychology practice going for years.

Cathy pushed aside the towels. Way in the back, behind the bottle of Scope and Liquid Plummer, was a small ceramic jar with a cork lid. She pulled this out. The jar felt cool in her hands. She pried open the tight fitting lid. Inside was a Zip-loc baggy. And inside that was exactly what the doctor ordered. Bud directly from Humbolt County in Northern California, or so Nikki Tomlinson had promised when she'd sold it to her. Whether Nikki was telling the truth or whether she was full of shit, it was the best weed Cathy had ever smoked. And in the last year, she had become somewhat of a connoisseur.

She tipped the jar over and felt the small pipe tumble into her hand. Normally she would have stuffed the pipe and the baggy in her pocket and snuck into the forest behind her house before she lit up. But she didn't feel like it. The dark splotches had her freaked out, and she needed a hit. Her therapist, a friend of her dad who had been at the wedding, had explained that her behavior showed that she wanted to be caught by her father, that it was acting out, a cry for attention.

Cathy thought it was bullshit.

Anyway, she wasn't worried about getting caught by her father anymore. What was the worst he could do? Hate her? Well, that was already pretty much the case anyway, so she figured she had nothing to lose. Besides, even the doctor treating her disease had said it would be all right to smoke if the nausea from the medicine got too bad. She didn't think her father knew about the medical okay, and that was fine by her. The less he knew the better.

She plucked a few buds from the baggy, breaking them up just a little by rubbing her fingers together, and packed them into the pipe. Using the lighter from the jar, she lit the pipe and sucked back the acrid smoke, holding her breath to let the pot do its magic. Soon her brain mercifully floated away, and the stress dripped like wax off a candle. She looked in the mirror. The purple marks still registered in her mind as a bad thing, potentially a really bad thing, but the pot took the edge off. She knew what she had to do, what she should have done when she first noticed the marks.

Reluctantly, she packed the pipe away and sprayed half a can of Lysol into the air to cover her tracks. As she dripped Visine into her glazed eyes, she made the decision to wait until after school to make the phone call. Better to do it outside the house. The last thing she wanted was for her dad to hear her on the phone and freak out like he always did. Someday he'd treat her with the respect she deserved. Until then she would sneak around behind his back.

Well, unless it turned out it was really serious, then she'd tell him. Asshole or not, he was still her dad.

Cathy grabbed her backpack from her room and headed downstairs. She just hoped she'd be able to see her doctor after school and get back home before anyone noticed. Since no one in the house seemed to care about her, the chances for success looked pretty good.

THIRTY-THREE

Dr. Stanley Mansfield removed his glasses and dug a thumb into the corner of each eye. He pressed hard, trying to relieve the sinus headache that had gathered momentum since he woke up that morning. Even his hair seemed to hurt. He knew he wasn't ill. Just a bad case of nerves and stress. Maybe it was time to take a vacation. Get away and do a little fly-fishing. He smiled at the ridiculous notion. It had been years since he had taken a break from his work. Then again, he thought, maybe that was why he found himself stuck.

The phone rang and killed all ideas about vacations and mountain trout. He considered ignoring it, but the shrill ring was too much for his headache.

"Hi, Stanley. It's Lauren."

Dr. Mansfield leaned back in his chair. "Lauren. How are you? How are Jack and the girls?"

"As well as can be expected, I guess." Lauren's voice tightened. He could tell she was trying to hold back her emotions, but they were getting the better of her.

"What's going on?"

"Still a little shaken up over everything," Lauren replied after a long pause, her voice trembling.

"Take some time off. I'll cover any cases you have here. Take time to be with your family."

"I'll probably take you up on that. I might take the kids for a trip. Get their minds off things a little, you know?"

Take the kids. He noticed she didn't mention Jack. "Sure. Whatever you need, you know that." There was no answer. "Are you still there?"

"Yeah, I'm here. I'm sorry. You see, I…"

"Go on. Tell me what's bothering you."

"I need a psych referral. Someone good."

"For the kids?"

"It's not for the kids. It's for Jack. This whole thing has really shaken him up. He's had some hallucinations."

Dr. Mansfield chose his words carefully. "I heard about his…uh…episode in Nate Huckley's room. You know it's normal for someone who's been in a crash like this to have short term psychological effects. Post-traumatic stress often occurs when the subject endures the kinds of event Jack went through. Especially when there are children involved."

"I know all that," she snapped. "But it's just a little harder when it's your husband and not some textbook study."

"Yes, of course. I'm sorry," he said.

Lauren sighed, "No, I'm sorry. I'm on edge. Jack doesn't know I'm calling you, and I'm not looking forward to the battle to get him to see someone. Do you know anyone good?"

"Yes, actually there is someone right there in Prescott City. I've known him a long time. He's good and you can trust him. I'll email you his information."

"Thanks. Is there any way you could pull some strings and get him in today?"

"If you think it's necessary, of course I'll ask."

"Please. I'd appreciate it."

"I don't want to intrude, but are you in any danger?"

"No. Why would you ask such a thing?"

"These hallucinations haven't led to violent behavior, have they?"

"No. Of course not," Lauren shot back a little too quickly. She seemed to realize it, too, and paused to collect herself before continuing. "Look, thanks for the help. And I appreciate the offer for some time off. I'm going to stop in later today to check in on Felicia Rodriguez, and then I'll probably leave tomorrow for a few days, maybe a week."

"God, I thought someone called you."

"Called me about what?"

"Felicia Rodriguez suffered a massive coronary yesterday afternoon."

"Damn, why didn't someone call me? What's her condition?"

Dr. Mansfield cleared his throat. "I'm sorry, Lauren. She died."

THIRTY-FOUR

The room didn't look like a typical therapist's room. Jack based this evaluation not on any personal experience, but from scenes in countless movies and TV shows. They always showed puffy leather chairs, cheap wood paneling, and the obligatory couch where pathetic people stretched out while they spewed their problems to a paid stranger.

There was no couch in this room, though. Besides the executive leather chair behind a sprawling antique desk, the only furniture was a pair of sturdy wooden chairs, with thick armrests, facing each other in front of a fireplace. One personal photo sat on the fireplace mantle – a picture of a teenage girl standing next to a horse. Jack stared at the photo as he sat in one of the wooden chairs waiting for the therapist to show up. Unlike the rest of the room, the photo at least had a warm feeling to it. The girl faced the camera with an ear-to-ear smile, one hand holding the reins, the other patting the horse's forehead. Staring at the picture relaxed him a little. And that was exactly what he needed to do. Unwind the tension. Slow things down. Get a grip.

Lauren had been diplomatic in her approach to get him to this session. When he'd agreed without a fight to see the therapist, her surprise hadn't been lost on him. It was the fear in her voice that did it. And his own fear too. He still couldn't piece together what had happened last night. All he knew was he had ended up with a baseball bat in his hand and had come out of his trance, or whatever the hell it was, just in time to stay off the evening news as a serial murderer. So when Lauren explained that Stanley Mansfield had arranged an appointment with a shrink for him, he had agreed right away. He also agreed that Lauren should take the kids down to their friends' house in Baltimore. Just for a while. Just until he was sure he wasn't going crazy.

Jack stared into the fireplace and watched small flames lick at the wood. He hadn't slept since the crazy events of last night. How could he? The whole experience was so vivid to him, as clear as any waking memory. Each time he closed his eyes the images came back to him, *that voice.*

"Hello, Jack. How are you?"

Jack pushed himself up from his seat and spun toward the door. Dr. Scott Moran, dressed casually in cords and a tan button-down shirt, held his hands up. "Easy there. Didn't mean to startle you." He crossed the room and held out his hand. "I'm Scott Moran. Good to meet you."

Jack smiled as he shook the doctor's hand. "Sorry, I didn't sleep much last night."

"I guess that's why you're here," Moran said as he motioned Jack back to his chair. "If you want, I could prescribe some sleeping pills and just call it a day. Maybe go golfing together? What do you say?"

"What?"

"Do you golf?"

"Yeah, a little."

"So. What do you want to do? Golf or therapy?"

Jack sized up Scott Moran. The psychiatrist seemed only a little older than himself, maybe in his mid-forties. His sandy blond hair was either expertly dyed or just hid any grey hairs the man possessed. He had a dark complexion, one of those rare blonds who tanned well. Moran had a runner's build, lean and muscular. He carried himself with a fluid, country-club self confidence. Jack was used to this kind of easy-going arrogance. It was practically a required attitude in Southern California, but that didn't mean he liked being around it. Besides that, he wasn't in the mood for jokes, so he sat and waited for the psychiatrist to continue.

135

Moran sighed. "I guess we'll scratch clever banter off the agenda then." He took a poker and stirred the fire until the flames crackled and spit. He spoke without looking at Jack. "Listen, I know you're a reluctant guest. But from talking to your wife, I think it's a good thing you're here."

Jack shifted uncomfortably in his chair. He noticed Moran study him out of the corner of his eye. Jack cleared his throat. "Thanks for making a spot for me on short notice. I appreciate it."

Moran shrugged. "I wasn't busy. Between you and me, I'm not a very good therapist."

Jack gave him a thin smile. Under different circumstances, he might have given Moran a break and played along with the weak comedy act, but the psychiatrist's shtick was getting on his nerves. The guy was like a golf course pro crossed with a Vegas lounge act. Not exactly a confidence inspiring combination. Still, Jack forced himself to continue. "So what did Lauren tell you?"

"That you're crazy." Moran waited a few beats, watching Jack's serious expression. Finally, he said, "I'm just screwing with you, Jack. You've got to lighten up a little."

Jack shook his head and started to stand up, "Maybe this–"

"Post-traumatic stress disorder. That's what's causing these hallucinations. You're not crazy, Jack. You're just a little freaked out by what happened to you. Happens all the time."

"Lauren told you–"

"No details. Just that you've had troubling dream-like images. Sleep walking. The works."

Sleepwalking? I took a baseball bat and almost beat my dog to death in front of my family, and she told you I was sleepwalking?

"You want to tell me the details of what you saw?" Moran asked.

Jack shifted his eyes and stared into the fire, his fingers tapping the wooden armrest.

Moran changed tack. He spoke in a lower, softer voice. "Jack, whatever you saw compelled you to walk around the house and do some things you didn't want to do. I'm guessing there is no way you would be here right now unless whatever you saw and whatever you did scared you and your wife pretty bad. I can help you. I really can. But that only happens if you let me in on the details."

"I haven't even told Lauren everything."

"Doesn't matter. Tell it to me. What's the worst case? That I think you're nuts? You don't give a damn what I think of you, right? So that's not a big deal. Best case, we figure some stuff out, I give you some answers, and you get better. You're a businessman. That's a low cost of failure with a huge upside potential. Listen, I have a family too." He pointed to the picture on the mantle. "A daughter, Cathy. I know what it's like to be a father. The responsibility you feel. I can help you with this."

Jack glanced at the photo of Moran's daughter. She smiled back at him and made him feel better. Then he remembered Lauren's look in the bedroom. She had been so scared of him. Worse, he hadn't been able to reassure her. He didn't know what he might have done next with the bat. He had no control over his actions. Over the hallucinations. Moran was right about one thing. He did owe it to Lauren and the kids to at least try. Without taking his eyes off the fire, Jack recounted every detail he could remember.

THIRTY-FIVE

"I won't be very long," Lauren assured the emergency room nurse who volunteered to watch after the girls. "Page me if you need me or if you get busy."

"Take your time, Dr. Tremont. We haven't seen a patient here all day," Nurse Haddie said.

Lauren kissed each of the girls on the cheek. They were already tearing through the box of medical supplies the nurse had given them. Lauren knew how the game went, and soon Band-Aids and gauze would be everywhere as the girls took turns being the patient and the doctor. It always made a mess, but she preferred it to when they played house. She wanted her daughters to know from an early age that they could do anything they wanted. She didn't believe in pressuring them, and she respected women who stayed home to raise their kids, but it secretly delighted her whenever the girls said they wanted to be doctors like their mom.

"Just remember that you ladies are going to clean up whatever mess you make." The girls paused for a second and then went back to their game with a new set of giggles. "Be good." She turned to the nurse. "They had Krispy Kreme doughnuts for a treat on the way here. Good luck."

The sounds of the girls playing faded as Lauren walked down the hallway toward the elevator. With the waning sound, Lauren felt her mind shift from being a mother to being a doctor. And one persona was no less protective than the other.

She had promised Jack that she would drive straight down to Baltimore, but she couldn't resist making this quick stop at the hospital. A patient of hers had died, and she wasn't satisfied with the answers she was getting.

She flipped through Felicia Rodriguez's file as she waited for the elevator to arrive. She saw the notation where the blood was drawn to be sent to the CDC. Below that were notations by various nurses regarding IV changes, temperature, blood pressure readings. All seemed normal. Then the entry that made her stomach turn. "Massive coronary. Attempts to resuscitate unsuccessful. TOD 17:14 hr." TOD stood for time of death. Lauren recognized the handwriting. Dr. Stanley Mansfield.

She shook her head. Something felt wrong. Felicia was her patient, and no one had called her when it happened. Stanley had even been the attending physician when the girl died, and still he hadn't called. She rationalized that Stanley had just been looking out for her, trying to give her time to be with her family. But still, something felt out of place. As she worked through the problem, it did occur to her that with so little sleep and the stress from last night, the only thing out of place might be her.

The elevator door opened. Lauren walked in, thankful to have the elevator to herself. She didn't think she could bring herself to engage in small talk today. She pressed "B," and the elevator dropped down toward the basement, down to Midland Hospital's morgue.

The basement was one area untouched by the renovations to the building over the years. The walls were still bare brick just as they'd been for over a hundred years. A maze of pipes ran in crisscross patterns overhead, attached to the ceiling with thick metal brackets drilled into the masonry. The floor was painted a no-skid industrial yellow in a poor attempt to brighten up the gloomy surroundings. The morgue was at the far end of the hallway that extended from the elevator. To get there, corpses were treated to a gurney ride past laundry rooms, supply cabinets, and storage areas.

The end of the road for the bodies was a large stainless steel door, similar to an oversized subzero refrigerator, large enough to fit a gurney through. The door appeared surprisingly modern in the turn of the century basement, more a high-tech bank vault than a door. On the other side of the sub-zero doors, bodies found refrigerated temperatures and a choice of ten separate "beds" for their temporary resting places. Morbid as it was, Lauren knew that the nurses and orderlies who had access to a key sometimes came down here on their breaks during the hot summer days. A strange place to eat a sandwich, but at least it was cool. The morgue was small, but Midland had only run out of room once.

Stanley Mansfield had told her the story on her first day. There was a freak storm in early December back in 1986. A freezing rain coated everything with a full inch of ice, turning the Interstate into a demolition derby. A semi-truck lost control and did the most damage, wiping out a whole row of cars pulled over to the side of the road to wait out the storm. After rescue workers sorted through the mess, all ten beds in the morgue were spoken for. Somehow, two terminal patients, a Mrs. Gunther and a Mrs. Brookside, both ready to get on with dying, found out about the predicament. The women were southern belles of the old breed, and they proclaimed they would not die until a space was available. True to their words, they held on for a few more days. They died the same day they were told the morgue was ready for them. Stanley swore that he believed they would still be alive today if he had just kept telling them there was no room in the morgue.

Like many of Stanley's stories, it was charming, but always with a disturbing undercurrent. Lauren brushed it aside. Most of the doctors she worked with developed gallows humor over time. It was just a way of coping with some of the horrible sights that came with the job. She had just never become comfortable with the jokes. She never laughed about death.

Lauren fished in her pocket and found her keys. The morgue was always kept locked because security into the basement was minimal. The days of bodysnatching were long gone, but the morgue was kept under lock and key because of an overeager reporter eleven years earlier. The reporter, a kid from the local paper, snuck in through the basement and photographed the bodies. He thought it would make a great story about lack of hospital security. Instead, the prank landed him in jail for a few weeks. Still, once the story got out, there was a public outcry for better security, which led to the space age doors in front of her. Lauren smiled. Another Stanley story with a twist.

There was a soft *whoosh* of air as she opened the stainless steel door. She stepped inside and closed the door behind her. She checked the log book to find which drawer contained Felicia Rodriguez's body. With a grunt, she pulled open drawer three and slid it from the wall. Empty.

Lauren slid the drawer back in and rechecked the log book. She had read it correctly. Felicia was supposed to be in number three. Lauren sighed. Someone must have entered the wrong drawer. It happened sometimes, but it was sloppy.

She heaved on the handle for drawer number one. Empty. Drawer number two. Empty. Again and again, she tugged open the heavy drawers only to find them empty. By the time she got to number nine, there was sweat pouring down her face and she was out of breath. She pulled hard at the handle and groaned on seeing that the drawer was empty. She laughed in spite of herself, wishing she'd started with drawer ten instead. "Murphy's law," she said to herself, pulling open the last drawer.

Empty.

Lauren went back to the logbook. It clearly indicated the date and time when the body was brought down to the morgue. There was no indication that the body had been removed for any reason. There were strong protocols in place when bodies were moved, especially when the body posed a possible public safety threat. She and Stanley had discussed that on the phone. The body would need to be kept at Midland until results of the blood work were back from the CDC.

She threw the logbook back in place and went to the door. She pulled on the handle. The door didn't move. She tried again.

Nothing.

She was locked in.

She grabbed the handle and leaned her weight on top of it. She grunted with the effort. No matter how hard she pushed, the handle wouldn't budge. Someone must have locked the door from the outside.

She stepped back from the door, tears welling up in her eyes. She was trapped. She felt her heart thumping in her chest. Her hands shook.

Then she noticed the sign on the side of the door. She rubbed her eyes to clear away the tears and started to laugh. God, she was tired. She needed to be careful that she didn't make any mistakes that could hurt someone. She promised herself that she wouldn't treat any patients today. Definitely not today. Not until she got some sleep. Not until she got a hold of herself.

She reached over and pushed the large button marked, "Open Door." The morgue door clicked and swung open.

Lauren sucked in a deep breath to calm her frayed nerves. There was too much going on. Jack's hallucinations, Sarah's bizarre writing, strangers stalking her house and now her patient's body going AWOL. She was stretched too thin. Maybe Jack was right. Maybe she should have gone straight down to her friend's house in Baltimore. She needed to get some perspective and a little time and distance would give her a chance to sort things out, come up with an explanation for what was happening to her family. But she felt a responsibility to Felicia too. She needed to understand what had happened to her.

As strange as the last few days had been at home, she expected to deal with emotional issues there. It was part of marriage and part of raising a family. She and Jack had brought their marriage back from the edge of the cliff they had found themselves on in California. All the resentment and alienation brought on by their jobs and fast lifestyle seemed now like a lifetime ago. Seeing Jack deal with the death of Melissa Gonzales and helping him cope with it had reminded her of how much she loved him. The result of that horrible experience was that they were a team again. The decision to move to Prescott City and work on rebuilding their lives proved it. She started to believe that they could handle anything life threw at them, just as long as they stayed together.

But the hospital was supposed to be different. Her work was her constant. The calm methodology of science was her refuge. Now, when she could really use the reassurance of normalcy, she faced another mystery. As tired as she was, she wasn't about to give up. If anything, her lack of sleep had made her more emotional. Now she was beyond being curious. She was angry.

Lauren headed down the hall back to the elevator, the heavy clacking of her low-heeled shoes hitting the concrete floor, telegraphing her mood. She had every intention of finding out what had happened to Felicia Rodriguez's body, and she knew where to start asking questions.

THIRTY-SIX

Steam rose up through the small hole in the coffee lid as Joe Lonetree raised his cup to his lips. He slurped at the hot liquid, savoring the bitterness of the dark roast. There was a time when he wouldn't have allowed himself this caffeine fix, but that was also a time when he wouldn't have needed the pick-me-up either. He'd only slept eight hours in the last forty. That much sleep would have once seemed a luxury, but he felt the fatigue wearing on him. Now, sitting in the Ford Bronco across from Dr. Scott Moran's office, he fought against the urge to nod off. When this was all over, he planned to sleep for a week. Some place warm with white beaches and fruity drinks.

The last year was a blur to him, a series of bizarre revelations that led him to this sleepy mountain town from half way around the world. He'd come a long way in a little time. And the change in geography was nothing compared to the other changes he had endured. In the last twelve months, his belief system had been stripped bare and then rebuilt with the old stories he thought he'd abandoned long ago. The old beliefs, for years sealed away in a remote corner of his mind, had escaped their banishment and lived once again. His father would have been proud to know his wayward son had finally returned to him, finally believed in his life's work after so many years of doubt.

Too bad the old man wasn't around anymore.

A quick look through the parking lot confirmed that Jack Tremont was still in the shrink's office. Lonetree leaned his head back and allowed his eyes to close. They burned at first, but the darkness soothed his tired eyes and the burning faded into a comfortable inkiness.

He allowed his mind to wander through the flashes of childhood memories that had been dredged up since returning to America. Small flashes of his father's face, snatches of conversation, images from a past he had worked hard to forget. There was the living room back in Arizona. Not in the nice house they lived in before his mother died, but the other place. The place his father took them to hide. A couch that slumped in the middle from broken springs. Fake wood panels that peeled off the trailer walls. Bright orange carpet that didn't reach all the way across the floor. A few landscape watercolors that hung on the wall, each one hanging at a crooked angle, the frames covered with thick dust. And brown bottles everywhere. Old Milwaukee. Empty, but with enough left in them to fill the air with the reek of stale beer. His mother would never have allowed the house to look like that. When she was alive, they had dignity as a family. After her death, they were poor. Worse, they were reservation poor. Two boys, six and ten, with a father who seemed intent on living out every Native American stereotype he could.

There, in that living room, his father had sat him down and explained his mother's death to him. His father was a big man, wide enough to have to turn sideways to fit through the trailer's small doorways. Tall so that he had to bow his head to walk in his own house. That day he bowed his head even though he was sitting on the couch, his face dark and brooding, his breath stinking from alcohol and cigarettes. Lonetree still remembered every second of the encounter. It was the first time he had been scared of his father. And ashamed of him.

After explaining how cancer had taken his mother away, his father made him kneel to the floor and pray with him. He asked forgiveness for being away from home so much during her illness. He prayed that she understood the importance of his work. Then, slurring his words and swaying unsteadily, he made his case to his son why he ought to be forgiven. He explained his life's work in a disjointed, rambling lecture. The story that came out that day was a bizarre tale, so strange and bewildering that young Joe Lonetree could do nothing but stare open mouthed through it all. Even with his ten year old imagination, he could not bring himself to believe what his father told him. It wasn't like his other stories of chiefs and tribes and mountain gods which his father used to tell with a grin. His father told *this* story with a shaking voice and darting eye paranoia. This wasn't just mythology or legend to him. He thought it was real.

At the end of the story, the big man grabbed his son and held him close, promising not to let the bad things hurt him or his brother. The little boy in the dirty trailer hung limp in his father's embrace, crying into his shoulder. Not from fear, but from understanding that he had not only lost his mother, but now his father as well. One to a disease he did not understand; the other to booze and a story he refused to believe.

Before his mother died, his father was a college professor, an author, a stable figure in his life. All that remained of that man was a delusional drunk, a paranoid fool who had lost his mind. Little Joe Lonetree wept in the trailer with his father. It was the last time they shared an embrace.

Lonetree opened his eyes with a grunt. He looked around to orient himself, blinking back against the dull winter sun. He glanced at the dashboard clock. Ten minutes had flashed by. He checked the parking lot. Tremont's car was still there.

With a sigh, he took off his sunglasses and rubbed his eyes. He felt sick to his stomach from his daydream. At least he'd woken up before what had happened next. Before he called his father a drunk and a liar. Before he blamed him for his mother's death. An accusation he never recanted to the old man while he was alive. It amazed him how far from that living room he had to travel before he understood his own father. The world he'd inhabited since his eighteenth birthday was different than anything he'd ever imagined, and in some ways as terrible as the fantasy world described to him that day.

The atrocities he'd seen in service to his country were as bad as any dream, especially now, surrounded by the picture perfect Americana of Prescott City. He glanced around him. Store fronts with neatly painted wooden signs. Wrought iron lampposts that, at night, lit clean sidewalks filled with clean people. Nicely trimmed grass in the open areas. Nothing out of place. Everything just so.

This was what the military told him he was protecting. But he doubted the happy residents of Prescott City would sleep well if they knew the things that he had seen and done on their behalf. The mangled embrace of corpses heaped together in the mass graves of Bosnia. The back walls of caves in Afghanistan covered with a red slime punctuated by the occasional white tooth, the residue of Taliban soldiers smashed against rock by thermobaric shock waves. An encampment of Abu Sayyef militants in the Philippines reduced to bubbling flesh by hemorrhagic fever. All images witnessed, and sometimes caused, by Lt. Joseph Lonetree, United States Navy SEAL. He felt out of place in Prescott City, like a Hell's Angel who had wandered onto the Andy Griffith show. Then again, he knew all he had to do was sleep and the images from his past were just a nightmare away.

At least the war zones where he'd lived for the past fifteen years had looked the part. Bombed out rubble, deep cave bunkers, hot jungles. They all fit his idea of enemy territory. But in this place everything seemed normal. The enemy blended in perfectly and, in his mind, that made everyone a suspect. Lonetree started to feel the entire town was somehow unnatural. Too clean. Too perfect. Walking down the street felt like watching a living history demonstration, as if everyone were in on a collective agreement to create an image of normalcy.

He wondered what the shrink Jack Tremont was talking to would think of this particular paranoia. The thought brought a smile to his lips. He knew he would make an interesting case for a team of psychiatrists. The Navy had offered him counseling a dozen or more times, a product of a kinder, gentler military. But it was common knowledge in the ranks that the offer wasn't serious. To accept was to be done with fieldwork, a sign you couldn't hack it. Paranoia was an asset in the field. It had kept him and the men who followed him alive through impossible situations, even though his reputation pointed to something more than simple paranoia as the key to his mission effectiveness. The rumor was that Lonetree had "special gifts" that kept his men alive.

The rumors followed him from assignment to assignment. Whispers trailed him whenever he walked through a mess tent. A spark of recognition attended any introduction to another Special Forces member. Men volunteered for missions when his name was attached to them. It was more than the deference given by soldiers to the true warriors in their midst. The rumors said that the lieutenant *knew* things in the field. And his knowing kept his men alive. A sixth sense. Indian magic.

Lonetree knew a sniper was waiting in the next building.

Lonetree sensed a cave was rigged to blow.

Lonetree knew his old man was dead of a heart attack back home...a day before the phone call came.

Nothing was ever said to his face, but he knew the stories were out there. He didn't think it was anything more than being careful and following his instincts, but he did nothing to dispel the speculation about his strange powers. The stories gave his men more confidence in him. And they ensured people left him alone. Just the way he liked it.

A year ago, after news of his brother's death reached him during a tour in Afghanistan, he'd ended his military life. His commanding officer, Colonel Goldman, was shocked when Lonetree didn't re-up. But he didn't put up a fight. After the things Lonetree had seen and done, the colonel understood if he wanted to go home. He'd shaken the man's hand and wished him luck on his new life, told him to call if he was ever in trouble and needed some help. Lonetree sensed the emotions behind the lie. The colonel knew the stories, and feared the Native American as much as respected him.

Now Lonetree was solo, but he still was on-mission. And he intended to stay alive through his current engagement. At least until he settled some scores. He'd led a life of killing and death, somehow knowing that he was chasing away the demons that had surrounded him from childhood. The demons his father had told him about. The same demons that he now believed he was close to catching. The ones he had sworn to destroy.

After the horrors that filled his life, evil forced on him by his military masters from above, it seemed infinitely just that he could now use his killing skills for personal vengeance. He was a hunter-killer, and he meant to finish the job that both his father and little brother had died attempting. He would avenge their deaths and send the demons back to Hell where they belonged.

Jack Tremont was somehow linked to his mission. Like so many things, Lonetree couldn't articulate how he knew it – he just did. And instinct was what he trusted more than anything. Except his instinct didn't tell him how Tremont fit into it all. Was he a potential ally or an enemy?

Lonetree knew the demons came in every disguise, but Tremont's actions so far indicated he didn't know what he was involved in. Lonetree had a feeling that, one way or another, Jack Tremont would prove useful, maybe even pivotal in bringing things to a conclusion. He knew impatience led to mistakes, but he felt he had waited long enough. It was time to take some chances. It was time to make a move.

THIRTY-SEVEN

Jack sat back in the chair and eyed the psychiatrist. He told the man everything that had happened over the past two days. Scott Moran listened quietly throughout the story, asking only minor clarifying questions, never offering any analysis or theory to explain the strange occurrences in the Tremont household. Jack noticed that no sign of incredulity passed over the man's expression either. Moran listened to the bizarre series of events as if they were the same things he heard day in and day out. Then it struck him. Moran probably did hear these kinds of paranoid delusions all the time. From other people who were going crazy.

Even now that the story was done, the psychiatrist kept the passive expression he'd held during the entire session. Jack placed the heel of his hand under his chin and forced his head side to side until the vertebrae in his neck cracked. Moran winced at the sound.

"So what do you think?" Jack asked.

"I think you need a chiropractor more than you need me." Jack smiled, only because he felt obliged. Moran rose from his chair and threw another log on the fire. "Trust me, Jack. I've heard stories that make your stuff seem boring." He used long tongs to stack burning embers around the new logs. The fire flared, crackling and spitting sparks into the room.

"I'm glad to hear there are people in town crazier than I am. That makes me feel safe."

Moran grinned and fell back into his seat. "Not crazy. They have issues to sort out, that's all. Nothing a little therapy won't help."

"Is this when you tell me my time's up and I need ten more sessions to get at the problem?"

"Nah," Moran waved a hand at him. "I don't think it's that complicated. You've had a pretty big shock, a traumatic event that's gotten under your skin. You never really recovered from the trauma of the accident you had in California."

"I've dealt with that. It's behind me."

"What was the name of the girl who died that day?" Jack looked away. He hadn't spoken her name for a long time. It made it too personal. Too real. He couldn't say the words without seeing her face. Scott Moran let the silence draw out long enough to make his point. "You see what I mean? You ran away from the problem by moving here, but you never faced it."

Jack nodded. "But how does this tie into what's happening now?"

"Maybe this is you facing it. Finally dealing with this demon in your past. You obviously feel responsible for Melissa's death. Buried guilt may have given rise to a hero fantasy about saving another girl, this one you say you saw in Nate Huckley's car. No, hear me out before you argue against it. This girl hit the windshield of your car just like Melissa Gonzales. A little too coincidental, don't you think."

"It's coincidental. But it doesn't mean it didn't happen."

"All right, let's put that to the side then. Once it became clear that you couldn't save the new girl, there's this paranoia that someone is after your daughters. Once again, you have a chance to save them."

"But you have it backward. Huckley was after them before I saw the girl. So your theory can't be right."

Scott Moran shifted in his chair. "All right, Albert James then."

"What about him?"

"The man died in your lap with a massive head wound. Didn't Melissa die of a head wound in the accident? Everything happened right after Albert James died, right?"

Jack felt the pull of Moran's argument. The logic drew him in. For the first time that day, he felt like a rational explanation might be within reach. "How do you explain the tangible evidence?"

"Such as?"

"The numbers written by my daughter. There were pages with Huckley's room number all over them."

Moran leaned in closer, like a doctor delivering bad news. "You may not like this question, Jack, but it's important that I ask it. Did anyone else see her write the numbers?"

Jack stared. It took him a few seconds to process the insinuation. He felt his face heat up in anger. "No, I guess...but you don't think I..." His hand involuntarily went to his mouth as he thought it through. Could he have written the numbers himself and not realized it? Was it possible? Could he be that sick? He would have sworn he had seen Lauren and Becky dead in their bed too. Maybe...maybe...

"And the visitor at your door. This strange man warning you about Huckley."

Jack seized on the suggestion. Something to steady himself, orient him to the real world. "Yeah, how do you explain that away?"

"Did your wife see him? Did she hear the conversation at all?"

Jack wrung his hands. "No, she didn't see him, but she heard the knock at the door. I'm sure she heard his voice." Moran sat back and said nothing. He let Jack make his own connections. "You think it could have been someone else and I just imagined the whole thing? Hallucinated this Lonetree guy?"

Moran shrugged. "Maybe. I doubt it though."

"You doubt it?"

"I wouldn't rule it out, but it might be explained by something a little simpler. It could have been someone who knew what happened to you and was using your situation to live out his own delusion. Someone from the hospital, maybe? Even someone who heard about your story from a friend over a couple of beers."

"Great." Jack said, shaking his head. "So this guy's some crazy living out a fantasy? That's supposed to make me feel good?"

"Who knows? Could be some scam artist who heard about your episode in Huckley's room. He shows up offering to help you, confirms the hallucination you think you saw, next thing you know he's asking for money for continued help. Believe it or not, there are people out there who do that kind of thing."

Jack leaned back in his chair and ran his hand through his hair. Moran seemed to have all the bases covered. Everything was a delusion triggered by watching Albert James die and dealing with guilt from the accident. He started to think about the night of the crash. The girl in the trunk of Huckley's car. Wasn't there a chance his eyes had played a trick on him? Hadn't Lauren and Becky looked real in the bed covered with sores? Maybe the whole thing was in his head. Maybe..."

"Jack, are you with me?"

Jack shook his head. "Yeah, I'm here."

"Listen, I'm not trying to scare you. If anything, this should be good news."

"How do you figure?"

"Well, think of the alternative. If these aren't delusions, then your daughter is a psychic who can hear people in her head, and Nate Huckley is haunting you while he's in a hospital bed in a coma."

"It does sound crazy, doesn't it?"

"Oh, we don't use that word. Let's just say it sounds very, very improbable. You tell me what seems more likely. You're experiencing psychological distress triggered by witnessing Albert James' death. This distress has led to hallucinations and acute paranoia which feeds into both your parental need to protect your children and your guilt over the girl killed in the car accident in California."

"And option number two?"

"Option two is that the boogey man is out to get you. And I hope it's option one because therapy and a little Lithium will help the delusions, but I'm afraid there's nothing in the pharmacopoeia to battle against supernatural cults trying to steal your kid."

Jack smiled. It did sound crazy. He actually felt embarrassed that he'd invested himself in such a story. Mentally, he tried out the new rationalization, and it felt good. It was based on rational thoughts. Time lines. Cause and effect. Cloaked in this logic, it felt reasonable. Red faced, he asked Moran for a prescription and another appointment time. A little therapy. A few pills. And everything would get back to normal.

Yet, even though Jack admitted the explanation felt good, there was something nagging at him. While Moran checked his appointment book, Jack wrung his hands and tried to push the feeling away, but it kept coming back to him. The new explanation was rational. It was logical. It was just that deep down, Jack didn't believe it was right.

THIRTY-EIGHT

Lauren walked into Dr. Mansfield's office without knocking. The old man was on the phone. He glanced up at Lauren and put his hand over the handset.

"Lauren. What are you doing here?" Before she could answer, he held up his other hand. "Can you give me a minute?"

"This can't wait."

Dr. Mansfield squinted at her. "You're here about Felicia Rodriguez."

Lauren noticed it was a statement, not a question. "Her body is missing."

"Yes, the body is gone. Hold on one minute." He uncovered the phone. "Hello? Are you still there? Yes, I'll be here this evening. Why don't you come on by around seven and we'll see what's going on. All right?" He paused. "Come alone if you want. Yes, that's fine. Call me when you get close."

After he hung up the phone she blurted out, "You know about Felicia already? Why wasn't I told?"

Dr. Mansfield finished writing a note into his planner, not looking up as he answered her. "Felicia's body was released to her family."

"But the CDC–"

"The results came back from the CDC. Negative for all known pathogens. Felicia Rodriguez posed no public health risk. We had no right to stop her body from being released."

"There should be an autopsy. We don't know what killed her. It could be something we've never seen before."

"You know we can't force the family to agree to an autopsy if there is no evidence of a crime or a public threat. I tried talking with Mr. Rodriguez, but he wanted nothing to do with it."

"How can you say it's not a public threat? The way her body broke down. The symptoms. The lesions. We need to find out what it was."

Dr. Mansfield handed her the report from the CDC. "Look for yourself. She came back clean."

Lauren scanned the document from the CDC. In a world full of biothreats, the CDC had become very quick in their lab work. In fact, many of the improvements were a result of her own work on the Homeland Defense Medical Council during her time at Johns Hopkins.

But she knew the CDC procedure well enough to know its limitations. Vigilance against bio-attacks had turned the lab into a sprawling bureaucracy with hundreds of technicians working through a constant flood of samples. The sheer volume meant it was impossible to test for everything, so the screens were limited to contagions that posed a significant public risk. Still, the list of tests on Felicia's blood work and DNA sample ran several pages. All negative.

"So cause of death unknown?"

Dr. Mansfield handed over a document. "The medical examiner's report will show massive coronary as cause of death."

Lauren threw the folder back on the desk. "This is bush league medicine and you know it."

The doctor rocked back in his chair, eyes narrowed. Lauren regretted her comment as soon as it was out of her mouth. She respected Dr. Mansfield, but this lapse of judgment was unconscionable. They had no idea what they were dealing with here. It wasn't the time to get sloppy.

Dr. Mansfield pursed his lips together. Lauren noticed his knuckles were white as they clutched the side of his chair. He was fighting to control himself. She saw a flash of anger in his eyes, something she had never seen before in him.

"I'm sorry we don't measure up to your standards, Dr. Tremont." The words came out clipped, each syllable snapped off like it was frozen. His voice rose as he spoke. "Good people work at this hospital, and they do an excellent job with the resources they have. I'll not have you or anyone else disparage their efforts to save that little girl."

"I'm sorry. It's just...it's..." she blinked hard, surprised to feel tears rolling down her cheeks. She wasn't sure if it was the shock at Dr. Mansfield's harsh tone or the stress of the last few days. Regardless, the tears came, pouring faster than she could wipe them away with the back of her sleeve.

Dr. Mansfield held up his hands and sighed. "I'm sorry. Really. Look, I understand you're upset. I get attached to my patients too. In fact, I was just on the phone with one of them. It's hard when they don't respond well to treatment." He got up from his desk and walked over to her. "We're both a little spent here. Let's just chalk this up to stress, all right? No hard feelings?" He opened his arms for a hug.

Lauren shook her head. She suddenly felt ten years old. She wanted the embrace, wanted to cry on his shoulder, but she wouldn't let herself. Smiling weakly, she said, "Thanks. I'm fine. I don't usually get so emotional."

"You're human. Emotional is okay."

Lauren smiled. "Yeah, I guess." She recognized his tone. It was what she called his grandfather mode, his voice full of comfort, his eyes sympathetic, the smile just enough to show he cared.

It was the Dr. Mansfield she was used to, but his flash of anger only seconds before left her unnerved. No amount of country charm could shake her surprise at the dark cloud that had covered his face. It made the old gentleman doctor routine seem just that, a routine.

Then again, he had said that the phone call he was on when she walked into the room was a patient who wasn't doing well. Maybe it was the stress.

Still, she suddenly felt uncomfortable being in the room alone with him. She wanted to get out of there as soon as possible. Besides, she was anxious to call Felicia's parents.

"I'm going to try again with the family to get them to authorize an autopsy. I have good rapport with the father. I think I'll be able to convince him." She turned to leave, but was stopped by Dr. Mansfield's low baritone voice.

"You're too late. The body was taken directly to Westlawn. Felicia Rodriguez was cremated earlier today. I'm afraid this particular matter is closed."

THIRTY-NINE

Jack fingered the white piece of paper as he waited for the red light to change. The prescription was scrawled out in the indecipherable handwriting that seemed to be universal among doctors. With a little imagination, he could see the word "lithium" buried within the loops and squiggles from Dr. Moran's pen.

There was a pharmacy a couple of blocks down the street. Leaving the psychiatrist's office, he decided to get the prescription filled and head home. Maybe read a book for a while. Go for a hike. Catch up on the consulting work that was due at the end of the month. Anything to get his mind off things.

He glanced at the prescription.

The turn for the pharmacy came up. He removed his foot from the gas and it hovered over the brake. The car slowed as it coasted, but Jack's foot remained suspended over the brake. The shopping center with the pharmacy slid by.

A voice in his head chastised him for being stubborn. That much he knew about himself. But there was something nagging him from his meeting with the psychiatrist. The whole meeting seemed contrived. Moran was too plastic, too ready to suggest answers to everything. Didn't psychiatrists try to get their patients to make their own breakthroughs? Establish their own conclusions?

The rational part of his brain laughed at the thought. What did he know about therapy, anyway? He had not gone after the accident in California. He'd just dealt with it. That was who he was, the guy who could deal with anything.

"You're doing a hell of a job with that, aren't you?" he muttered to himself.

It was ridiculous for him to second-guess Moran. Still, he couldn't shake the feeling.

He usually had a good feel for people, his success in business had depended on it, and he'd gotten a strange read from Moran. But given the circumstances, he decided he didn't have the luxury of playing hunches or letting his feelings get in the way. The psychiatrist had given him an explanation he could live with, and a prescription to help him cope. He needed to follow the advice and get on the medication. He owed it to Lauren and the kids to do it.

He glanced over his shoulder to merge left and make a U-turn back to the pharmacy. There was a black Ford Bronco positioned just off his rear left bumper that blocked his way. Jack turned on his signal and sped up. When he looked back, he saw that the Bronco had also accelerated, staying on his bumper.

Jack groaned. Probably some high school kid, he thought. He didn't have the patience to play around. He slowed down to allow the Bronco to pass. But it matched his speed again, staying right behind him.

"What the—" Jack twisted in his seat to get a look at the driver. His heart thumped hard in his chest when he recognized the man behind the wheel. Joseph Lonetree. He felt as if the air in his lungs had turned to cement. Clenching the wheel with his left hand, he grabbed the phone to call the police.

But as he dialed, the initial shock wore off. His adrenaline rush transformed his panic into something else. Anger. Not only because of the man following him, but because he had allowed himself to feel intimidated. This man was a threat to his family. He wasn't going to run away from him. And he wasn't going to wait for Sheriff Janney to ride in and save him either.

Jack cancelled the call and threw the phone on the passenger seat. He pressed a button on his door and the automatic window slid down. Jack extended his arm out of the window and waved the man forward. Once the Bronco pulled up even, Jack motioned for Lonetree to follow him. The Bronco fell back and followed Jack's lead off the main road and into an EZ Mart parking lot.

He parked at the far end of the lot away from any other vehicles and threw the car into park. Jack climbed out of the car as the Bronco pulled into the space next to him. He walked up to the SUV and squinted through the tinted side window, trying to see what the man was doing. When the automatic window rolled down, Jack had his answer.

The handgun was positioned by Lonetree's waist so that it wasn't visible through the front windshield. But Jack had a perfect view down the gun's dark barrel. A view, he realized, only made possible because the gun was pointed directly between his eyes.

Jack couldn't believe it. He was being held up in the middle of the day in a grocery store parking lot. This sort of thing happened in Columbia, or even in South Central L.A., but in Prescott City?

Jack looked up from the gun into the face of its owner. Lonetree was expressionless, his mouth a straight line, his eyes hidden behind impenetrable sunglasses that reflected Jack's alarmed face back to him.

"What is this? What do you want with me?"

The barrel of the gun wagged in the air. "Get in. I want to show you something. I'm not going to hurt you."

"Then why do you need the gun?"

Lonetree shrugged. "You seem like the kind of guy who needs to be persuaded."

"I'm not going anywhere," Jack said with more confidence than he felt.

There was a metallic click as Lonetree slid his thumb over the top of the gun. Jack didn't know much about firearms, but he was pretty sure the click was the sound of the hammer being cocked. Lonetree's voice came soft but unmistakably firm. "Just so you know, I have no problem shooting you if you refuse to come with me."

"What's this all about? Money? What?"

Lonetree waved the gun. "Last call. Get in the car."

Jack wondered whether Lonetree could get a shot off if he dropped to the asphalt. Maybe if he stayed low next to the car he could escape.

It only took a few seconds for him to throw out the option as too risky. As crazy as it was to get in the car, Jack decided it was an even worse idea to resist. Something about the man's voice told Jack he wasn't lying. He was willing to shoot, and doing so wouldn't bother him one bit.

Besides, Jack was curious. Lonetree had predicted Huckley would try to contact him again and it had happened. It occurred to Jack that perhaps the prediction was the seed that caused his hallucination in the first place.

At least that was what Moran would likely say.

But Jack didn't buy it. Somehow Lonetree knew what Huckley was up to and that was enough to make him interesting.

Jack opened the door to the Bronco and climbed in. Lonetree shifted into drive and pulled out of the parking lot, heading south.

"So, where are we going?" Jack asked.

Lonetree glanced over and gave him a crooked smile. Jack considered that the smile might have been meant to reassure him, but coming from a man who had just kidnapped him at gunpoint, Jack felt less than comforted. They drove to the Interstate in silence, leaving Jack to wonder if he had just made the worse mistake of his life.

FORTY

"Mommy," the girls shrieked on seeing Lauren round the corner. They pushed away their piles of Band-Aids and gauze and ran to see her. Lauren knelt down and gave them a squeeze. On a normal day, they would have only given her a quick glance and gone back to their playing, as if not noticing she was there would mean they could play longer. Their excitement reminded her that this was no normal day. After last night, Becky and Sarah were confused and scared, just like their mother.

"Have you been good for Nurse Haddie?"

"Yes, ma'am," the nurse answered from behind them. "They've been sweet. Playing right there the whole time. I think you have a couple of future docs on your hands."

"Well, they're certainly bossy enough."

Nurse Haddie laughed. "Are doctors bossy? I don't know what you're talking about."

"I have a few more things I need to do. If they're—"

"No, leave 'em here. It's not a bother at all. Keeps me from being lonely. It's dead around here today."

Sarah tugged at her mom's sleeve. "Becky's not sharing."

"Am too. Shut up, you little baby."

"I'm not a baby."

Lauren glanced up at the nurse. "Are you sure you don't want me to take them with me?"

163

"Shoo now. Go do what you need to go do. Nurse Haddie's got it covered."

The girls giggled at their mom being shooed away. Lauren thought they might get anxious over her leaving, but they were already walking back to their play area. "I won't be long. Then we'll get in the car and head down to Baltimore."

"And see the dolphins?" Becky asked.

"At the quarum?" Sarah added.

"It's the aquarium, dummy."

Lauren leaned down and gave each of them a kiss on the head. "Don't call your sister names. We'll see if there's time for the aquarium when we get down there. Play nice now." With a wave and a mouthed thank you to Nurse Haddie, she headed back toward her office.

Lauren wasn't sure where to start. All she had was a bad feeling that something was very wrong. It wasn't only the botched protocol on Felicia Rodriguez's body that had her bothered. She felt like Dr. Mansfield was hiding something. Maybe he had made a mistake. Administered the wrong drug, something. She'd seen things like it before. It happened more often than the general public would care to know. Working on little sleep and surrounded by stress, tired docs and nurses made mistakes. And sometimes the mistakes killed people. It wasn't that they were reckless, it was just a fact of life. No one was perfect. People expected their doctors to be infallible, but to hold doctors to a standard where they were not allowed to make errors was unrealistic.

As Lauren ran through these old arguments in her head, she couldn't help wonder if she was making them for Dr. Mansfield or for herself. Felicia was her patient and she had died. Was it her own failure she was trying to wash away? If it was, it wasn't working.

She dug into a pile of papers by her computer and pulled out a photocopy of Felicia's admittance records. Cradling the telephone between her shoulder and her ear, she dialed the number listed as Felicia's home. There was a long pause and then the phone rang. Panic seized her as she realized she didn't know what she was going to say. She reached for the button to disconnect the call, but before she could do it someone answered.

"Hola?"

"Uh, hello. This is Dr. Tremont. Is this Mr. Rodriguez?"

The voice erupted in a torrent of Spanish, too fast for Lauren to understand. It came across loud at first and then faded, as if the person had dropped the phone and was shouting at it from a distance. Lauren couldn't understand the words but the tone was unmistakable. Anger. Mixed with grief. In her line of work, she was an expert in that language. Suddenly a new voice was on the line.

"Hello. Can I help you?" a woman said. She sounded young.

"Yes, my name is Dr. Lauren Tremont. I was treating Felicia. I'm so sorry for your loss. Is this her mother?" Lauren could still hear the man shouting in the background.

"Look, this isn't a good time."

"Is this Mrs. Rodriguez?"

"I'm Felicia's sister. Rosa."

"Rosa, I know this is hard. But I'm trying to understand what happened to your sister. I need to know what happened so I can stop it from happening to other people. Do you understand what I'm saying?"

"Look lady, don't talk down to me like I'm some illegal just over the border. I was born in this country, okay? I go to college."

"I'm sorry, I just – I just want to find out what happened."

"You're sorry, huh? I've had enough with you people. You come after us because we're poor, offering us money. Then when things go wrong, you act like you don't know what happened. You said you were her doctor and you're calling me to find out what happened? That's pretty screwed up, lady."

"Wait, I don't understand. Who offered you money? For what?"

"And now Felicia is dead. Okay? Dead. I say fuck that, lady. Fuck that you don't know. Just leave us alone, all right. Leave us alone."

The voice was gone, replaced by dead air. Lauren sat in silence, absorbing the sting of being accused of Felicia's death. The girl was right – she was Felicia's doctor. She should be calling the family with answers, not questions. But she couldn't let that stop her. Lauren hit the redial button. Busy. She tried again with the same result, busy. The phone was probably off the hook.

Lauren replaced the receiver on the headset with a shaking hand. The silence in the room felt cold and sterile. Her heart pounded in her chest, and the blood thudded through her eardrums like boots marching on pavement. What the hell was going on?

She reached down to the filing cabinet drawer on the lower level of her desk. She pulled it open and flicked through the headings until she came to the one marked CDC. Pushing the other files out of the way, she pulled the manila folder out and slid the drawer back in with her foot. When she looked back up, Dr. Mansfield was in front of her desk.

"Hello, Lauren," he said.

Lauren jerked back in her chair, startled at his sudden appearance. "God, you scared me."

"Seems I've been doing that a lot recently," he said with a smile. "Sorry about that."

Lauren caught her breath. She turned the CDC file face down on her lap so the label wasn't visible. "What are you doing here?"

"Funny, I came by to ask you the same question. I heard you were still in the building. You're supposed to be on the road, aren't you?"

"Yes, I'm just…just finishing up some paperwork," she said, hating how unsteady her voice sounded. She wasn't sure if it was because of their last conversation or how he'd just given her a scare, but she felt nervous being in the room alone with him.

"Are you all right? You seem a little shaken." Dr. Mansfield edged around the desk toward her.

"No, I'm fine. I – I was talking to Jack. You know, he's a little confused right now."

"Oh, I see. Is there anything I can do?"

"You know, I'd like to be alone for a while, to tell you the truth. Pull myself together a little before I go get the kids. A nurse is watching them for me."

"I understand." Dr. Mansfield squinted at her. "Are you sure there's nothing else? Are you all right about Felicia Rodriguez?"

Lauren straightened up in her chair. A flush of anger pushed back the nervousness she felt. "To tell you the truth, I'm not all right with it. She's dead. And I still think there ought to have been an investigation. Luckily, the CDC will still have her samples so we can run more tests."

Dr. Mansfield nodded. "I was thinking the same thing. You made a lot of sense earlier. We should have done more. After you left my office, I talked to the medical examiner. I found out he took two postmortem blood samples. I've had them sent to the CDC along with a request for additional screening on the first batch."

Lauren felt the tension drain from her shoulders. It was exactly what she wanted to hear. She suddenly felt foolish for letting her imagination run away with her. She didn't even know where the train of thought had been leading, but if Dr. Mansfield was willing to pursue additional tests, then her suspicions of some kind of malicious cover-up were blown out the window.

"That's great. That makes me feel much better."

"I figured it would. Now why don't you get out of here? Leave me a number where you're staying, and I'll call you if anything interesting comes back." ·

Lauren nodded and scribbled a number on a piece of paper. "It's a friend of mine from Hopkins. We'll be down there for a week or so." She handed the phone number to Dr. Mansfield. "Jack's going to meet us down there," she added, not sure why she felt a need to explain.

Dr. Mansfield folded the paper and put it in his pocket. "Good. I'll call you if anything happens. Try to get some rest and take care of your family."

Lauren hadn't intended to ask the question, but as Dr. Mansfield turned to leave she decided she had nothing to lose. "Do you know of anyone doing any drug trials up here?"

Dr. Mansfield turned, a little too quickly Lauren thought. "What a strange question. Why do you ask?"

"One of the nurses asked me about it."

"Drug trials in our little area? I don't think so. Which nurse?"

"Excuse me?"

"Which nurse asked you?"

Lauren didn't like the hard edge back in his voice. The same impulse that made her lie about a nurse asking her the question made her self-conscious of how she played off her answer now. "You know, I don't remember. They kind of all blend in." She wanted to look away because his eyes were boring into hers, but she knew how it would look. Didn't liars always look away? So she met his stare. The seconds creaked by, punctuated only by the internal clock of the blood surging through her system.

"Right, well, like I said, I don't think so. But I'd want to know if there was something like that going on. You know, we're supposed to be informed if someone is doing a trial in case there are side effects. Let me know if you hear anything about it."

"Will do."

"Right then. I'll see you, later." He paused like he wanted to say something more, but then turned and left the room.

"Thanks. See you later."

Lauren slumped back into her chair. She didn't know what was wrong with her. She wondered if she had been infected with Jack's paranoia. There was a logical explanation for everything Dr. Mansfield had done and said. Even his response to the drug trials was appropriate. He was right. As head of the hospital, he ought to know if there were medical studies being performed in the area.

Still, in her mind, something was out of place. What Felicia's sister had said on the phone rattled around in her head. Someone had offered them money. A drug trial was the first thing that had come to her mind. Even at Hopkins, it was well known that poor people and college kids were the only ones who responded to the open calls for clinical trials of new drugs.

But now she thought of another possibility. What if someone had offered them money after Felicia died? What if it was someone trying to cover-up a mistake?

"Jesus, Lauren. Why don't you just accuse the man of murder?" she said to the reflection in her computer monitor. She knew she was stressed out, knew she wasn't thinking clearly. Less than a day earlier, she had thought Jack was losing it for exactly the same kind of paranoid ideas. Still, no matter how crazy it sounded, she couldn't let it go.

She opened her file on the CDC and leafed through the papers until she found what she was looking for. She turned on her computer and waited impatiently for it to boot up. While Microsoft icons appeared on the screen, she walked over to her door and locked it. Just a precaution, she thought to herself, same as the email she was sending her friend at the CDC to double-check Felicia's results. Probably nothing would come of it, but precautions never hurt. And maybe it would let her rest a little easier.

FORTY-ONE

The bleeding started around lunchtime. Gertie Howell was the one who noticed it first. Chewing on the carrot that she limited herself to in an attempt to meet the standards set by the fashion magazines stacked next to her bed at home, she suddenly wrinkled her nose at her friend.

"Gross. What d'ya do? Pick a scab or something?"

Cathy Moran heard the words, but their meaning was slow to register. She'd been like that all day. She was so tired she could hardly keep her eyes open. Her second period teacher had given her a break and allowed her to slump back in her chair and doze off while the rest of the class broke into project groups. She felt a little better when she woke up, but the feeling was temporary. Now her eyelids hung heavy and her body ached to lie down.

"Cathy? Did you hear me?" Gertie leaned forward and whispered, "Hey, you're boob's bleeding. Come on, it's kinda disgusting, all right?" Gertie's tone ensured that Cathy understood. Even if *she* didn't care that a splotch of blood was spreading across her white sweater, it was embarrassing her friend.

Cathy's head sank down, and her eyes lolled in her head until they came to rest looking down at her sweater. Gertie was right. There was a circle of blood about the size of a quarter just above her left breast. Suddenly, the lunch table tipped precariously, and she had to slap her hand on the table to keep from sliding off onto the floor.

Gertie, whose side of the table hadn't moved at all, glanced around to make sure no one else was watching. "Hey, you all right? You're acting like a freak."

Cathy pushed herself up from the table, the cafeteria swiveling around her on an unseen axis. She grabbed her books and held them tight in front of her.

"I'm fine…fine. Just need to go to the restroom."

"Maybe I should go with you," Gertie said without making any movement to put the words into action.

"No," Cathy said. "I'm fine. I'll…I'll just see you later."

Cathy walked unsteadily across the cafeteria, the hum of a hundred teenage conversations pelting her head like pressure waves. She wanted to put her hands to her ears to block the sound, but she didn't dare move the books that covered her chest. She lowered her head and shuffled out the door as fast as she could.

She walked past the bathroom nearest the cafeteria. Too busy. Dragging her shoulder along the lockers to keep her balance, she made her way to the P.E. locker room. At lunch, it would be deserted. She didn't want anyone else around.

By the time she made her way to the locker room, her arms were stiff from clinging so tightly to her books. In front of a mirror, she forced her arms down inch by inch, afraid of what she would find.

The front of her sweater was soaked through.

There was blood everywhere.

Tears started to pour down her cheeks.

Taking a deep breath, she lifted her sweater up over her head to take it off. Her fingers were numb, like they'd been dipped in ice water, so her effort was clumsy. When she looked in the mirror, her face was smeared with blood. The shock of it paled next to the rest of her image in the mirror.

Large sores pitted her skin, blisters ripped open. Blood and pus oozed in time with her pulse — small rivulets of blood dripped down her breasts and fell to the floor. The bruises that had that morning only covered her chest now extended over her midsection, across her abdomen, and down past her navel.

She pushed down the front of her jeans. The bruises continued down into her pubic area. She turned and saw in the mirror that the same dark spots covered her back.

No one can know about this.

The thought screamed at her, warning her of the consequences if she told anyone. If she went to a teacher, then whatever doctor they took her to would discover the disease she carried. They would find out she was getting the special medicine, the medicine her dad said was the only thing saving her life. He'd told her it was experimental and that if anyone found out, they would have to stop giving it to her. Looking in the mirror, she imagined how much worse it would get if she couldn't have the secret drugs.

She searched the locker room until she found a black sweater left behind by a sweaty P.E. student. It stank, but Cathy pulled it on anyway, hoping the blood wouldn't show on the dark color.

Using paper towels, she did her best to clean the blood from her face. The bigger problem was her blond hair, now flecked with bright red blood. She found a ball cap in a locker and tried her best to tuck her hair into it.

She was satisfied with the result. It was good enough to get through the hallways. Luckily, she had sneaked out of school enough times to ditch class that she knew exactly what door she needed to head for.

Wiping her eyes, she tried to focus on the task at hand. She had to get to a payphone and call her dad. It was all that mattered. He would help her. Sure they had their problems, but she knew he would do anything for her. He had gotten her the medicine to begin with, right? Maybe she needed a bigger dose. Or maybe they gave her the wrong shot last time. Whatever it was, he would take care of her.

Cathy straightened up and pulled herself together. She walked out to the hallway and carefully made her way to the fire exit, praying that no one would see her and that her dad would answer the phone when she called.

FORTY-TWO

Lonetree exited Interstate 70 only ten minutes out of town. They drove a couple of miles through grazing lands dotted with cows huddled near one another for warmth. There was no sign of a building of any kind in sight. Soon they turned onto a gravel road. Large ruts cut across the downward slope of the road, scars from years of heavy rain. The Bronco's suspension creaked and groaned in protest as Lonetree hit the deep holes without slowing.

The forest was thick even though most of its foliage already lay decaying on the ground. Both sides of the road were walls of towering maples and birch, mostly sticks now with only a scattering of determined red and gold leaves not yet willing to fall. The trees had twisted masses of thorny brambles filling the space between their trunks. Jack had some of the same thorn bushes on his property and he knew they were almost impossible to break through.

They continued bouncing down the path for more than twenty minutes. Jack observed the road had a slight incline and the composition of the forest changed as the truck climbed. Large clumps of rock appeared through the underbrush, made up of the rounded granite found throughout the Appalachians, vestiges of a great mountain range once larger than the Rockies, now worn smooth by centuries of weather.

Lonetree yanked the wheel and turned into an opening between the trees. Branches scraped paint off the sides of the

Bronco as it pushed its way down the narrow path. Lonetree leaned forward, looking carefully at the passing trees on their right, occasionally slowing to scrutinize an area more thoroughly. Then, without warning, Lonetree jammed the brakes and the Bronco shuddered to a stop. He turned the ignition, grabbed his gun, and jumped out of the truck.

Jack looked around the truck for something to arm himself with. He suspected that his captor wouldn't be that sloppy, but he didn't want to miss an opportunity. He opened the glove box and poked through the contents. Nothing.

His door opened. "C'mon. We're almost there," Lonetree said.

Jack didn't move. "Forget it."

"What's that?"

"I said forget it. I'm done with this." Jack turned in his seat and looked Lonetree in the eye. "Tell me where we're going. I want to know what's going on."

Lonetree hesitated, then raised his gun until it was pointed at Jack's chest. Jack continued to stare the man down. With a sudden movement of the wrist, Lonetree flipped the gun so that the butt pointed toward Jack.

"Safety's on. But it's loaded," he said. "Take it."

Jack didn't believe the offer. He reached out for the gun, expecting it to be pulled back from him at the last minute. Once he slid his hand over the handle, Lonetree released his grip and pulled his hand back. Jack turned the gun sideways to figure out the safety lock. He found the safety and disengaged it. Without hesitation, he aimed the gun and pulled the trigger.

The blast was louder than he expected, especially in the quiet forest. The recoil jammed the gun back into his hand, but it felt solid. Felt like power.

Lonetree looked up as if checking out the target Jack had just shot in the sky. His expression never changed. He waited to see how Jack would react to the trust he'd just given him.

Jack fought down the urge to demand the keys to the truck and get the hell out of there. He reset the safety lock and faced Lonetree. "All right, so it's loaded. Why'd you give it to me?"

"Call it a goodwill gesture. I need to know whose side you're on."

"I'm sure as hell not on your side," Jack said.

"Yeah, but you're not on their side either. I'd be dead right now if you were."

"What do you mean their side? *They* who? How is Huckley involved? What does he want with my daughter?"

"Slow down. *They* are the bad guys. Huckley and the others."

"What others?"

Lonetree paused. "Not yet. I'll tell you eventually, but not now."

Jack rolled his eyes. "Okay. So there are these bad men. What do they want with Sarah?"

"To be honest, that's what I'm trying to find out. This is a smart group. They don't make very many mistakes. Huckley attacking you in that rest area was way out of bounds. He already had the girl in the car, so his hunting trip was successful."

"What do you know about the girl in the car?"

"I know Janney tried to make you think you had imagined the whole thing."

"Yeah, he said there was no body. I know he's lying. The body had to be there."

"No," Lonetree said, "he wasn't lying. He didn't find the body. I did."

"I don't understand. You were there?"

"I was tracking Huckley. Saw the whole thing."

"But why the hell would you—"

"Hide the body for him? It didn't fit in my plan for him to get picked up by the regular police. Besides, I'm sure it's driving them crazy not knowing where the body is."

"But the girl. Her family. You can't just hide the fact that she's dead."

"These guys hunt runaways, druggies, kids without families or friends to miss them when they disappear. She was already dead, so she didn't care."

Jack saw the girl's face pressed up against his windshield. So terrified, so aware that she was about to die.

"You said they hunt runaways. What do you mean 'hunt'?"

Lonetree waved the question away. "We're getting ahead of ourselves here. My turn for questions. Has Huckley been in contact with you? Shown up in a dream? Anything like that?"

Jack pressed his lips together in frustration. This man knew too much about him and he knew nothing. He was getting sick of playing catch-up. "Who are you?"

"Has he been in contact with you?" Lonetree insisted.

"Yes, yes he has. The bastard was in my head. Laughing at me. Almost made me take a baseball bat to my family. Now who the hell are you? What do these bastards want with my family?"

"I don't think you'd believe me right now if I told you what was really going on. Let's just say there are good guys and bad guys. I'm one of the good guys."

"Not good enough," Jack said. "I want the whole story."

"Well, you're in luck. That's exactly why we're out here."

"What is this place?"

"This place? This place is where the bad dream starts, Jack. A really bad dream. To make you believe what I have to tell you, I have to show you the proof. It's the only way you'll buy into it."

"Try me."

Lonetree shook his head. "No dice. You come along for the whole ride or you get nothing. Your decision."

"Why should I trust you?"

"Because your little girl is in real danger. Huckley should never have taken the chance he did, which tells me there's something special about your daughter these guys want. And when they want something, they won't stop until they get it."

"But what could they want with her?"

"I haven't figured that out yet. But make no mistake, when they do get her, they'll kill her. That I know for certain."

Jack's mind reeled. A few days ago, he would have reacted differently to what the man had just said. He would have declared the man crazy, used the gun to demand the keys to the Bronco, and headed home to call the police. What Lonetree was saying was insane. Nate Huckley was in a hospital bed in a coma. How could he harm his family?

But the last few days had provided Jack with a thorough introduction to the surreal. He lacked the confidence to declare with certainty that Lonetree was lying.

Hadn't everything that had happened over the last few days been impossible? That was the problem. It was, but it had still happened.

He didn't know if it was stress-induced or something else – all he knew was that somehow Nate Huckley was hardwired into his brain. Lonetree thought he knew what was going on. Whether delusion or reality, Jack decided the man might shed light on what was happening. Amazingly, he found himself ready to listen to the lunatic in front of him.

"Okay. Let's say for a second that you're not some delusional psychopath. Why do you care what happens to my family?"

Lonetree shrugged. "I don't. Your problem is my opportunity. That mess you made on the highway has brought some rats out of the sewer, ones that I've been hunting for over a year. But the head rat is still hiding. He's the one I want. Our working together is a matter of convenience, nothing more. If I have to choose between saving your family and getting my revenge, I won't think twice about the decision."

Jack squared his shoulders to the huge man. "If you get in my way of taking care of my family, I won't think twice either."

Lonetree broke the tension with a broad grin. He was starting to like this guy. "Okay. Pissing match over. We don't have much time, and it takes some work to get where we're going." Without waiting for an answer, he headed up the trail.

Jack hesitated. Even though he still had the gun in his hand, he was reluctant to blindly follow this strange man into the woods.

Then again, his other option was to fill the prescription for lithium still in his pocket and pretend nothing had happened. Faced with a choice between action and medication,

Jack knew what he had to do.

He followed Lonetree down the trail. He laughed out loud when the Robert Frost poem popped into his head, something he used to have on a plaque in his office.

I chose the path less traveled and that has made all the difference.

In the back of his mind, he wondered at his choice. On what path was it that he now traveled?

That of discovery?

Or the path of madness?

He worried that the two had somehow become one and the same.

FORTY-THREE

The nurses at Midland General rotated floors every few weeks. Officially, it was for cross training, but Anna Beaufort didn't care what they called it as long as she got to be on the third floor every so often. Most of the nurses thought this was the worst rotation because nothing ever went on – except when someone died, of course.

But Anna loved it. Being on the third floor gave her time for her real passion – reading. She always had a book with her, tucked under the pile of charts as she did her rounds or hidden in the drawer of her desk when the docs showed up unannounced to check on a patient. With her books, she went on journeys across the globe, fell in and out of love several times a week and, best of all, solved mysteries. Her new discovery was Catherine Coulter. Not enough graphic sex for her taste, but the quality of the writing more than made up for it.

Down the hall from the nurse's station where Nurse Beaufort sat solving the latest murder in her book, old Mrs. Haig was dying. It was the cancer. In her lymph nodes this time, they told her. A few years before, she gave a breast to the disease, but it hadn't been enough. The voracious disease wanted all of her. And this time she had decided to give it.

With her husband dead six months now, Ruth Haig no longer felt the pull of the world to keep her alive. There were her children and grandchildren, all healthy and loving, but she missed her Daniel. And she was tired. So tired. She had endured the pain and sickness that went with the chemotherapy treatment for breast cancer. Endured it to stay with Daniel. She couldn't stand the thought of leaving him behind and making him manage without her. But now it was almost time for her to go. Time for her to meet her husband and the let the new generations go on without her.

So when the cancer was discovered a month ago, she refused treatment. Both of her sons begged her to change her mind, but eventually they came to understand her decision. Or at least accept it. With the decision came a sense of peace that Ruth hadn't felt in months. It was a familiar sense of comfort. The feeling of being curled up next to Daniel, his arms wrapped around her. She knew she would be in those arms again soon.

Ruth smiled in her sleep, tucked under her blankets, deep into a dream where she and her lover were together, young, with a lifetime ahead of them. It was the younger version of Daniel that came to her in these dreams. But she had always seen him that way when he was alive too, even in the last days when he walked with a bent back and shuffling feet. For her, he was always the youth that courted her, romanced her, loved her. She could stay forever in this dream world if she were allowed.

But the pain would not allow it. Always her constant companion, the pain scratched on the door of her mind, demanding entrance. She blocked it out, not willing to leave her delicate fantasies. But the scratching became a knock. And soon the impatient visitor was banging on the door as waves of pain wracked her frail body.

Her eyes flitted open, the sweetness of her dream lingering for only a second before it evaporated under the heat of the pain. She lolled her head to the side. Her left hand moved automatically, stiffly patting the bed until her fingers closed around a round plastic pad with a large button on it. Her thumb pumped away at the button, signaling the device next to her bed to pour morphine into her system.

It didn't take long. Almost immediately, the edge wore away. As the seconds ticked off, the pain continued to fade until it was once again manageable. The pain never left completely. It always hung nearby, a reminder of the disease eating away the flesh inside her. She knew the end was near. She only needed to hang on for a few more weeks, she told herself. One more Christmas and then she could go.

She settled back in her bed, trying to take deep breaths and relax her body on each exhalation. Her mind wandered, as it often did these days, back through the stacks of memories stored within her. She enjoyed thinking about the good times of her life, her wedding day, the kids' birthdays, so many happy times.

Her favorite memories were of Christmas. Even though her sons lived all over the country now, they nearly always managed to make it home for the holidays. And it had only gotten better over the years as the flock of grandchildren grew. A new generation of kids had stared in wonder as Daniel walked across the front lawn in his Santa suit. She took pictures as her sons put their kids on the same sleighs they had used when they were growing up and sledded down the hill in the back yard. Afterward, they'd all thaw out by the fire, chomping on her famous cinnamon sugar cookies as they laughed at the stories of the day.

Now they were all coming home one last time. Everyone knew it was her last Christmas. It was the last thing she wanted to do before she passed on. One last time to see all the faces. Hear their laughter. Listen to the stories one more time. She mumbled a regular prayer to her late husband. *One more Christmas, Daniel. One more Christmas with the children, then I'll come to you.*

She caught a movement from the other side of the room. She craned her neck forward to see what it was.

"Hello, Ruthie," said a man's voice, soft and gentle.

"Who's there?" Ruth asked.

In the corner of the room, from the dark shadows, came a soft glow of light. Pale at first, but growing in intensity, it throbbed as if keeping time with a pulse. Ruth squinted as the light became bright enough to illuminate the entire room.

Within the light, she could see the outline of a form, but it wasn't until the light started to move toward her bed that she realized what she was seeing.

"Oh, Daniel," Ruth whispered, knowing that it was her husband come to collect her. "You're beautiful."

The man said nothing. Light streamed around the edges of his body, obscuring his face. He continued toward the bed.

"Daniel, honey, I can't come yet. It's not time. I need one more Christmas. Please. Can't I just have that?"

A hand reached out from the light and hovered over the bed. Ruth reached out to touch it, mesmerized by the luminescent skin, in rapture over the idea of holding her Daniel's hand once more.

The hand seized hers. It closed, in a claw-like grip, crushing the bones in her hand. Ruth cried out, first in pain and then in terror from the face that leered in front of her.

"You're not Daniel," she whimpered.

"Sorry, Ruthie," Huckley hissed. "Nothing personal. But you have something I need."

Ruth tried to pull back her hand, but the man's grip was too strong. Huckley squeezed harder, his lips turning up in pleasure as she groaned.

"Don't hurt me," she begged. "Oh God, please don't hurt me."

A buzzer went off next to Nurse Anna Beaufort. The sudden burst of noise in the silence made her jerk back in her chair and nearly drop her book. A quick look at the monitors arrayed in front of her explained the cause for the alarm. The heart monitor in room 302 was flat-lining. She felt a pang of sadness. It was Ruth Haig's room, one of her favorites. She had grown quite fond of the tough old bird.

The nurse opened a binder positioned on the shelf next to the monitors. She already knew the answer to her question, but she felt obligated to look it up to be sure. The binder had tabs on the side listing the patient's names that were on the floor. She flipped open the book at the tab designated for Ruth Haig. She used her finger to trace the space between the heading and the written entry on the page. She was right. There was a DNR order, 'Do Not Resuscitate.'

"Aww, that's a shame." Nurse Beaufort had come to know Mrs. Haig a little over the past couple of weeks. She knew how much she was looking forward to Christmas with her family.

She picked up the phone and dialed an extension. The doctor picked up on the third ring. "Dr. Brendel."

"This is Nurse Beaufort on the third floor. Ruth Haig just passed."

There was a pause. Anne thought maybe the news had hit the young doctor hard. But then she heard him answer a question put to him by someone else in the room. He wasn't even listening. Then he was back on the line. "Ruth Haig? She has a DNR, right?"

"Yes, doctor."

"All right. I'll be up when I can. Wait until I come up before we notify the family." Then the phone went dead.

Nurse Beaufort snorted. Docs were all the same, pompous asses every one. That Dr. Tremont was better than the male docs, but she still had an attitude.

The nurse reluctantly marked the page in her book and headed down the hall to Room 302 to start to prepare the body. There was no one else there to cover the desk for her, but she didn't think twice about it. It was a slow day. Nothing much really happened on the third floor anyway.

FORTY-FOUR

They hiked through the forest along a narrow deer trail, just wide enough to permit them passage through the prickly underbrush. The crunch of dry leaves and small twigs accompanied every step. Squirrels chattered nervously above them, hopping from branch to branch, alarmed by the intruders and uncomfortable with the lack of coverage afforded them by the naked branches of the winter trees. In the distance came the unmistakable honking of Canadian geese. The asynchronous chorus grew louder until the flock heard the tramping men below and veered away, their angry calls fading quickly into the air.

Lonetree set the pace. The only supplies they had were whatever contents Lonetree carried in the pack strapped to his back. The large man had refused any of Jack's attempts to pry out more information about Huckley, so he had finally quit trying and resigned himself to walk in silence.

After ten minutes, Lonetree stopped and shrugged off the backpack. He pulled out a black handheld device with a LCD screen above a series of buttons.

"Is that a GPS?" Jack asked.

"Uh huh," Lonetree acknowledged, working the buttons for the global positioning system. The device was a little different from those found at the local Radio Shack. Even with its compact size, it could pinpoint their location to within one meter. That in itself was no technological wonder. What made the unit special was its ability to withstand being run over by an armored division and come out of it unscathed. That and a special signal dispersal algorithm that ensured anyone interested in his whereabouts couldn't trace him back from the GPS contact with the satellites. It was one of the little toys that had gone missing when he left the SEALS.

"You're quite an outdoorsman," Jack baited. Lonetree grunted but otherwise ignored the comment. "And quite a conversationalist," Jack muttered.

Lonetree threw the device into his backpack and slipped the straps over his shoulders. "We're a couple of minutes away. Let's go. I want to get you back before they notice you're gone. I don't want to make them nervous."

Before Jack could question his last statement, Lonetree turned sideways and pushed into the thicket guarding the side of the path. Jack could hear the branches snapping, but Lonetree himself disappeared completely from sight, as if the forest had swallowed him whole. He walked up to the point the big man had disappeared and saw that there was another path faintly traced on the ground running perpendicular to the path they were on. Jack put his hands up to guard his face from the scratching thorn bushes and pushed forward.

Twenty yards later, the bushes thinned and it was possible to walk without the dry thorns snagging his clothes and skin. Lonetree picked up the pace again and Jack struggled to keep up. He thought he was in good shape, but he realized that he was no match for the man he was following. Jack estimated that Lonetree had him by five inches and at least sixty pounds, yet the man wasn't even breathing hard.

Finally, Lonetree stopped and waited for Jack to catch up. He pointed in front of him. "This is it."

Jack looked carefully where his guide pointed. Behind a thin cover of vines, he saw a black gaping hole that opened up into the earth. He crept down the slope that led to the opening and pulled back the vines. Jagged rocks hung suspended in the dark earth that ringed the fissure. It was a rough circle about twice the width of a man. The floor of the cave disappeared in a dark slope littered with loose rock. Jack's eyes could penetrate no more than a few feet into the gloom. It reminded him of an animal's lair. The kind of cave he threw rocks into when he was a kid – right before he and his friends ran like hell in case something came out after them.

Lonetree slapped a huge hand in the middle of Jack's back. "Hope you're not claustrophobic." Jack looked down and saw Lonetree's other hand in front of him. It held a hardhat with a miner's lamp attached to the front.

"Welcome to the entrance of Hell."

FORTY-FIVE

Lonetree dumped out the gear from his backpack on the ground between them. He separated the equipment into two piles, stuffing some of the items back into the pack for later use. He threw Jack knee and elbow pads, a hardhat with a miner's lamp attached, and a pair of overalls to put over his clothes. Jack pulled on the overalls, fighting back the rising panic he felt over going into the cave. He didn't like to label himself as claustrophobic. He just didn't like tight, dark spaces where he couldn't breathe. The prospect of crawling into a cave did not appeal to him at all.

Lonetree looked him over, tightening the elbow pads until they pinched at Jack's skin, and demonstrating how the miner's lamp worked. "Ever been spelunking before?"

"Yeah, I took my kids to the Luray Caverns."

"The big cave with the concrete sidewalks for tourists and the little light show? That's not spelunking. That's walking."

"Okay. So I haven't been spelunking before. Anything I should know?"

"Yeah." Lonetree scrambled into the cave opening. "Don't get lost. And don't get stuck."

"Thanks for the advice," Jack said, but he doubted the big man heard him. Lonetree was through the opening and out of sight. With a deep breath, Jack followed.

Past the mouth of the cave, the temperature dropped several degrees. The air was moist, like after a thunderstorm, and smelled of freshly tilled soil. In fact, after the bed of loose rock at the opening, the floor of the cave turned to slick mud. The cave, more like a tunnel, slanted down at a sharp angle. Jack followed Lonetree's example and used the mud to slide down on his backside, steadying himself by dragging his hands along the tunnel walls.

When the tunnel curved enough to block out the little light that had been filtering down from the cave opening, Jack had to fight back a wave of panic. Gravity was pulling him down into the earth, but it seemed to push the walls of the cave in around him as well. He closed his eyes and took several deep breaths, blocking out the horror images flashing through his mind. Trapped underground. Running out of air. Buried alive.

He focused on Lonetree's back moving away from him, surrounded by a halo of light from his miner's lamp. The image of the space closing in around the descending figure only made it worse. He tried to take his mind off the constriction by examining his new environment more closely.

The miner's light attached to his helmet danced around as it illuminated the space in front of him. He saw that the mud ran along the sides of the wall. He realized it must be from runoff from recent rains that had carried soil down the tunnel like a drain.

Jack tried to remember details from a semester of college geology, wishing that he had actually paid attention. The sides and ceiling of the tunnel were solid rock. He assumed that the walls were limestone. There were entire networks of limestone caves throughout the area, especially over in West Virginia, where the ex-miners made a cottage industry catering to adventurous tourists from around the country.

Every now and then, the local paper ran a short story about spelunking. Occasionally, there was a piece about some new system discovered or a human-interest story on a local guide. Most of the stories were about deaths. Usually amateurs who went down for a short afternoon and never returned. The local writers failed to hide their contempt for the out-oftowners who tromped through the caves every year decked out in their brand new Patagonia outfits and shiny helmets.

Search parties made up of guides and serious cavers were organized and sent out with every disappearance. The success rate for search parties was not good. Going against the basic tenets of survival, the lost cavers never stayed put after they realized they were lost. Whether from panic or optimism, the amateurs kept on looking for a way out and kept going, as if thinking that if they traveled far enough, they'd walk out of their nightmares. In reality, all they did was walk deeper into them.

It suddenly struck Jack that he was no different. Wasn't he just going farther and farther into this crazy story on the slim chance of stumbling across something that might help?

He stopped in his tracks. What the hell was he doing? It was crazy to follow this lunatic down this tunnel. Crazy to have even gotten into the car with the man. What he needed to do was get back to the surface and get back to town. He needed to get down to Baltimore and make sure the kids were safe. He had to get out of there.

Jack reached out to the walls for balance and readied himself to turn his body around in the confined space to head back to the surface. Before he made his move, he noticed Lonetree had stopped below him.

Grunting from the effort, the big man managed to wiggle out of the backpack. He looked back at Jack, raising his hand over his eyes. "Watch your torch. If you look right at me, your light is in my eyes."

"Sorry." Jack cocked his head to the side so that the beam hit the wall.

"How are you doing?"

Jack sat down on the muddy floor. Hearing Lonetree's voice, the urgency to turn around started to fade. He sucked in a deep breath through his nose and exhaled through his mouth, willing himself to relax. "Just tell me whatever is down here is worth it."

Lonetree didn't bother with an answer. He reached up and switched off his light and pointed at Jack's helmet. "We need to let our eyes adjust a little. Turn the switch on the side of the helmet. No, it's on the other side."

Jack turned the switch and the world went black. The cave walls disappeared, replaced with a pure darkness unlike anything he had experienced. It oppressed his senses, as if it were actually sucking light out of him. He waved his hand in front of his face and had no sensation of movement. The claustrophobia returned. He imagined being lost in the void, left alone to struggle through the cave, a blind, pale worm burrowing through the earth looking for the sun. A shudder ran through his body.

Lonetree's voice rose up from beneath him. "We'll wait about five minutes for our eyes to acclimate. When we put the lights back on, avoid looking straight into the light so you can keep as much of your night vision as possible."

Jack gave a thumbs up. He immediately felt foolish. He couldn't even see his hand himself. "Right, five minutes." Jack closed his eyes and mentally tried to put himself somewhere else. Somewhere above ground. Some place with sunshine and open spaces.

Lonetree's voice dragged him back into the cave, rising up from the tunnel like the rumble of an earthquake.

"My brother died about two years ago. I was on assignment in Afghanistan, Navy SEAL. Doing pretty much what we're doing now, crawling through tunnels looking for bad guys. Only better armed."

The tone in Lonetree's voice made Jack crane forward as if he were a kid at a campfire and the storyteller had just started a tale. He sensed this was what he had come to hear.

"Anyway, I find out he's dead in a radio check with the surface. There aren't many details, only that he's dead – car crash they think. The radio operator tells me he's sorry. His brother died in Iraq and he feels for me. Which was good, since I figure someone should feel something. I can't. I'm just frozen solid. Can't move. Can't breathe.

"See, the night before, down in the caves, I had a crazy dream about my brother. I was used to strange dreams. It's part of the drill when you've been in a lot of combat, especially when you run the kind of missions I have. But it's even worse when you're hunting underground, alone in the dark, hours of silence for your mind to turn in on itself."

Jack noted the use of the word "hunting." It wasn't lost on him that Lonetree's prey had been human. Terrorists or not, the thought still made Jack uncomfortable.

"This dream was different though," Lonetree continued. "I remembered every detail, every word that was said. He was in the cave with me. There was no light, but I could see him without a problem, as if we were standing in the middle of a field at high noon. The strange thing was that it didn't shock me. It seemed the most natural thing in the world that my kid brother would appear out of nowhere a thousand feet below a mountain range in Afghanistan. I remember so clearly not wondering how he had done it. I just accepted it. The same way you accept it when you fly in a dream, you know?"

"What did he say?" Jack asked.

"He told me things, many things. I'd heard it all before. From my old man when I was a kid. Most of it sounded insane. But I didn't mind. It was a dream. What did I care if he talked a little nuts? My kid brother had crazy in his bones. Part of the family tradition, I guess." Lonetree paused, just long enough to steady his voice back into its low, rolling rumble. "I wouldn't have given the whole thing a second thought except for one little detail."

The hairs on Jack's neck tingled. He realized he was gripping the rock walls next to him as though trying to hold on to the real world.

"You see, in this dream, this clear, lucid dream a day before I talked to the surface, my brother came to me in that cave to tell me he had been killed." Lonetree paused. Jack strained his ears to pick up any sound coming from the passage beneath him. After a full minute of silence passed in the dark passageway, Lonetree's voice rose up once again. It was full of emotion, not pain, but seething hatred. "He told me how it'd been done. He told me every sick detail of how they tortured him. Most important of all, he told me who was responsible."

Jack couldn't see the man's face in the darkness, but the emotion in Lonetree's voice was so intense that his imagination created what his eyes could not see; a mask of pain and anger and an almost animal savagery, lips twisted into a terrible sneer as they spit out the words.

Jack's own words came out as a whisper. "Why did they kill him?"

An explosion of light erupted around him, making him wince and shield his eyes. It was Lonetree's helmet lamp. The light jumped up and down as the big man struggled to move the position of his body. Soon he had reversed the location of his feet. Instead of sliding down the tunnel feet first, Lonetree was positioned to crawl forward on his hands and knees. He shoved the backpack ahead of him and started to edge forward.

Jack knew that the answer to his question lay at the end of the tunnel. That recognition brought out a mix of emotions – excitement to find out what was causing all the bizarre events of the last few days – yet trepidation that the answers were more than he was prepared to deal with. Still, for the first time that day, Jack had no thought of turning back. No second-guessing what he was doing there. Whatever secret lay buried in this cave was somehow connected to Huckley and the hallucinations. He could feel it. And finding out about Huckley and whoever his accomplices were put him one step closer to protecting Sarah from harm.

Curiosity and determination to protect his daughter overwhelmed all other emotions. He needed to know what was at the end of this strange journey. What kind of secret was so important that it had been buried at the bottom of a cave? And by whom? These were questions he was no longer willing to leave unanswered.

He twisted his body until he was face down on his stomach, the smell of the mineral-rich mud so strong that it stung his nostrils. As he scrambled forward, he calculated that Lauren and the girls were probably just reaching Baltimore. He thanked God he and Lauren had agreed she would take the girls down to her friend's house. At least they were safe, away from all this madness. Safe where no one could find them. With everything going on, at least he could take comfort in that.

With a grunt, he pushed off with his elbows and heaved himself toward the retreating light ahead of him.

FORTY-SIX

Sarah was mad. Becky was hogging all the cool bandages, the ones with the Sesame Street characters on them, leaving her the very uncool regular Band-Aids to play with. And whining wasn't changing her sister's mind one bit. The whole thing just served as a reminder that big sisters were horrible sometimes, a fact she pointed out to Becky in a pouting voice. In response, Becky called her a baby and gave her hair a hard tug. Tears welling up in her eyes, Sarah got up to go tell Nurse Haddie. And if things weren't bad enough, as she walked over to the nurse's station she realized she needed to go to the bathroom.

She poked her head around the corner and saw Nurse Haddie talking on the phone. Her mom always told them never to go to the bathroom alone in the hospital. "What if you fall in?" she always asked. The comment predictably broke the girls up into a round of giggles and promises to flush each other down the toilet at the first chance. But they always followed the rule. As funny as it sounded, the idea of getting stuck in the toilet was kind of scary.

But Nurse Haddie had her back to Sarah. She was twirling her hair around her finger and laughing into the phone. Her voice sounded funny, like her mom did sometimes when her dad called on the phone. All giggly and soft. Adults were weird, Sarah decided. After a full minute of waiting, her bladder won out over her pride, and she went back to ask her big sister to go with her.

"I told you you're a baby," Becky teased. "Can't even go to the bathroom by yourself."

That was enough. Sarah scrunched up her nose and stuck out her tongue. Since that didn't have the effect she wanted, she bent down and picked up the pink rubber ball they'd brought from home. She raised it in the air as if she was going to hurl a pink fastball at her sister's forehead. It worked. Becky let out a shriek and covered her face with her hands.

Sarah lowered her hand, turned and walked away. After a few steps, she turned around and, with a roll of her eyes, said, "Becky, you're such a baby." She kept walking, a huge smile spread across her face.

After one last hopeful look into the nurse's station to see if Nurse Haddie was off the phone yet, Sarah set off for the bathroom. She'd been to the hospital enough to know where it was, just through the door that led out of the emergency room and down the hall to the right. She walked to the door with her head down, trying to bounce the ball with alternating hands, the pink ball looking extra bright against the lime green floor.

Through the door, out of the ER, and right into temptation. On the other side of the door was a long, empty hallway. Shiny linoleum stretched out in front of her like an airport runway, completely clear of any obstacles and totally absent of any adults. The hall almost begged for her to throw the rubber ball. It was clear all the way down to the elevator at the far end. She could just imagine how cool it would look with the ball skipping along the linoleum, bouncing off the walls the whole way down.

But what if someone walked out of the side rooms and saw her? And what if they told her mom?

She chickened out. Her mom would be really mad if she Sarah threw a ball around the hospital, especially since she wasn't even supposed to be in the hallway by herself to begin with.

She spotted the blue sign for the bathroom three doors down the hall. Seeing the sign, her urge to pee took on a new urgency. She hustled down the hall to the door and was about to go in when a different urge hit her. She turned and faced the direction she had just come from and chucked the ball down the hall toward the emergency room door. It bounced around in a satisfying way, careening off the white walls and making neat squeaking noises when it hit the linoleum. After bouncing for a bit, it rolled to a stop against a wall, well out of the way of where anyone might step on it. Sarah decided to leave it there and pick it up on the way back.

She leaned all her weight against the heavy bathroom door until it swung open, and she went inside.

A few minutes later, she reopened the door, pleased with her accomplishment. She couldn't wait to tell her mom that she had gone all by herself, even though she weighed the possibility that she might get in trouble for it too. She'd just blame Becky. After all, she had asked her sister to come with her and she was the one who said no. Maybe she could find a way to get her sister in trouble and brag all at the same time.

Sarah's plotting was interrupted when she glanced down the hall. She felt a pit form in her stomach as she realized she might get in trouble from her mom after all. Her ball was gone. Someone must have walked by and found it while she was in the bathroom. Busted.

Something hit her between the shoulders, not too hard, but enough to scare her.

She let out a yelp and spun around.

It was her ball.

And there was no one in the hallway.

"Hello?" she called out. There was a soft echo in the hallway, a sound effect that made her feel very alone. She felt nervous, like someone was watching her. It was time to get out of there. She bent down to get her ball, but as she reached down, it started to roll down the hall.

Scrunching her eyebrows together, she watched as the ball came to a stop a few feet away from her. She stepped closer to it, but again it rolled away just out of reach. "Who's doing that?" she demanded of the hallway. Nothing. Not even the echo this time.

Squish. Squish.

Footsteps on linoleum.

Right behind her.

195

Sarah turned around at the sound. But the hallway was empty in that direction too. Holding her breath from being so scared, she turned back and saw her ball rolling away from her. And it wasn't stopping this time. In fact, it was speeding up as it went. Sarah stared, watching it go farther and farther down the hall, all the way down to the elevator.

Just as it was about to hit the metal doors, they slid open. The ball shot inside and bounced off the back wall of the elevator.

Sarah stepped back against the side of the hallway, wishing she could blend right into the wall. Whoever was in that elevator would definitely tell her mom.

But no one came out. The ball bounced around, hitting the different walls, and then came to rest. Sarah knew the elevator doors usually closed after a while, but these didn't. The elevator stayed open. The ball right in the middle of the floor.

Sarah waited to make sure no one came out of the elevator. She looked back the other direction to see if she could spot whoever was responsible for the ball's strange behavior. Still no one.

She took a few faltering steps down the hall, trying to gather her courage. She looked over her shoulder again, wishing there was someone else around. The hospital was never very busy, but usually *someone* was around. A nurse or a cleaning person. But there was nobody. The hall was empty. She thought about going to get Becky or Nurse Haddie, but part of her knew Becky was somehow responsible for all of this. Sarah pictured her sister hiding at the end of the hall, waiting for her to chicken out so she could call her a baby again.

The image of her sister was enough to get her feet moving. Thinking the quicker she moved the less time she'd have to get caught, she broke into a run and hurried down the hall as fast as she could, the squeaks from her sneakers the only sound in the dead air.

By the time she reached the elevator, she was out of breath. She stopped. Now that she was there, so close to getting the ball, she started to get nervous again. Too scared to rush right in, she wiggled her toes right up to the edge of the entrance and peered in. Her ball was the only thing inside.

Balancing on one foot and holding on to the side of the open door, Sarah stretched her other leg into the elevator, trying to reach out for the ball. Her toe just barely touched the side of the ball. Shifting forward a little, she was able to get a better angle and place the side of her sneaker on top of the ball.

Carefully, she pulled her foot back toward her. It was working. The ball was rolling toward her. Suddenly, her foot slid off and the ball skidded to the back of the compartment.

Sarah groaned. The last thing she wanted was to go into the elevator. She couldn't explain why, but it scared her. Maybe she should just leave the ball where it was. She would get into a little trouble, but it wouldn't be that big a deal.

But the image of her sister stopped her. Sarah imagined her laughing and singing – *Baby. Baby. Sarah's a baby.*

Sarah took a deep breath and wrung her hands together. She needed to get her ball.

Reaching out with her right hand, she wished as hard as she could that the ball would just roll to her. She imagined she could reach all the way to the back of the elevator. She pictured her arm stretching out until her hand floated over the ball. In her mind, she lowered her hand until it wrapped around the ball.

To her surprise, she felt the pressure on her fingertips. She felt the texture of the ball. Carefully, she pretended to pull the ball toward her. Her eyes went wide.

The ball moved.

It rolled one full turn towards her.

Then it stopped.

Another roll closer.

Then it stopped again.

Sarah smiled. She was doing magic. She wasn't sure how, but she knew it was cool.

Then the ball stuck. No matter how hard she tried, it refused to move. She concentrated, but the ball not only wouldn't roll toward her, it went back the other direction.

She cocked her head to the side. It felt like something had pulled at her hand when the ball rolled back. She tried to make the ball move again.

Nothing.

She relaxed her concentration.

As soon as she did, something wrapped around her wrist and yanked her arm.

She flew forward into the elevator, hitting the floor hard.

She scrambled to her feet, knowing she had to get out of the elevator. She had to run back into the hall as fast as she could. Get back to the emergency room. Back to Nurse Haddie. Back to her sister. Back to safety.

There was a hiss. Then a roar. The heavy metal doors flew in from the sides and crashed together with enough force to shake the compartment.

Sarah ran at the door and tried to force her fingers into the seam and pull the doors open. It was too late. She was trapped. The elevator was already going up.

FORTY-SEVEN

The tunnel was a tighter fit than Jack had expected. If he hadn't seen Lonetree disappear through the hole in front of him, he would not have believed it possible. He kept reminding himself how much larger Lonetree was than himself. If the big man could fit through, then he ought to be able to get by without a problem.

But it was a problem. He was stuck. The passage was all smooth rock now. The absence of the mud ought to have made the going easier, but Jack had only moved forward a few feet after over ten minutes of struggle. The rock pressed in on him from all sides. The ceiling was so low that he had to turn his head to the side to pass through. It was impossible to turn to face the opposite wall. His helmet would get wedged between the floor and roof if he tried to change positions.

The small space felt suffocating. Over and over, Jack forced back waves of panic. But seeing Lonetree slide through so easily helped him psychologically. He started to feel more frustration than fear. He wasn't used to having to be wet-nursed through a physical challenge.

The area around him was illuminated by both his own light and Lonetree's. He now crouched at the end of the section of the tunnel and coached Jack on how to get out of the tough spot.

"Jack, rest for a second and just listen."

Jack stopped straining and did as he was told, lying flat on the cool rock, the sidewall of the passage inches from his face.

"You can't fight a rock. You're not going to win. This stuff is all technique. Here's what's happening. Notice how the passage is so much lower on the left than the right? There's half the vertical height on that side than the high side. See what I'm saying?"

"Yeah, I see that."

"Okay. When you're moving forward, your body is sliding downhill and lodging into that wedge down there. Slide back a little. Then push off with your left hand and foot and keep on the high side."

Jack dug his toes into the rock and pulled himself backward. He jammed his hand and foot into the left wall and shifted his body to the high side. Keeping his body weight on the left, he edged his body forward, crab walking through the passage. He was amazed at how much easier it was. Less than a minute later, he reached the end and climbed out of the tight tunnel into an open gallery.

The gallery was long and narrow, just wide enough to walk through. On either side, the walls soared up into the darkness. Jack craned his head backward to shine his light upward. The smooth rock walls towered above them, the beam too weak to penetrate up to the ceiling. The stone was a pale white that seemed to absorb the light from the intruders and give off its own soft glow. Wide streaks of dirty brown and green glistened when the light hit them. Jack reached out and felt the wall. It was slimy with algae growth and ground water oozing through the rock.

"How far up does that go?"

Lonetree threw Jack a bottle of water from his pack and glanced up. "Hundred feet or so. The ceiling is interesting."

"How so?"

"It's alive. Crawling with bats. Thousands of them." Lonetree opened some water for himself. "The walls look like that from the guano."

Jack lifted a foot off the ground and felt the sticky floor suck his boot down. "Nice."

"Can't hurt you. Makes a hell of a fertilizer."

"How could you have found this place?" Jack asked in between gulps of the warm water. "Did you grow up around here or something?"

"No. But I grew up in caves like it. My father taught me and my brother."

"Oh yeah?" Jack said as he tossed the water back to Lonetree, a little surprised at Lonetree's sudden chattiness. "He was into caving?"

"Archeology. Growing up, he dragged us around the country to different caves. Always trying to prove his grand theory."

"What was his theory?"

Lonetree took a deep breath as if wishing the conversation had gone another direction. "He was convinced that there was a whole undiscovered record of early North American civilizations buried in the caves throughout the U.S."

"How did he come up with that?"

"Early cultures on every other continent went into caves for rituals, for burials, to record their lives with paintings. There are more being discovered all the time. Sometimes miles deep into cave systems. But the record left by early Native Americans seemed minimal compared to what had already been discovered around the world in other civilizations."

"Makes sense. So did he find what he was looking for?" Jack asked.

"He made some important finds. Nothing flashy, you know. Nothing that ended up in National Geographic or anything. But they were enough to keep getting grant money and get him tenure at the University of Oklahoma. For years, he kept looking, sure his theory was correct. Then, finally, he made the find of a lifetime."

"This cave."

Lonetree nodded. "This is it. He came in the same way we're going right now. So did my brother. And what they found changed everything they believed."

Jack looked around the gallery, again arching his neck to shine his light upward. "So, what did he find?" But when he lowered his head, Lonetree was already walking down the gallery and pulling the backpack over his shoulders. Jack hustled to catch up with him and then fell into line behind him. He was about to ask his question again when he noticed the floor of the gallery.

They were following a well-worn path. Jack at first thought there had to be another explanation for the feature so far underground, but the more he studied it, the more it seemed to him to be a trail worn into the solid stone by years of heavy use. Based on the little Lonetree had just told him, he guessed that he was walking on the path carved by ancient Native Americans. But why here, so far underground? Jack had no answers, something he was starting to get used to. But with the appearance of the path, he felt as if he was finally close to getting some.

FORTY-EIGHT

The elevator doors on the third floor of Midland General Hospital slid open. Sarah Tremont stood in the center of the elevator, her pink ball clutched with both hands. Even when the doors were open she hesitated to run out, though she wanted nothing more than to be out of the spooky elevator. All she could think about was how fast the doors had closed when she was locked in, how they had smashed together. What if that happened again? What if the doors slammed shut right when she was getting out and squished her in half?

She leaned forward to get a better look at where the elevator had taken her, too scared to move her feet. There was a nurse's station, just like there was on every floor. But, as far as she could see, there was no one there.

"Hello," she called out. "Anyone there?"

Silence.

Focused on looking for help outside the elevator, Sarah didn't notice at first when the lights above her started to dim.

Then they flickered, as if surges of electricity were throbbing through the wires. A low hum filled the small compartment.

Sarah looked around nervously, but she couldn't pinpoint where the sound was coming from. It seemed to come from everywhere.

The floor beneath her started to tremble.

Suddenly, the floor dropped from under her feet, throwing her off balance. The floor rose back up with a jerk. The elevator bucked wildly, as if it were a wild horse trying to shake a rider. The lights flashed off and on. Gears squealed, metal on metal. A howl like angry wind through a tunnel filled the compartment. The noise rose until it was so loud that Sarah covered her ears.

Sarah screamed and ran to get out of the elevator, squeezing her eyes shut as she approached the door. She lost her balance as the bucking elevator floor dropped out from beneath her. She fell forward onto the floor outside the elevator, landing hard on her knees, scraping them both. Just as she cleared the door, the elevator slammed shut with a crash and the noise was gone.

Sarah picked herself up off the floor. She whimpered from fear, too scared to cry. Blood trickled from her knees and small droplets splattered on the floor, bright red against the green linoleum. Once she steadied herself, she ran to the nurse's station, hoping that someone would be there to help her. The desk was empty.

She called out in the loudest voice she could manage, "Hello. Is anyone here?" No answer.

Then she saw the phone.

She ran behind the desk and picked up the receiver, relief beating back her fear. Help was only a phone call away.

She held the phone to her ear and heard the dial tone. She typed "0" for the operator, but nothing happened. The dial tone blared dully in her ear. She hung up and then tried punching some of the other numbers. Each time she pressed a button, she heard the beep on the line, but the dial tone hummed over it. Frustrated, she put the phone back on the hook and slouched in the chair.

The silence made Sarah nervous. It was weird that no grown-ups were around. She couldn't remember the hospital ever being so empty. The whole thing was spooky. She started to cry softly, too scared to make much noise. She never should have left her sister.

The phone rang. The bright peal of sound seemed to shatter the air around her. She jumped in the chair with a high-pitched squeal. She stared at the phone, waiting for it to ring again. Nothing. The same eerie silence returned.

Tentatively, as if it were a hot iron she might burn herself on, she reached out for the phone. She picked up the receiver and held it to her ear. There was no dial tone.

"Hello?" she whispered.

"Hello," the voice said.

Sarah swallowed hard. "This is Sarah Tremont," she said, managing to stop crying and use the polite tone she always used with adults she didn't know. "I'm looking for my mom."

"Where are you, darlin'?"

"I don't know." She started to cry.

"Shhh now, sugar. Don't you cry. Look around you, what do you see?"

Sarah did as she was told. "I'm at a nurse's station on the top floor."

"Good. That's good." The voice flowed in soft tones. "Look at the doors, now. What numbers do you see?"

She leaned to the right to see around the desk. "I see room number 311."

The voice chuckled. "Well, sugar. You're just down the hall from your mommy. Only a few doors down."

"Really? Where's she at?" She felt like she might cry again, from relief this time. She didn't care if she got in trouble. All she could think about was getting a big hug from her mom.

"You know the room you saw?"

"Uh-huh."

"Go on over there and turn to the right. You know your left and right don't you, sugar?"

"Yes."

"Good. That's real good. Go to the right and keep watching the numbers on the doors. They should be getting bigger."

"What number is my mom in?"

"Room 320, sugar," Nate Huckley whispered through the phone. "Hurry now. We're waitin' for you."

FORTY-NINE

Jack heard the rushing water even before he cleared the tight passage leading into the next gallery. The cave was wider than some of the others they had passed through, a good ten yards across. Jack noticed the water with interest, but the enormous missing section of the cave floor was what really caught his attention.

"Step to the side there," Lonetree instructed. "The middle of the floor could collapse with too much weight."

Jack nodded and crept along the wall to where the underground river came out of the rock. The water was moving deceptively fast. Shining his lamp on the surface, he thought it looked like a giant black snake sliding lazily past him, but reaching down and sticking a finger in the river let him know there was nothing lazy about the flow. Water splashed at him, and his hand was knocked away by the force of the current.

"Hey, the water's warm," Jack called out.

"A natural hot spring feeds into it. Keeps it a reasonable temperature. You can smell the sulfur."

The river was only about twenty feet wide, but it transected the passage they were in. Jack looked over to Lonetree.

"It's moving too fast to swim. How do we get around this? Swing over like Indiana Jones?"

"You got it."

"I was kidding."

Lonetree angled his light up to the rock ceiling over the center of the river. There was a metal hook embedded into the face, and a black nylon rope extended to the wall next to Lonetree.

"Isn't that rust on that hook up there?"

"Yeah, don't worry though. It held me, so it'll probably hold you too."

"Probably?"

"Well, you never know about the longevity of these things. It might just give way one day. Just fall out."

"Great," Jack said. He shone his light down the length of the river until it disappeared into the opposite wall. "So if I fall in, where does this thing take me?"

"Well, that depends."

"On what?"

"On your religious beliefs. Because if you fall in, you're dead." He held out the rope. "You want to go first?"

"No, why don't you go ahead."

Lonetree nodded. He removed his backpack and secured all the latches. Satisfied everything was intact, he tossed it across the river, easily clearing it by several feet. "There's a smaller rope attached to the main rope. It's there so we could still retrieve it if one of us accidentally lets go of the rope after we cross." By "one of us," he obviously didn't mean himself. "Just make sure it's not tangled on anything before you swing across."

"Check."

No sooner was the word out of Jack's mouth than Lonetree was airborne. He kicked his legs out at the lowest part of the arc and arched his back just in time for a perfect landing on the other side. Jack clapped softly for the acrobatics.

"Here, grab the rope," Lonetree said.

Jack reached out as Lonetree sent the rope back over the river. He grabbed onto it with both hands. "Got it."

"All right. Now, try to swing at an angle. The floor is weakest in the middle."

Jack nodded. He tugged on the rope to test his grip, shining his headlamp at the metal ring in the rock roof. He rocked back on his heels and, not wanting to give himself time to change his mind, leapt forward over the water.

The rope had more give than he thought, and he had to lift his feet up to keep from dragging them through the river. He tried to swing his momentum forward, aiming toward Lonetree's light on the far side, but he could tell he was going to come up short. An image flashed in his mind of being swept away in the black waters beneath him. Down through the earth to God knew where. With a cry, he arched his back and stretched his feet out to the rock floor on the other side.

His feet hit solid rock, but he was too horizontal. Momentum gone, he started to fall backward.

Lonetree grabbed his waist and pulled him forward. Jack let go of the rope and fell safely to the floor of the cave.

"Well, that was graceful," Lonetree said. He recovered the swing by pulling in the guide rope. He attached it to a hook in the wall.

Jack dragged himself to his feet, realizing that Lonetree had just saved his life. "Thanks, I owe you."

"No problem. Just know that I collect on my debts. Come on. This way."

The passage made a ninety-degree turn and then continued on a downward slope. The going was easy, and they were both able to walk upright down the trail. Jack checked his watch. Time seemed non-existent underground. He couldn't believe they had already been in the cave for almost an hour.

Lonetree crouched by a fissure at the base of the rock face at the far end of the gallery. When Jack looked down into the narrow slit, a nervous laugh escaped from his throat. The hole Lonetree pointed to was impossibly small. There was no way they would be able to fit through it.

"You can't be serious." Jack said.

"It's not as bad as you think. I'll guide you through it. What we came for is on the other side of this wall."

That made Jack stand up straighter. The downward climb had become an endless series of galleries separated by tight spots, or squeeze holes as he'd come to think of them. Each one presented its own challenge and its own sense of accomplishment after he pulled himself through it. Now there was only one more squeeze hole between him and the mystery that had brought him this far.

Still, the spot Lonetree hovered over was no more than a crack on the rock, a limestone rabbit hole. Worse, the hole went straight into the floor of the cave and then turned like an elbow joint. How could they crawl through that angle?

As if reading his mind, Lonetree began his instructions. He jumped down and stood in the hole. Lowering himself carefully, he threaded his feet and legs into the crevice. "You have to go feet first to get through this bend here. Sit down in this hole and push your feet into the passage as you slide down, just like this."

"Why feet first?"

Lonetree shrugged. "To get through this first curve head first, you'd have to start upside down, doing a handstand. Besides, it's possible to get stuck on this one. This way you'll have more leverage to pull yourself out."

Jack groaned, wishing his caving partner hadn't felt the need to be so truthful.

"Now once in, you'll need to rotate on your right hip and curl your legs. It's an "S" curve, so you need to adjust back to the left side when you hit the other curve. Got it?"

"No. But let's do it anyway."

Lonetree curled his hand into a fist and bounced it a couple of times off the top of Jack's boot, like an athlete psyching up his teammate when they needed a big play. Jack appreciated the gesture. He hated to admit it, but he was starting to like the big man. Then, with a wide grin, Lonetree clutched the rock face around the opening and pulled his body into the wall.

FIFTY

Lauren couldn't stop her hands from shaking. The trembling had started with the call from the emergency room nurse. Usually an unflappable woman who was calm under the most extreme situations, Nurse Haddie's panicked voice on the phone had been intense enough to make the bile rise on the back of Lauren's throat. The nurse's words still crashed around in Lauren's head as she ran down the stairs to the first floor of the hospital. Each word was like a nail being pounded into her brain.

I can't find Sarah, Dr. Tremont. She's gone. I can't find her anywhere.

The doctor in her rifled through a hundred rational explanations for her daughter's disappearance. A game of hide and seek. A trip to the bathroom. A fight with her sister.

The mom in her screamed the alternatives. She was hurt and couldn't call out for help. She wandered outside and was hit by a car. And the worse fear. The unspeakable fear. Somebody had taken her. It happened thousands of times every year. But it couldn't be happening to her baby. No, not her baby.

She thought about calling Jack but decided against it. Sarah could be around the corner or pouting somewhere because she was in a fight with her sister. Why worry Jack until she knew what was going on? Besides, he might not be able to handle any more stress right now. The thought made her grimace. She had just gotten used to counting on Jack again. Now, she felt the old feelings of abandonment return. She suddenly felt very alone.

Lauren shoved at the heavy metal door at the bottom of the stairs. She turned left and broke into a run toward the emergency room. She could hear voices down the hall, loud and with an edge of panic. Two male orderlies walked down the hall toward her, calling out for her little girl like they were looking for a dog that had run off. When they saw her, they shook their heads. Lauren recognized one of them, Ned Brickman, a kind old man, the resident grandfather. He had over a dozen young grandchildren. From the pain on his face, she could tell he was living through the nightmare scenario with her as if Sarah were one of his own.

"We'll find her, Doc," the old man reassured her. "Probably jus' run off to play or somethin'. You know how kids get. Don't you worry, now. We'll find her."

Lauren forced a smile, but Ned's concerned expression only made her hurry faster to the emergency room. The nurse was there, trying to calm Becky down and ask her questions at the same time. Becky shouted when she saw her mother and ran over to her, tears covering her cheeks. Lauren wrapped her up in her arms and squeezed her tight. She looked up at the nurse. "What happened?"

"I was watching them. I swear it. They were playing fine so I walked over to get my charts. Then the phone rang and I…" Her voice trailed off as she fought back her own tears.

Lauren didn't have the patience to wait for the woman to pull herself together. "How long? How long were they out of your sight?"

"Five minutes. Ten tops. Then Becky came in and asked if I'd seen her sister around. I looked all over this floor, all the bathrooms, called the other nurse stations. No one's seen her. That's when I called you. I'm so sorry, I–"

Lauren shot her a look that ended the apology. She didn't need Becky to hear any more panic. She hugged her daughter just long enough to calm her down, then pushed her back and held her in front at arm's length.

"Becky, we just need to find your sister. Okay?" She waited until Becky nodded. "All right. Can you tell me where you saw her last?"

Becky made a few false starts, each time her voice catching in her throat as the tears continued to pour. Lauren rubbed the girl's back and pushed back the stray hairs from her face.

"I dunno…she said she had to go potty. She wanted me to go with her, but I didn't. I'm sorry, Mom. I'm sorry."

Lauren hugged her. "It's okay, sweetie. We'll find her. She's just somewhere in the hospital. It's not a big deal, all right? I don't want you to worry." Becky nodded. "Good. Now I want you to stay here while I go look for your sister."

"Noooo," Becky whined, grabbing onto her mother's clothes. "I want to stay with you."

"Listen, I need you to stay here in case she comes back this way, all right? I won't be gone long." She hefted Becky into the air and sat her down on the padded receptionist's chair. She turned to the nurse and snapped, "Watch her."

The statement came out loaded with accusation. The nurse lowered her eyes to the ground, and Lauren immediately felt a pang of guilt. She couldn't help feeling angry even though she knew it was unfair. How many times had she left the girls alone for ten minutes while she worked down the hall from her office? A dozen times? Two dozen?

She made a mental note to apologize to the nurse later, but for now she had no time to think of anything except finding her baby. With one last smile at Becky, she left the emergency room and walked back out to the main hallway. She could hear Ned Brickman and the other orderly still calling out Sarah's name. Lauren wondered if Sarah would come out if she heard these men calling for her.

She tried to think through the likely scenarios that would make her daughter hide. Purposely, she threw up a mental wall to block out the image of her little girl being abducted, giving other possibilities top priority. But no matter how thick and high she built the wall to block out the thoughts, she felt them building force inside her mind. Kidnapped. Molested. Murdered. It seemed so unlikely, though. There were people everywhere in the hospital. Someone would have to be crazy to try to take her here.

"Ned!" she called out, running down the hall until she caught up with the old orderly. "Ned, can we put someone at every door. You know, in case—"

"Already done it, ma'am," he said, his eyes showing none of their usual good humor. It was obvious he was taking Sarah's disappearance seriously. "I locked some 'a the doors an' put nurses at the other ones. Jus' being careful, you know. Don't think anything like that happened, you know. Lotsa good people 'round here to look out fo' her."

Lauren smiled. She appreciated his calmness. It was exactly what she needed. "You're probably right. Thank you, though. For the doors."

Ned nodded and continued his walk down the hall, calling out Sarah's name. Lauren headed the other direction and did the same. She'd go floor by floor. She knew by now there were nurses on every floor looking for Sarah, but she wondered if so many people calling her name would just scare her and make her hide. Maybe she thought she was in trouble. Maybe she had wet herself and was embarrassed to come out.

She fixed on the idea. She had told her sister she had to go to the bathroom. If she couldn't find one, or didn't make it in time, that would explain why she might not come out from wherever she was hiding.

Lauren felt herself calm down. The more she thought about it, the more rational it seemed. Once Sarah heard her mother's voice, she'd come out, all red-faced about having an accident. It was just a matter of getting within hearing distance of wherever she was hiding.

Lauren set off down the hall, struggling to hold on to her confidence that it would be a short search.

FIFTY-ONE

The squeeze hole was worse than Jack had imagined. Much worse. Ten minutes to move less than twelve feet, his flesh crammed into any pocket of space available, his breathing made shallow as the rock coffin around him pressed hard on his ribs. Finally, he heard Lonetree's voice urging him on, giving him instructions. Then a hand grabbed his boot and Lonetree pulled him through the last section.

He sensed that this new cavern was larger than anything they had yet seen. The acoustics were different. The air moved to its own current. Water dripped in the distance, sending echoes bouncing off the rock walls. It was a hollow sound, as if its disjointed rhythm measured time in this place. It sounded far away but reached them clearly through the dead air. He strained to see into the void in front of him, but their helmet lights did little to push back the dark. He tilted his head back until his light pointed straight up. Again, the light was too weak to show anything except the wall stretching up behind them out of sight.

"I can't see anything," Jack said, not quite sure why he was whispering. "What is this place?" He started to take a step forward but was jerked back by a tug on his overalls.

"I wouldn't do that," Lonetree said. He pointed his light toward where Jack had been about to step. They were on a platform of some kind, a ledge on the side of a cliff that dropped straight off only feet from where they stood. One step forward and Jack would have tumbled down into the abyss.

"Watch your eyes," Lonetree warned, holding up what looked like a stick of dynamite.

With a twist, the end of the stick erupted into a brilliant white phosphorus light. Jack could feel the heat from the flare even though he stood several steps away from it. With a grunt, Lonetree chucked the flare up into the black void in front of them. It sailed through the air, so bright that it created an eerie aftereffect in their eyes, a long tail that tracked its trajectory, as if the light burned a hole in the air as it traveled.

Jack stared at the light tumbling end over end through the air. He thought his eyes must be playing tricks on him because at the peak of its arc, high above the platform where they stood, the flare slowed in mid-flight and slowly righted itself, a candle held upright in the air by an invisible hand.

The slight side-to-side sway of the light's descent gave away the secret. The flare was attached to a parachute, designed to deploy at the peak of its arc. Jack tore his eyes away from the flare and surveyed the chamber now lit for them to see.

It was larger than he'd suspected. Even with the light of the flare, the far wall of the cavern remained hidden in shadows. What he could see was immense. The rock platform they were on was twenty or thirty feet above the floor of the chamber, and the roof soared at least three times that distance above them. Gigantic stalactites hung from the top of the cavern like an inverted forest of dead trees, glistening from moisture still seeping through the rock. Some reached down to meet their stalagmite siblings, looking like giant redwoods or like ornate columns holding up the roof. The bright light of the flare reflected off crystal structures embedded in the rock walls and brought out brilliant reds and browns of the formations.

After absorbing the dimensions of the chamber, Jack turned his attention to the floor of the cavern. The slow sway of the flare as it descended cast long moving shadows across the floor, making it hard to discern the structures spread out beneath him. As the flare closed the space between it and the floor, the light revealed more of what was beneath it. Then the air around the flare grew still, and in that moment, the cavern revealed its secret.

Jack took a step back, reaching behind him to find the rock wall. "My God. What is this place?" he muttered.

Lonetree didn't answer. He stood like a statue as if the terror of what he saw turned his blood cold. He lit another flare once the parachute hit the ground, this one less intense. He held it in front of him like a torch. "Follow me. And stay close."

Jack forced himself to look away from the scene laid out below him. He turned to watch Lonetree disappear down the side on the ledge. At first inspection, it looked like the rock ledge dropped off at a ninety-degree angle, straight down to the cluster of stalagmites below. Now that he stood looking down at the edge of the platform, he saw that there was a slight slope. Lonetree was making good time down the rock face aided by the hand and footholds carved into the smooth rock. Obviously, they weren't the first to use this entrance.

Jack descended the rock ladder, testing each handhold before shifting his weight to it. The grooves carved into the rock were rough and uneven, as if hacked out by a pickax or a crude chisel.

Jack jumped the last few feet and landed next to Lonetree. His light wobbled through the air until he steadied himself. But once he shone his light on the stalagmites rising from the ground in front of him, he wished he'd been a little more careful coming down the ladder. The limestone pillars were chiseled to a point, arrayed along the base of the ledge like an animal trap. Jack suddenly felt very unwelcome. They were the animals the sharpened stone spikes were meant to kill.

"Step where I step," Lonetree said. "I've found some nasty traps down here, things you definitely want to avoid."

Jack nodded.

In only a few steps, they cleared the line of stalagmites and came up to the first of the strange structures he'd seen from the platform. And the first pile of skeletons.

FIFTY-TWO

One of the nurses had called the police. Officers from the Midland police department were the first to arrive at the hospital. As soon as they were told the situation, Sarah's description was broadcast over the radio net. Available officers were instructed to patrol the area and keep an eye out for the little girl. Sheriff Janney radioed ahead that he was coming down to personally organize the search.

Lauren sat in the nurse's break room, her eyes red. Once again, she picked up the phone and dialed Jack's cell number. The phone rang five times and switched over to voicemail. Lauren slammed the phone back down. She'd already left messages.

Dr. Mansfield had stayed by her side the entire time, not saying much, just staying close for support. She appreciated his presence. He knew most everyone in the room by name and had been an advocate for her. Lauren tried to smile at him but couldn't manage it. She couldn't take her eyes off the object sitting in the middle of the table in front of her. Sarah's pink rubber ball. Found on the third floor. And worse, they had found blood on the floor. Of course there was no way to be sure it was Sarah's. That would come later as part of the forensics done on the case. But Lauren didn't have to wait for a DNA test. She felt it in her bones. It was her baby's blood on the floor. Someone had taken her. Someone had hurt her.

What if they've already killed her?

Lauren shook her head as if that alone could sweep the thought away. She couldn't believe this was happening to her. And that it happened in the hospital of all places. Too many things had worked in the kidnapper's favor. Sarah had walked away from her sister. The nurse watching her hadn't noticed she was gone. The nurse on the third floor had been in a patient's room and hadn't seen anything. The chances were astronomical that anyone could have carried it off. Still, someone had.

Lauren blamed herself. How could she have come back to the hospital after what had happened at home? She should have just packed up the kids and taken them down to her friend's house in Baltimore. Four hours there and four hours back. She could have returned the same day to help Jack sort things out.

But now her baby was gone. And it was her fault.

Sheriff Janney strode into the room followed by the Midland police chief, a balding, lanky man who didn't do much to fill out a uniform. He looked relieved, and Lauren felt a surge of hope. Janney pulled a chair up to the table and sat next to Lauren. She scanned both the sheriff and the police chief for any hints that they might know something new. It had been that way for the last hour. Every time someone walked in the room she was seized with terror that they had bad news. *We found your daughter, Mrs. Tremont. I'm sorry to inform you that…*

But Janney had nothing new to say. He just wanted to reassure her that everything that could be done was being done. That the officers and deputies involved were professionals and would find Sarah. Most importantly, the police chief had agreed that Sheriff Janney would be the head of the investigation and have jurisdiction over the case.

Lauren glanced over to the police chief and understood the reason for his relief. He was off the hook. Janney was running things now. The news surprised Lauren. She always thought of law enforcement as eager to keep jurisdiction, not give it up. But looking at the Midland chief, she wasn't shocked. The man looked as if busting a jaywalker might give him a panic attack, let alone with a kidnapping. Lauren decided it was a good move. At least until the cavalry showed up.

"When does the FBI get involved?" she asked.

Janney shook his head. "I called them, but they're letting us take care of this for right now. Said most of these things resolve themselves. Usually it's a misunderstanding or something."

"What do you mean a misunderstanding? What's to misunderstand? She's gone. She's—"

"Now before you get upset, let me just say I agree with them. I bet we'll find her playing outside or hiding somewhere in the hospital. There's nothing the FBI could do for us right now anyway, except get in the way," Janney explained in a calm voice.

"I want to talk to someone at the FBI. She's not just playing outside somewhere. There was blood up there. Someone took her, God damn it! This is a kidnapping, not some misunderstanding."

"Lauren," Dr. Mansfield said, "I agree with the sheriff. You should let the professionals handle this. They know what they are doing."

Tears flowed down her cheeks but she didn't brush them away. She didn't know what to do. Over and over, she saw Sarah's face and fought down the thought of never seeing her again. It was overwhelming. "Just find her. Please find her."

"We'll do our best," Janney said.

A nurse cleared her throat behind them. Dr. Mansfield twisted in his chair, saw who it was, then turned back to face Lauren. "That patient I told you about earlier, the one on the phone? She's just come and—"

"Go see her. I'll be all right."

"I could cancel. Reschedule for later."

"No, I'll be fine. Really. Go take care of her."

Dr. Mansfield patted her hand. "I won't be long. Have them find me if anything happens. "

Janney shifted his weight uncomfortably in the chair as the doctor left the room. The sheriff turned to Lauren. "Look, I understand this is a hard time, but trust the pros on this one.

Usually these things are not what they seem. Usually they are something else entirely."

Lauren caught the insinuating tone in his voice and noticed him wringing his hands. "Do you have a theory, Sheriff?" she asked.

He cleared his throat and placed the palms of his hands delicately on the table. "Mrs. Tremont—"

"Dr. Tremont," the police chief corrected him.

Janney gave the man a thin smile, barely hiding his irritation at the intrusion. "Yes, I'm sorry, Dr. Tremont. Like I said, I think we'll find Sarah in no time at all. This whole thing will be old news by tomorrow morning." Lauren waited for the sheriff to come to the point. "But, I want to think through every possibility here. Make sure we're not missing anything. I'm not sure if you know this, but many children go missing every year, almost 10,000 just last year."

Lauren sat stiff in her chair. "I'm aware of that."

"Well, the number one reason for child disappearances, especially in this age group, is that they're taken by a parent or family member." He paused to allow her to say something, but Lauren sat stone-like, her eyes fixed on him. He continued. "Now I know that your husband has been having some troubles recently. Some emotional troubles." He tapped the side of his head as if to make sure he wasn't being too subtle. "Do you think there's any chance that he…" Janney's voice trailed off, leaving the accusation to hang in the air. Unsaid but delivered.

Lauren felt every eye in the room focus on her. Where seconds before there had been a buzz in the room from the two dozen or so officers, deputies and hospital staff hanging around, there was suddenly silence. All conversation ceased as if on a secret cue. She knew that given the size of the community and how fast good gossip traveled, it was likely that every person there knew the events of the past few days as thoroughly as she did, probably with some interesting exaggeration thrown in for good measure. Only in the silence did she finally understand that everyone in the room thought her husband had abducted their daughter. Janney waited for a response, but Lauren offered none.

Slowly the focus of the awkward silence turned back to Janney. He withered under Lauren's intense stare. "I mean, have you heard from him? Been in contact with him since you found out she was missing?"

"No, I haven't," she said. She almost added that Jack thought she and the girls were down in Baltimore visiting a friend, but she stopped herself. She didn't like Janney's smug attitude, and she wasn't going to make it easy on him. Even the slightest insinuation that Jack would do something like that made her angry. How could all these people think that? What did they know about their situation? True, Jack was going through a tough time with the accident – things were strained right now – but he would never do something like this.

Then again, she never thought he would show up beside their bed with a baseball bat either. What if it were possible? Could he have come and stolen her out of the hospital under some kind of delusion that he was saving her? Could he have had another hallucination like last night? It would explain why no one heard Sarah scream when she was taken.

Lauren stopped the thoughts flooding her mind and refocused herself. When she looked over at Janney, she saw the trace of a smile on his lips, now there, then gone. She knew he had caught the play of emotions across her face. He had seen the doubt and for some reason he liked what he saw. Lauren broke eye contact with him and looked around the room. Conversations immediately started back up as if they had never stopped. Not a single set of eyes made contact with hers. She felt the cold sting of isolation and it unnerved her.

They all think Jack took her.

Janney stood. "Let me know when you hear from him, all right? And don't worry, we'll find Sarah for you." Without giving Lauren a chance to comment, he walked out of the room, followed by the police chief. Lauren sat alone at the table. For how she felt, she might as well have been alone in the world.

FIFTY-THREE

Narrow rock pillars formed the walls of the cage. They were spaced at irregular intervals, though none of the spaces between the bars were large enough to push more than a fist through. The pillars extended over fifteen feet into the air where thick rope weaved in and out between the bars, binding them together. The rope was now broken and frayed, in some places hanging limply in dried tangles.

Jack walked around the entire cage, exploring it from every angle. He felt that something was missing, but he couldn't place it. Then it occurred to him. There was no door. No opening of any kind. Whoever was put in this cage was meant to stay in it for a long, long time. Given the contents of the cage, it seemed the presumed sentence was forever.

There was a pile of bones in one corner, heaped up like the discard pile at a rib house. Balanced on top of this pile was a skull, clearly human, the black holes of its eyes staring at them, intact teeth set in a disturbing grin.

It was confusing at first, there were so many bones, but Jack's eyes slowly picked out a pattern. It wasn't just a random pile. There was a story in front of him. One large skeleton sat in the corner, its legs straight out, back upright against the stone bars. Gathered on top of it, Jack counted four or five smaller bodies. Children. Small skeletons of children. Some of them babies.

"Oh my God. They were just kids." He moved closer. "The adult. It's a woman, right? Their mother?" Jack asked.

"I assume she's their mother. All the adults here are female." Lonetree looked around the cave. "Every single one of them."

Jack could imagine their deaths. The mother, imprisoned, maybe abandoned in this dark underground pit, gathering her children to her as they died one by one. Or did the mother die first? Her children climbing on her. Crying. Trying to shake her awake as they lost energy and finally their will to live. Either way, it was horrible, too horrible.

Jack jumped, the image of the deaths vaporizing as Lonetree tapped him on the shoulder. He pointed to an arm of one of the small skeletons, the child buried beneath the others, maybe the first to die. Jack saw gouges in the bones, but he didn't understand what it meant. "What is it?"

"Bite marks. By the end, they were eating the dead to stay alive."

Jack saw that he was right. The marks were all over the bones. Judging how small the skeletons were, the gouges could only have been caused by the adult.

He looked back into the vacant eyes of the skull. Her head was cocked at an angle toward him, and she stared him down as if daring him to judge. A chill passed through him as cold as the thought filtering through his consciousness. *Did you wait until they were dead? Did you at least wait for that?*

"Let's keep going," Lonetree said.

Jack was thankful to leave the cage and its tragic occupants behind. He wanted to remove the skull from his memory, but it lingered with him, floating around him in the dark like a black sun burned into his retina. But there was no sun in this place, no warmth, only cold night that lay over the bones like a death shawl.

The flare hissed and spat in the void ahead of them, a circle of red light that cast wild shadows across the cavern floor. Jack knew what to expect after his initial view from the platform, but seeing it up close was a different matter. Cage after cage filled with skeletons. There were hundreds of them. The same scene replayed over and over with only slight variations. A female adult with several children. Caged like animals. All left to starve to death.

They walked in awkward silence, like reluctant guests at a stranger's funeral. Every now and then, they would point to a scene in a cage that was different, a variation of suffering. One woman died lying in the center of the cage, the bodies of her children laid out in a circle around her. Another had her children stretched out on the floor in peaceful repose, each skull caved in from where she had used the rock walls as a weapon of mercy to end her children's suffering.

Another skeleton had her arms stretched out through the cracks in her rock cage, her face pressed to an opening. Jack approached to take a closer look. He froze when he felt the crunch beneath his feet, like stepping on a pile of insects. He looked down, hoping he was wrong about what he would find there.

Crushed under his boot was a tiny skeleton. Jack tried to step back, but his feet were caught in the rib cage and his attempt to avoid the skeleton only desecrated the remains further. He regained his footing and carefully shook off the bones that clung to his foot. His shame for violating the grave of this little girl was harder to shake off.

Somehow this girl had escaped but stayed next to the cage until she died. Jack wondered why she hadn't run away, but then looked around and imagined the cavern as the little girl would have experienced it. Complete darkness filled with the screams and moans of dying people. Where was she supposed to run? If they were all abandoned down here, where was the girl to go? She had escaped from one prison only to enter another. Jack imagined the woman in the cage holding the girl's hand, soothing her as they died together.

What had it been like? All these people starving to death in the dark, aware of what was happening to them and helpless to stop it. Had they screamed? Cried for help? Begged for forgiveness from their captors? How long could a person scream before it was impossible to scream anymore? Then quiet. The end had to be quiet. They would be too weak at the end.

"Don't try to imagine it." Lonetree's voice came out of the darkness. "No matter what you imagine, you wouldn't do it justice."

Jack turned his headlamp toward the voice. The flare had died out and Lonetree's own light was turned off, as if he preferred the security of the dark. He seemed disturbingly at home among the cages, among the dead. "What happened here? Why were they in these cages?" Jack asked.

"To control them. To use them." Lonetree's voice was distant, as if lost in a daydream, here but gone.

"Used them for what?"

Lonetree held up a notebook, bound in thick brown leather. "These are my father's notes, added onto by my brother. When he came to me in the cave, he told me where he would hide them. Made me repeat it over and over so I wouldn't forget." He slid his hand over the cover. "It tells what happened here. I think it explains what's happening to your family. The contents of this book were the reason my father and brother were killed. Knowing that, are you sure you want the answer to your question?"

Jack reached out for the book and Lonetree allowed him to take it. He flipped through the pages, thick with writing, illustrations and charts. "Tell me," he finally said, closing the notebook. "Tell me what happened here."

FIFTY-FOUR

Lonetree threaded his way through the maze of stone cages. Jack knew instinctively where they were headed. He had noticed a low circular building near the center of the cave when they first entered the chamber and used the parachute flare. His guess was confirmed as he turned the corner around a cage, careful to avoid the bony hand that extended out toward him. Lonetree stood in front of the strange structure, waiting for him to catch up.

Lonetree removed a tube from his backpack. A foot long, it had black rubber nubs at each end with the center made of plastic that shone a pale yellow in the beam from the helmet light. Lonetree twisted the stick with a loud crack and shook it. The stick glowed a brilliant yellow, creating a round ball of light for them in the center of the cave.

"Turn off your helmet light to conserve the battery," Lonetree said, turning his own light off. "This is a high-intensity stick, so it's only going to last fifteen or twenty minutes."

Jack did as he was asked and walked up to the structure. The edge of the roof was right at eye level, but it rose at a steady slope to create a dome over a large circular wall. It looked like an overturned, shallow bowl. He estimated that the center of the dome reached only ten or twelve feet.

The building was carved out of a solid mound of white limestone, but whatever craftsmen had created it used a technique that left no sign of their work. The surface of the roof glistened, flawlessly smooth and perfectly proportioned. The curved wall of the structure, however, was covered with detailed engravings that stretched around the bend and out from the reach of Lonetree's light.

Jack looked closely at the carvings directly in front of him. He recognized the scene. Tall pillars arranged in circles formed cages, the same cages arrayed behind him in the dark. But in the carving, ladders rested against the side of the cages and prisoners were being put into their cells. Off to the side, rows of women and girls stood attached to each other by chains. Waiting their turn. The faces of the women were carved in high detail, their wailing and crying so real that Jack felt he could almost hear them.

"These carvings are the story of what happened here," Lonetree said. "I wouldn't have been able to understand it all without my brother's notes. Wouldn't have believed it without seeing this place." He pointed to an area on the rock wall in front of them. Bodies were stacked, one on top of another, next to a pyre with flames consuming bodies, the smoke rising to cover the roof of the cave. "Some of it doesn't need an explanation. Mass murderers always get rid of the evidence. Maybe even the most evil men feel shame of what they do," Lonetree said, his voice distant.

"It's so savage. So primitive."

"Modern man isn't far behind. Think of the Nazis in WWII. The Serbs in Bosnia. Khmer Rouge. Taliban. Chechnya. The list goes on. It's all the same. Mass murder followed by cover-up. Nothing changes."

Jack heard the bitterness in Lonetree's voice and knew it was more than a history lesson. It was personal. He guessed Lonetree had seen atrocities like the ones depicted in the carvings, not frozen in rock, but live with real blood and real screams. The images were bad enough. Jack could hardly imagine what it meant to see it as it happened. He wondered what an experience like that did to a man. "Where does the story start?" Jack asked.

"Over here." Lonetree pointed to a panel to their left. The scene was like one from a children's history book. It was an Indian village; simple tee-pee structures, a few domestic animals, people at work tending crops, tanning hides, dancing. "This is before what my father called the Visitation. Here, in this next panel, is when everything changed."

Jack crouched down and ran his fingers over the carving. It was the same village, but now a giant man stood in the center of it. The entire village gathered around this visitor, kneeling before him. Jack leaned in and examined the figure. He ran his hands over the spot where the man's face ought to have been. Instead of a face, there were deep gouges chiseled into the rock.

"Why   is   the   face   gone?"

"It's that way on every panel. Removed after the fact."

"Why?"

"It's common when a ruler falls out of favor for his image to be eradicated. The Romans did it. Egyptians. Try to find a statue of Lenin in East Germany after the Soviet Union collapsed."

"So who was he?"

Lonetree raised his finger in the air like a parent hushing a child who keeps asking how a movie is going to end while they are watching it. Jack followed the narrative in pictures as Lonetree kept on with the story.

"The stranger is shown here wearing the skin of a mountain lion, the sign of a shaman, a magic man. In my father's notes, he named this person by his title, Shaman. There is no other record to indicate his name. But the way he is depicted, he doesn't appear to be one of their tribe."

"What were these? Cherokee or something?"

Lonetree smiled. "Cherokee were about a thousand miles from here. It's amazing how little you people know about the indigenous people here. No, these weren't Cherokee. No one knows for sure, but my father thought they were the Sumac."

"Sumac? Never heard of them."

"Doesn't surprise me. They're more myth than anything else. A warrior people found in the legends and folklore."

"These don't look like warriors to me. Looks like a peaceful little village."

"The tribe changed after Shaman arrived. He made them change."

He pointed to the next panel, holding the glo-stick close to the wall. The shadows skirted away to reveal a massacre. Bodies lay strewn across a field. Arrows filled the sky. In the center of it all was Shaman, hand outstretched with a severed head in each hand.

"This guy wasn't messing around," Jack breathed.

"Again, going by my father's theory, after Shaman took control of the village, the Sumac became brutal warriors and attacked the other tribes in the area. Indian warfare, in North America in particular, was typically not the kind of massacre you see here. Life was too precious to destroy like this."

"So what was the deal?"

"Shaman was not one of them. For some reason they followed his instructions with religious frenzy. Look here, you can see what happened next."

They moved on to the next panel. It showed Shaman leading his warriors back from the battlefield walking over the bodies of their enemies. Behind them was a line of women chained together. The next panel showed Shaman leading the tribe in a ritual sacrifice of their prisoners. The chained women were being led to a stone table where blood poured off. Body parts were heaped in a pile. Around the table, the tribe danced and drank the blood of the murdered women.

"Jesus, they killed them all."

Lonetree nodded. "Ritual sacrifice. Happened all over the world. There are scenes just like this from the Aztecs down in the Yucatan. I mean, just like it. But until this discovery, archeologists had not ever found anything like this so far north."

"Wait a second, you're losing me. Are you trying to say this Shaman guy was an Aztec? That's not possible, is it? I mean, that's like four thousand miles away."

Lonetree shrugged. "My father and brother thought he might have been Olmec, a civilization that predated the Aztec. But there's no solid proof. Besides, after the other discoveries here, that seems almost trivial. Look at this." Lonetree pointed to a spot on the carving. "See the Sumac warriors line up in front of Shaman after the ritual? He lays his hands on each of them. This is where the god gives the gift to his followers."

"I don't follow," Jack said.

"Look at the carvings. None of the battles show a Sumac dying. Even old men are fighting like they are young warriors. My father believed that the Shaman gave the warriors special powers. Powers that made them all but invincible."

Jack groaned and shifted his weight uncomfortably.

"I know how it sounds," Lonetree said. "I'm straight-edge military. I spent fifteen years in a world of hard and fast rules. You don't think I know this sounds crazy? Stay with me though. Just keep an open mind. I mean, just look around you for a second. Remember what's happened to your family in the last few days. This is some strange shit, but it's real. It's going to test your beliefs big time. But it's real."

Jack took a deep breath. "All right. Go on. I'm listening."

Lonetree shuffled over to the next panel, about halfway around the circumference of the stone structure. Shaman was depicted horizontally, surrounded by warriors hacking at his body. "Wow, looks like they got tired of whatever this guy was giving them," Jack said.

"Or greedy for more of it. No one knows, but my father's theory was that the warriors demanded something and the Shaman refused, so they decided to force it from him."

"And so they killed him," Jack said.

"According to the notebook, that didn't end the terror. The Sumac continued the ritual sacrifice. With one small addition." Lonetree pointed to a scene where decapitated bodies were stacked up. Next to the table stood a round hut, a smaller version of the stone structure in front of them.

"What's that?" Jack asked.

"A new part of the ritual they incorporated after the shaman. An idol. A temple, something like that. My father wasn't sure. He thought maybe they put the Shaman's body there. Whatever it was, it's obviously an earlier version of this structure here in the cave, so it had to be important to them. Anyway, to keep the rituals going, they needed more victims. For years, they lived in a constant state of war, ranging far to find new tribes, killing the men and capturing the women. My father studied Native American folklore all over the Eastern seaboard and up into the Great Lakes. Over and over, he found stories that matched up with this. Even the plains Indians of the Midwest have references in their mythology of a tribe of cruel and evil warriors. A tribe who enslaved women and who could not be killed by an arrow. They called the Sumac the 'ones who walk with dark spirits.'" Lonetree cleared his throat. "Anyway, it wasn't long before the Sumac destroyed the tribes nearby. Others moved away to avoid the danger. So without an easy source of people for their sacrifices, they had to get more creative."

"So they grew people. Like growing a crop," Jack muttered.

"They bred them in captivity. Primarily women since that was what the ritual called for. They no longer had to hunt. They had a renewable supply for their sacrifice. This worked for years until a man from a distant tribe discovered their secret." Lonetree pointed to a spot on the carving. "It shows it here. This warrior goes back to his own tribe and returns leading a war party."

"To free the slaves?"

"It's a nice thought, but unlikely. The tribe probably wanted the power for themselves. In any case, they failed. You can see it right there. At the end, there isn't a single man from the invading tribe standing. The Sumac slaughtered them all. But the village sustained heavy losses themselves."

"I thought you said they couldn't be killed," Jack said.

"I don't think they thought so either. But with massive enough injuries, they died like normal men. There's a difference between infinite longevity and invincibility. They could live forever, but they had to be careful. Accidents, war, anything that could inflict a massive trauma could kill them. Understanding this changed everything."

Jack traced his fingers over the rock, resting his hands over the scene where the crowds of women were herded into a hole in the ground. "So they went underground to keep it secret," he whispered.

"And to keep out of harm's way. Look, it shows they brought the round structure down with them. They must have built this new building later."

"But how did they get in here? They couldn't have come the way we just did."

"Maybe, this whole area is unstable. Most of the tight spots we came through are that way because of cave-ins. There might have been an easier way in that's since collapsed."

Jack looked around at the great cave, especially at the jagged stalactites pointing down at them from high above. "So this place could cave in at any time?"

"Possible, but unlikely. The smaller tunnels are a greater risk. This whole area is a giant catacomb. There's a similar system in West Virginia that's over a hundred miles long. Who knows how far some of these tunnels go?"

"But it's stable?"

Lonetree shrugged. "The drought this year makes cave-ins more likely. The water table is low and that can cause shifts."

"Shifts are bad?"

"Yeah. But I wouldn't worry about it. This place has made it this long, right?"

Jack pushed aside the thought of being crushed by millions of tons of rock and returned his attention to the stone structure. "How long did they use this place?"

"See these panels here? These moons represent time. There are seven hundred and ninety of them." He held up the notebook. "My father assumed they were months, that the cave was used for about sixty years."

Sixty years. Jack couldn't imagine it. If true, it meant that generations of children had been born and lived their entire lives underground. Most would have been sacrificed in the ritual, but others would have been spared and allowed to grow to adulthood. These would be the breeding stock. His thoughts turned to the adult skeleton in each cage. The poor souls. Jack couldn't imagine an entire lifetime down in this place, imprisoned in a cage. "You said your father assumed the moons in the carving represented months. The way you said it, you made it sound like his assumption was wrong."

Lonetree cleared his throat. "My brother was methodical where my father was more instinctive. It made sense that it would be months. Almost every primitive society learned to mark time by the waxing and waning moon. But my brother wasn't satisfied. And he had access to more sophisticated instruments. He conducted more tests. He was always careful, always needed specifics..." his voice trailed off.

Jack turned away from the rock wall and moved into Lonetree's line of sight to get his attention. "And?"

"They're not months. The moons are years. Each one is a year."

"You mean to say that..." Jack turned in a circle to look at the cave. Its stone cages. Its darkness. Its terrifying isolation.

"That's what I'm saying. If my brother's calculations are correct, humans were bred in this cave for almost eight hundred years."

FIFTY-FIVE

Jack refused to believe what he had just heard. His mind blocked out the revelation as long as it could, trying to put off the implication of what Lonetree was saying. But it crept in, unbidden and unrelenting.

Was it possible? Eight hundred years? How many would have been killed during that time? How many babies would have been born in this hole? Generation after generation unaware that the world above even existed. Raised like cattle for the slaughterhouse in the bowels of the earth. Veal locked in cages, blinded by the dark, flesh white from lack of sun, mutated by life without light.

"Then what happened?" he whispered.

Lonetree waved the glo-stick at the panels next to the rows of moons. Smooth rock extended beyond the curve of the structure. "Then nothing. The carving stops. But from the look of how they died," he swept his glowing wand at the vacant stares of the skulls glowering at them from behind their bars, "it looks like the Sumac abandoned the place in a hurry. There's no sign of a fight in the cave and no male skeletons anywhere."

"Didn't your father have any theories?"

"According to the notebook, his best guess was that they were struck by the same disease that hit the rest of the native cultures around that time in history."

Thinking back to his early American history, Jack remembered that whole populations of Indians were decimated in only a few months after the arrival of European settlers. Suddenly he felt a little glimmer of reality filter back into his life. "Didn't Indians die from small pox? It was an epidemic, right? Well, if these Sumac could be killed by small pox, then this whole story must be wrong. Maybe this whole thing, the cave, the cages, everything, was just some demented religious ritual. You said yourself that this was common with the Aztecs."

"I'm not talking about small pox. Their bodies were not affected by disease."

"What then?" Jack said, exasperated that his rationalization was about to disappear. "What did he think it was?"

"Black powder. White men with guns. They could not withstand the kind of damage a gun does to a body."

Jack still held out hope that Lonetree was wrong. He searched for a breakdown in the logic. He seized on the missing link. "Okay. Let's suppose all of this is true. The shaman. The lost tribe. These life-giving powers from the rituals. Let's just say this incredibly implausible and unbelievable thing is true. What in the hell does any of this have to do with my family?"

Lonetree held out his brother's notebook. "My brother discovered that this is more than history. This is alive. This is happening now. Someone found the cave and started the rituals again."

"Huckley? He's doing this?"

"The girl you saw in the trunk of his car? She was on her way here to be sacrificed."

Jack's throat was dry, painfully so. He dragged his tongue across his lips. He didn't want to ask the next question, but he couldn't hold it back. "And they believe…"

"That the ritual prolongs their lives. Gives them powers. So you see, it doesn't matter if you believe me or not. It doesn't really matter if you believe the ritual works. All that matters is that they believe it works. They believe they've found immortality."

"But – but that doesn't explain why they want Sarah. You said yourself that Huckley took an unbelievable risk going after her like that. Why do they want her so bad?"

Lonetree shook his head. "I don't know."

"Bullshit. You know and you're not telling me."

"I wish I did, Jack. It would be helpful. All I know is that Huckley sensed something about her that made the risk worth it. You've found out that Huckley isn't normal. He's psychic, a telepath. Look, I know this is hard to swallow. This supernatural hocus-pocus drives me crazy too. But some things are certain. Men are using this cave for ritual human sacrifices. These same men tortured and killed my brother because he was getting too close to their secret. These same men are after your little girl, and they will not stop until they capture her and sacrifice her."

"Why don't you kill them? That's what you want, right? What's stopping you? Why are you bringing my family into this?"

"I told you before, I don't know who all of them are. I know Huckley and a few of the others. But I know there are more. I know there's a leader, but he's careful not to expose himself. Even the others only refer to him as the Boss. I need a way to flush him out in the open."

A pit formed in Jack's stomach as he realized Lonetree's plan. Finally, he understood why Lonetree had brought him to this place, why he needed his help.

"You want to use Sarah as bait," he whispered.

"It's in your interest, Jack. The only way they'll stop is if they're dead."

"Are you crazy? I'm not going to – you're out of your mind."

"Who knows how many people they've killed? Look at this." Lonetree dropped to his knees and spread out the bundle of loose papers that had been stuffed in the notebook. They were missing person notices. All young girls. All from states bordering Maryland. "This is only from the past few years. My brother plotted the missing persons reports over the past ten years on a map." He slapped the map over the other pages. It showed a section of the U.S. from Maine to South Carolina and west to the Mississippi. Little dots pinpointed where girls had gone missing. Little clusters appeared around major cities, but most noticeable was a bulging ribbon of color stretching up into Pennsylvania and down into West Virginia and edging into the neighboring states. At the center of the ribbon was the nexus of the disappearances, Prescott City.

"How could the authorities not notice this?" Jack asked.

"Multiple jurisdictions. This cluster covers five different states."

Jack stood up. "We've got to call the police. Tell them everything."

"And watch these guys disappear? No, we've got to do this ourselves. Don't you get it? If we don't stop them, they will get Sarah eventually. And they'll go on killing these kids. Sarah is the perfect–"

"Never. I'm not going to put her in danger. I – I would never – what the hell?"

Jack's voice trailed away. He felt the muscles in his stomach tighten. Up on the wall behind the stone structure, he saw a light. Dim at first, like a reflection off shiny rock. There, then gone. His first thought was that there was someone else in the cave. But the light glowed brighter. It was coming *from* the rock.

Lonetree turned to follow Jack's line of sight. "What is it?"

"Don't you see it? A light up on the wall."

"Where?"

"There. Right in front of you. Don't tell me you can't see it."

"I don't see anything. What are you talking about?"

Jack didn't reply. He was mesmerized by the light, glowing brightly now, rolling down the side of the cave wall. It was beautiful, like how he imagined an angel might appear when he was a child. He felt the heat of it against his face and breathed in deep as if he might fill his body with its warmth. He could hear Lonetree yelling at him but couldn't understand what he was saying. He tried to tell him to speak more clearly, but when he tried to turn toward Lonetree, Jack realized he couldn't move.

Jack willed himself to move, but his body didn't respond. He was helpless as the light moved closer and closer toward him. It pulsed, growing larger with each beat. He no longer felt any warmth from the light. It was replaced by a cold fear that something terrible was about to happen.

FIFTY-SIX

Stark branches faded into grey ghosts behind the fog heralding the approach of night. The cold air rolled over the mountains, damp and heavy, an invisible wave about to crash against the homes lying in the valley. The sun slipped below the horizon without fanfare, the only testament to its passing a slight darkening in the shade of grey that blanketed the sky. It was the worse time of year for living things. The time of the longest nights, where the sun escaped its life-giving responsibilities by drifting south, day after day, relinquishing its province to the night.

And the cold. The ever-present chill that seeped through any protection Nature devised to guard herself. Thick fur, layers of feathers, rough bark, all impeded the intruder but never stopped it. This was not a time for comfort, not like the fair days of the other seasons. This was a time for survival, a concept foremost in Lauren's mind as she readied her eldest daughter to leave.

Becky allowed her mother to adjust the straps on her coat, fix the stocking cap that pulled down over her ears, push her gloves up over her fingers. She didn't say a word and averted her eyes whenever her mother's face drifted in front of her.

Lauren took her little girl's gloved hand, gave it a squeeze, and walked her out the door. She had exhausted every way to make her daughter understand why she had to go but without luck. Becky still pouted as she shuffled her feet toward the waiting car. Lauren wished she could make her understand, but ultimately all that mattered was that she was going to be safe.

Lauren loaded her daughter into the back seat of Sushma Bhasin's Lincoln Navigator, made her promise to call when she got safely to Baltimore, and gave Becky a kiss good-bye. Sushma, her diminutive frame and youthful dark skin making her look more like a hospital intern than the leading women's health specialist that she was, stood a few steps away, careful not to intrude on their time. When Lauren closed the door, Sushma pulled her friend into her arms and hugged her tightly.

"Thank you for coming up, Sushma. You don't know how much I appreciate it."

Sushma stepped back and looked Lauren in the eye. "Don't even dare thank me. I'll take care of Becky. I'll let her do all the things you won't. She'll love it."

"It's just that she's been at your house before, and she knows you and..."

Sushma held her much taller friend at arm's length. "Listen. It's all going to work out. Okay?"

Lauren smiled and wiped away the tears she hadn't realized were sliding down her cheeks. "How'd you get so tough?"

"Medical school. Brings out the animal in all of us."

They shared a soft laugh, the reality of what had brought them together hanging over them like the remnants of a nightmare. They hugged and said goodbye. Lauren waved at Becky and told her she loved her. She wasn't surprised when her daughter gave her the cold shoulder. Not surprised, but still it hurt.

She watched as the car pulled out of the lot and disappeared into the fog. A thread of doubt flapped around in the torrent of thoughts flooding her head. Was she doing the right thing sending her away? Making that decision without talking to Jack about it first?

She stopped pulling the thread. It was done. Becky was safe, far away from what was happening here. She trusted

Sushma completely. As a doctor, her mind was trained to compartmentalize problems, focus on the patient in front of her, not the patient that came before or the one that came next. With Becky safe, she pushed that worry into a box, closed the lid, and moved on. The next compartment to open was like walking into a double trauma without a staff to assist her. Jack and Sarah both missing. Her husband in the middle of a bizarre emotional crisis. Her baby stolen out from beneath her.

She needed to get a hold of herself. Exhausted even before she had come to the hospital, the emotional ride of the last few hours had pushed her to the edge. In her frazzled state, the conversation with Janney kept replaying in her head. The faces of the other police in the room, so poorly hiding their judgment of Jack. Maybe she was the one being blind.

She hated herself for the doubts that crept through her head, but she couldn't deny the possibility. On some level, she hoped it was Jack. Even if this was a continuation of his delusions, they could work on it, get him help. At least their baby would be safe. There was no way he could ever hurt their little girl. Nothing in the world could make him do that.

A sob caught in her throat. She tried to hold on to her emotions, but she was losing her grip. Out of view of the police, the nurses, the other doctors, the locals who had gravitated to the hospital as word of the missing girl spread through the town, Lauren allowed herself to break down. As she cried, the same thought came to her again and again, *God damn it, Jack. Where in the hell are you?*

FIFTY-SEVEN

"**J**ack! JACK! What do you see?" Lonetree shouted, waving the glo-stick above his head.

Jack wanted to answer but he couldn't. He was frozen in place, only able to move his eyes to track the glowing ball of light rolling down the wall toward them. The orb was a brilliant white, intense enough that it was painful to look at. Jack felt his eyes burning from the exposure to it, but still he couldn't turn away.

Halfway down the wall of the cave, the orb detached from the rock surface and hung suspended in the air. Then, drifting slightly as if it were at the whim of the gentle air current in the cavern, it moved steadily toward Jack.

Lonetree watched the expression on Jack's face change from amazement to rapture. "What's going on? I don't see anything!"

The ball of light floated over their heads. Jack strained his eyes upward to watch the strange apparition. As it came closer, he saw a spinning vortex at the center of the light, as if it were white-hot lava draining back into the earth. Here, deep within the stark white light, Jack thought he saw vague forms and shadows rising and falling back into the light. As he watched, a swirl of vapor extended out from this churning mass, folding in on itself until it became an amorphous cloud outside of the white orb. Slowly, like clay being pushed into a form by invisible hands, the cloud changed shape. Soon the basic features of a face covered the front of the cloud. It was nondescript, androgynous, but beautiful in its simplicity.

Then the eyes opened.

Jack felt fear cascade down his spine. The eyes were aware. Not the eyes of a statue or a mask, they were alive. They darted about, like a newborn taking in its first sights outside the womb. But when they saw Jack, the eyes stopped and bore down on him.

Slowly, the apparition's mouth stretched open. The luminescent wisps of light swirling around the orb began to pour into the black cavity as if there was some irresistible gravity inside. Soon strands of light were being sucked down into the mouth, both from the glowing orb and from the glo-stick still held in Lonetree's hand.

A body started to form, building from the inside out, as if the light devoured by the mouth was simply revealing a translucent body that had been invisible in the dark.

The digestive tract appeared first, shimmering organs disconnected from the malformed head that hovered above it. Then lungs. Arteries. Veins. A twitching heart that pumped yellow light. The mouth opened wider and pulled in the last traces of light. A skeleton materialized around the floating body parts. Layers of skin appeared, translucent so that Jack could still see organs jostling together inside the body. The apparition closed its mouth and lowered its head, the last details of its facial features filling out.

Nate Huckley.

The blood drained from Jack's face. He felt like he was underwater. Pressure forced in on him from all sides. His ear drums felt as if they might burst, shredded from the force pushing against them. He desperately wanted to claw at his ears to scratch away the pain. But he couldn't move. The world was frozen. Everything except the approaching form of Nate Huckley.

"Can't move?" Huckley asked with mock concern. "That's too bad. Feels kind of helpless, huh? Kind of like – oh, I don't know – lying in a hospital bed in a coma."

Jack strained against the invisible force that held him in bondage, but he couldn't move.

"Yeah, that's what it feels like. You will yourself to move but nothing happens. Frustrating, isn't it?"

Huckley spat into Jack's face. The spittle was sparks that danced across his face like a Fourth of July sparkler. Huckley smiled, pleased with his new trick.

"See, I was a little upset at you at first. I mean, you almost killed me. I take that personally. Why couldn't you have been a good boy and left well enough alone? I was leaving the rest area, wasn't I? Sure, I would have gotten your little girl later, but I was leaving. But you had to be the hero, right, and come after me on the highway like a goddamn cowboy."

"Jack, what's wrong?" Lonetree shouted.

Huckley ignored him. "As you can imagine, it took me a while to figure out what was happening after I woke up in the hospital. I could feel my body, but I couldn't make it work. I was trapped. It's a horrible feeling. Horrible. Well, you know what I'm talking about, right?"

Huckley walked around behind Jack.

"But then I found I could leave my body behind and travel without it. It's very liberating, actually. You wouldn't believe the things that go on when people don't think anyone else is there."

Huckley spun around in front of Jack so that the two men's faces were nearly touching.

"But, here's the thing, Jack. My time's up. I gotta get back into my body so I can take care of a little unfinished business. Seems some things just require you to be there in the flesh and blood. And besides, while this whole out of body experience is fun and all...I WANT MY BODY BACK."

The words came out as a roar and blew into Jack like a hurricane. The eyes on the face bulged out as if they would explode. Huckley's body shone bright as if the light gauged his anger.

As fast as the fury had appeared, Huckley's maddeningly calm demeanor returned. "I'll give it to you. You had me scared. I thought you put me in that coma for good. Thought they were gonna have to rewrite the medical books. I would have been a medical miracle. I can see it now, 'Man lives two hundred years in a coma.' Of course, that never would have happened. The Boss would have taken care of me before that. Finished the job off, so to speak."

"Jack, what the hell is going on?" Lonetree shouted, keeping his distance.

Huckley moved around behind Jack and leaned into his ear. "That would have been a shame. I would have missed out on all the fun we're going have with your little girl. There's something very, very special about her. The Source has promised me things, wonderful things, if I bring her to him. Powers beyond my imagination, he says. What do you think makes her so special?"

Huckley paused as if waiting for an answer.

"Oh right, you can't talk. Shame. There is something about your little girl, though. I thought my brain had ripped in two when I sensed her in that rest area. It was intense. Lucky for me, I've figured out how to get back into my body. Just in the nick of time, as it turns out." His lips curled back in a half smile, half sneer. "Because we already have your little girl."

Jack struggled against the weight pressing in all around him. No matter how much force he exerted, he couldn't move. He couldn't help but flash an image of Sarah in his mind's eye, a grisly scene of what the monster in front of him might do to her. Without meaning to, he pictured the car crash back in California, the little girl on the windshield, the blood pouring down the broken glass. But it wasn't Melissa Gonzales this time – it was Sarah.

I'm responsible. I'm responsible for both of them.

Huckley moved around in front of him, his smile slanted like a drugged up carnival barker. "Yes, that's right. You're a killer too. Aren't you? A kiddie killer just like me. That's too good. Too good." Huckley's tongue lolled out of his mouth and circled his lips. "Well, I'd love to stay and talk shop, one killer to another, but it's time I got back. And don't worry about your little girl. We're going to have to go really slow with her, make sure we don't make any mistakes. It hurts more that way, but what can you do?"

I'll kill you. You son-of-a-bitch. Touch her and I'll kill you. Jack screamed in his mind. Panic seized him. An image of Sarah danced across his mind, sweet, beautiful, innocent.

Huckley laughed. "Not for long, Jack. She won't look like that for long." The apparition turned his back and walked away, leaving Jack's line of sight open to Lonetree who still stood in front of him waiting for an explanation. "Now you're going to do me a favor. Lonetree here is a trouble-maker, just like the rest of his family. For some reason, I can't touch him. Indian magic or some such bullshit. That's where you come in. First him. Then yourself. Careful. Guns can be dangerous in the wrong hands."

There was no warning. Jack felt no sensation of release before his body reacted.

He saw Lonetree's expression turn from concern to shock. With his peripheral vision, Jack saw his own arm rise from his side and aim the gun Lonetree had given him. He pointed it at the big man's chest and squeezed the trigger.

The discharge of the gun exploded in Jack's ears, but it had to compete with the screams coming out of his mouth. The horror of his actions didn't stop his trigger finger from pulling again. And again. Aiming at the chest. Then the head. Back to the chest.

His finger pulled until the magazine clicked empty.

Control of his body returned.

Huckley was gone.

Jack dropped the gun and stared in disbelief at the damage he'd inflicted on Lonetree's body.

FIFTY-EIGHT

The Boss let himself in through the old delivery doors in the southeast corner of the hospital. It was dark out, and he was sure no one had seen him. He would have sensed it. Not that he pretended to have the abilities of Nate Huckley, but he had acquired a higher sensitivity to things over the years. They had all experienced byproducts from the ritual. While Huckley's natural psychic abilities obviously were augmented by his contact with the Source, the Boss's new gift had been harder to notice.

At first, he thought the changes in how his mind functioned were a result of his continued studies. He had always been blessed with a superior memory, but soon after the ritual sacrifices started, he was able to commit whole passages of text to memory after only a few readings. Then after only one reading. Soon, in an advancement that left him unnerved, he started to perfectly retain information after only a quick visual scan of a page. And the recall was absolute. All he had to do was close his eyes and the words appeared. He consumed information like other men consumed air or food. Books, always more books. For years, nothing but cramming facts about a civilization into his head until he thought he might go mad from the knowledge.

But his excitement turned to frustration as the limitation of his new power became apparent – a limitation that stole away his dream of ultimate intelligence. In the end, his power amounted to little more than a parlor trick, of no more use than a good online encyclopedia. It wasn't until the computer age that the Boss had the analogies he needed to explain his situation. Like a computer, he was able to store infinite information, but the limitation was the synthesis of information into ideas and conclusions. Information was power, and he was able to make significant progress in any field he pushed himself to understand. But the true genius he craved was always just out of his reach.

He dared to believe the Tremont girl could change all that. The Source had finally promised to grant his wish if the girl was brought to him.

It was why the Boss had come to see things for himself.

He glanced up the hallway of the stripped-down basement. With soft squeaks of his leather soled dress shoes against the painted concrete, the Boss crossed the hallway to the vault-like door of the morgue. If Huckley was right, the other side of the door was his salvation, the culmination of a lifetime of work.

He punched in a special code and slid back the stainless steel door. Air whooshed out from the seal as if the morgue had been holding its breath just for his arrival. He stepped into the cool room, the smell of antiseptic rising up from the shiny linoleum floor.

The Boss closed the door behind him and locked it in place. With one hand on the metal door, he held himself still, even skipping the next two breaths to ensure absolute silence. Perfect. He couldn't hear a sound. Satisfied, he walked over to drawer number ten, the bottom right hand corner of the wall of temporary resting places for the dead of Midland and surrounding communities. He'd had enough of dead people recently. Too many of them, and not the right ones. He was looking for life in drawer number ten. He dragged it open. Empty. Just as he expected.

He pulled the drawer all the way out until it hit the stops, like an office filing cabinet. The Boss knew he could crawl through the opening with the drawer still in the wall, but he was a large man, so he disengaged the drawer and hefted it to the side. On his hands and knees, he pushed himself into the space in the wall, elbowing his way to the back. His body wedged tightly into the space and blocked the light from the room behind him, but he knew what he was doing. He found the small clasp on the panel in front of him, twisted it, and opened the hatch.

The space beyond was another drawer just like the one he now lay in, except warmer. It had to be. Sometimes they needed to keep bodies here for days until they were ready to be taken out of the hospital. Stored at the cold temperatures, the people could never be kept alive for long. The drawer was also brightly lit by a row of halogens recessed into either side, giving it the look of a food warmer at a restaurant. The Boss knew the door opening triggered the lights and that usually the drawer was dark as any grave, especially because the thick soundproofing ensured no ambient light made its way in. Some of the people, put here when they were drugged, woke up in a panic and screamed for hours.

The Boss had tapes of it. The more interesting ones decided that they had died and that the darkness was the afterlife purchased by their sins. An eternity of black night, sitting in your own waste, hungry, thirsty, praying for salvation until you went insane. The Boss guessed that if released, the people who ended up in that drawer would have had a new appreciation for both life and religion. Of course, he would never have allowed a person to be released from the drawer, but it was a thought.

The Boss stared at the small form sleeping in front of him. The drug administered to her was strong enough that she wouldn't wake up until after they moved her. He wished Huckley understood more clearly why the Source wanted this particular girl.

The Boss knew he had to trust Huckley's intuition on these matters. The fact that Huckley delivered the message as an apparition while he was in a coma gave his opinion on the supernatural added credibility.

Remembering Huckley's appearance caused a shudder to pass down his spine. Even with everything the Boss had been through, the sight had shaken him, not only because of the complete supernatural strangeness of it, but for the first time ever, he had been afraid of Huckley. Afraid of what he was becoming. Afraid that his own power no longer matched that of his underling. Looking at the blonde-haired girl sleeping in front of him, he found it hard to believe that she represented the key to understanding the Source.

Free from limits, was what Huckley had said the Source had promised. *She will set us free from limits forever.*

But what did it mean? That sacrificing her would yield a serum so powerful they could stop the ritual? Or did it mean they would finally have true immortality where no weapons could kill them? The most exciting possibility, the grail which the Boss had been chasing for nearly three centuries, was to be able to reproduce the serum himself. To, in effect, become the Source.

All guesses. In reality, none of them knew what *free from limits* meant, and they wouldn't until they sacrificed her in the cave. Regardless of how it turned out, whatever free from limits meant, the Boss had decided this was the last adventure for his psychic friend. Huckley had served him well, his abilities were even the reason they found the cave to begin with, but now he was becoming too strong, too independent. And no one should be more powerful than the Boss. It was unacceptable.

With a shaking hand, the Boss reached out and stroked the sleeping girl's hair. He let his fingers dance over her face, touching her closed eyes, nose, then brushing against her slightly parted lips. He closed his eyes and tried to sense the power inside the small body.

There was nothing at first – at least he thought it was nothing. He assumed the hum in his ears was from the lights right next to him, but slowly the noise grew. He resisted the urge to withdraw his hand and listened, not only with his ears, but with every sense he possessed.

The hum throbbed in a steady rhythm until the Boss realized he was hearing the blood moving through the girl's veins.

Then a bolt of electric pain tore through his arm.

His eyes opened and the world turned white, as if a photographer's flash had erupted inside his eye.

Another bolt of pain screamed up his arm and embedded itself deep into the center of his brain.

A hundred white flash bulbs went off until the world was purple with the after-effects.

The Boss cried out. Rising up too fast, he slammed his head into the metal ceiling of the drawer. He fought to remove his hand from the girl, but couldn't move it. The shafts of pain continued, one after the other, the same strong hum from before – the girl's heartbeat.

Using his free hand, the Boss rammed his frozen arm at the elbow joint. The arm doubled over, and his hand fell away from the girl's face.

The Boss lay still for a few seconds, panting hard from the pain, glowing circles still dancing across his vision. Once his strength returned, he pulled the latch shut and shimmied out of the morgue drawer as fast as he could. He didn't understand what had just happened, but he sensed that the girl had almost killed him. And he couldn't have been happier. She was unlike anything he had ever encountered – Huckley was right about that.

Free from all limits. The Boss didn't care what the risks were, he had to find out what that phrase meant. He had to find out soon.

FIFTY-NINE

The trees rushed past in a blur of motion. Jack held on tightly as the Bronco bumped down the gravel trail leading back to the main road. The overalls from his muddy climb up through the cave lay in the back; the earthy smell of them permeated the cab. The climb out had been quick even though the tight spots were more challenging working against gravity. He was a fast learner, and the technical aspects of climbing through holes were the same going up or down. Besides, the way down had been a hesitant path to the unknown, while the journey up was spurred by the promise of fresh air and open space.

And the fear that Huckley really did have his little girl.

He tried to make himself believe it wasn't true. Couldn't be true. Huckley was in a coma at Midland hospital. Lauren and the kids had left that morning and were going straight to Baltimore. Even assuming that the ghostly apparition of Huckley was real – which Jack found harder to believe outside of the cave and back in the real world – there wasn't even the opportunity for Sarah to have been taken. Not unless the men stopped them on the open road out of town. But that seemed too audacious even if these men were as intent on getting Sarah as Lonetree said they were. Then again, what *wasn't* audacious about the events of the last two days? Was anything really out of the realm of possibility?

Jack took stock of the situation. A cult was trying to abduct his daughter for some bizarre ritual involving human sacrifice. There was a secret underground chamber filled with skeletons in the backwoods of Maryland. And now a psychopath in a coma was haunting him from his hospital bed and was able to take physical form?

He wanted to laugh at it all, pass it off as a grand delusion worthy of university study. But the images of the cave were too clear in his mind to be laughed away. A chill passed through him as he pictured Huckley's apparition in front of him. The complete helplessness he'd felt with his body immobilized.

He absently rubbed his right wrist and hand, the one that had held the gun. The skin wasn't broken, but a deep bruise had already developed. Purple and red smudges covered his wrist and lower forearm.

The irony was that Jack was thankful for the bruise. At least it was something he could see. Something he understood. Proof that this wasn't all in his head but that *it*, whatever it was, did exist – at least in some small, painful, bruised measure – in the physical world. His world. But even as the bruise comforted, it confirmed his worse suspicions.

However Huckley had engineered his activities outside of the hospital room, he was getting better at it. This was the first time Huckley had the strength to take form and use force. But he hadn't been able to sustain the force for long.

Jack wondered how long it had taken to empty the chamber into Lonetree. Five or six seconds? Then the force gripping his wrist had disappeared as if the energy required for the action drained Huckley, forcing him to retreat back to his own body. It was all theory, but it seemed likely. Jack was starting to get a better feel for his enemy. If it had been possible, Huckley would have stayed around to gloat over Lonetree's corpse. Not only that, but Huckley had said "first him, then yourself." Huckley had intended the last bullet for Jack. Whatever the reason, Huckley hadn't been able to finish the job and was forced to leave as Jack discharged the gun at Lonetree.

Jack smiled as he pictured Lonetree's wide-eyed expression when Jack had raised the gun and started firing. The ex-Navy Seal still had sharp reflexes, but nothing was fast enough to dodge the blasts from such a short range. Lonetree had reached the same conclusion in the few hundredths of a second between the time Jack first raised the gun and the sound of the first shot exploded into the cave. Years of training hardwired into Lonetree's nervous system made him drop and roll for cover to avoid the gunshots. By the time he hit the floor, Jack had already fired three times. If there had been real bullets in the gun, Lonetree would have been dead.

Lucky for both of them, Lonetree was a liar and a cheat. The whole scene before they started down the cave, handing Jack the gun as a sign of trust, had been a scam. Blanks. From the beginning, the gun was loaded with blanks. Lonetree had played him for a fool.

Lonetree wasn't apologetic for his deception. After the reverberations of the gun shots finally died down, he'd looked up at Jack standing over him, shrugged, and said, "Didn't think I'd trust you with bullets, did you?" And that was the end of the conversation about the gun.

Jack looked over at the driver's seat and wondered what else the man had lied to him about. He pushed the thought from his mind. The last few hours had been a nauseating ride of emotions, and the last thing he needed was to wander through the minefields of his own paranoia. He needed to trust someone, and Lonetree at least knew something about what was going on. An old saying about strange bedfellows tried to work its way through the clutter in his mind.

Lonetree interrupted him. "You might get cell reception right about here. The main road is around that bend."

Jack took the phone from Lonetree and flipped it open. He watched the Sprint icon flashing, *Searching for signal.* Another fifty yards up the road, the message blinked off and a single bar appeared. He punched the speed dial number for Lauren's cell.

Busy.

He knew the hospital had a back-up pager to reach Lauren in an emergency. He needed that number.

He dialed Midland General and waited impatiently through four rings before the on-duty nurse picked up.

"This is Jack Tremont. I need Dr. Tremont's pager–"

"Mr. Tremont, they've been looking for you," the nurse blurted out.

Jack felt a wave of nausea. Something must have happened. *Please tell me Lauren's not there. Please tell me she's not there.* "Is Dr. Tremont in the building?"

"Hold on. I'll get her."

Jack's stomach dropped with the words. Then the line went dead. For a second, he thought she'd disconnected him by accident. Then a sharp beep signaled that he was on hold. The beep only sounded twice before Lauren was on the line.

"Oh God, Jack. Where are you?"

Jack tried to answer but his throat was suddenly too dry. The panic in her voice answered his question. They had his little girl. It wasn't a lie. Only then did Jack realize how well his subconscious had created a parallel explanation for everything that had happened, a carefully constructed rationalization that would lead him and his family back to their simple, quiet lives. But it all balanced on this phone call, on hearing that Sarah and Becky were safe, that they were in Baltimore watching the dolphin show at the National Aquarium. That the whole thing was a nightmare, a sticky cobweb that he had walked through, messy and hard to get out of his hair, but nothing a hot shower and a change of clothes wouldn't fix.

"Jack! Are you there?"

"Yes," Jack shouted into the phone, as though the volume of his voice would somehow clear up the choppy cell connection. "Are the girls with you? Is Sarah safe?"

Lauren said the words he expected but still could never prepare himself to hear. "Sarah's gone. Someone took her." She broke down and started crying.

Jack wanted to soothe her, tell her they would get her back, that nothing bad would happen. But he felt numb and couldn't speak.

Lauren's sobs stopped and she cleared her throat. "Where the hell are you? I've been trying to call you all day. And…" the tone of her voice changed, lowered as if she were guarding her words from someone nearby. Even over the bad connection, the words came across edged with trembling accusation. "How did you already know about Sarah?"

"Listen carefully. I know who took Sarah."

"Jesus. Who? Where is she?"

"Huckley. Nate Huckley took her. I know this sounds crazy, but I saw him and he told me what he was going to do."

There was dead air. He could hear her breathing, so he knew he hadn't lost the connection. Lonetree tapped his shoulder to attract his attention, but Jack ignored him. He shouted into the phone. "Did you hear me? It was Nate Huckley. And there are others involved. Janney's one of them. You're in danger. You've got to believe me."

"Oh, Jack," Lauren moaned.

With those two words, the bottom fell out of his world. He had been in a free fall all day, and now Lauren had yanked away the safety net. She didn't believe him. "Listen, I'll be there in half an hour, okay? Half an hour."

More dead air. Then Lauren's defeated voice. "Sheriff Janney wants to talk to you. I think you should do what he asks you."

"No. I'll be there in–"

"Hello, Jack, this is Sheriff Janney. How are you?" He talked slowly, pleasantly, like a hostage negotiator asking the bad guy what kind of pizza he wanted while the SWAT team took their positions.

"Janney, I know you're in on this. If you hurt my little girl I swear to God I'll kill you."

"Now, there's no reason for threats here. Let's just calm down now. Why don't you tell me where you are? I can have one of my men escort you in. That way, you won't get slowed down, you know, get lost or something like that. This is, of course, assuming you are planning to come here."

Jack sensed the sheriff was playing to the people around him, including Lauren. Threatening to kill the man when he didn't know who else was listening on the line probably wasn't the best PR move. "Just don't hurt her. I'll do anything to get her back. Anything."

The sheriff paused for a beat. When he did reply he was still soft spoken, in control. "I'd like you to come in and talk. I have some questions for you. So does your wife."

Jack didn't answer. There was nothing in Janney's tone to suggest negotiation was possible. He wondered how much the sheriff knew about the last two days. Had Lauren told them about last night? About the baseball bat? Had they convinced her that he was on some hallucinogenic binge? Then it hit him. How had he been so stupid not to see it sooner? He knew there was something in Lauren's voice that bothered him, and it was more than disbelief over Huckley.

"Put Lauren on the line," Jack said, barely managing to keep his voice steady. "Right now, Janney. Put her on the line."

"She's not available. Tell me where you are, Jack. If you didn't do anything, then you have nothing to worry about, right?"

"You son of a bitch. You're trying to make Lauren think I kidnapped my own daughter."

"Are you coming in or not?"

"I'll be there in twenty minutes, you bastard. You better be there." He slammed the phone on the dash of the Bronco. "Godammit!"

Lonetree looked over at him. "That went over well."

"Yeah, real well."

"You know you can't go to the hospital, right? If you show up, he's going to figure out a reason to arrest you."

"At least I could tell the story. Tell people about the cave. The missing girls."

"Every person there already thinks you're crazy. Including your wife. What do you think would happen if you showed up talking about ritual sacrifices and underground caves full of skeletons? Straightjacket time. Not only that, but within an hour of being in custody, you'd be dead. Probably shot while you were allegedly attacking a deputy or attempting to escape."

"No one would believe it."

"Are you kidding? After your performance on the phone? People would think it was a damn shame, but they wouldn't lose sleep over it."

Jack shook his head. "This is crazy. I know who has Sarah, but you're saying not to do anything about it?"

"I didn't say that. You didn't want to use Sarah as bait, but it's already happened. Now we have to use it to our advantage."

"You mean your advantage. Don't act like you care what happens to Sarah. Don't play me."

"Okay. Fair enough. But we do have the same interests here. You may not believe in the ritual performed down in that cave – hell, I have a tough enough time believing it myself – but there's been enough strange shit to make me believe it's at least possible. Somehow, every sacrifice makes these bastards stronger. And, if they're willing to take all these risks over Sarah, then..."

"Then what?"

"I don't know. Maybe she's some kind of key for a whole different level of power."

Jack rolled his eyes. "This is nuts."

"Think about it. Why else would they take so many risks? You told me that Huckley said something about her being the one they were looking for, right? What do you think that means?"

"I don't know," Jack admitted. "But I still don't see how this helps."

"Huckley said they're planning to bring Sarah to the cave, right? So, we know they have to keep her alive until then."

"Okay," Jack said. "So we get back to the cave and wait for them."

Lonetree shook his head. "If it was just Huckley, maybe. He's impatient and brash enough to go ahead whether or not he knows where we are. But there's the leader of the group, the one Huckley called the Boss. He's careful. Careful enough to keep his identity secret. So I'm guessing he's smart enough to tie up loose ends before he allows Sarah to be brought to the cave."

"So what are you saying?"

"I'm saying we need to force the issue. Go on offense. Make this Boss guy do something. Hope for a mistake."

"That's our plan? Hope for a mistake?"

"Well, we could call them up one by one, tell them we know who they are and threaten to kill them. Worked well with Janney."

"Listen, I don't care about your revenge. I just want to get my girl back."

"Fair enough."

"You still haven't told me where we're going."

Lonetree reached into a stack of papers wedged into the space between the driver's seat and the console. He pulled out a folder and tossed it over to Jack. "Take a look at that. You'll see why I still need you."

Jack flipped through the papers Lonetree had tossed him. The last page was a large photograph. It took his breath away. "Is this for real?" he asked.

Lonetree nodded.

"Jesus," Jack whispered.

"You're going to get one chance at this. You have to be ready for some dirty work if you want to save your daughter. Tonight might be your best chance to get her back alive. Your only chance."

Alive. Before that moment, Jack hadn't contemplated Sarah being anything other than alive, and the idea of his little girl being hurt in *any* way made it difficult for him to breathe. The thought of her being killed was not within his ability to process.

Jack took a deep breath and studied the photograph he held in his hands. Just when he thought things couldn't get any worse. "All right. Tell me what I have to do."

SIXTY

$\mathbf{A}$ half hour had passed since the phone call and still no Jack. Lauren tried his cell a half-dozen times, but it went directly to voicemail without ringing. Janney hovered nearby whenever she picked up the phone. Each time she hung up in frustration, he gave her a thin, patronizing smile. She wondered if that was the effect he intended. If it was an attempt to comfort her, it didn't work. If anything, Janney's presence, his squinty eyes and creepy smiles, made her more anxious. What was she doing trusting the sheriff's judgment over Jack's?

She looked over and saw Janney on the phone in a nurse's station. A glass window separated them, but the door was open so she caught snippets of the conversation. He was giving a detailed description of Sarah and telling whoever was on the other end of the phone what had been done so far to search for the girl. When he was done, he gave a full description of Jack. Janney turned in mid-sentence and made eye contact with Lauren through the window. She looked away and couldn't shake the feeling that Janney had turned to make sure she could hear him. Maybe she was just being paranoid. Then again, she scolded herself for the hundredth time that hour. If she had been *more* paranoid about leaving her children alone, none of this would have happened.

"Dr. Tremont." The voice shocked her out of her thoughts. It was Janney, back from his phone call. "I have good news. That was the FBI. They're treating it as a kidnapping now."

"Wh-what does that mean?"

"They don't work kidnapping as much as they did before they became primarily anti-terrorism. But they still have great resources available. They'll check all major transit points, train stations, buses, airports, you name it."

"I want to talk to them. Do you have the number for the agent in charge?"

Janney lowered himself into the chair next to her. He reached out to take her hand, but she pulled it back away from him. "Listen, you let them do their job, all right? They'll find them," Janney said.

"You mean her. They'll find her."

"Yeah, that's what I mean. They'll find her." He tapped the table with his fingers, drumming out a slow, methodical beat, his eyes never leaving Lauren's face. "Have you had any luck reaching Jack?"

Lauren didn't answer. The sheriff already knew she hadn't. She shifted her eyes to look out the window. Janney pressed on. "You know, it seems strange to me that a man whose daughter has just gone missing wouldn't..." He let the sentence hang, his fingers still thumping the table. Lauren didn't take the bait. She turned her back to the sheriff, not wanting to give him the satisfaction of seeing tears welling up in her eyes.

Dr. Mansfield spoke from behind her. "Lauren, there's someone I'd like you to meet." She turned in her chair. A man stood next to the doctor, dressed casually in slacks and a button down, looking very uncomfortable. There was no color to his face, and he wrung his hands as he waited to be introduced. "This is Scott Moran. He saw Jack earlier today."

Lauren accepted the psychiatrist's outstretched hand. It was cold and clammy, like shaking hands with a cadaver. Even in the midst of her own emotional agony, she couldn't help feeling sorry for the man. Something weighed heavily on his mind, and she suspected it had to do with Jack.

"Please sit. Tell me what you know," Lauren said.

"Sheriff, I was supposed to tell you that one of your deputies needed to speak with you right away. Sorenson, I think his name was," Dr. Mansfield said.

Janney looked to the door impatiently. He was obviously unhappy about missing whatever the psychiatrist had to say. To Lauren's surprise, Janney got up to leave. "Moran, you come find me later and fill me in. You got that?"

Scott Moran nodded. Then he and Dr. Mansfield each took places around the small square table that Lauren had used as her base of operations throughout the long night. Moran grimaced as he sat down as though he were in physical pain. Lauren wondered if she looked the same way to the people around her. It was how she felt anyway.

"First let me say I'm sorry for your loss," Moran started.

Lauren felt her stomach muscles clench. *My loss.* Dr. Mansfield cleared his throat impatiently.

"I mean, there's still a chance they'll find her, of course. I'm sorry. I…"

"You'll have to excuse Scott," Dr. Mansfield said. "He's had some bad news in his family today."

"I'm sorry to hear that," Lauren said, feeling bad that, in fact, she wasn't sorry to hear it. She just felt sorry that it interfered with the man's ability to tell her about her husband. It was a selfish thought and she chastised herself for it, trying hard to find some sympathy. "I hope it's nothing serious."

"It's my daughter, she—" Scott Moran's voice trembled, and he bit his lower lip in an effort to control himself. Lauren looked up at Dr. Mansfield for an indication of what the man was talking about. The doctor scowled at the psychiatrist.

"Come on, Scott. Pull it together here," Dr. Mansfield said.

Lauren caught the irritation in his voice and assumed that he thought the man was overreacting to whatever was happening with his daughter. Ungracious thoughts poured through her as she waited for him to continue. *My daughter's missing. If yours is dead or dying, all right. Otherwise, shut the hell up.* The thoughts made her feel like a terrible person, but she couldn't help herself. It was all she could do to keep from reaching over the table and shaking the man until he told her what he knew. But her lack of control over her thoughts didn't extend to her actions. She sat quietly, feigning patience and empathy she didn't feel.

"Go on. Tell Lauren what you told me."

Scott Moran nodded his head. "Of course. I'm sorry." He turned to Lauren. "You know my conversation with your husband would normally be bound by doctor-patient privilege. But since you are his spouse, and since it involves the commission of a crime, I'm not–"

Lauren waved her hand in the air impatiently. "Wait, wait. What do you mean commission of a crime? What did the two of you talk about?"

"Well, you know about the hallucinations, right? First, the one with Huckley here in the hospital, then later at your house. The baseball bat?"

"Yes," Lauren said softly, ashamed for the embarrassment she felt, as if Jack's obvious mental illness were a dirty family secret instead of a medical problem.

Scott Moran whispered so quietly that Lauren was forced to lean across the table to hear him clearly. "So you know he thinks he heard Nate Huckley's voice telling him what to do. He actually believed that Huckley caused his actions. That he was being haunted by him."

"I know all this. What else did he say?"

"That Sarah heard Huckley too. That she was special. He went on and on about psychic phenomenon and these strange powers Sarah possesses. Do you know where he could have gotten such an idea? Has anything strange happened involving your daughter recently?"

Lauren thought of the pages of numbers Sarah had drawn. The number 320 over and over. Huckley's room. She wasn't ready to talk about that. "No, of course not," she said.

"Well, the idea fascinated him. He believed that Huckley was after her to try to steal these secret powers. On top of that, he was the only one who could save her. I mean, it was really paranoid stuff."

Lauren swallowed hard. "All right. So how does this make you so sure that Jack's responsible for abducting her?"

"Now I never said that, not directly."

"You said you were telling me this because 'it involved the commission of a crime.' I think those were your exact words. What crime would that be, Dr. Moran? Hallucinating?"

"Lauren, easy," Dr. Mansfield said. "Scott is trying to help."

Lauren smoothed her hair back and took a deep breath. "You're right. I'm sorry. I'm just getting a little tired of people who don't even know Jack already convicting him."

"Well, that wasn't all he said."

"Okay, what else did he say to convince you he's a criminal?"

"There was one thing that shocked me enough to write it down word for word." Scott Moran took out a piece of paper from his pocket. "Here you go. 'I'd rather Sarah were dead than be captured by those bastards. She'd be better off being dead, that's for sure. I just hope I have the guts to do it if it comes to that.'" Scott Moran folded the piece of paper.

Dr. Mansfield put his hand on Lauren's shoulder. "It doesn't prove anything, but I thought you had the right to know."

"C-can I see that?" Lauren asked, pointing a shaky finger at the paper Scott Moran held. He handed it to her, and she read through it, still unable to imagine the words coming from Jack's mouth. "What did you – what was your recommendation to him?"

"I told him to admit himself for hospitalization. I thought he was a suicide risk and might pose a threat to others. He just laughed at me. Told me I was the crazy one. I didn't push it because I thought he would become violent."

"I just don't understand," Lauren said, her lower lip shaking. "How could it go this far so fast? I don't understand."

"On the contrary, I don't think this was fast at all. If anything, it was very slow. He told me about the accident in California. The little girl who died."

"That wasn't his fault though."

"But that's not what he thinks. He holds himself responsible. He is carrying enormous guilt. Something like that held inside long enough starts to take on a life of its own. It manifests itself in unexpected ways. Depression. Hallucinations. Split personality. All it took was a trigger."

"And what was the trigger?" Lauren asked.

"Could have been anything. Some obvious ones are the man he saw killed by lightning. Could be because of Max Dahl's daughter having a terminal illness. Could be he saw a pickup truck the same color as the one in the accident. What I'm trying to say is that it could have been anything."

Dr. Mansfield stood up. "Thank you, Scott, for coming to us. Why don't we let Lauren think about this for a moment?"

Scott Moran took his cue, slid his chair from the table, and stood. "I'm sorry I couldn't have done more. I really am."

Lauren tried to smile but felt as if she would lose control again. She remained seated and nodded her acknowledgement. Dr. Mansfield lowered himself to her level. "I have to talk to Scott about a few other things. Will you be all right?" Lauren nodded, not at all sure if she would be or not. The doctor patted her on the shoulder and told her he would be back shortly.

Across the room, Janney saw the meeting with Lauren Tremont breaking up. He still seethed at missing whatever Scott Moran had told her. How was he supposed to handle the situation if he didn't have all the information available? Before he could work up a real rage about being excluded, Deputy Sorenson appeared in the hallway. Janney dragged him to a private corner for an update. "What do you have?"

Sorenson stared at the floor. "Nothing. Not a trace. The guys are still out looking."

"Godammit!" Janney ran his hands through his hair. "We need to find Tremont and Lonetree. We're running out of time." He steadied himself. He made it a rule never to look concerned around his men, never show weakness. He was used to dealing with situations like this, but this one had him worried. Janney had intended to use this problem to make a case for being the number two guy instead of that idiot Huckley. Maybe even to argue to the Boss that Huckley was a liability. But for that to happen, he needed to contain this problem quickly. It would boost his stock and, more important, give him a chance to make Huckley look worse. But the Tremont woman made things difficult. If he hadn't faked the phone call to the FBI earlier, he was sure she would have called them herself. And that would have complicated things.

"What do you want me to do?" Deputy Sorenson asked.

"Set up outside. They might be heading this way."

Sorenson leaned in close and whispered, "What about the other thing? Do you want me to do anything with that?"

Janney looked up and down the hall, impatient with the deputy's lack of discretion. "No, let it alone. I'll take care of it. Just get outside and keep your eyes open." He watched as the deputy turned and strutted down the hall, one hand resting on the handle of his gun. "Goddamn cowboy," Janney muttered.

If he was right about Lonetree, this might be the last time he had to deal with Sorenson. He felt a tinge of regret, but not because he felt any affection for the man. Sorenson had been a mistake. Like always, Janney had recruited him from out of state. The fewer local ties the better. Criminal record, ex-military, the man had seemed the perfect addition. And in the past year Sorenson had done everything asked of him. Of course, the kid thought he was involved in nothing more than old-fashioned police corruption. A little drugs. A little prostitution. He didn't have a clue what he was really mixed up in. They never did until the very end.

But Sorenson was too cocky for his own good, and Janney knew that would eventually lead to mistakes. The same way Huckley's arrogance kept driving them to the brink. He decided to retire Sorenson after the current problem was cleaned up. That is, if Lonetree didn't take care of him first.

Janney headed back toward the cafeteria where Lauren sat waiting for her husband to appear. With any luck, Janney thought, this whole mess would be resolved by the end of the night. If only the resolution could include getting rid of Huckley, permanently. Even if the Boss didn't agree to it, it didn't mean it was impossible. He pushed the thought around in his head, savoring its implications. Life without Huckley. Life without the hassle and complications that followed the man. Life without the risk that he put them all through. Just imagining it brought a smile to his lips. Suddenly he felt a new sense of promise and opportunity. He whistled a little tune as he walked back to the hospital cafeteria, the seeds of a plan to destroy Huckley taking root with each step.

SIXTY-ONE

Even through his shirt, Jack felt the cold metal of the gun against his stomach. He reached down to his belt line to make certain it was still secure after his sprint across the lawn. The downward angle of the gun pointed the business end of the weapon straight into his crotch, so he had checked a dozen times to make sure the safety was engaged. He pulled back his sweater and felt for the safety catch again. Just in case.

He tried to control his breathing. He was panting far harder than he should have for the small exertion he'd made. He had to relax. A couple of deep breaths as he crouched in a shadow against the brick building, and his pulse started to slow and even out.

I'm going to kill a man.

The thought didn't startle him – it just oozed its way into his mind. *I'm going to kill a man.* The simple statement had replayed in his mind since he and Lonetree had worked out their plan. These six words formed the soundtrack to his actions, looping around his brain until they dissolved in the background and made way for the other voices that clamored for attention in his head. Angry voices, angry because they knew Jack held out hope that killing would be unnecessary, that mercy would ultimately prove a better strategy than revenge.

Especially to this enemy.

The voices insisted the man Jack hunted was not really a man at all, but a monster that killed women and children. Tortured them in bizarre rituals. Had these victims been shown mercy? Of course not. So then, why shouldn't such a monster be killed? Why should he be afraid to do it?

The voices were compelling, but Jack still hoped he wouldn't have to take the safety off the gun.

He ran down the length of the building, careful to check each window for watchful eyes before he passed by it. The grass crunched beneath his feet, frozen by the cold. Each footstep sounded impossibly loud in the still air, like he was sneaking around with a string of empty soda cans tied to his feet. But he knew it was his mind playing tricks on him. No one could hear him. He hoped.

A door around the back was unlocked, just as he expected. He turned the knob slowly, careful not to make a sound, and inched it open to minimize the creak of the hinges. The room was dark, so he walked in and eased the door shut behind him.

Forward through the room, down the hall, he moved on the balls of his feet. It reminded him of playing hide-and-seek as a kid, tiptoeing through a dark house, not knowing who was going to jump out of a shadow to scare him. The difference was that as a kid it was fun to get scared. He wasn't having any fun tonight.

With sudden clarity, he realized that his prey might not go quietly. Until that moment, he hadn't fully appreciated the possibility that the man might find him first. That on turning the next corner, a tire iron might crush into his face. Or a flash of light from a gun could be the last thing he saw before being enveloped in darkness forever. Jack had the uneasy feeling of a hunter whose role has been reversed, that the panting beast no longer ran ahead of him trying to escape, but now stalked him from behind waiting for the moment of ambush. Some of his resolve melted into fear and paranoia, but he kept moving through the house.

Jack took the gun from his waistband and held it out in front of him, the muzzle pointed up to the ceiling, just like he'd seen in the cop shows on television. Heeding Lonetree's advice, he left the safety on but kept his thumb on the mechanism so he could release it in a hurry if he needed to. The instant it took to disengage the safety could cost him valuable seconds, but he also knew it gave him the time he needed to avoid shooting the wrong person. He appreciated that Lonetree's suggestion was clearly an act of self-preservation.

Jack moved into the next room. Still dark. There wasn't a light on in the place. The prey was either gone or expecting them.

Jack squinted to interpret the shadows in the room, but the curtained windows blacked the moon out. There could have been a gun positioned three feet from his forehead, and he wouldn't have known it. Despite the impenetrable darkness, he felt something was different about this room. He knew without light, without hearing a sound. He knew something was wrong.

Someone is in the room. Someone is watching you.

A brilliant light flashed on overhead. It burst through his dilated pupils and turned the world glaring white. He raised his left arm to shield his eyes and his right hand to point the gun at whatever was in front of him. Blinded and scared, he pulled the trigger. Hard. The gun didn't fire. He hadn't removed the safety.

He crouched to the ground on reflex and fumbled with the gun, sliding the safety to the side. By the time he raised the gun again, his eyes had started to adjust to the light and his brain had caught up with the action. No one had shot at him. He wasn't being attacked. Instead, the person who had turned on the light was sitting in front of him, regarding him with interest, as if curious whether Jack would figure out the safety on the gun or not, and once he did, if he would fire the weapon.

Satisfied after a few beats that Jack would not shoot, at least not yet, Max Dahl withdrew his hand from the light switch on the wall and sat back in his leather chair.

"I thought you might come by tonight."

Lonetree moved expertly around the corner from the front of the house, his gun trained on the space between Max's eyes.

"And I see you brought a friend. Joseph Lonetree, right?" He lowered his hand back to the armrest of the chair and sat smiling at them both. "I don't suppose we could do this over a drink, could we?"

"Are Kristi or the kids here?" Jack asked.

"They're gone. At her mother's in Annapolis."

Jack took a step forward, his knuckles white from his grip on the gun. "Where's Sarah? Tell me or I'll kill you."

Jack thought he saw a momentary flare of indignation in Max's eyes. But it was there only for a second, as if his friend suddenly remembered the charade was up and he was no longer entitled to trust.

"I swear to you, I didn't know anything about it. I just heard about it tonight. After they'd already taken her."

"Do you know where she is?"

Max shook his head. "I know where they'll take her eventually. But they won't do it right away. They'll want things to calm down first. I'm so sorry. I understand how it feels to know you're losing a daughter."

Jack searched for any sign that Max was lying. The seconds stretched out as the two men stared each other down. Jack knew it was insane to believe anything Max said. Their entire relationship had been a lie. Lonetree had shown him the proof. Max was the enemy. He was a vicious killer, a predator. Jack had expected to feel rage at this moment. Rage for the lies Max had told. Rage for the betrayal of a friend. Rage for the evil that Max took part in. But his emotions were different than he expected, and he could not find the anger he knew he was entitled to feel. Something about Max had changed. His shoulders were slumped forward, his eyes circled with dark rings. Jack noticed the slight shake in his hands. Despite everything, Jack still felt pity for his friend. No matter the monster he was, right now he was just a broken man. The father of a little girl who was dying.

"How about that drink?" Max asked.

Jack hesitated. He and Lonetree had agreed that he would get the first crack at getting Max to help them. If he wasn't successful, Lonetree would take over the interrogation. Jack wondered how long the big man would wait before he took matters into his own hands. He decided to see how far he could use his and Max's friendship to make him talk. Lowering his gun, but knowing Lonetree still had him covered, Jack walked over to the small bar where he knew Max kept the good bourbon. He took out two tumblers, clinked some ice into each, and poured two fingers of auburn liquid. He crossed the room and handed a drink to Max.

"Here's to the truth," Jack said.

Max paused, then raised his glass slightly toward Jack. "The truth." He slugged back the glass of bourbon with a satisfied moan.

"I'm sure you know most of the story already, considering the company you're keeping." Max nodded toward Lonetree sitting behind Jack. "By the way, I met your brother a few times. He was a good man. Not that it makes any difference, but I was against removing him."

Lonetree's face was a mask. Jack remembered the story about Lonetree's brother telling him who had killed him. Lonetree gave no indication that he accepted Max's assertion or knew anything to the contrary. He simply stared and waited. A professional soldier on a mission.

"Who else is involved, Max? Who has Sarah?"

"I'll tell you what I can, but you have to understand, Jack, I can't tell you everything."

"But—"

"But nothing. You don't know these people. They'll go after Kristi and the kids. They'll punish me through them. Even if you kill me, if they think I betrayed them, they'll still take their revenge on my daughters. I won't risk that. Not for you. Not for Sarah. I'd rather die."

Lonetree stood up and raised his gun. "Sounds good to me."

"Wait," Jack yelled. "He said there are things he can tell us." He turned back to Max. "Right? There are some things you will tell us?"

Max shrugged. "Sure, but it won't do any good."

"Why do you say that?"

"Because it's hopeless, Jack. You can't stop these people. Make no mistake, they will kill Sarah. They've decided they need her, and that's the end of it. Nothing will change that now. The only question is whether or not you're going to die trying to save her."

Rage tore through Jack's system from hearing his daughter's life dismissed so easily. The gun, still in his right hand, seemed to throb, begging to punish Max for talking about Sarah in such a way. Jack felt the danger in such power. He carefully placed the gun on a side table. "You could help us, you know. Help us destroy them."

Max grimaced. "It's too late for that. Much too late. Besides, if they thought I helped you, they would take my family. I won't risk that."

Lonetree crossed the living room so Max could see his eyes as he spoke. "What makes you think your family is safe from me? You think I've never killed a woman? That I would hesitate to kill the child of a monster like you? Look at me and tell me if you think your family is safe."

Max stared at Lonetree. "What I'm worried about is worse than death. Much worse."

"All right," Jack said. "Tell us what you can. After that, we'll decide what to do with you."

Lonetree backed away and leaned against the fireplace mantle, a brooding statue waiting for his chance to take action. Max took a deep breath and told them what he dared.

SIXTY-TWO

"There were fifteen of us at the beginning. Only a few of us are still in Prescott City. There were others. Some moved on. Others...well, some of them are no longer around."

Jack didn't want to turn this into twenty questions, so he let the pause stretch out until Max continued with the story.

"We were a pretty rag-tag group. We met up in Baltimore, by chance mostly. Men who didn't have anything to lose. All willing to do whatever it took to make our fortunes. We figured there would be safety in numbers. You know, bargaining power for supplies, better in a fight, that sort of thing. Like in any group of men, leaders emerged. I was one of them. So was a big German named Hans Boetcher – you know him as Jim Butcher – our friendly Piper's bartender. Janney was another, a personal favorite of the Boss."

"The Boss?" Lonetree prompted.

"Yeah, he was the real leader. He was different from the rest of us. Well-educated, a society man from up north, judging by the accent. No one knew what his story was, and no one was brash enough to ask. Without a vote or any kind of agreement, we all started calling him the Boss and deferred to him on decisions. It was the Boss who brought a strange looking man named Nate Huckley into the group.

"Even at the beginning there was talk about whether we were comfortable having Huckley along. You know what I'm talking about. That white skin and those pale blue eyes that wander around in his head like he's watching everything at once. And his temper. Some men you can just tell have violence coiled up inside of them. Nate Huckley was the same back then as he is now. He had so much tension in him that you could almost hear his body hum if you stood too close to him.

"But the Boss said he was in, and that was the end of the story. The same reasons we were uneasy with Huckley also made him the best front man for the group when we negotiated with the supply stores. He was also the one who came across the old man with a mining claim to sell. Supposedly the mine was a producer, but the old man couldn't do the hard work anymore. The Boss organized us all to go in together and buy it. The plan was that half of us could work the mine and the other half trap furs until we struck a vein. With all of us working, we thought that we couldn't help but strike it."

"When did all this happen?" Jack asked.

"I still remember the date we left." Max shook the ice in his glass and poured the final drops of bourbon into his mouth. "I don't expect you to believe me. It was September 3, 1819."

Jack reached into the breast pocket of his jacket and pulled out a yellowed photograph. He held up the photo so Max could see it. "Lonetree gave me this on the way over here. I'm not saying I believe you. Just that I'm willing to listen."

Max leaned forward, his eyebrows raised as he looked over the photograph. A group of men lined up in front of a clapboard shack. Burlap sacks were stacked up behind them. Some of the men were dressed in light colored suits, with waist coasts and hats, but most were working men dressed in coveralls. Scrawled across the bottom was the date, September 3, 1819.

"Where'd you get this?" Max asked.

"Lonetree showed it to me when I refused to believe you were part of all this. It was mixed in with his brother's files. Of course, it could be a forgery, but given everything else that has happened, I'm willing to believe almost anything. That picture was probably why Lonetree's brother was killed, right?"

Max ignored the question and looked at the picture more closely. Jack figured he was picking himself out from the group.

"Haven't aged at all, have you?" Jack said.

Max looked at the photo, his expression almost wistful. "No, I've aged. You might not be able to see it, but I've aged a great deal."

"Which one of these is the Boss?" Lonetree asked.

Max smiled. "He's not there. Even then he kept a low profile. Like he knew what was going to happen all along. In a way, I guess he did."

"Listen. I need to know what's going on here. Sarah is gone. Nate Huckley is haunting me from a coma. And it's like he's getting stronger every time he makes an appearance. I don't have time for games. I need to know who's involved and how all this works."

Max nodded as if hearing that Huckley was haunting his friend was the most ordinary thing. "We've all had different reactions to the ritual over the years. Huckley was always sensitive, kind of a psychic, but nothing like he is now. I think even the Boss is afraid of him now. He's a little off-balance."

"Tell me about it." Jack said.

"Still, Huckley won't be quiet long. His body would have recovered by now. I imagine he's chosen to stay in the coma for his own reasons. Out of body experiences would be his thing, that's for sure."

Jack shook his head. "I still can't wrap my brain around it all. How does this work? How did it start?"

"You don't know?" Max looked up at Lonetree. "We thought you already knew. I'm almost certain your brother knew the details, or at least he suspected them. Unfortunately, he didn't tell us much at the end. He was strong. Something about your brother made it so Huckley couldn't read his mind. Indian magic or something. So Huckley tried to persuade him the old-fashioned way. But your brother refused to tell us what he knew or where his notes were. All that pain, and still he kept his secrets until the end."

Lonetree looked away at the mention of his brother, his neck and face reddening. "Keep going, Max," Jack said, wondering if Max was deliberately antagonizing Lonetree.

Max exhaled a long breath and shook his head. "The group left Baltimore the day that photo was taken, and we headed up into the mountains to work the mine and try to make a go of things. Nothing much happened for over a year. During that time, the Boss and Huckley would disappear for weeks at a time to explore the area, but no one else knew what they were looking for. When they were in camp, they spent hours poring over maps and strange books. Then one day, they came back from a trip and you could tell they'd found something. They didn't say anything, but it was written all over their faces. The next day, the Boss picked six of us and we headed off due west, mules loaded down with shovels, mining lamps, and rope. Two days later, we reached a hole in the ground, and the Boss told us we were going down to a deep cave where treasure awaited all of us. That was the beginning of the nightmare."

"I know," Jack said. "I've been in that cave."

Max arched his eyebrows. "Really? How did you—" He slumped forward in his chair. "I guess it doesn't matter anymore. But if you've been there, you know how horrible it is. While the rest of us stood there in the middle of that dark graveyard crossing ourselves and praying to God that we could get out of there, Huckley and the Boss walked around with smiles on their faces. Then we found the Source and Huckley really got excited."

"The Source? The round structure in the center of the cave, right?" Lonetree said.

"Yes, we didn't start calling it the Source until later, until we finally understood what it was. At first we weren't sure. The Boss and Huckley were fascinated by the carvings. Almost like they were expecting to find them. The rest of us wanted to get the hell out of there, but the two of them kept walking around the carved wall, holding their lanterns up close to the carvings and muttering back and forth. I edged closer to them, trying to hear what they were saying. I overheard Huckley whisper, 'It's talking to me. Shut up so I can hear.' Then the real horror started."

"What?" Jack asked.

"Huckley did it for the first time. Not the whole ritual, of course, we didn't know anything back then. But he did a Taking."

"What do you mean, Taking?"

"How about another drink?" Max asked, raising his glass hopefully. Jack obliged by filling the glass from the decanter. Max downed half the glass in one gulp. He nodded appreciatively. "Taking is what we called it. I suppose it's easier to digest that way."

Lonetree snorted. "You guys murder little kids but can't stomach calling it killing?"

Max winced but otherwise ignored the comment. "Anyway, the first sacrifice was one of the guys with us, a friend of mine actually, named Frank Jeter. Huckley discovered a loose rock on the stone structure. It was circular, not more than a foot in diameter. Huckley pried it loose and pulled it out, revealing a hole that went right into the structure. The Boss told Jeter to go throw a rock into the hole. He did and the rock bounced inside, confirming our hopes; the structure was hollow.

We all thought the same thing. No one would go through all the trouble to build such a thing unless it was to keep something safe inside. Something valuable. Gold, we thought. I guess Jeter thought the same thing. The Boss didn't even have to tell him to look inside. Jeter did that all on his own.

"He wasn't looking into that hole for more than a few seconds when it happened. Even now I can't think about it without cringing. It was the shock factor, you know. None of us expected what was going to happen, and that made it all the more terrible to watch."

Max tipped his glass back until the ice tumbled against his lips, and the last of the booze dripped into his mouth. He sucked in one of the ice cubes and crunched it between his molars.

"Whatever Jeter saw in there, it was the last thing he used his eyes for. No more than three or four seconds after he put his face up to the hole in the rock, Jeter's body lurched forward like he was trying to force his face through the opening. He beat the palms of his hands against the rock, trying to push back. A few of us laughed. Jeter was always playing jokes. This one was in bad taste because we were so scared to begin with, but it was still funny. That is, until he started to scream.

"Then his legs shot out straight under him, rigid like electricity was going through them. The scream became garbled as his face wedged deeper into the hole. I went to grab for him. But I was standing next to the Boss, and when I moved forward he reached out and took me by the arm. His eyes never left Jeter's writhing body, but I understood. Whatever was happening, the Boss wanted to see the thing play out.

"Right then, Jeter's feet jerked off the ground. I mean both of them, like he was levitating in some magic show. But he wasn't floating. Violent spasms tore through his body as it rose up into the air until his legs were parallel to the floor.

"Jeter's face was still pressed into the opening, so as his body rose higher we could hear the *pop-pop-pop* as his spine cracked into pieces. Even so, he was still alive.

"His torso suspended in the air, like a pole had shot out from the hole and skewered the length of him. That was exactly what it was like, a living piece of meat on a rotisserie, limbs flapping spastically in all directions.

"Then, as if seeing him like that wasn't enough, I could see something moving under his clothes. Where it was exposed, I saw bulges moving under his skin. I thought whatever was underneath would rip through the flesh and pop through.

"You want to know what I thought it was? Rats. Can you believe that? I thought maybe it was a bunch of starved rats that had crawled in through Jeter's mouth and were going to town on the poor guy's insides. Sounds nuts, but as horrible as that was, it was still better than the other option. If it wasn't rats doing it, it was something outside of my understanding. Something evil and powerful. And sure to kill me just like it was doing Jeter.

"Then, in the middle of my panic, without any warning, Jeter's body went limp and slumped to the ground.

"No one moved. We just stared at the man's destroyed face, no more than a mushy plump with strands of his entrails hanging from his mouth. Janney turned and threw up at the sight. But not Huckley. And not the Boss. While we were scared for our lives and our sanity, they were enthralled. Like they had made some great discovery. Turns out this was exactly what they had been looking for all along. Seeing Jeter die just confirmed things for them."

"What do you mean they were looking for it? How could they know?" Lonetree asked.

"They were just like your father and brother," Max said. "They had done their research, pieced together the folklore and the Indian legends. They went searching for the lost tribe of the Sumac. And they found them. Or what was left of them anyway."

Jack cut in before Lonetree could say anything about the implied insult of his family being grouped together with Huckley. "So what was in the stone structure? You call it the Source, but of what?"

Max looked at his empty glass and swirled the ice. Jack wondered how many drinks the man had had before they arrived. Dark bags hung under Max's eyes and his pupils were glazed over. When he started to speak again, Jack heard the slur in his voice.

"Well, after watching Jeter die, we all wanted to get out of there. All of us except Huckley and the Boss, of course. They were pointing to the carvings on the walls and arguing back and forth. We couldn't tell what the argument was, only that the Boss gave in and agreed with Huckley. Then Huckley walked back, ripped the clothes from Jeter's body, pulled out a knife and started cutting. Piece by piece, he fed the body through the hole in the wall. None of us helped, not even the Boss, but none of us left either. We were too afraid and too awed by what we saw when Huckley cut into Jeter's body."

Max paused. He must know he had his audience well-salted and seemed to enjoy stretching out the moment. Finally, looking disappointed neither of his captors had begged him to go on, he continued. "You see, when Huckley cut into Jeter's flesh, there was no blood. Not a drop."

Jack clenched his hands into fists from frustration. He knew he needed to hear this but he couldn't beat back his incredulity. Things like this simply were not real. There had to be a rational explanation for it all. Jack couldn't shake the sensation that everything that had happened to him was a massive practical joke, and at any minute someone would jump out from behind a curtain, point to a hidden camera and laugh. *You fell for that? What an idiot!*

A body drained of blood. This was the stuff of late night cable television, not real life. But still, he ticked off the tangible evidence in his brain. There was the photograph of Max. Huckley's appearance in the cave. The fact that Sarah had been kidnapped just like Huckley had said. There was too much evidence *not* to believe. And to believe part of the story meant he had to take all of it. Bloodless corpses, supernatural forces. All of it.

What bothered him most about the story, he realized, was that Max was describing the same ritual Sarah would be subjected to if he didn't save her in time. As Max described the grisly scene, Jack saw his daughter in place of the man. Thinking of her death was hard enough, but hearing the torture she would have to endure was too much to bear.

He tried to refocus on Max. The slur in his speech was more pronounced now, and his eyes drooped as if he fought off sleep. Jack wondered if he might have taken something more than alcohol before they arrived. He hoped Max's condition would loosen his tongue.

"I think you're full of shit."

Max blinked hard, as if focusing on his old friend was a particularly hard thing to do. "You do, huh? Well, you weren't there, were you? You can kiss my ass if you don't believe me."

"Make me understand then. How does it work?"

Max smiled and wagged a finger at him. "You're trying to get me to tell you all the little secrets. Very clever, Jack. Very clever. Hell, I'll tell you. It'll cost you another glass of bourbon though." He waited until Jack filled his glass before he continued. "After Huckley pushed the body through the hole, we waited for something incredible to happen, but nothing did. Minutes passed and still nothing. There was no sound inside the structure. The silence was more unnerving than any sound I could imagine. Then finally, Huckley cried out and pointed to a spot on the wall. We all saw it. A thin line of blood dripping down the rock face, as if the stone itself was bleeding. We crowded around it, holding our lanterns in a circle. The Boss inspected the area and found a small hole out of which the blood oozed, as if from a small scratch. The Boss and Huckley were ecstatic, talking about how it was just like the carvings. Then Huckley did it."

"Did what?" Jack asked.

"The thing that changed all of our lives forever. The thing that might change the world eventually. He completed the ritual and did the Taking for the first time."

SIXTY-THREE

Max sipped the last of the bourbon from his glass. He considered the leftover ice as if perplexed where all the booze had gone, then, defeated, sat the glass on the table beside him.

"Huckley reached out with a finger and wiped the blood off the wall. I remember holding my breath, thinking the substance might start burning him, that maybe it was acid or poison. But Huckley knew what he was doing. He held the finger up to the Boss, showing off a little, then held out his other arm for us all to see. Huckley, like the rest of us, had scratches all over his body from the hard climb down to the cave. He located a fresh cut and wiped the blood on his finger into the wound. We thought he was crazy and cried out to stop him, but he just kept rubbing it. Then he wiped away the blood on his shirt and held his arm back up for us to see the results for ourselves. The cut was gone. It had healed completely. That's when we started to understand what we had found. The cave was the Source of healing. The Source of eternal life."

"The only catch is that you have to murder innocent little girls to get it," Lonetree said.

"And that's quite a catch, isn't it? Everything has its price. It seems almost fitting that something so miraculous should come so expensively. The carvings and the skeletons in the cave made it clear that women were the desired sacrifice. It was over a week before we could capture one and bring her down to the cave. The Taking went the same way, but the life-

283

giving blood that had trickled after poor Jeter was killed now gushed from the rock after the girl was sacrificed. This time Huckley drank from it, suckled the hole in the rock wall like it was a teat. No one else dared until we saw what it did to him."

"Which was?"

"You still don't get it, do you? This stuff is the cure-all. The ultimate antibiotic. The fucking fountain of youth. No disease or virus can touch us. The cells in my body don't break down. I don't age. Watch." With surprising quickness, Max grabbed the glass on the table and smashed it with his hand. It shattered, sending shards of glass deep into his skin. Max held up his hand and pulled out the glass, wincing as he did so. "Still hurts like a bitch, though." Blood gushed from his wounds, running down his forearm. Slowly, the flow of blood tapered off, then stopped altogether. He held the hand out toward Jack. "See, look at the skin. It's already growing back."

Jack leaned forward and saw what he was pointing to. The wound closed in on itself. Within seconds
it was completely sealed.

"Dear God," Jack breathed.

"Neat trick," Lonetree said. "Want to see how you do with a bullet through the chest?"

Max nodded. "He's right. We're not immortal, not by a stretch. Cut off my head or shoot me through the heart, and I'm as dead as the next guy."

"I guess the movies about vampires were right, huh? A wooden stake through the heart and all that," Lonetree said.

"You might laugh," Max said, "but I've spent a lot of time wondering if the myths about vampires don't have some truth to them."

"Come on," Jack said.

"No, I'm serious. Not flying bats, pointy teeth, and that bullshit, but the root mythology. The idea that beings exist who are biologically capable of transforming the energy of other living things into a reusable resource. And that blood is the bridge to make it happen. The myth is all over the place when you start looking for it. Think about it. Isn't this really about the blood being transformed into life? What do you think Christians do every time they take communion? Doesn't the catechism talk about the blood of Christ being the source of life and salvation?"

"I think it's a stretch," Jack said.

"Maybe, but there are other cases. The statues of the Virgin that cry tears of blood. Healing tears, Jack, just like the blood from the Source. The Aztecs sacrificed hundreds of people a day to their gods. They ripped still-beating hearts from the chests of their victims. Wasn't that blood cult the same thing? The same mythology of giving blood to a god in return for life?"

"So what are you trying to say? That the Source is a god?"

Max lowered his head into his hands. "I don't know. I don't know anymore. I'm just trying to make sense of it, you know. Maybe if there was a higher purpose, then it would all make sense." Max was still coherent, but it was obvious he was having trouble focusing. Jack wondered how much time they had left before their source of information passed out.

"You mean the killing you've done would make sense," Lonetree said.

Jack tried to move Max's attention away from Lonetree. "If you've already had this serum, why go on killing?"

"The Source always wants more sacrifices. And we need to drink the transmuted blood regularly for it to work."

"And Sarah. Why her?"

Max shook his head. "I'm not sure. Huckley and the Boss have been working on some project together for years. Maybe Sarah has something to do with that. One thing I can tell you is that Huckley's psychic abilities have gone to a different level recently. I mean, over time, each of us developed something almost like a mutation. Kind of like a gift from the Source. For Huckley, it was his special abilities."

"What was yours?" Lonetree asked.

"What do you mean?"

"You said you all changed from Taking. How about you? What was your gift?"

Max's eyes drifted to the back of the room. Both Lonetree and Jack checked over their shoulders to make sure no one had sneaked in behind them, but there was nothing there. When Jack turned back, he recognized Max's expression as the same one he had seen at Piper's when they were talking about Jesse's heart disease. Max was in a different time and place, somewhere far away, before his girl was sick, before his world came to an end.

"Max?" Jack said.

Max jerked his head back as if he had been slapped, as if the force of his return to the here and now was more physical than emotional. "My gift? It was nothing. Nothing important."

Jack decided to leave the obvious lie alone. He was getting impatient. Every minute spent trying to coax information out of Max was a minute lost in the race to save Sarah. "Huckley then. Tell me more about Huckley."

"I never really understood his powers. Honestly, I never tried. I'd like to tell you I was curious about all the odd things that happened, but I can't. If anything, I prayed to know less than I did. Maybe that makes me a coward, but it's the truth. I never asked for this. Not even back then."

"But that didn't stop you from Taking, did it?" Lonetree said.

Max nodded. "Eternal life. Life without sickness or disease. The temptation is too great. You can both sit there and judge me all you want, but you weren't there. It wasn't offered to you. And until it is, you can't ever understand the power of it. Immortality is a narcotic – it lures you in and makes you a slave until you'll do anything to have it." Max looked away again. "You'll do things you wouldn't believe."

Jack fought down his revulsion. He wanted to ask Max why his life was so much more important than the victims he took to the cave. Why other men's daughters were less valuable than his own. But he left the questions unspoken. He didn't have time to preach or judge. He just wanted answers. "You said Huckley has greater psychic powers. Like what?"

"He claims to talk directly to the Source all the time, which, for him, is just like talking to God. The only reason I can imagine that he risked what he did to get Sarah was if he thought the Source itself made him do it. True or not, if Huckley believes it, then things don't look good for Sarah. I'm sorry, Jack. I really am. But Sarah *is* going to die. And there's nothing you can do about it."

Jack walked over to the fireplace and stared at the ashes and bits of burnt wood piled up under the metal grate. He wished there was a fire going. Everything felt suddenly cold and dark. "I don't understand, Max. How do you all get away with this? How do you live this long and no one notices?"

"That part is easier than you think. At first we thought we would have to move every couple of decades, make pilgrimages back to the Source. But it's never been a problem."

"Don't people notice? Don't they ask questions?"

"People see what they want to see. They believe what they want to believe. If their eyes show them something impossible, their brains step in and make the adjustment for them. We all get comments about how little we age, how good we look, but it never goes beyond that. If it does, then we take care of it."

"You kill them," Lonetree said. "And you have the perfect set-up. Janney runs protection. Butcher listens at his bar for people to talk about their suspicions after they have a few drinks."

Max nodded. "The Boss set that up. His smartest move was having Scott Moran get credentialed as a psychiatrist."

"Jesus, Moran's one of you? I told him everything."

"That's the way it's supposed to work. People bring in a sixty-year-old photograph of one of us, and Scott convinces them they're delusional and paranoid. Medicates them into submission." He nodded toward Jack. "Almost worked on you."

"But the women. The girls," Jack said, his voice cracking as he pictured Sarah in his mind. "How do you...I mean, how could you–"

"Murder innocent people?" Max said. "Be responsible for so many deaths and stay sane?"

Jack turned back to look at the ashes in the fireplace. "Yeah. How do you do that?"

"You might as well ask a crack head on the street why he killed someone for a pair of Nikes. Why? Because he could sell them on the street for fifteen bucks and get one more hit. I can't explain it any more than any addict can explain why he drinks, snorts, shoots up, or whatever. I need it. And when the need comes, I'll do anything to get it."

"But you killed *children*. I've seen how much you love your own kids, and I don't get it. Or was that a lie too? Was all that crying on my shoulder about Jesse's heart disease just an act like everything else?"

"I did it for her too," Max tried to shout. It came out as a bubbling slur, saliva dripping from the corners of his mouth. "Don't you understand? The Boss said he would break the rules and let me bring Jesse to the cave if I helped them take care of you. If I helped them get Sarah."

"I thought you said you didn't know anything about this."

Max blinked hard, then arched his eyebrows and blinked again as if something had floated into his eye. "But I couldn't do it, Jack. I – I couldn't d-do that. Not e-e-ven for Jesse. Besides, I...I found ana-anoth'-other way. I used...used my gift."

Jack's eyes narrowed as he watched Max struggle through his words. He was disoriented. The corners of his mouth drooped down and his chin trembled. With a cry, Max's hands flew to his eyes and rubbed them as if someone had just thrown a handful of salt in them.

"Are you all right?" Jack asked.

Max stuck his thumbs in the corner of his eyes and pressed in hard.

"Jesus, you're bleeding. Your eyes are bleeding," Jack cried out as tiny trickles of blood ran down Max's cheek. When Max pulled his hands away, Jack saw that the whites of his eyes were dark red, as if every blood vessel in them had simultaneously exploded. "What the hell..."

"Get...a mirror...please," Max mumbled, pointing to the fireplace.

Lonetree grabbed a round mirror off the fireplace mantle and walked it over to him. Max took it and held it up to his face with shaking hands. He turned his head side to side to view his face from different angles. His face was changing so fast that between oscillations, new blotches and marks appeared. The skin around his eyes was now gouged with deep lines. His nose swelled. Then whole sections of it melted away, as if it were being devoured by a runaway cancer. With each turn of his head, handfuls of hair fell onto his shoulders, leaving the pale white flesh of his scalp exposed.

"So fast. I didn't expect it to 'appen tho fast," Max groaned, raising a liver-spotted hand to his mouth. He parted his lips and felt his teeth. They sank into soft, rotten gums. He closed his mouth in horror and covered it with his hand. He moaned in pain. Forcing himself to confront the damage, he raised the mirror and opened his mouth again. A flow of blood poured over his bottom lip and drained down the front of his shirt. Rotten teeth, mixed with the gore of black gums and the lining from inside his mouth, slid down his chin.

"What's happening to you?" Jack whispered.

"I saved 'er," he struggled to say. Another bloody tooth tumbled down his chin. "Is my gif' from tha Source. I th'aved Jesse."

Jack shook his head that he didn't understand. It was Lonetree who guessed it. "He said they all changed from Taking. His mutation, his gift, must have been the ability to transfer his life energy to someone else. Looks like it was a one-time deal. I think we're seeing time catch up with your friend here."

A gurgling sound rose from the back of Max's throat. His legs started to thrash in wild spasms. Jack watched his friend deteriorate before him. His skin drew in on itself, like shrink wrap on wet plastic. His bones stuck out, in some places breaking through the now brittle skin. Max was turning into a corpse right in front of them.

"I don't get it," Lonetree said. "He's had to have killed hundreds of people over the years. Why would he give up now to save one little girl?"

Jack didn't have the same question in his mind. He knew. He knew because he also was a father and understood the bond. Understood a father's willingness to sacrifice himself so that his daughter could live. Max wasn't just saving a little girl, he was saving *his* little girl. Jack knew he would trade his own life in a second if he could get Sarah back safely. He leaned in so that Max could hear him. "That's it, isn't it? You did this for Jesse?"

Max nodded, but his eyes were unfocused. His head dipped as if he were drifting off to sleep.

"Listen. I need your help. Please, for the love of God, tell me who the Boss is. Tell me where they've taken Sarah." Max was drifting away, so Jack reached out to shake him awake. But when he grabbed his arm, his fingers sank into rotten flesh until he clutched bone. He pulled back his hand in disgust, bile rising in the back of his throat.

On a violent exhalation of breath that sent blood and spittle flying through the air, Max tried to form a word.

"Come on. Say it. COME ON."

Jack pleaded as he watched Max's eyes turn into pale blue clouds as clusters of cataracts grew like crystals.

"How do I stop them?" Jack shouted. "How do I stop them from killing my daughter?"

It was too late. Max was dead.

SIXTY-FOUR

They didn't have a plan. They parked around the corner and kept to the shadows as they jogged up to the hospital grounds. There were a half dozen cop cars in the parking lot, but only one of them was running. Lonetree pointed out the fire escape he'd used to break into the third floor on his first visit to Huckley. Framed in the window was the silhouette of a man in uniform. Lonetree looked through his field binoculars.

"That's a cop watching the window."

"Now what?" Jack asked.

"Don't worry about him. A little diversion in the front of the hospital, and he'll go check it out."

Jack asked the question that had been nagging at him. "Why didn't you kill Huckley when you sneaked in there the first time?"

"I needed to find out who would protect him. I knew about Janney, Max and Butcher, but I needed to see who else came out of the woodwork. The Boss is the one I'm looking for. You have to understand, I don't want to just kill these people. I want to punish them. What happened to your buddy Max back there is fine with me."

Jack didn't argue. As long as Lonetree was after the same people he was after, he didn't care where he got his motivation. Besides, if the unthinkable were to happen and Sarah were killed, he would welcome any punishment Lonetree meted out. In fact, he would be right next to him. "From what

Max said, it sounds like Huckley has turned into a loose cannon. I'm surprised someone didn't finish him off while he was in the coma."

"I've thought about that. I'm guessing the Boss has a use for him. Max said Huckley can communicate with the Source. Either Huckley is insane and imagining things, or the Source possesses some kind of sentient intelligence. Either way, I think it's time to screw with the Boss's plans. He wants Huckley alive. For me, that's a good enough reason to kill him. At least it will force the Boss to react."

Jack nodded, vaguely aware how he now talked about death and killing as easily as if he were planning strategy for a road trip. Still, something bothered him about Lonetree's first visit to Huckley's hospital room. "So if you weren't trying to kill him, what were you doing in his room?"

Lonetree looked away uncomfortably. "I did a ritual my father taught me when I was young. Wards off evil spirits."

"Huckley said there was something stopping him from getting to you. Called it Indian magic."

Lonetree shrugged his shoulders. "He hasn't bothered me at all."

"Except for almost killing you in the cave."

"I blame you for that. Maybe I should do the ritual to keep me safe from you and that trigger finger of yours." Lonetree's smile stood out in the dark.

Jack laughed. "Don't try to bond with me." Then his tone turned more serious. "If Janney's here, then I've got to get to him and make him talk."

"You think all those deputies with guns are going to let you do that?"

Frustrated, Jack said, "All right, you're the commando military guy. What should we do?"

"Like I said, it's time to do away with Huckley. Once he's gone, we might have a better chance to spook the others into the open. Maybe even give up your daughter."

Jack realized it was the first time Lonetree had mentioned Sarah in any of his plans. He appreciated the gesture but wondered if the big man was patronizing him. "Why would they do that?"

"No one wants to die. But I imagine guys who have the opportunity to live forever want to avoid death that much more. With a choice of facing me or releasing Sarah, they might let her go."

"But you're not going to stop if I get Sarah back."

"They don't know that, do they?" Lonetree said with a smile.

A shiver passed through Jack's body, and every hair stood upright on the back of his neck. He reached down for the gun Lonetree had given him and held it out. "Maybe you should take this. What if it happens again? What if Huckley forces me to use it on you?"

"He hasn't tried anything since we left the cave, so…" Lonetree shrugged. They were both in uncharted territory, the blind leading the blind. "Besides, the first mention of glowing bodies floating through the air, I'm going to shoot you in both arms. Just to be on the safe side."

"Before you do that, try disarming me first."

"I'll try," Lonetree said, his tone suggesting that his solution was much easier and more likely his first choice.

Jack looked back at the squad cars in the parking lot beneath them. He saw two uniformed police walk by the glass doors that led to the emergency room. "How about a plan?"

"Well, that depends on you."

"How so?"

Lonetree nodded to the gun in Jack's hand. "It depends. Would you rather go to the front of the hospital and create a massive diversion and then hold off about two dozen cops who will be trying to kill you?"

"And option two?"

"Climb up that fire escape, sneak into Huckley's room, and squeeze off five or six rounds into his chest."

Jack thought through his answer. A week ago he could never have contemplated taking another man's life. But things were different now. The bastard had his daughter. He nodded toward the fire escape. "Option two. I'll take Huckley."

"Are you sure? We're only going to get one shot at this. I can't have you getting in there and finding you don't have what it takes to pull the trigger."

"He wants to torture and kill my daughter. Trust me, I won't have a problem."

Lonetree stared into Jack's eyes for several long seconds. Finally, as if satisfied with what he saw in his companion's expression, he clapped him on the shoulder. "All right. Here's the plan."

SIXTY-FIVE

Lauren hung up the phone with Sushma, thankful that at least Becky was safe. Her eldest daughter had been quiet on the phone but didn't seem mad at her anymore. Lauren figured it was one more thing to thank Sushma for. She imagined that her friend had used the three hour car ride to help Becky understand that her mom was just looking out for her.

Whatever she said, it had worked. The last words her daughter said were, "I love you, Mom. Find Sarah for us."

It had taken everything Lauren had to keep her composure. She managed to talk in spite of the few tears that broke through the emotional wall she'd erected around herself. She told Becky she loved her too and that she would call again in the morning.

She looked around the room. Police and hospital staff were scattered around, all trying very hard to appear that they had not heard the whole conversation even though the room was small enough and quiet enough that not hearing every word was impossible. It was an act of kindness, this false privacy, but, like everything that night, it took on a devious quality in her mind. Instead of politeness, their faked indifference seemed like spying to her. How gullible did they think she was anyway?

A quick glance at the clock told her it was almost midnight, six hours since her phone call from Jack. She was beyond rationalizing the meaning of his disappearance. Five hours ago, she'd been convinced that he was in traffic somewhere. That he didn't want to take the time to pull over to a pay phone.

Four hours ago, she'd thought he might be in a car accident, again without a phone. She was worried for him and listened to the police scanners in the room, sure that word of a terrible accident would be announced any second. After that, her excuses for his absence ran out. She'd spent the last couple of hours facing the fact that perhaps her husband's mental illness was worse than she thought. Maybe Scott Moran wasn't a liar. Maybe Jack's delusions were really a leading indicator of more profound psychological issues. He'd sounded so manic on the phone. So paranoid.

Maybe he did take Sarah.

The thought welled up in her mind despite her insistence that it stay away from her. When the possibility first occurred to her, she'd prayed for it to be so, hoped to God that Jack had come in and taken Sarah away. Even delusional, she could never have imagined that Jack would ever hurt their little girl. But now, with hour after empty hour to contemplate Jack's bizarre behavior, she couldn't be sure. Maybe Jack was capable of hurting their baby. She hated herself for thinking it, but how could she not wonder? What mother wouldn't at least wonder?

The many police scanners spread throughout the room suddenly erupted in bursts of voices and static. Lauren couldn't understand the tinny radio voices, but the police and deputies in the room reacted immediately to what was being said. They surged out of their chairs and headed toward the entrance of the emergency room. The ones with their wits about them hung back with their guns drawn.

"What is it?" Lauren shouted to a deputy passing her. "What's going on?"

"Someone's shooting outside," the deputy said. "One of our guys is hit."

"Who's shooting?" Lauren called out.

But the deputy was already moving toward a window on the far side of the room. He braced himself in position and knocked out the window with the handle of his gun. Just as the last shards of glass hit the floor, Janney strode into the room.

"What the hell are you doing?" he shouted at the deputy. "What is this, a shootout in the Wild West for shit's sake? That window doesn't even look out over the parking lot, you moron!" He grabbed the deputy by the collar and pushed him toward the emergency door. "Get out there and see what's going on."

The voices on the scanner lost their edge of panic and Lauren started to get a feel for what was happening. A gunman, maybe more than one, was taking shots at the patrol cars in the parking lot. No one could tell where the shots were coming from.

Janney grabbed the scanner. "Sorenson? Are you hit?"

Static, then Sorenson's voice came over, "It's just glass. I thought I was hit, but the son-of-a-bitch blew out the windshield, and the glass nicked me in a few places."

"Nicked me in a few places," Janney mumbled under his breath, his rising temper evident to everyone in the room. He pressed a button on his walkie-talkie. "Find out who it is and take him out. Copy that? Lethal force is authorized." Janney marched toward the exit, striding past Lauren on the way out.

"I know what you're thinking," Lauren called out. "But you're wrong. Jack's never fired a gun in his life. There's no way that's him."

To Lauren's surprise, her words stopped the sheriff in mid-step. He stood with his back to her for a few seconds and then spun on his heel to face her. She was surprised to see a smile on his face. Janney walked up to her. "You know what, Dr. Tremont? I think you're right. Come this way, please." Ignoring her demands to be released, Janney grabbed her by the arm and pushed her past the open-mouthed hospital staff as they marched together toward the elevator.

SIXTY-SIX

Getting onto the fire escape had been a challenge. Only after four attempts and two banged up knees was Jack able to use the wall for leverage to reach the lowest metal rung. Lonetree made enough noise for a small army in front of the hospital. The gunshots echoed through the valley until it sounded like the forest around Midland General Hospital was reprising its role as a Civil War battlefield. *One hundred and thirty six Union and Confederate dead*, proclaimed the granite monument in the town square. Jack just hoped Lonetree was making sure the body count was slightly lower than that tonight.

He also hoped Lonetree was right, and that the guard on the third floor had left his post when the shots started. He tried to not think about what he would do if some young cop pulled a gun on him. Instead, he focused on not falling and killing himself on the fire escape.

The old metal walkways groaned under his weight and shifted uncomfortably as he pulled himself up. The window that opened onto the second floor was framed by the weathered painted words, "ESCAPE ROUTE. DO NOT BLOCK." He tried the window. Locked.

Not a good sign. Lonetree had said that both the first and second story windows were unlocked last time. If the third floor was locked too, he would have to break the glass and attract unwanted attention to himself.

Deciding to deal with it when he got there, Jack climbed the ladder to the next landing. The metal was rough and flaky, the whole apparatus a giant piece of rust, likely to collapse at any minute and send him crashing to the ground in a twisting tangle of metal shards.

He shook his head to clear the image. The ladder did sway slightly under his weight, but it felt secure enough. He kept climbing and reached the third floor landing.

The window was open.

Not just unlocked, but wide open.

Jack ducked into the shadows. There was no reason for the window to be open. It was a freezing night, and the hospital controlled its temperature precisely. He twisted back and forth to look into each dark shadow on the fire escape, sure that he would find someone lying in wait for him. There was no sign of the deputy.

Wanting to be sure, Jack craned his neck to look up to the roofline. Nothing. Maybe the cop had opened the window when he heard the first gunshots, trying to gauge where they were coming from. Then, realizing he was out of the action, had gone downstairs so he wouldn't miss out. After all, as a deputy in Midland, what were the chances of another shootout? Jack figured the scenario seemed plausible enough. He prayed it was true.

He tentatively stuck his head through the window and looked down the hall. Every muscle in his body was tense. If a cop or a nurse saw him, he would have only a few seconds to jump back down the fire escape – and lose his chance to kill Huckley – or climb through the window and somehow subdue whoever he saw.

Subdue. It was the word Lonetree had used. Jack wasn't sure if a nurse on her rounds would be someone he could bring himself to subdue or not. Pushing the doubts out of his mind, he climbed through the window and into the third floor hallway.

There was no question what room he was looking for. The number had been burned in his mind the day Sarah wrote it a thousand times with her crayons. The thought of Huckley taking control of Sarah's little body, of imposing his will on her, strengthened Jack's resolve to take action.

He jogged down the hall, his eyes darting back and forth looking for any movement. His hand slid under his shirt and pulled out Lonetree's .357 Magnum. *Anything smaller might just make him angry*, was Lonetree's explanation for the large caliber gun.

"Oh my God!" a woman called out from behind him. "Is that you, Mr. Tremont?"

Jack stopped breathing. He recognized the voice. He could picture the nurse's face but couldn't remember her name. He turned, careful to move the gun behind his back as he did so.

The nurse closed the door to the patient's room she had been in. "Thank God you're here. Dr. Tremont has been so worried. She – she..." The nurse's voice trailed off, and a puzzled expression replaced her joy of discovering him. Jack noticed her eyes darting down to where he held his hand behind his back. He was trying to stash the gun in his beltline, but it kept getting snagged on his sweater.

"Yes, yes," he stammered, "I got here as fast I could. I'm sorry. I don't remember your name."

The nurse didn't move forward. Her uncertainty was clear as she shuffled her feet in place. "Lucy Brookes. We've only met a couple of times," she said.

"That's right. I'm sorry. I'm terrible with names. I–" He lost his grip on the gun, and it fell onto the linoleum floor with a dull thud. Both he and the nurse stared at the gun. And then at each other. The color drained out of her face, and she started to shuffle back down the hall. There was more gunfire outside, and the nurse looked down the hall as if just then recognizing what the sounds meant. Jack reached down, grabbed the gun, and walked toward her with open arms, the gun pointing down at the floor.

"Listen, I can explain. It's not what you think." He checked behind the nurse to make sure his memory served him right. There was no stairwell at the end of this hall. Only five more rooms and then the window leading out to the fire escape.

"I don't think nothin'," Nurse Brookes promised, her eyes full of tears.

"I want you to go into this room right here and just wait in there. Will you do that?"

"What are up to? Are you after Dr. Tremont?"

"No, Lucy," Jack said in the most soothing voice he could muster. "I'm not going to hurt her. Please believe me."

The nurse had stopped moving. "I'm not going anywhere until you tell me what you're doing in my hospital with that gun."

Jack decided he'd been too calm. He raised the gun and barked, "I don't have time for this, Lucy. Either get in the room, or I'm going to shoot you in the Goddamn leg. Now what's it going to be?"

He knew he could never shoot her, but he counted on the nurse not knowing this fact. The threat and the sight of the barrel of a gun was enough to convince Lucy to give up her standoff.

With a shriek, she ducked into a room and slammed the door behind her. Jack went to the door to see if he could lock or wedge it closed somehow. As he approached the door, he heard Lucy talking excitedly to someone. At first he thought there might be a deputy in the room, but then he realized his mistake.

"Stupid. Stupid," he cursed out loud to the empty hallway. Each room had a phone. The nurse had already let them know he was there.

The window to the fire escape was only feet away from him. He could easily escape in time. Even if they thought to send someone over to the fire escape, Lonetree had them pinned down inside. But then Huckley would still be alive.

Jack made the decision in a matter of seconds. He had to finish what he started.

He turned and ran down the hall, making sure that the safety was off the gun. He reached room 320 and threw open the door.

The room was dark, illuminated only by the orange glow of life-support monitors. He didn't bother with the light. He didn't have time. Without pausing, without thinking, he ran up to the bed and pulled the trigger.

The explosion of the .357 Magnum jerked the handgun back in his hand. He steadied it and fired again. Each shot so loud in the small room that he thought he might go deaf.

The entire bed bucked when each slug slammed into it. Pieces of shredded cloth flew into the air. Sparks poured from the electrical equipment hit by shrapnel and threw bizarre shadows over the carnage.

Jack fired all six shots into the bed. He screamed through it all. A release of the tension and the frustration of the last days welling up inside him and coming out as a primal yell.

Then silence. Out of bullets and out of emotion, Jack simply stared at the scene in front of him.

"Hello, Jack."

When he turned, he felt like his brain turned in on itself.

There, standing in a row against the back wall, were Janney, Lauren, and Nate Huckley. Huckley wasn't in the bed. He was fully awake and dressed.

"Surprised to see me?" Huckley cracked.

Lauren pointed at Jack and shouted a warning. Too late, he realized she was pointing behind him. A flash of pain exploded in the back of his head. He felt himself falling. Then nothing.

SIXTY-SEVEN

"**W**ake up! WAKE UP!"

The words seemed to have solid form and beat against his brain like sonic chunks of concrete. The shouting was accompanied by a drum roll of dull metallic thuds. It wasn't until he opened his eyes that he could place the sound. A police baton being dragged across metal bars. The fuzzy outline of a face drifted on the other side of the jail cell. Slowly, it materialized into a smiling Deputy Sorenson.

"Hello, Mr. Tremont. I thought we might get to see each other again."

Jack sat upright and groaned from the sudden movement. He swayed in place as he waited for the blood rush to pass so he could reclaim his equilibrium. The world slowed its orbit around him, and he was able to focus enough to wish bad things on the deputy harassing him from the other side of the bars. An unexpected grunt behind him made him twist around to see who he was sharing the cell with. His worst fears were confirmed as he watched Joseph Lonetree roll over on the bunk in the corner.

Jack crawled over to Lonetree and poked him in the ribs. "Wake up," Jack said, surveying the many cuts and bruises on his face. "Jesus, you look how I feel."

Lonetree squinted and looked around the cell. "Is this the best room they have?"

"Great plan. We didn't accomplish anything and now…now look at us."

"Tell me you at least got Huckley."

Jack quickly explained what had happened. When he was done, Lonetree shook his head. "I knew I should have done it myself."

"Hey, looks like you're in this jail cell with me, buddy. How did *you* get caught by some small town cops?"

Lonetree shrugged. "Must be getting old." He pointed to Deputy Sorenson standing outside their cell. "That piece of shit got the drop on me from behind. Not much you can do when you have a gun pointing at your head."

"This guy is the one who roughed you up like this?"

"That was when his buddies showed up. I guess they were a little bent out of shape from me shooting at them. They hit like pansies though." Lonetree laughed and pointed to Deputy Sorenson. "Especially you, shithead. Complete pansy."

Sorenson started digging in his pockets for the keys, "You son-of-a—"

"Sorenson!" Janney shouted as he entered the cell block. "What the hell are you doing?"

The deputy, looking like a whipped dog, stuttered, "N-n-nothing...I was just—"

"Just about to open that door, get your ass kicked, and let these prisoners escape."

"I—"

"Get out of here," Janney growled, wrinkling his nose as if the deputy's incompetence were something he could smell. He waited for him to sulk out the door before turning his attention to Jack and Lonetree. "So hard to find good help these days." He grinned as he walked up to the cell. "What are we going to do with the two of you?"

Jack tried to contain the emotion in his voice, but still it came out trembling. "Where is Sarah? What have you done with her?"

Janney smiled. "Attempted murder. Assault against a police officer. Illegal firearms. Aggravated assault. So many charges, so little time." He leaned in close to the bars. "But we'll worry about that later. I brought a special visitor for you."

Jack looked to the door, expecting to see Lauren. Instead, he saw a man dressed in jeans and a white dress shirt, with skin so pale that his neck and shirt seemed to run together. Blue eyes stood out from the white flesh of his face, and two blood-red thin lines sufficed for a mouth. These two lines were twisted together in a wicked smirk as Nate Huckley strode into the cell block.

"Hello there. Good to see you again," Huckley said, draping one hand over the crossbar that ran across the center of the cell wall and waving the other through the air in an accentuated gesture. He looked over to Lonetree. "We haven't met. But I knew your brother well. He was…fascinating. I've never met a man with such endurance for pain."

Jack turned to Lonetree, expecting the man to run at the bars, maybe even tear through them and rip Huckley's throat out. But he stayed where he was. His chest heaved and his hands clenched at his sides, but he seemed to know that a lunge would be futile, probably even pleasing to his tormentor.

"Smarter than your brother. Not as hot headed," Huckley said. "Surprising. I would have thought the opposite, you being the family grunt and all." He turned his gaze on Jack. "And you. You've made your wife very unhappy. Don't you know it's extremely bad taste to kidnap your own daughter and then try to murder one of your wife's patients? I don't think she'll be visiting you any time soon."

"Where's Sarah?" Jack demanded. "What did you do with her?"

"Ummm, little Sarah. You know, she really is quite an interesting little girl. Not much to look at when you first see her, but when you get in here," – he tapped the side of his head – "my, my, my. Now that is a different story."

Jack charged up to the bars, "If you hurt her, if you touch her in any way, I'll–"

"You'll what?" Huckley laughed, waving his hands at the jail cell. "If I were you, I wouldn't spend the little time I had left to live making idle threats and fantasizing about saving my daughter. I suggest you take responsibility for your sins and ask for forgiveness before you die."

"Sins? What are you talking about?"

Huckley stared open mouthed. He looked over to Janney who took the cue to shake his head in disgust. "What sin? You can't be serious. You *trespassed* against me. You almost caused me to die." He reached for his throat as if the word alone caused him pain. "You sinned against me. And sinners must be punished."

"You're insane," Jack whispered. "What do you think you are? A god?"

Huckley laughed. "Think? No, Jack. I don't think I'm a god. I know it."

Movement behind Huckley caught Jack's attention. He looked at Janney just in time to catch a facial expression that he hadn't expected. His lips were curled back in unmistakable scorn at what Huckley said. Leaving one hand still wrapped around the cell bars, Huckley glanced over his shoulder to follow Jack's line of sight. The second he turned, Lonetree made his move.

Going from a standstill to full speed in one step, Lonetree jumped through the air, his right leg outstretched in a martial arts kick. The heel of his boot slammed into Huckley's knuckles, mashing the bones and flesh into the metal bars.

Huckley howled in pain. He raised his mangled hand in front of his face, looking at the shafts of bone sticking out from the skin. What had been a hand was now reduced to an unrecognizable claw.

Lonetree was back on his feet, admiring his work. "Now you're a one-handed god, you sick son-of-a-bitch."

Deputies clamored outside the door to the cell block, shouting questions through. Janney, unable to suppress a grin at Huckley's wailing, crossed over to the door and called through it, "Everything's all right. Don't worry." Then to Huckley, "Keep it down, will you?"

Huckley snarled at the command, for a moment more animal than man. But then he seemed to catch himself. He straightened, still cradling his destroyed hand against his stomach. Jack noticed the bleeding had already stopped. "Maybe you'll die with a little more dignity than your brother." He reached his good hand out. "Janney, give me your gun."

"No way. You're not doing it here." He nodded to the door that led out of the cell block. "Too many Midland cops here. Not possible."

Huckley closed his eyes and took a deep breath. He whispered, "You're right. You're right." It was quiet. Huckley stood with his eyes closed as if listening to soft music that only he could hear. When he opened his eyes, a wide smile spread across his face. "Little Sarah is ready," he said, slowly turning to face Jack. "Love to stay and talk, but there's work to be done."

Jack was desperate. "Wait. What is it about Sarah? You need a life, take mine. Trade her for me."

"You have no power to bargain. If I wanted your pitiful life, I'd just take it. I have the control here. You don't have a clue about your little girl, do you? What her true value is?"

Jack fell to his knees in front of Huckley. "I'll do anything.   Just   don't   hurt   her."

Lonetree gripped his shoulder. "He's not going to change his mind. Don't make this better for him."

"Don't listen to your Indian friend here. I encourage begging. It's so much like prayer. Still, he's right about one thing. I'm not going to change my mind. Your daughter is one in a million. I don't know, maybe she's entirely unique. I didn't understand why the Source wanted her so badly at first. In fact, it's still somewhat a mystery. I'll tell you this much though. After the accident, I woke up in a dream world as black as any cave. I was terrified, but then I saw your daughter. I saw her as the Source must see her. Sarah blazes with light. She's like a forest fire among candles. Psychic energy like I've never seen before. When she is put through the Taking ritual it will be unlike anything we've ever done. It will be magnificent." Huckley stared off into the distance. "I'll be free from all limits. I will be a god."

Jack felt the blood drain from his face. "She's just a little girl."

"Yes, a little girl that will change things forever. I can only imagine the kind of power I will get from her. Even people like you will not be able to deny my divinity."

Lonetree shouted to the sheriff. "You don't believe this bullshit, do you Janney? You think Huckley here is a god?"

Huckley held up the hand Lonetree had mangled. The injury had already completely healed. "Nothing can hurt me," Huckley said. "Nothing." Then he turned to Janney. "I need to go. Everyone knows to be there?"

"Everything is set up." Then in a lower voice he added, "Are you sure this can't wait? There are a lot of outsiders around. If we just–"

Huckley held up his hand. "The Boss gave the order. This happens tonight."

Jack leaned forward to hear Janney's reply. "It's not worth the risk."

Huckley patted the sheriff on the cheek, a little harder than necessary. "Janney, how would you know? Besides, you're to follow orders. Let us do the worrying, all right?" He motioned back to Jack and Lonetree. "And Janney–"

"Yes?"

"Make sure they suffer before they die."

This comment seemed to brighten Janney's mood. "Not a problem."

They left the room together, leaving Jack and Lonetree behind to guess at their fates.

SIXTY-EIGHT

Lauren sat back in her chair and rubbed her temples. The three Tylenols she had taken an hour earlier barely touched her throbbing headache. It originated in a knot of twisted muscles and nerves at the base of her neck, shot out across her skull, and seemed to be digging a hole behind her right eye. She needed rest, but she knew sleep was impossible. Her daughter was still missing. Her husband, now a cold-blooded would-be murderer, was incarcerated in the Midland jail three blocks away. She could hardly sit still for a few minutes, let alone lie down. Sleep, she decided, would have to wait.

Her call to the FBI had gone nowhere. It was like no one had ever heard of her case, or it was such a small priority that they couldn't be bothered to remember. She pictured a busy room full of agents, computer screens, phones ringing, and, on a corner desk that no one really used, a tiny Post-it note with Sarah's information scribbled on it. Just one more little girl missing. One of thousands abducted each year. Abducted and never found. At least an agent had told her he would dig around and call back once he found out who was on the case.

She crossed the hospital cafeteria which had become the impromptu command center for the dual investigations of the kidnapping and shootings by the two madmen the police had taken into custody. *Madmen. My Jack was one of them.* Even though she had been right there, seen the rage in his face as he screamed and fired the gun into the bed, even though she'd seen all of that, she could hardly believe it. Deep down, the analytical part of her understood why she was so reluctant to accept Jack's actions.

If he was capable of that, then he could have taken Sarah. Could have hurt her. Could have...

She wouldn't allow herself to go any further. She couldn't handle that right now. She couldn't handle that ever.

The automatic coffee maker finished perking, so she slid the glass pot off of the heating element and refilled her mug. She usually drank it black, but she reached for the cream and sugar to cut the bitterness of the dark roast. Her stomach was already rebelling over the first eight cups she had downed that night. She circled the spoon around the mug, allowing herself to be mesmerized by the dark brown coffee giving way to gentle tan swirls of cream.

The same questions filtered through her mind that had nagged her all night. How could Jack go so far, so quickly? The car accident with Huckley had been a few days ago. The waking dream – and the scare with the baseball bat – was just two nights ago. She cursed herself for agreeing to move from California, agreeing to help Jack run away from the memory of the *first* car accident. Maybe Moran was right and it really had started back then. Maybe by moving to Maryland, Lauren had helped set the actions in motion. Thick layers of blame wrapped around her conscience. And it felt right; felt like it belonged there. After all, she was responsible for Sarah, and now she was gone. No matter what, the responsibility for that would always come back to her.

Still, something bothered her. Obviously, Jack had psychological problems, his actions since his accident with Huckley showed that. But he had still been coherent. Still Jack. More paranoid, sure, but still rational. So how did he turn into that animal she'd seen in Huckley's room in just one day?

The only blessing was that Huckley had revived from the coma earlier that afternoon. The charge against Jack would not be murder, only attempted murder. But Huckley's sudden recovery was another strange part of the story. It wasn't that uncommon in strictly medical terms. Patients in comas quite often regained consciousness after a week or two. Some even did so after more than a year. More rare, but still it happened.

The strange thing about Huckley's case was the speed of his recovery. Patients in a coma for a period of time usually woke up weak, disoriented, and required several days of rest to recuperate. But Huckley was packed and ready to leave just hours after he regained consciousness. He acted as if he'd been in the hospital for nothing more than a routine checkup.

Dr. Mansfield had conducted the examination, and Lauren had taken little notice when word filtered through the hospital of the bizarre recovery. While his case on a normal day would have been an irresistible medical curiosity, it couldn't compete with the unfolding tragedy of Sarah's disappearance.

Now, with so many empty hours and nothing to do but let her mind wander, and with Huckley more linked to her family than ever, she gave the man's sudden recovery more thought. Especially after the strange moment between her and Huckley last night.

Lauren had only made eye contact once with Huckley during the ordeal of Jack's arrest. Janney had stood between the two of them as they waited for Jack to appear. She had been both indignant and scared. Mad from being dragged to the third floor against her will. Terrified that Jack might actually show up.

It was after the horror of seeing Jack fire the gun at the pillows stuffed under the covers of Huckley's bed that she caught the look from Huckley. It happened when Janney was handcuffing Jack, sprawled unconscious on the floor from the blow administered by one of the Midland cops. She turned her head, not trying to look at anything, just to look away, when her eyes locked with Huckley's.

He had been staring at her, she was sure of it. And he was smiling. Not a self-satisfied smile of triumph, but a licentious crooked turn of his lips, an unwelcome appraisal of her body that made her feel naked, violated. On her skin, she had imagined she felt the foreign touch of strong fingers moving their way up her leg, up her back, across her chest. She had reached for her clothes, pulling on them as if spiders crept across her skin. But, just as suddenly as it had started, the sensation disappeared. And when she looked up, Huckley was no longer looking at her. He was following Janney and Jack out of the door. But as she watched him leave, Huckley had raised one hand and waved his fingers in what seemed to be a slow, mocking farewell.

Lauren noticed her knuckles had turned white from gripping her coffee cup as she relived the encounter. She took a sip and rested the rim of the mug against her lips, inhaling the steam, letting it soothe her.

This waiting around was killing her. As a doctor, she always had a course of action. There was always another test to run or more research to perform. There was always hope for a cure and a sense that somehow she could contribute to that cure.

But this was different. Sarah was gone and there was nothing she could do to bring her back. Except wait. Wait and let the professionals do their jobs. And that was the other problem. The professionals were not quite the varsity team of law enforcement. The Midland police were only slightly better than the Keystone Kops. Janney was an egomaniac who seemed more interested in prosecuting Jack than finding her daughter. And if her phone call was any indication, the FBI didn't give a damn.

She had cried enough. Now she was getting angry. She had given the police their chance. She had done everything they asked, including not visiting Jack in the jail. But listening to the police had accomplished nothing. If Jack kidnapped their daughter, she needed to talk to him, needed to reach out. Maybe she could get him to tell her where their baby was hidden. Lauren decided she didn't give a damn what the police said. She was going to talk to Jack whether Janney liked it or not.

SIXTY-NINE

Jack stood on the bed to look out of the barred window set high in the wall. The jail was one of the town's historic landmarks, old brick and mortar walls and open beamed ceilings that belied the fact that it was still a functioning police station. But improvements had kept it up with the times. In the rear of the building, away from the tourists, the metal bars were the same forged steel found in any big city jail, and the floor was covered in shiny institutional linoleum for easy clean-up after locking up the drunks on Friday and Saturday nights.

The window gave him a decent view of the Savage River as it flowed through town. Besides thick metal bars, the window was secured by two sheets of thick Plexiglass, one bolted inside and the other outside. Someone had spent their jail time etching deep grooves in the plastic. Jack wondered if they had been bored or actually pathetic enough to think they could escape.

The door to the cell block opened. Since he and Lonetree were the only prisoners, he assumed the visitor was for them. He felt his heart beat in his throat when he realized who it was.

"Thank God." He cried as he crossed to the bars. Her expression was cold and severe, but he didn't care. At last he'd have a chance to explain things to her. But then another figure followed her into the cell block. Janney.

Lauren turned to the sheriff. "I told you I want to see him alone." Janney hesitated. "What? Are you afraid I'll slip him a file and break him out of here?" she snapped.

Janney nodded. "Five minutes. That's it, all right?" he said as he left the room.

"Jack," she said, forcing a smile. "Have they given you medical treatment?"

Jack waved off the question. "I know who has Sarah." Lauren nodded for him to go on. He noticed her expression wasn't hopeful. Jack's words tumbled over themselves, "It's Janney. Janney and Huckley working together."

"Sheriff Janney?" Lauren said slowly. "You think the sheriff kidnapped our daughter?"

Jack heard the condescension in her voice. He took a deep breath and gathered his thoughts. "Listen, what I have to tell you is hard to believe. I didn't believe it myself until I saw the evidence. I need you to trust me." He reached out and gripped her hands. She held on loosely.

"I'll try. But—"

"No," he whispered. "Don't say anything else. Leave it at you'll try."

"Okay. Tell me."

Jack hesitated. He needed to make Lauren understand. "This is Joseph Lonetree. He's the man who came to the house a few days ago, the same night that I had those hallucinations. He's who I've been with since I left Dr. Moran's office yesterday afternoon."

Lauren's eyes shifted over to the hulking man in the corner. He smiled and nodded as if the gesture alone validated Jack's story. "Go on."

"Lonetree's father and brother were both working on an archeological theory before they were murdered by people interested in keeping their past a secret. He came back to get revenge for their deaths. It just so happens that the people he wants revenge against are the same ones who have been screwing with our lives. The same ones who took Sarah."

Lauren shook her head. "I don't understand. They were killed over a theory?"

"This is going to sound crazy," Jack winced at his own choice of words, "but keep an open mind until I'm done. The theory *was* the truth. It revolves around an ancient Indian tribe..." Jack gave a short version of the story related by the rock carvings in the cave. He described the cave itself and, finally, the story Max Dahl had told about Huckley. When Jack started telling about Max's sudden death and his body's deterioration, Lauren held up her hand for him to stop.

"I can't do this," she sobbed, "I just can't listen to this anymore. I don't know how this man has made you believe all of this, but it's sick. You need help." She gently took his hand again. "And I want to help you. I'll get the best doctors and we'll work through this, all right? But right now I need one thing from you." She pulled his hands until she brought him face to face with her through the bars. "Where's Sarah? Tell me where she is so I can go get her. Please. Will you just do that for me?"

Jack pushed back away from her. "You still think I took her! It's Janney and Huckley. And someone they call the Boss. They're taking her to the cave tonight. They're going to kill her, Lauren. They're going to kill our little girl."

"Listen to yourself. Now there's someone called the Boss trying to..." Lauren put her hands to her head and squeezed her temples. "Look, I don't want to argue. I want to help."

"You saw the numbers Sarah wrote on those papers at the house. Huckley's room number. You know something strange is going on."

"I talked to Dr. Moran last night. The psychiatrist. He told me you admitted to him that you wrote those numbers yourself."

"Jesus. Moran's one of them! You can't trust him. He's lying. Can't you see what they're doing? They're trying to turn you against me."

"Just tell me where Sarah is. Please, honey. Will you do that?"

Jack shook his head. "I swear to God all of this is true. You have to believe me. You're the only one who can stop them now."

With one last pained look, Lauren turned and walked to the door. It opened as soon as she knocked.

Jack shouted after her, "YOU HAVE TO STOP THEM, LAUREN. YOU'RE THE ONLY ONE WHO CAN!"

Once the door slammed shut, Lonetree grunted from the corner, "That went well."

Jack pressed his head against the bars and squeezed his eyes shut. Never before had he felt so alone. It was already mid-morning. In only a few hours his little girl would die. And there was nothing he could do to stop it.

SEVENTY

The day passed with tortuous certainty. Each minute followed the next no matter how hard Jack prayed for a reprieve. Lonetree kept a respectful silence and distance from his cellmate as if he knew better than to offer any consoling words. Jack sat on the top bunk and alternately stared at the ceiling and out the window at the approaching storm.

Low, black clouds came down from the north, which this time of year meant snowfall was a possibility. These clouds weren't the soft grey of early season snow, but the angry darkness of massive thunderstorms the valley was known for. Jack thought it fitting. The growing weather matched his mood.

Around four in the afternoon, the rain started. A soft *pat-pat-pat* against the Plexiglass rectangle that served as their window. Trees started to jag back and forth as the wind gusted from multiple directions. Thunder rumbled down the length of the valley, far off, but still strong enough to make the Plexiglass shudder like the skin of a beaten drum. Jack peered out of the window. Judging from the sky, it was going to be a bad night. But then again, he'd known that before he looked out the window.

The door to the cellblock opened, and Janney came in to check on his prisoners. He looked freshly showered, his still-damp hair combed back, his face clean-shaven. *Like he's ready to go to church*, Jack thought.

"Just wanted to make sure your stay with us is comfortable," Janney said.

"Don't do this. I'll do anything. Just let her go."

Janney looked pleased, as if he relished taking over Huckley's tormentor role. "Just let her go, huh? You think that would be a good idea?"

Lonetree pulled himself to his feet. "You're wasting your time. Huckley and the Boss call the shots. The sheriff here can't take a crap without asking first. Isn't that right, Janney?"

Janney's obvious pleasure at Jack's groveling disappeared, and his usual scowl returned. "No one tells me what to do. Not Huckley. Not anyone."

Lonetree continued to bait him. "Yeah, that was obvious today. Huckley's a god, right? What does that make you then? His servant? Are you going to worship him when he tells you to?" He sneered at Janney. "Did Huckley ask you to take a shower? He probably likes his worshippers nice and clean, huh?"

"You're already a dead man, Lonetree. You're just choosing how painful it's going to be."

Lonetree spat through the bars. "You're pathetic. You're just going to sit there tonight and watch Huckley acquire more power over you. Him and this Boss character. Who is this guy anyway? Is he even around here? Do you let him order you around too? Maybe that's your deal. You like taking orders."

"Shut up."

"Yeah, that's you, Janney. Playing the bitch for all the big dogs."

Janney's nostrils flared and color rushed to his face. Jack watched him finger his gun and wondered if the temptation would prove too much. Maybe that was Lonetree's goal. A quick death instead of the slow torture promised them.

"You don't know anything. The Source gives us all power. Tonight we'll all get a fix, not just Huckley."

"But the Boss and Huckley most of all, right?" Lonetree smirked. "God, you're pathetic."

Jack thought Janney might pull his gun and shoot Lonetree on the spot. Instead, he slid the palm of his hand over his head, smoothing his hair down flat against his scalp. A broad smile broke out across his face. "You're something else. A real prize. I'm going to enjoy watching you die. Slowly." He turned and walked down to the door leading out of the cell block. He called out, "Take care, boys. It might be a rough one for you." Then he was gone.

Jack turned to Lonetree. "What the hell were you doing?"

Lonetree sat on the lower bunk and started to take off his boots. "Some of that stuff was just to make him mad, but there was a lot of truth to it. You can tell Janney hates playing second string to Huckley. I'm just trying to help that resentment along."

"So what does that do for us?" Jack said.

"Two things. First, a wedge between Huckley and Janney is something we might be able to exploit later. I wanted to put it in the front of his mind. Second, he just confirmed where they are all going to be tonight, right?"

Jack replayed the conversation in his head. "At the Source. In the cave. But we knew that."

"Not really. They could have called it off because of the police presence. The storm. Anything. We assumed they were going to the cave, but now we know. Not only that, but we know they'll all be there together. He told us both Huckley and the Boss will be in the cave. It's a great opportunity. Once again our interests match up, Jack. All the bad guys I want and the little girl you want will all be in the same place tonight."

"Great. Good information to have while we sit here in jail." He turned to look at Lonetree tugging at the heel of one of his boots. "And what the hell are you doing with your boots?"

The heel snapped off. Lonetree held it out toward Jack who shrugged his shoulders at the solid piece of black rubber. Lonetree grinned as he slowly turned it over to reveal a hollowed out interior filled with a light grey substance. He stuck one of his fingers into the heel and scooped out some of the contents.

"What is it?"

"This, my friend, is C-4 plastic explosive."

"You walk around with plastic explosive in your boots?"

"Sure, doesn't everyone?" Lonetree grinned. "The Navy told me it was guaranteed to put a spring in my step." He lowered his voice and turned serious. "Now that we know where the bad guys are going and that Janney's already left, what do you say we break out of this shit hole?"

Jack grabbed Lonetree by the arm. "Wait. You had the ability to break out of here all day and you didn't tell me about it?"

"I needed the Boss to think I was neutralized. Otherwise he might have disappeared. Besides, if I had told you about the explosives this morning, Huckley might have been able to read your mind and the whole thing would have been blown. Besides, would you have been willing to wait all day like we needed to?"

"You son-of-a-bitch. They could have killed Sarah already."

"But they didn't."

"You didn't know that for sure," Jack said.

"Listen, nothing is ever for sure. I figured it would be hard for everyone to sneak away until the night. There has to be media everywhere out there. Kind of hard for the sheriff to disappear in the middle of the day for a quick human sacrifice."

Lonetree took a deep breath. "Look, we can keep talking about this, which will accomplish exactly nothing, or we can break out of here. What do you want to do?"

Jack forced himself to let go of his anger. Lonetree was right. It was already done. "Okay. Just promise me that you'll keep me in the loop from now on. Agreed?" Lonetree nodded, but Jack knew his companion would continue to inform him of his plans on a need-to-know basis. Without any other option, he realized he would have to live with it.

"Before I ask what the plan is to break out of here, I want to point out that the last two times you were in charge of our strategy things didn't turn out so well. One plan left behind a decomposing body and the other landed us both in jail."

Lonetree smiled. "Let's hope the third time's the charm."

SEVENTY-ONE

Lauren didn't know where to turn. Her visit to the jail that morning had been a disaster. Jack's raving story only made things worse. He saw enemies everywhere he looked, enemies with supernatural powers. He believed that he, alone, had the information that could stop terrible events about to destroy them all. Clearly her husband was suffering from paranoid delusions. Even a first year med student could have made the diagnosis.

It didn't make sense. Even with the problems in California, there had never been anything like this. Jack had never acted paranoid before or reported hallucinations of any kind. She thought there would have at least been warning signs. Something to indicate a meltdown this extreme was possible. She searched her memory but came up blank. And that's what scared her. There must have been *some* sign, and she had missed it. Coils of guilt wrapped tightly around her. She was stunned by her failure as a mother and a wife. How could she have been so oblivious? How could she have let this happen?

She shook her head to clear her bout of self-pity. The hospital cafeteria was empty now. The police and sheriff's deputies had moved out once they took Lonetree and Jack into custody. As far as they were concerned, the police had the kidnappers, and now it was just a matter of making them talk. The police had all avoided making eye contact with her as they packed up their things. She wasn't sure if it was pity for her lost child or scorn for her helplessness.

Even the hospital staff was uncomfortable around her, scurrying by with heads down. She didn't fixate on it. It wasn't like she was being shunned by lifelong friends. In reality, the people here were strangers to her, more associates than friends. And that's what made her feel so alone.

She tried to call Sushma to check on Becky but reached her answering service. She left a short message for her daughter assuring her that everything was going to be all right. Lauren's throat constricted as she told the lie into the lifeless machine. Everything wasn't going to be all right. Nothing would ever be all right again. She hung up the phone. The halls were silent as she walked up to her office. She closed and locked the door. She needed privacy.

She sat at her desk, her thick padded chair wrapped comfortably around her. Without thinking, she snatched up a pen and started twirling it in her hand, a nervous habit left over from medical school. With a kick, she spun the chair around so it faced the credenza covered with framed photos of her family. She leaned forward, picked up a large metal frame and laid it on her lap.

The photo was from their trip to the Grand Canyon. Taken from the canyon's edge, it showed all of them together, even Buddy with his long tongue hanging out the side of his mouth. They'd gone in the late fall when the desert air had a cold edge. The girls' cheeks were red from the chill. Both Sarah and Becky beamed with jack-o-lantern smiles as they waved at the camera.

Lauren turned the picture over. This wasn't helping.

She picked up the phone, hesitated, and then punched in Dr. Mansfield's extension. After five rings she hung up and called the on-duty nurse.

"Yes, Dr. Tremont?" the nurse answered.

"I'm looking for Dr. Mansfield. Is he in the hospital?"

"Let me check." There was a muffled noise as Lauren heard the nurse ask someone if they had seen him. She came back on the line. "He's downstairs. Said he wanted to be notified when they came to get the Rodriguez girl's body."

"That can't be right. He told me they took her yesterday. That she'd already been cremated."

Again, muffled voices before the nurse was back on the line. "I've got the file right here. Felicia Rodriguez. TOD 22:14 hr on Thursday. She's being picked up today. I'm sure if it." The nurse paused. "Do you want me to send someone down to get him? Dr. Tremont? Hello?"

But Lauren was gone, already out her door and headed for the stairwell. It was only two flights down to the morgue, and she meant to get there fast. Lauren took the stairs as fast as she could, her mind running full speed as she clambered down.

She couldn't understand why Dr. Mansfield had lied to her. She wanted to believe there was a mistake. That she would get to the morgue and find a different body being removed, not Felicia Rodriguez.

But she was suspicious. The way Dr. Mansfield had handled Felicia's death had bothered her from the beginning. One thing was for sure, if it *was* Felicia he was discharging for burial, there were going to be problems.

She jumped the last few stairs and yanked on the basement door. Locked. The stairwell doors were never locked. It was against fire code. Luckily she'd brought her keys with her, which included a master for the hospital doors. She slid it into the keyhole and cranked it. When she heard the bolt slide back, she turned the handle and yanked open the door.

The stairwell door was next to the elevator at the end of the corridor opposite the morgue. She looked to her right at the elevator first. A metal folding chair was jammed between the doors to keep them open. She knew the "Hold Elevator" button could be overridden by an emergency key that every doctor had in case they needed to move a patient. Even though this override function was rarely used, someone wasn't taking any chances that the elevator would be called away.

She swung her head around to the left, looking down the hallway. At the far end, the door to the morgue was also propped open. Her first thought was that she was too late. They had already transported the body. But a quick glance back to the elevator changed her mind. No, they had to still be down there. Dr. Mansfield had to be in the cooler getting the body ready.

On the way down the stairs, she had imagined how she would confront the old doctor when she saw him. Demand to know what he was doing. But now, standing alone in the basement, dark shadows in every corner from the poor lighting, she felt her nerve slipping.

It wasn't that she believed Jack, not at all, it was just – *Just what?* she asked herself. So, maybe some of Jack's paranoia had rubbed off on her. That was no reason to shrink away from her duties as a doctor. This was a question of protocol. If Dr. Mansfield was trying to cover-up something about Felicia's death, it was her responsibility to find out what it was.

Still, when she heard Dr. Mansfield's voice rumble down the hall, she instinctively reached behind her for the door and twisted the handle. Fear spread down her spine like freezing water. With one foot already back in the stairwell, she watched Dr. Mansfield emerge from the morgue pulling a gurney.

Go get the police, Lauren. Don't do this by yourself.

No sooner had the thought torn through her mind than she saw who pushed the other end of the gurney. She had only met him once, but she would not forget Scott Moran's face for a long time. His words had devastated her conceptions of her husband. Hell, his short conversation with her had devastated her life. She just couldn't understand what he was doing in the morgue. It didn't make any sense.

Neither of the men had seen her yet. Giving in to her instincts, she hurried back into the stairwell and pushed the door shut, hoping the final click of the lock engaging didn't sound as loud in the basement as it did to her.

With the door closed, she turned and ran up the stairs. She burst through the door into an empty hallway on the first floor. Earlier that day there had been police everywhere, but now the place was deserted. Running toward the cafeteria, she tried to get her thoughts in order. What was she doing? Wasn't it plausible that the nurse had made a simple error? That Lauren hadn't heard of one of Dr. Mansfield's patients dying last night? Was grabbing a cop to confront and accuse a respected doctor of hiding a body really what she wanted to do? God, she was so confused. And exhausted. She needed help.

Styrofoam cups still littered the cafeteria tables, but all other signs of the command post for Sarah's search were gone. The room was empty. As far as the police were concerned, the case was solved. Now it was just a matter of finding a body. Dragging the river. Looking in dumpsters. Before her mind could go too far down that path, Lauren decided to go to reception. There had to be someone in this Goddamned hospital.

She spun around and ran straight into Sheriff Janney. It shocked her and she let out a short scream.

"Whoa there," Sheriff Janney said. "I didn't mean to sneak up on you."

Lauren took a few steps back, getting herself back in control. "No, I'm sorry. Just a little jumpy is all."

"Listen, can I get you anything?" he asked. "Have someone drive you home, maybe?"

She shook her head. Janney hadn't been her favorite person through this ordeal, but now, given how things had turned out, she wrestled with the fact that the sheriff had been right. Jack had been the threat. Grudgingly, she recognized that Janney had just been doing his job.

"Mrs. Tremont," he said softly, genuine concern on his face. "How can I help you?"

"There is something," she finally said, making her decision to trust him. She told him about Dr. Mansfield.

Janney nodded as she expressed her concerns, both for what the doctor might be doing and how it would look if she were accusing him unjustly. "Tell you what," Janney said, "we'll go down and see what's going on. Just you and me. No need to tell anyone else. That way if it's no big deal, it's no big deal. Sound good?"

Lauren nodded. After voicing her concerns about Dr. Mansfield, she felt self-conscious, suddenly sure that the whole thing was a result of her overwrought mind. "Thanks, I really appreciate it."

"No problem," Sheriff Janney said, following Lauren back to the stairwell. "In fact, you wouldn't believe how glad I am that I ran into you."

SEVENTY-TWO

"**I**s that enough?" Jack asked as he leaned in to get a better look. To him, the thin ribbon of what looked like grey play-dough wrapped around the thick steel bar seemed inadequate.

"The shape of the charge is more important than the amount of explosive used," Lonetree explained as he curved the C-4 into small half-moon shapes. "These little guys will cut through the bars and probably won't spray shrapnel on us at all."

"Probably?"

Lonetree smiled. "It's more an art than a science." He handed a few of the small crescents to Jack. "Wrap these around the inside base of the bar. One per bar." He noticed Jack's nervousness handling the material. "Don't worry. It can't go off until I put in the blasting filament."

Jack looked at the wire curled up on Lonetree's lap. "Looks like fishing line."

"It's made special for booby traps. And that's what we're making."

"We agreed no killing if possible, right?" Jack asked.

"Don't worry. We're going for minimal collateral damage."

"Some of the cops out there are hardly more than teenagers."

"They might get banged up a little, but nothing too serious."

Together, they rigged the explosives. Within five minutes they were ready. Transparent wire connected each of the charges, ran along the floor to the back wall of the cell, and terminated in the trigger device in Lonetree's hand. After getting Lonetree's signal, Jack reached up and pressed a large red button on the door of the cell. They'd been told to use the call button sparingly, or it would be turned off. He breathed a little easier when he heard a ring in the outside office.

No one came.

He hit the button again.

They waited a full minute and still the door remained closed.

Jack and Lonetree exchanged looks. Jack guessed they were thinking the same thing. What if Janney had left instructions that no one go into the cell block? If so, the whole operation became trickier. They could get out of the cell but not without alarming however many police were in the next room. By the time they set the charge and blew the door that led out of the cell block, there would be a wall of guns lined up against them.

Jack thumped the buzzer with his fist. Hitting it repeatedly and yelling at the door.

Finally, the door opened.

Jack recognized the man. He was one of the Midland police, tall and lanky, probably in his twenties even though teenage acne covered his neck and cheeks.

He closed the door behind him and did his best to look impatient. "What d'ya guys want?"

Jack backed away from the bars. "We're getting hungry."

"You just ate. What d'ya think this is? A hotel?" He walked closer, snorting from his own joke.

Lonetree waited until the young cop reached the far corner of the cell, then he yelled, "NOW!"

Jack turned his back and covered his ears. Lonetree punched the detonator. There was a flash of light, then a series of explosions. Jack's ears stung from the concussion wave even though his hands clutched the side of his head. Blue-grey smoke hung suspended in the cell, and the air burned from the chemicals in the explosives.

Lonetree rushed past him, waving his hands to clear out the smoke. Most of the bars they had fixed with C-4 had shorn off cleanly and now lay on the floor. Two bars still hung in place, but a well-placed kick from Lonetree sent them crashing to the ground.

Jack surged forward and followed Lonetree through the smoke. The young cop was on the ground, holding his ears and moaning. Blood covered his face.

Lonetree dragged the cop to his feet, deftly grabbing the gun from his holster. "Tsk, tsk. You should know better than to bring a weapon into a jail cell." He turned to Jack. "Thank God for small town cops."

"Is he all right?" Jack asked, waving his hand in front of the dazed man's face.

"Only scrapes. No real injuries that I can tell." He put the gun to the young man's head just as the door leading to the police headquarters opened. "STOP RIGHT THERE. WE HAVE A HOSTAGE."

Jack followed Lonetree out of the cell block into the exterior room. There were six police that they could see. The office space was set up without walls, so there was no place for anyone to hide and the window shutters were pulled shut. Finally, luck seemed to be on their side.

In less than five minutes, they disarmed the officers and herded them into the still intact jail cells. Lonetree dragged the young cop around with him and barked at the others to follow in order to save their friend's life. Jack checked the officers for weapons and removed their radios to make sure they couldn't call for help.

With all the police in one cell and the door closed behind them, Jack and Lonetree took a minute to catch their breaths.

Lonetree slapped Jack on the back. "You did good. Kind of wild, huh?"

"Actually, yeah. It was a rush."

"The looks on their faces..." Lonetree laughed.

"I wish we had on that on video."

"If you ask nice, maybe they'll give you a copy." Lonetree nodded up to the corner of the room. Jack looked up to see a camera mounted on the wall, the red light on.

"Great. How about we get the hell out of here?"

"Right." Lonetree started searching through the desk nearest him. "Look for car keys."

Jack turned and patted the papers on the desk. "I've been thinking about access to the cave. There has to be an easier way. There's no way Huckley and the others are going in the way we did."

"There's another entrance. I've seen it from inside the cave. There's an elevator going up a crude mineshaft. Using GPS, I figure the entrance is somewhere on Huckley's property. That's how we'll go in. Even if they hear us coming, they won't be able to escape without running right into us. Find any keys?"

Jack raised his hand in the air and shook a plastic container full of keys. "I think this is what we're looking for."

Lonetree walked over and took the container. "Perfect. I'll drive."

SEVENTY-THREE

Sheriff Janney opened the basement door for Lauren. When she hesitated, he smiled and offered to go first. Lauren shook her head and stepped into the basement. The corridor looked the same as when she had left. Both the morgue and elevator doors were jammed open. But now there was a gurney in the elevator. Lauren assumed it was the same one Dr. Mansfield and Scott Moran had been pushing. Faint noises came from the morgue at the end of the hallway.

"I'm going to see who that is," Lauren whispered, pointing to the elevator. She hoped she could take a quick look, see that the body was actually one of the terminal patients from the third floor, and sneak back upstairs without Dr. Mansfield ever finding out about her suspicions. Janney nodded and followed closely behind her. Lauren stepped over the chair that held the doors open.

Lauren inched her way toward the cadaver's head. The body bag zipped vertically, so Lauren only had to unzip a few feet to expose the face.

She pulled slowly, noticing that her hands trembled as she did so. The stench from the rotting body wafted into her nostrils as soon as the bag's seal was broken.

Under her breath she whispered, "What are you, back in med school? Afraid of a cadaver? Get a grip, Lauren." With a final tug, she pulled down the zipper to the body's chest, pushed away the edges of the bag, and stood back.

The body was in horrible condition. Dark sores had eaten deep into the flesh, especially across the girl's chest. Clusters of raised bumps covered the neck and jowls, like massive spider bites that had been scratched until they bled. The cadaver's face was swollen and blotched with crimson rashes that looked like burn wounds, making the girl's features almost unrecognizable. Lauren stood with her back against the elevator wall. The type of pustules were the same. The rash. The discoloration. All the same.

But it wasn't Felicia.

It could only mean one thing. This girl was another case of the same disease that had killed Felicia. The disease was contagious, and Dr. Mansfield was trying to keep it a secret. But why? What the hell did the old man think he was doing?

"What is it?" Janney asked from outside the elevator. "Is it your patient?"

Lauren was going to re-zip up the body bag, but it really didn't matter now. The hospital would have to be quarantined until the pathogen was identified. If it was an airborne contagion, they were already exposed anyway. She left the bag open, the girl's face staring blankly at the elevator wall. "No, it's someone else."

"So there's no problem."

"No, there's quite a large problem," Lauren said, not ready to scare Janney with the details quite yet. She felt her confidence return to her. This was the type of situation she had been trained to deal with. Something that required an ordered medical response. First, she had to find out if there were other cases. The answer to that was down the hall in the morgue with Dr. Mansfield. "Come with me, Sheriff."

"Yes, ma'am," Janney said, falling into step behind her.

Lauren hoped the noises coming out of the morgue were enough to cover the sound of their footsteps as they marched down the corridor. With a deep breath, Lauren turned the corner and walked into the morgue.

There was a gurney in the center of the room. Judging from the outline visible under the white sheet, it held another cadaver, this one smaller than the one in the elevator. *That's Felicia*, Lauren thought. *It has to be.* She tore he eyes away from the body and looked up at the man who had violated her trust. Dr. Mansfield was bent over one of the body drawers, helping Moran pull himself out. They both froze in place when she appeared.

"What you are you doing here?" Dr. Mansfield demanded.

"What am I doing here? Jesus! What are *you* doing?" She noticed his eyes dart behind her as Janney walked in. She was glad she had thought to get the sheriff before she came down. "What is he doing in there?" she said, pointing to Scott Moran.

The psychiatrist finished extracting himself from the body drawer. When he did, Lauren walked over and leaned down to look into the drawer. The back of it was gone and it opened into a small room behind the wall of body drawers. "What the hell is this?" Lauren said.

Dr. Mansfield looked down at her. "I wish you had stayed upstairs. This is really unnecessary."

"Unnecessary! You've covered up a potential viral outbreak here. This is insane."

"You don't understand."

"You're right. I don't." Lauren squinted at the impassive doctor. "You never sent the blood work to the CDC, did you?"

"I didn't need to. I know what killed your patient."

"What do you mean? How could you possibly..." Lauren's voice faltered as she looked from Dr. Mansfield's face to Scott Moran's and back again. They weren't scared. They had been caught in a major cover-up, yet they weren't scared at all.

An alarm sounded in her head. There was no reason these men should be so calm. Unless...

She spun around to look at Janney. The sheriff shrugged and blocked the doorway.

"Oh God. What are you all doing?"

"Science. Advancing civilization." Dr. Mansfield kicked the body drawer closed with his foot.

"Are you conducting experiments on these girls? Is that it?"

Janney cleared his throat behind her. She turned in time to see him pointing at his watch. "Sorenson has the ambulance upstairs. We should get going before people start asking questions."

"Where are you taking them?" Lauren cried out. Then it hit her. The thought that should have occurred to her from the beginning. Her voice came out no more than a whisper. "Did you have something to do with Sarah disappearing? Do you know where she is?"

Dr. Mansfield looked as if he might answer her but then thought better of it. He looked past her to Janney. "You're right. We'll take her with us." His voice had changed. Gone was the smooth gentility of the country doctor. His words came out in a clipped tone, with the stern confidence of someone used to having orders followed without question. "Make sure there's a cover story and her car is removed from the parking lot."

"I'll take care of it, Boss."

Dr. Mansfield straightened up as Janney said the words, his eyes darting to Lauren. Janney caught the unspoken reprimand and stared down at the floor.

Lauren noticed the interaction. Slowly, she made the connection of what Janney had said. She turned and stared open-mouthed at Dr. Mansfield. "Jack said someone called the Boss was responsible for all this. For taking Sarah. Is that you? Are you the one they call the Boss? Are you the one doing all this to my family?"

Dr. Mansfield looked at Janney again, a wave of anger flashing in his eyes. When he turned back to Lauren, he was back in control, his voice calm. "Your daughter is safe. If you come with me quietly, I'll take you to her."

Lauren broke down, sobbing. "How could you? How could you take my baby? What's wrong with you?"

"I've always liked you. This wasn't personal. If you knew what I do, you might appreciate the decision I had to make. I will explain things to you, but right now we have to go. Scott here will medicate you for our little trip. It's only sodium butabarbital. You may not believe this, but you can still trust me."

"Screw you," Lauren said. "Screw you and your trust. If you hurt my baby, I'll kill you."

Lauren watched as Scott Moran produced a syringe from a bag and indicated that Janney should hold her. She relaxed her body as the sheriff grabbed her arms.

Thinking that Lauren had given in, Janney loosened his grip. As soon as he did, Lauren twisted forward and kicked, hard, into the man's groin. His grunt told Lauren the heel of her shoe had found its mark.

Quickly, she spun to the side and used Janney's momentum from bending over to push him headlong into the room. Her path to the door clear now, she ran into the corridor and sprinted to the elevator at the end. She tried to ignore the shouting behind her. And then the heavy footsteps as the men ran after her.

Stairs or elevator? Find the right key to unlock the door, or wait for the elevator to close? She chose the elevator just as she reached the end of the corridor. With a fluid movement that surprised even her, she launched herself over the chair that blocked the door, hooking it with her foot as she did to drag it into the elevator. She spun around and slammed her fist into the buttons to close the door.

She backed up against the rear of the elevator, tears obscuring her vision. Janney and Moran were running down the corridor, racing to get to the elevator before the metal doors slid shut.

They were too close.

She wasn't going to make it.

She cursed under her breath, pleading for the doors to move faster. She looked around the compartment for a weapon, but there was nothing. If they got there, she was dead.

Please God. Please God.

Janney's face filled the narrow gap between the doors. He reached out with his hand to force the elevator back open. Lauren shut her eyes and cried out.

Then silence. She opened her eyes and saw that the doors had closed. The elevator lurched as it started its slow climb to the first floor.

She would have allowed herself a sigh of relief, but there was movement on the gurney next to her. She looked over reluctantly, not really wanting to look at the disfigured face again. The body bag was still unzipped as she had left it, but the head had lolled to one side. Now the poor girl's face stared right at her.

She reached out an unsteady hand to zip the bag up. There would be police and hospital staff everywhere once she got out of the elevator. They didn't need to see this.

As she tugged on the zipper, she glanced down to the girl's face. A single open eye stared back at her.

Then the eye blinked.

Lauren jumped back, screaming. The eye roamed around, searching her out. The girl was alive.

The elevator shuddered to a stop. Then, groaning under its age-old machinery, it started back down to the basement.

"No, no," Lauren whimpered, taking her eyes off the girl long enough to beat on the control panel with her hand. She should have known better. Dr. Mansfield had an emergency override key. Of course he would use it to stop her.

She screamed at the ceiling, praying that someone upstairs would hear her. That someone would come and save her and save this poor, diseased girl who was impossibly still alive. Lauren didn't stop screaming until the elevator stopped back in the basement and the door slid open to reveal Mansfield, Janney, and Scott Moran waiting for her. The second gurney was positioned behind them, a white sheet still covering the body on it.

Janney had pulled out his gun and now trained it on Lauren's chest. She caught her breath and held her hands in front of her as if they would be able to deflect a bullet if he decided to fire at her.

"We've lost enough time." Dr. Mansfield motioned the sheriff and Moran forward. Lauren struggled when Janney grabbed her by the arms, his fingers digging into her arm this time. Scott Moran tapped the syringe, then calmly walked toward Lauren.

"You're crazy. You're all crazy," Lauren said. She felt a little stab of pain from the injection in her arm.

Dr. Mansfield ignored the comment. "Perhaps when I explain everything, you'll think differently."

The drug took effect immediately. Her muscles relaxed and black walls appeared on either side of her vision. She tried to step forward but stumbled. Dr. Mansfield grabbed her arm and steered her toward the second gurney in the corridor. She tried to say something, but her mouth wouldn't respond.

Then she was in front of Janney. He was saying something to her. She heard the sound, but it reached her brain as a low, indistinguishable rumble. She saw he was laughing and pointing to the gurney where he had lifted the sheet that had been draped over it.

She looked down, too disoriented to be shocked, too numb to react. It wasn't Felicia Rodriguez they were hiding. It was a little blonde-haired girl in a white gown. She lay stretched out, her hands folded neatly across her chest.

So peaceful. Lauren thought, barely lucid. *Dear, sweet Sarah. You look so peaceful.*

Unable to fight off the drug any longer, the world turned dark and she collapsed.

SEVENTY-FOUR

Jack hung a sign on the police station door that told anyone who might stop by that it was closed for the night. It was a long shot, but they figured they might get lucky and buy themselves a little extra time before anyone found the officers locked in the jail cell in the rear of the building. Next, they found the keys to an unmarked sedan parked behind the station and drove out slowly so as not to attract any attention.

They made a quick stop at Lonetree's Bronco. He had parked it far enough away from the hospital that the police hadn't connected it to him. Still, they decided to keep the sedan, thinking it less conspicuous than the SUV. Jack stayed in the car as Lonetree rummaged around the back and emerged with a duffel bag.

Jack raised an eyebrow at Lonetree as he climbed back into the sedan.

"New boots," Lonetree said, gunning the engine. "And a few other supplies."

As they drove away, Jack spotted Midland Hospital down the street and felt a pang of guilt. Lauren had to be going through hell. He ought to be with her, comforting her. Or at least he ought to let her know that he was going after their daughter. But she would never believe him. The way she'd left the jail, he was sure – if given the chance – she would turn them in.

A flash of lights behind them shook him from his thoughts. He grabbed the door handle in a panic. They had two choices if it was a cop: turn themselves in or take the cop out. He knew what Lonetree would do. What scared him was that he would go along with anything in order to keep going. Nothing would keep him from reaching the cave.

Fortunately, the flashing lights weren't from a police cruiser but from an ambulance rushing away from Midland Hospital. Lonetree pulled the car over to the side and slowed down, telling Jack to hide his face. The ambulance whipped past them, all sirens and lights. He tracked the vehicle as it hurried up the road ahead of them, fighting back a feeling that the ambulance should mean something to him. He shrugged off the intuition, chalking it up to the guilt he felt over leaving Lauren behind at the hospital.

Her abandonment made sense on a rational level. He wondered whether he would act any differently if they reversed roles. Still, no matter how much he rationalized her reaction, it hurt. The look on her face when she walked away, the one that convicted him of taking their little girl and doing God knew what to her, would stay with him forever.

Crouched in his seat, waiting for the ambulance to pass was all the time he needed to have the emotions wash over him again. It was a waste of energy, and there was nothing he could do about it now. The only things that mattered were getting to Sarah in time and making the sons-of-bitches pay for what they had done to his family. After that, he and Lauren would be able to sort things out. For now, it was better if she didn't know what was going on. Better if she were safe in the hospital where she could take care of Becky. Then a thought occurred to him that sent shivers up his spine.

If he died tonight, Lauren would never know the truth. She would live the rest of her life believing that he kidnapped their daughter. And Becky. The poor girl would grow up as the kid whose dad had gone crazy, chopped up her sister, and stuffed her in a hole somewhere. Little girls didn't grow up right after something like that, did they?

"It's gone now. You can get up," Lonetree said. He shifted the car back into gear and they rolled forward.

"Have you been to Huckley's house?"

Lonetree nodded. "Yeah, staked it out from a distance. Your friend Max confirmed what was in my brother's notes. He said that Huckley was a bona fide psychic and that the Taking ritual had only made him more sensitive. I think it was how they finally caught up with him. One of his last entries was how he suspected Huckley could even hear thoughts at some level. I didn't want to get too close in case he felt he was being watched."

"Did he ever notice you?"

"Every time. I'd be watching him move around the house through binoculars, and he'd turn and look right at me. It would only be for a second or two, more of a reflex than anything else, like when you see an animal in the wild. He knew I was there. I'm sure of it."

Lonetree pushed the sedan up to seventy miles an hour on the freeway. They needed to hurry, but the last thing they needed was to be pulled over for a traffic ticket in a stolen police car. It would be hard to talk their way out of that one.

Ten minutes later, Lonetree exited the freeway and wound through back roads until they came to a stop at the end of a dirt road.

"This is it. There's a farmhouse about a quarter mile back. There are a couple of barns and outbuildings. I'm guessing the elevator for the mineshaft is set up in one of them."

Jack peered down the driveway. Something was nagging at him. "How far are we from the tunnel where you took me the first time?"

"Less than ten minutes on back roads. Why?"

"Something you said back at the jail has been bothering me," Jack said. "You said even if they hear us coming, they'll have to come through us to get out."

"Yeah, so?"

"Well, they're definitely going to hear us coming, aren't they? We're going down a mineshaft in an elevator. Not exactly stealth mode."

"What are you trying to say?"

"I'm saying that it's a good plan if our goal is to get into a gun fight and try to kill these guys. But if the goal is to save my little girl, then we should be sneaking up on them through the tunnel. Right?"

Lonetree cracked his neck side to side. "You know what my purpose is," he said coldly. "I'm here to kill that son-of-a-bitch who killed my brother. This Boss person is down there. If we go in the other way, they could be coming up the main entrance as we're going down. We could miss them altogether, and I still wouldn't know who he is."

"To save my daughter, we need to have surprise on our side. The tunnel's the only way to do that," Jack argued. "If we miss them, you can kill Huckley and the others later, but I only get one chance to save Sarah."

"I've been working for a year to find the Boss. He's down there right now. All of them are together. How can you ask me to pass that up?"

Jack didn't give an answer because he didn't have one. Lonetree looked down the road in front of him, the road to Huckley's, the road to his revenge. Jack watched as the veins in the big man's neck stood out from clenching his teeth together. Jack stared at him. And waited.

He understood the battle that raged inside Lonetree. He guessed they felt the same emotions. Somewhere inside, in a dark corner where all the horrors of his imagination were trapped and pent up, Jack did not believe he would ever see his little girl alive again. This thought, so terrible that his sanity could not give it any credence, had borne a dark, brooding offspring – revenge. He wanted to inflict horrible violence on Sarah's captors. Make them endure the most unspeakable tortures he could create. Lonetree's revenge was for an actual loss. Both a brother and a father. And this loss had fermented for years.

The difference was that Jack still held some hope. To move forward, he had to cling to it and massage it back to life when hopelessness washed over him. Now, he was asking Lonetree to subordinate his revenge to Jack's small hope of recovering his child. He knew it was a lot to ask, but he prayed it wouldn't be too much for Lonetree to give.

341

They sat in silence, the sedan's engine providing the only background noise to their quiet battle of emotions.

Without comment, Lonetree suddenly threw the sedan into drive and gunned the engine. The car's tires spun on the gravel road, caught traction, and lurched forward toward the driveway leading to Huckley's house. Jack sagged forward in his seat, the weight of his failure almost too much to bear. But right before they entered the narrow lane, Lonetree yanked the wheel to the left, causing the rear tires to slide out. The sedan spun a hundred and eighty degrees. With expert skill, Lonetree corrected the spin and accelerated the car down the road.

Lonetree looked over to his passenger. "You better move fast through that tunnel, Jack."

"You don't have to worry about that," he replied, nodding his head toward the back seat. "I just hope you have some nasty tricks in your duffel bag for our cave friends."

That seemed to make Lonetree feel better about the decision he'd just made. A smile stretched out across his face as they bounced down the road in silence. "You bet your ass I do."

SEVENTY-FIVE

Jack was amazed by how much easier it was to navigate the tunnels this time. A downpour started before they reached the cave opening and had made a mess of the first hundred feet of the passage. Slippery mud coated the ground and the two men had to rake their fingers along the walls to control the speed of their descent.

Except for themselves being covered with thick mud, once they were farther into the cave, there were no other signs of the rain. It was good news, Lonetree told him, since many caves were prone to flooding during hard rains.

They moved quickly. The combination of adrenaline rushing through Jack's system and the experience from the first trip allowed him to make short work of sections where he'd languished before. He noted with satisfaction that Lonetree didn't have to wait at all. In fact, since Lonetree had to push the duffle bag in front of him, Jack often found himself waiting for the space ahead of him to clear.

In less than half an hour, they reached the gallery with the river. Only one tight passage remained between them and the main cave. Walking up behind Lonetree, Jack heard the big man groan as he shined his light on the river.

"What is it?"

"This is a problem," Lonetree said.

Jack edged next to him and pointed his own light at the swollen river rushing in front of them. The river was nearly twice as wide as the last time they'd been there. The few feet of water directly in front of them was shallow, without much current, but beyond that the river flowed full force. Jack looked up at the rope swing. The spot where he had jumped from before was now a good ten feet into the river. He judged the height of the ceiling and the new width of the river. The geometry wasn't good. He looked at the sidewalls. Both were sheer faces that went straight into the water and seemed impassable.

"What now?" Jack asked.

"Guess we're going to have to earn this one," Lonetree said. "Here, shine your light over here."

Lonetree sat his backpack on the ground and started to remove its contents, stacking the small arsenal of weapons on a rock shelf. Knives, handguns, hand grenades, C-4. There was other equipment Jack didn't recognize, but he didn't bother to ask questions. His curiosity was eclipsed by other worries. He wiped away the mud that covered his watch. Seven-thirty. The sun had been down for over an hour.

What if they already killed Sarah?

It wasn't the first time the thought had occurred to him. In fact, he'd thought of nothing else during their descent into the earth. And now, so close to the main cave, images poured over him of what they might have done to his little girl. Maybe it was happening this very second while he sat there catching his breath. Maybe he would push his head through the rock tunnel just as they killed her.

Lonetree shined his light at Jack, breaking him from his thoughts. He noticed Jack looking at his watch. "I think she's okay."

"How do you know?"

Lonetree shrugged. "Just a guess, really. But I usually have a sense about things like this."

While it didn't make Jack feel much better, he appreciated Lonetree's attempt to give him hope. "Just the same, let's get this thing going. Any thoughts on how we're going to do this?"

Lonetree nodded. "You're going over on the rope first. It's going to be a little tricky, but I think if I push you it'll be okay."

"You think?"

"I'm not going to B.S. you. This might not go so well. The other option is to climb back out of here and try to catch them at Huckley's property. You know the risk of that, though."

Jack searched for any sign of accusation in the big man's voice. It was, after all, Jack's plea for Sarah that had put them in this predicament. But if Lonetree held any resentment from the decision he had made, he was doing a good job disguising it. Jack forced a smile but couldn't repress a shiver as he looked at the black water rushing pass them. "Let's get over this river."

"All right," Lonetree said. "But there's a little something I haven't told you yet. Something I think you ought to know. Just in case."

Jack felt his stomach roll over. Something about Lonetree's voice worried him. He sounded too detached, too cold. "What is it?"

Lonetree pointed at the wall in front of him. "That thing in the cave over there has to be destroyed. I mean, even if we die doing it, we have to stop these guys. Otherwise they'll go on killing. That's the most important thing, right? That they're stopped and this kind of thing can never happen again."

Jack nodded. "What is it you're not telling me?"

"Last week, I rigged the cave with enough C-4 to take out a city block."

Jack stared at Lonetree. "That's a little something? Is there a big something that you're not telling me about?"

Lonetree ignored the comment. "The whole cave structure in this area is unstable, so when the charges go, the whole cavern should collapse. Everything in that cave will be buried under a few million tons of rock."

Slowly, Jack understood what Lonetree was implying. Once all the people were down in the cave, Lonetree could accomplish the mission with a push of a button. Of course, it would also mean that Sarah would be dead too. "I don't understand. Why didn't you use it already? Why didn't you just blow them up?"

"First, I have to be sure they are down there. If I blew the cave without seeing the Boss, I'd never be sure I killed him. But there's a technical reason too. I couldn't rig the explosives to detonate from up top. The cave is too deep and there is too much metal in the rock to get a clear signal. So I rigged a timed device that I could activate from down here." Lonetree held up a black box with three dials on it.

"Okay. So why are you telling me this?"

"Because anything could happen from here on out. We could get separated. One of us could be killed. If that happens, I want you to set off the explosives. I want to make sure you end this thing if I can't." Before Jack could agree, Lonetree held up his hand. "And I mean even if you're still in the cave. If there's a chance they might catch you, you have to detonate."

Jack nodded that he understood.

"I'll do it," he said. "Show me how it works."

"It's simple. Align all three dials to zero, press this button. That primes it. Turn the dials to five. Press it again and *boom*. Find out if religion is for real."

"What about this up here? What does that do?" Jack asked, pointing to an LED display and a touchpad.

"It's a timer. If we're going to get out of here alive, this is the way we do it. Up arrow on the left for minutes. Up arrow on the right for seconds. Once you start, there's no going back. Completely tamper-proof so even mind-reading a-holes like Huckley can't do anything if they figure out what's going on." Lonetree shoved the detonator into one of the backpack's pockets. "All right. Let's do this." Lonetree handed Jack a gun, knife, and box of ammo. He positioned twice as many weapons on various parts of his body and then stuffed the leftovers into his backpack. "Hope for good aim," he said with a smile. Rearing back, he flung the backpack over the river where it landed safely on the other side.

"You want to throw me too?"

"I'm going to try."

"Thanks, but I'll go with the rope." Jack said, wading along the wall toward where the rope rested on a hook. The water was cooler than last time, fed by the rainwater, but still felt like a lukewarm bath. He waded in up to his thighs, his feet spaced wide apart as he braced himself against the current. Not daring to go any farther, he stretched his arm out and managed to grab hold of the rope with his fingertips. Carefully he reversed course and carried it back as far as possible toward Lonetree.

"Okay. Remember last time you did this?"

"You mean when I almost fell in? Yeah, I remember."

"Well, this time has to be better."

"Thanks," Jack said, tugging on the rope and shining his light up at the rusted hook drilled into the ceiling. He listened as Lonetree described the plan, realizing he really hadn't been kidding earlier. With one last tug on the rope, Jack nodded. "Let's do it."

Lonetree stood behind him and took hold of his jeans on either side of his waist. Jack shuffled backward as the big man pulled him back. Then his feet were off the ground as Lonetree hefted him up in the air. Jack pulled himself up a little on the rope as he was instructed and held his breath. He heard Lonetree grunt as he was lifted even farther off the ground and then hurled forward.

Jack felt Lonetree shove against his back and then the pressure was gone. Everything was silent. The air rushed past his face. He felt himself reach the bottom of the swing's arc and kicked his legs forward to maximize his momentum.

He had to let go of the rope at just the right time and jump though.

The timing had to be perfect.

The difference of a second was the difference between life and death.

Wait, wait, wait, now!

Just as the thought to let go registered in his mind, the tension in the rope disappeared. Jack fell through the air, tangled in the rope that only seconds before had been his lifeline.

He hit the water on his back, knocking the wind out of him. Reaching down, he could feel the rock floor, but he could also feel the current pulling him toward the middle of the channel.

Gasping for air, he clawed his way through the water, struggling to get a foothold on the slippery rock beneath him. He moved on instinct, not even certain he was going the right direction.

But slowly the pull of the current weakened and the water became shallower. Out of danger, he turned and righted his helmet which had slipped backward on impact. He shone his light up to the ceiling. The rope was no longer suspended over the river. The rusted hook was gone, replaced by a gaping hole in the rock.

Jack shuddered at how close he had come to death.

"You all right?" Lonetree called over.

"Yeah, I think so," Jack said. He moved all his limbs to check for injury but found nothing. "The rope's gone. How are you going to get across?"

Lonetree's light danced across the rock face on either side of the river. It came to rest on the upriver side. "Grab the rope. It should still be attached to the guidelines. Those small ropes on the side."

Jack waded over and pulled on the guideline. Sure enough, it was still attached to the larger rope. Dragging it in against the current felt like fighting a big fish. Finally, he pulled in the end of the rope, including the clump of rock that still held the metal hook. Making sure Lonetree was ready, he threw the heavy end over and tied his end of the rope around his waist.

"Are you braced against something?" Lonetree asked.

Jack looked around the smooth walled tunnel. There was nothing he could use as a tie off. "Wait a second." He grabbed the backpack Lonetree had thrown across and slipped it over his shoulders. At least the weight of the pack would give him a little more ballast. Then he sat on the rock floor and dug his heels into a deep crack in the ground. It wasn't much, but at least he could brace himself with his legs if Lonetree fell in. "Go ahead," he shouted.

He watched as Lonetree's light bobbled through the darkness on the other side of the river. The progress of the light slowed and Jack knew the man was climbing the rock face. Jack took up the slack in the rope, careful not to pull hard enough to make Lonetree lose his balance.

"How is it?" Jack called out.

"Piece...of...cake."

Lonetree's response came in short, halting bursts. Jack knew the man was struggling. He had seen the rock face himself. It seemed impossible that anyone could climb across it. But he watched the light embedded in Lonetree's helmet slowly float over the river and wondered if anything really was impossible for Lonetree. The guy was like some action superhero. Jack was half surprised he didn't just leap over the water in a single bound.

This thought disappeared at the sight of the light tumbling down the wall. A fraction of a second later, Lonetree's cry reached his ears. The rope went slack in Jack's hands.

He watched in horror as Lonetree floated past him, beating his arms against the current.

Oh shit.

Jack realized what was about to happen and braced for it. When Lonetree reached the opposite side of the passage, the rope snapped taut.

Jack cried out from the pain of the rope cutting into his side. Leaning back so that he was almost parallel with the floor, he tried to absorb the weight in his legs, but he knew he couldn't hold it for long.

Within seconds he felt his feet start to slip. Lonetree was too heavy.

Slowly, inch-by-inch, the rope pulled him forward out of position. Soon, he was looking down the length of rope at Lonetree struggling at the other end.

White water splashed everywhere around Lonetree's hulking form. He was right at the mouth of the gaping hole where the river entered the rock wall. Working hand over hand, he was trying to pull himself up the rope, but the current was too strong. Lonetree's helmet light shined right into Jack's eyes, temporarily blinding him. When the light moved again, Jack could see Lonetree's right hand held a knife. He was trying to cut the rope to keep Jack from being pulled into the water.

"NO!" Jack shouted.

His feet slipped forward another inch.

He clenched his teeth and pulled back against the weight even as his brain surged with commands for him to stop.

Let go of the rope. You need to stay alive so you can save your daughter.

He ignored the warnings and cinched the rope tighter around his waist. He watched as his feet edged up the rock incline he was using for a brace. He had to readjust his position or he would lose all traction.

With a heave, he pulled back on the rope and tried to jam his heels back down to get a better grip.

His feet missed.

They slipped forward, and suddenly all his resistance to the rope was gone. With enough torque to squeeze the air out of him, Lonetree's weight yanked him forward headfirst toward the river.

Jack bounced along the rock floor like he was being dragged behind a truck. He reached out and clawed at the ground for something to cling to, but he knew what was coming next.

Jack sucked down a lungful of air just as his body plunged into the water. He closed his eyes and curled up in a ball the best he could with the rope still tugging at his midsection.

He knew that in less than a second he would disappear just like Lonetree had into the black hole cut into the rock. In that one second, a cascade of images burst through his mind – as if every synapse knew it was about to blink out forever and wanted to fire one last time. His family. His girls. His wife. And with the images came an unspeakably cruel understanding that he would never see any of them again. The black hole ahead of him was death. Cold, dark and silent. He focused on the images of his wife and daughters as he rolled end over end through the water, carrying his memories into the darkness with him.

He was sorry, so sorry, that he hadn't been strong enough to save his daughter. But it occurred to him that maybe he deserved to fail. After all, he had taken another father's child away when he ran over and killed Melissa Gonzales. Maybe God did exist, and He was settling a score, making sure all debts were paid off in the end.

Still, what kind of God would punish children for the sins of their fathers? Only a God who didn't care or didn't exist. Either way, Jack held no desire to meet Him. He expected that death would be as dark and lonely as the tunnel looming ahead of him.

Time snapped back into place, and the world moved again in full motion. The river carried him into the rock wall, his helmet scraping against the ceiling as he tumbled through the water.

The narrow beam from the waterproof helmet light cut through the dark water and lit up the smooth walls as they flew by. Jack knew he was a dead man, but still he reached out for something to grab onto. Gaining a handhold was the only thing keeping him from clawing back upstream and escaping the clutches of the river. Both times he managed to grab onto a crack in the rock, the rope around his waist tightened and ripped him from the wall.

It suddenly occurred to Jack that Lonetree might already be dead. The thought of being dragged through the dark tunnel tied to a corpse struck Jack as a particularly gruesome way to die. He idly wondered where the river ended and how long he and Lonetree would be joined together. Maybe forever. Buried underground. Their bodies seeping into the ground water a little bit at a time.

Jack choked down the little air left in his mouth and throat. His ears rang. He wanted to fight back, scrape and beg for every spare second, but he felt his muscles loosening, surrendering, as he started to float through the water instead of struggle.

The blood in his temples beat in a rising tempo, quickening. He couldn't hold his breath much longer. He had only seconds left before his body betrayed him and sucked the lukewarm river water into his lungs.

Then the rope around his waist went slack. The meaning of this worked its way through his oxygen-deprived brain. Lonetree's body was probably hung up in a crevice or wedged between rocks up ahead. Wherever it was, maybe there was an air pocket.

But the burning in his chest had gone from pain to desperation, and thoughts of survival disappeared.

Seconds later, even as he floated through coils of rope bunching up in front of him, his willpower gave way. With a choked inhalation, Jack's lungs filled with water. Deep inside the mountains of western Maryland, in a dark underground river without a name, his failing body floated with the current. As he lost consciousness, he wondered if his remains would ever be found.

His brain burned off the last remnants of oxygen still available, then, without fuel, ceased to function. The rest of his body did the same.

SEVENTY-SIX

Consciousness came like a sunrise viewed through antique glass, distorted and blurred. Pale shadows swirled in faded degrees of color. Muffled sounds reached her ears in undulating waves, like listening to a talk radio station through blown speakers.

"She's waking up," someone said.

She recognized the voice, but she couldn't attach a name to it. Hearing it made her feel comfortable. Made her feel safe.

Everything was confused, but she knew something bad had happened to her – she was sure of it. And the owner of the voice would tell her what it was. He would help her.

She squeezed her eyes shut and willed the pain in her head to go away. The voice came back to her through the velvet darkness and asked her how she felt. It was just like Stanley Mansfield to ask such a question.

That was it. That was who the voice belonged to, Dr. Mansfield.

It was just like him to look out for her. She smiled and tried to say hello, but there was something wrong. The words wouldn't form on her lips. She carefully opened her eyes, aware at some level that the bright light around her would be painful if taken in too quickly. Dr. Mansfield's face hovered in front of her, blurry at first, and then sharpening into focus as if someone were fine tuning the reception in her head. Then, in a rush of images, she remembered what had happened. She remembered the basement in the hospital. She remembered Dr. Mansfield was not her friend. He was the Boss. The person in the crazy story Jack had told her.

In an emotional plunge that left her stomach turning, she remembered seeing Sarah.

The burst of adrenaline from that memory pushed her consciousness through the thick drug-induced blanket around her brain. She pushed herself up off the floor.

"Sarah? W-wh-where's Sarah?"

Strong hands pulled her up to a sitting position. Dr. Mansfield's voice came at her from what seemed multiple directions. "Easy. The drug is wearing off."

Lauren smelled manure. And damp straw. She rubbed her eyes and looked around. They were in a barn. The interior was lit by massive halogen lights so that everything stood out in sharp contrasts. There, on the ground next to her, blonde hair fanned out around her head, was her little girl, curled as if she were asleep in her bed at home. But something was wrong. She was too still, too pale.

Lauren's heart thumped hard in her chest. She lurched forward but several hands held her back. She screamed in frustration and lashed out, but she couldn't break free. Rope appeared, and she sobbed as her hands and feet were bound, her eyes never leaving Sarah's unmoving body.

"Is she alive?" she sobbed.

Dr. Mansfield crouched down in front of her, putting himself into her field of vision as she continued to stare at her daughter. "Yes, she's fine. She's had the same medication I gave you. Now, try to calm down, all right? You'll feel the effects of the drug for a few more minutes."

"Why are you wasting your time with her?" Huckley asked, spitting on the floor. "She's going to die just like her daughter. What's the big deal?"

Lauren's eyes went wide. She struggled at her bindings until the rope started to cut into her wrists.

"You'll just make it worse. Please calm down." Dr. Mansfield said. "Please."

Once she stopped struggling, Dr. Mansfield rose and faced Huckley. Lauren tore her eyes away from her daughter and watched the two men standing only a few feet from her. No words were exchanged, but Huckley stared at the ground, his shoulders slumping forward like a kid pouting from a parent's reprimand. No, Lauren thought to herself, more like an animal's show of submission. The simple gesture confirmed to her that the doctor was not only part of the madness, but he was leading it. And if he was the leader, the one Jack called the Boss, was it possible that the rest of Jack's story was true? Was it possible that these lunatics meant to kill her daughter in some kind of ritual sacrifice? Lauren shook her head, willing the thoughts to go away, as if that alone could change the situation she found herself in.

"Moran and Butcher will need more time in the cave. Get the others around. Janney's over at the house. Tell him we're going down in half an hour." Dr. Mansfield gave a slight nod toward the door, and Huckley left the barn without comment.

Lauren started at the sound of the sheriff's name. Like snippets of a bad dream, scenes in the hospital basement pieced themselves together in her mind. The psychiatrist, Scott Moran, he had been there too.

Jesus, who isn't part of this?

Then she remembered her last meeting with Jack. How she had refused to believe him and had run away just when he needed her most. He hadn't been crazy, but trying to save their daughter. How horrible he must have felt when she turned on him while he was telling the truth.

It still didn't explain why this was happening. It didn't explain that poor girl on the gurney in the elevator. Or what Dr. Mansfield was up to. Lauren shuddered as she pictured the girl's one open eye staring at her. Confused and in pain.

"Will you tell me what the hell is going on? Why are you doing this?" Lauren asked. "What are you mixed up in?"

Dr. Mansfield sat next to her and ran a hand through his hair. "It's complicated. I'm just sorry you had to get involved. It wasn't supposed to work out like this."

"Whatever it is, you don't have to go through with it," Lauren pleaded. "You could let Sarah go. Help us get out of here. We wouldn't tell anyone. We would–"

"You don't seem to understand. Your daughter's here because I ordered it. Huckley found her, but this is my decision," Dr. Mansfield said. "I'm afraid you're asking the wrong person for help."

"This is crazy," Lauren said, mostly to herself. "This is all insane."

"I know it must seem that way. But you don't understand the magnitude of what's happening here. This is bigger than me or you. Or your little girl. This is something that could change the entire world. It could change everything."

"What are you talking about? In the hospital I asked if you were conducting human experiments, and you didn't deny it. Did you kill Felicia Rodriguez?"

Dr. Mansfield nodded. "And others like her. But they didn't die in vain. Some day they will be looked at as heroes. They were sacrifices for the greater good of society." He stood up and moved closer to her. "It's not like this is the first time it's happened. Louis Pasteur used human subjects in his experiments, many who died, but now he's revered. Would you have blocked the development of vaccines because of risks to the first human recipients?"

"What you're doing is wrong. No, it's worse than that. It's evil. You can't just rationalize it away."

"Spare me the ethics lesson. If you only understood what I was–"

"Nothing is worth killing innocent girls. Nothing."

"Are you so sure of yourself?" Dr. Mansfield stared up at the barn's ceiling for several seconds before he went on, his eyes never leaving some distant point far beyond the confines of the wooden beams above them.

"Suppose God came down to this barn and sat next to us. He says there's been enough pain in the world and He wants to put an end to it all. He offers you the ability to cure all disease in the world, all infections, all genetic defects found in the human race. In essence, God gives you the ability to end the suffering of the world. He gives you the gift of immortality to share with the world.

"But the gift comes at a price. To develop this universal vaccine, you have to sacrifice the lives of over a thousand innocent children. One thousand lives to save the suffering of six *billion*. As horrible as it sounds, who in their right mind would say no to such a proposition? Would you? Would you refuse to deliver to God His thousand deaths so that you might save the world?"

Lauren stared at the doctor, not aware at first that he was waiting for her to answer. The look in the man's eyes as he spoke had shaken her. It was the glazed, distant look of the fanatic, as if he had already created the world he described, and he was looking at it through a window visible to only his eyes. Gone was the reasoned, rational man she thought she knew, replaced by a lunatic with a religion to sell. Lauren decided he was already beyond help, and she'd be damned before she gave in to his vile logic.

"I think that if God asked for a thousand deaths, it would occur to me that it wasn't God at all. What you're talking about is evil. Unjustifiable evil."

"Saving six billion people is not justification enough?"

"You're not saving six billion people. This is crazy."

"Really? Do you want evidence? Would that make you understand?"

Dr. Mansfield produced a knife from his pocket. He held out his exposed forearm and slashed it with the blade. Lauren screamed as blood gushed out of the wound. The doctor grimaced from the pain but did not move his arm.

"It still hurts, but look. Look at what's happening."

Lauren didn't have to be asked. She had already noticed how quickly the blood flow had stopped. Now the skin regenerated at the edges of the wound. Within seconds, the gash was completely healed. Lauren stared open-mouthed. "How is it…what did you…"

"Now you understand what I'm talking about. I'm working on a serum that could give this to the world. And you're only seeing the surface of it. This same regenerative effect is taking place at the cellular level throughout my body.

The serum halts deterioration. My body is immune to all viruses and bacterial infections. And without cellular breakdown, the body doesn't age."

"Are you trying to say that you can't die? Are you saying you believe the same story Jack told me? About the Indians and the cave? That this is all about some sacrificial ritual that gives you immortality?"

"Immortality isn't technically correct. We're as close as we can get. There are limits, of course. Massive trauma can kill me if it's more than my body can regenerate. Anything wrong with my body before I took from the Source will not regenerate. A fact one-armed Jim Butcher didn't appreciate. But without being murdered or the victim of a terrible accident, I could theoretically live forever." He lowered his voice as if aware of how incredulous his next statement would appear. "In fact, I've already lived for over two hundred years and have yet to show any sign of physical deterioration."

Lauren matched Dr. Mansfield's serious look.

"So you're saying Jack's story is true?"

Dr. Mansfield nodded.

"You sacrifice people so you can be immortal, and you're trying to synthesize the effect in a lab so you can cure the world of all disease?"

The doctor nodded again.

"And you're going to sacrifice my daughter because you think she has some kind of special psychic powers that will help you with your study?"

Slowly, as if fearful of her reaction, he said, "Yes, that's why she's here."

"And you're 200 years old?" Lauren's face turned red as she spoke the words. When the doctor nodded this time, she erupted into laughter. "Jesus, you've gone off the deep end, you know that?"

Her laugh took on a maniacal quality to it, edged with tears and panic.

"What the FUCK is wrong with all of you? I mean, I don't know how you pulled off the little trick with the knife, but that's magic, not medicine. What's next? Are you...are you...I don't know, going to put a woman in a box, stick it full of swords, and when she pops out unharmed tell me you cured her?"

A dark cloud had come over the doctor's expression, but she didn't care. Tears poured down her cheeks. These men were insane. Both she and her daughter were going to die. Given the situation, she decided she might as well speak her mind. "This is the stupidest Goddamn thing I've ever heard."

Dr. Mansfield turned, took one step toward her, and raised a hand as if to strike her. Lauren cowered to the side, fighting the rope around her hands to fend off the coming blow.

Slowly, the doctor lowered his hand. "People don't speak to me like that. You're lucky I need your help." He knelt down until his face was level with hers. "This is the most important scientific find ever. You saw it with you own eyes and still refuse to believe it. How can you explain away what you saw?"

Lauren met his eyes and stuck her chin out in his direction. She decided if the bastard moved to hit her again, she wouldn't move. She wouldn't give him the satisfaction. "There are a thousand things. Hypnosis, for example. Or maybe you have developed a drug that put me into a hyper-suggestive state and are initiating my hallucinations," Lauren said. "Give me a few minutes and I could come up with a dozen explanations."

"But there wouldn't be a single one that felt right. Come on, you know what you saw. You're a scientist. Open your eyes to the evidence and let yourself look beyond the boundaries imposed by your limited knowledge of what is possible in the natural world. Make no mistake, this is a natural phenomenon. It's not ghosts and magic, but a biological process."

"This isn't science. What you're doing is murdering kids for an insane delusion."

"But hasn't science always been pushed forward by men who chased their 'delusions' and proved them right? Copernicus, Pasteur, Newton, Einstein. All delusional fools who found truth where others saw impossibility. Hasn't truth always been victimized by the limited creativity of the scientific minds charged with uncovering it? Progress stalls until someone is willing to challenge the boundaries. Newton was a heretic for saying Aristotle was wrong. Then Einstein came along and explained Newton was wrong. Then Stephen Hawking challenged everything once again. Think about it. Even our most basic understanding of life has changed. We had immutable laws that governed requirements for life to exist. Then organisms were found around volcanic vents at the bottom of the ocean, living in conditions that our laws told us were impossible. If it were up to you, scientists would have looked at the evidence and said, 'Hypnosis, drug-induced hallucinations,' and left the laws as they were. But we didn't. We rewrote the laws about what it meant to be alive."

"That's different. What you're talking about is—"

"Is what? Impossible? Or just against the natural laws that you learned from medical textbooks? Maybe there are no laws, Lauren, only frontiers that we've reached. The spot on the other side of the frontier is not impossible, it's just the unknown." He slid closer to her. "You're confused and scared, and that's understandable. But like it or not, I've found a way to take the life force of a human being and turn it into something tangible. Something storable. Something transferable." Dr. Mansfield lowered his voice. "Can you imagine what we could do if we gave this gift to the world? Can you imagine how it would change everything?"

"Jack described a cave where women were kept in cages. Bred for this insane idea. Is that what you mean by changing the world?"

"Yes, yes," Dr. Mansfield said with a wave of his hand. "A terrible thing. Very primitive. That's why my research is so important. Once I develop a synthetic method to replicate the function of the Source in the cave, we can use manufactured genetic material. With this done, the Source will no longer be needed. Huckley believes there's a supernatural force behind this, but I'm convinced it's a biological process. The Source is an organism that absorbs organic material for its own survival and produces a fluid as a residual by-product. This fluid, when ingested, actually changes cellular function to protect from disease and deterioration. Somewhat like oxygen produced by plants, the by-product sustains human life. I've tried to replicate the serum, but you've seen the results."

"Wait, you said manufactured genetic material. What do you mean?"

"Cloning, of course. That's why the time has come to reveal the serum to the world. Now that the human cloning has been successful, we can create specimens specifically for this purpose. Engineered for minimal brain function, subjects can be mass produced. An unlimited supply of material without the moral issues."

"*Without the moral issues?* Just because science can do something doesn't mean it should. Why can't you see that? Why can't you sense the evil in all of this?"

He ignored her. "I'm close, so close to understanding it. Once I can replicate the process, it will be possible to mass produce the serum. I'm so close. I thought I had it with the Moran girl, but think I know what was wrong. With more test subjects, I can—"

"Test subjects? Is that what you call Felicia Rodriguez? Don't try to make it sound respectable. She was murdered. She was just a baby, for God's sake, and you murdered her. And that poor girl in the elevator at the hospital was Scott Moran's daughter? Jesus, don't you understand, as soon as you go public they'll lock you away in an asylum? Or, if there's justice, they'll fry you in the chair. You are a murderer, nothing more. How could you go this far for this…this stupidity?"

Dr. Mansfield stood up. His cheeks flushed. "I thought you, of all people, would understand what I'm trying to do. Sometimes sacrifices have to be made for the greater good."

"I'm sure the Nazi doctors in the concentration camps said the same thing," Lauren said. "You can't justify murder. I don't care how you dress it up."

"Don't be naïve. We justify murder every day. What do you think about all those Iraqi civilians killed in the war? All those Afghans? Just collateral damage, right? Not really murder? But weren't they sacrificed so Americans could feel more secure? Weren't they murdered so you could live? Take it to a different extreme. Didn't a child die somewhere in the world today of starvation? Didn't someone die because they didn't get a ten dollar malaria shot? But you didn't do anything to stop it, did you? 'Not your responsibility' is the rationalization. For the price of the car you drive, you could have saved a hundred children from starvation, but you didn't. And you didn't sacrifice them for science. You sacrificed them for your own comfort. Your own hypocrisy damns your argument." He leaned forward and whispered, "This is science. It's not personal. I want you to listen, closely, to me. We don't have much time before the others come back in. There's a reason I've taken the time to tell you all this."

"And what's that?"

"Since you moved here, I knew you were meant to help me to finish my work. I need your insights to finish what I've started."

Lauren stared at him, incredulous. "You think I'll help you with this madness? That will never happen."

Dr. Mansfield glanced to the door and held a finger to his lips. "Before, when I asked you if you would sacrifice a thousand children to save the world, you said no. I wonder, does your conviction hold if we change the question to saving one particular child?"

Lauren choked back the emotion that surged inside her as she realized he was talking about Sarah. Only now, with this glimmer of hope, did she realize she had already given herself and her daughter up for dead. Maybe there was a way to save her. "Anything," she whispered. "I'd do anything."

"I can save Sarah. Huckley insists we sacrifice her. He believes she holds the key to freeing us from the limits we face, but I can control him." He dragged his tongue across his dry lips. "If I spare Sarah, will you help me develop the serum?"

Tears swelled in Lauren's eyes. Just the reference to sparing her daughter was enough to collapse the columns of morality that held up her belief system. Everything she had just argued against seemed to pale next to saving Sarah. Still, a force inside her fought against the abdication. How could she help a madman take innocent lives? What would her daughter's life mean if it came at that cost? Slowly, her conscience beat back her maternal impulse and concluded that she had to refuse. She had to make a principled stand. But when she opened her

362

mouth, the words that tumbled out were not angry defiance, but a mumbled defeat. "I'll do anything you want. Just don't hurt my baby."

Dr. Mansfield eyed her carefully. "I'll have to keep her somewhere until we're finished with the work. In case you change your mind, you see."

Lauren nodded.

"These other men, they can't know about our arrangement. Huckley has filled them with promises about how Sarah will change their lives."

"But I thought you were the leader."

"It's more complicated than that. With these men, I can't afford to look weak. I have to plan this carefully. If you want to save your daughter, not a word, understand? No matter what happens."

Lauren nodded her head, remembering the analogy Dr. Mansfield had used earlier about God. She looked up at the doctor and realized she had done exactly what she had accused him of doing. She had made a deal with the devil, and there was no going back.

She looked up as voices approached from outside. The door swung open, and she saw Huckley, the sheriff, and Deputy Sorenson, whom she recognized from the first night in the hospital with Jack.

Janney called out. "What about her, Boss? Are we taking her down with us?"

Dr. Mansfield shook his head. "She stays up here. I'm going to convince her to help with the project."

Huckley snorted and hawked a gob of spit against the wall. He wrinkled his nose at Lauren as if she were a spoiled piece of meat. "She'll never help." He nodded to Deputy Sorenson. "Maybe the kid here can break her spirit a little while we're gone."

Sorenson smiled. "Are you saying what I think you're saying?"

Lauren looked to Dr. Mansfield, but he avoided her eyes. He had his arm over Janney's shoulder and was walking him outside, talking softly in his ear. Huckley watched them walk out and then turned back to Sorenson. "You're a big boy.

I'm sure you can figure it out. Just make sure she's alive when we get back. Don't be too gentle, though. She won't learn her lesson unless you bloody her up at least a little."

"Don't worry. It'll be my pleasure," Sorenson said, stepping toward Lauren, his eyes roving over her body.

"Not right now, you idiot. Later, when we go down."

"How long's that going to be?"

Huckley shot Sorenson a glance that told the deputy his tone of voice alone was enough for Huckley to consider killing him. He shook his head. "We'll go when we're ready. When the two of them are done with their little secrets," he said, jutting a chin toward the doorway through which Dr. Mansfield and Janney had disappeared. "We'll head down in about fifteen, give Butcher and Moran time to finish up. And son, no matter what happens, don't you dare come down that elevator shaft."

Sorenson was still staring at Lauren, shifting his weight from side to side, dragging the palms of his hands across his chest. "Don't you worry about that. I have plenty up here to keep me occupied."

Lauren closed her eyes, praying that Dr. Mansfield wasn't lying and that there was still a chance she could save Sarah. She would endure any pain and indignity from these men, but only if it meant Sarah could go free. Otherwise she thought she would go insane from helplessness. She thought of her poor Jack, locked up in the Midland prison. How terrible the last day must have been for him. But at least he was safe, the publicity of his arrest probably the one thing keeping him alive. At least Becky would have one parent at the end of it all. It was a small consolation, but given the circumstances, it meant everything to her. *You stay alive, Jack,* she murmured under her breath. *You stay alive for our girls.*

Lauren jumped when the scream erupted on the floor beneath her. Her heart sank, knowing, as only a parent can, that the sound meant her daughter was in pain. She looked down and saw Sarah struggling to her feet, the shriek coming from her mouth reaching an impossibly high pitch. When Sarah turned toward her mother, Lauren shuddered. Her daughter looked right through her.

"Sarah. It's all right. Come here," she called out, trying to reach out toward her.

But her bindings made it impossible to move. Even without the rope around her wrists and legs, she would have frozen in place when she realized Sarah's screams were actually words.

The same words.

Over and over.

Daddy's dead! Daddy's dead! DADDY'S DEAD!

SEVENTY-SEVEN

At first he thought there was some kind of mistake. He had felt the water rush over his lips and slide over his tongue on the way down his throat. He remembered knowing the moment had arrived when there wouldn't be another moment to follow. Time was through with him. It was over.

But there he was, still in the tunnel. Still floating in the dark water. Everything was the same. Except the burning in his chest was gone. And he breathed freely. It didn't make any sense. It didn't make any sense at all.

Jack looked down at his hands and lifted them to his face. They shimmered like they were made of water. The beam of light from his miner's helmet shone right through them. With the sight came sensations of his new body. It was loose, not like free falling because that meant motion. It was more like how he imagined walking in space would feel. Smooth and effortless. He felt oddly comfortable with the sensation, as if he was in a place he'd visited before.

Before he had a chance to question where he was, a little girl came and took his hand. He mistook the girl for Sarah and felt a pang of guilt for wishing it had been her. His intuition told him it was better that Sarah was not there with him. It was better that his daughter was someplace else. Even if it meant he never saw her again, it was better than if it were her holding his hand and guiding him forward. Better that it was this strange little girl he didn't recognize.

He let the girl holding his hand lead him through the tunnel. Even without looking down he knew he wasn't moving his legs, but he still went in the direction he wanted. Forward. Toward the light ahead of him.

"Do you remember me?" the little girl asked.

Jack looked away from the light glowing in front of him and down at the pretty face staring up at him. "I'm sorry. I don't think I—"

Then the image hit him, fast like the beat of a strobe light. The side of the girl's head was caved in. Her face gouged by glass. Bright red blood poured down her neck and chest. Her mouth stretched wide in a scream. Then, a beat of the strobe light later, the girl was back, pure and beautiful.

"Oh, God." It didn't occur to him to pull his hand away or to be shocked by the little girl's identity. "I'm so sorry for what I did to you. I'm so sorry. So sorry."

The girl whispered back, "I know you are."

Jack didn't know what to say. Somehow he knew throwing himself at her feet and begging for forgiveness wasn't allowed. There were rules in this place. Nothing posted or written, but clearly there were rules. He could feel them.

"Did it hurt?" he asked.

The question felt somehow too personal, too intrusive. But he couldn't stop it from coming out. He'd spent every day for over a year wanting to know the answer to the question.

"Yes," Melissa whispered, "there was a lot of pain. Even after I came to this place."

"I'm sorry."

"I am too," Melissa said.

She tugged at his hand to continue forward, but he pulled back. He choked on his words on his first attempt. He needed to speak the forbidden words out loud.

"That day, the day I...killed you. Everyone said it was an accident. Just one of those tragedies. But that's not the truth." He let the tears fall down his cheeks. "It was my fault."

"You were reckless."

"Yes," he whispered. "I was rushing to a meeting about...something, I don't even remember what it was. Talking on the phone, not paying attention. I knew I was going too fast, but the meeting. I had to make the meeting." He tried to steady his voice. "I saw you on the bicycle, you know. All the way down the road, but by the time I was at the end of the street I forgot about you. It wasn't until you were lying there, bleeding to death on my windshield that I realized what I had done."

"Go   on."

"It wasn't enough that I killed you, but I let them cover it up. The police. They knew. There were eye-witnesses. But I let them cover it up. You were poor, so they looked the other way, and I let them. I let everyone believe I was innocent, even my wife. I didn't tell anyone I was doing seventy on a residential street full of kids. I didn't pay for my sin. I'm so ashamed."

The girl was silent for several seconds. "The people here told me I should never forgive you. That I should make you pay for what you did. I listened to them. It's the reason I'm still here."

Only then did Jack notice the dark forms of people moving in the walls around him. But they weren't really walls, just dark edges of his vision. The world there was different than where he walked hand-in-hand with Melissa. The place in the darkness was deep and thick with its own viscosity. A black environment where shadow creatures struggled like insects caught in the sinewy stickiness of a spider web. "What is this place? Who are those people?"

"Purgatory. Limbo. Ether. Choose a name. It's a place for those who are not ready to go home because they don't want to leave home. Do you understand?"

Jack looked down at the little girl, realizing the small figure was misleading. Melissa Gonzales, killed at the age of eight when she crushed her chest cavity against the front bumper of his car and smashed her head open on his windshield, was no longer a child. She was much more now.

"They   are   holding   onto   their   lives   before they…before…Melissa?"

"Yes, Jack?"

"I died in the river, didn't I?"

The girl stopped and pulled his hand toward her until his face was even with hers. Leaning forward, she kissed him on the cheek. When she pulled back, she gave him a smile so beautiful that Jack felt he might cry. "I forgive you for killing me. I forgive you for everything. I want you to know that."

Jack choked down a sob as the weight of his guilt dissolved with the girl's words. He felt shame at his reaction even as he felt awed at her gift to him. "I don't deserve it."

"We all deserve it. I learned that here." She grasped his hand tightly. "What I told you before was wrong. It doesn't work to run from the devil. You have to face him and defeat him. You can beat the devil, but only if you're strong for your family."

As she spoke the words, images flashed in Jack's mind. The pages of scribbled numbers Sarah wrote with the word "run" scrawled across the back. Albert James whispering in his ear, warning him to take his family away. The voice in his head the night Huckley almost made him take a baseball bat to his family. Jack put it together. "It was you? It was you all along trying to warn me?"

"I stayed to help you, to show that I've forgiven you. The men who want to use your daughter must be stopped. There are many here who cannot go home until those men are destroyed. You can stop them. You have to stop them."

The light ahead of them blossomed, a brilliant flower of light that reached out for them, begged them to walk forward, pleaded for them to surrender to it. Jack was mesmerized, but the girl tugged on his hand. She pointed behind them. Jack turned and saw a pale point of light, no more than a candle that seemed a mile away.

Motion. The sensation of falling. The point of light sped toward him, suddenly as big as the sun. And the heat. His skin burned. Jack covered his face to block the pain. But his lungs were filled with fire. It was melting his insides.

God, he was going insane from the pain. He had to get it out. He turned to his side and heaved, expelling the fire, expelling the pain.

When he inhaled, he expected more heat but found relief instead. It was air. Cool, sweet, beautiful air.

Lonetree's voice floated into his stirring consciousness. "There you go. Breathe now, breathe." Jack's eyes fluttered open, and Lonetree's face hovered over him, a wide smile pasted on it. "You had me a little nervous there. Thought you were gone for good."

Jack tried to smile, rolled on his side, and threw up again.

He was alive. And whether he deserved it or not, he had another chance to make things right.

SEVENTY-EIGHT

While Jack recovered, Lonetree told him about his own part in their shared adventure. Just like Jack, he had tumbled along with the current, sure that he was one lungful of air away from death. He saw small pockets of air on the ceiling, but the river moved too fast for him to take advantage of them. The limestone walls were worn too smooth for him to grab hold, but it didn't stop him from trying until the very end.

It was at the end, right when he thought his lungs might either collapse or explode, that the impossible happened. When he reached up to try and grab hold of the ceiling, his hand broke the surface of the water. With a violent kick, he pushed himself up just as his lungs gave way. Instead of sucking down water, he breathed air.

Getting his wits about him, he splashed his way over to the side of the channel, swinging the light from his miner's helmet over the rock face. It was only three or four feet high, but there was no way he could climb it, not with the current rushing him past it. But then he saw the steps carved into the rock. He swam toward them with everything he had left, knowing it was probably the one chance he was going to get to save his life. He reached the steps and caught his breath in time to pull in the rope as Jack's body floated by.

"You weren't breathing. No pulse. You didn't respond to CPR either. I worked on you for a while." Lonetree looked away. "To tell you the truth, I gave up on you. I'm sorry, but I thought you were gone. I had already pulled the backpack off your body and was checking my gear when you started to puke all over yourself. I pumped the rest of the shit out of you though," he added defensively.

"Thanks," Jack said. "I mean it. If you hadn't fished me out of the river I'd still be floating to God knows where. You saved my life."

They sat in the cave for a few seconds, both men alone with their thoughts. Lonetree decided to speak his out loud. "You could have let go of the rope when I fell in the river. I saw how you wrapped it around you. It wouldn't have taken much to get out of it."

Jack shrugged. Lonetree had made his observation the way someone might describe any commonplace thing. But Jack understood there wasn't a question buried underneath the statement, and there was nothing else to be said about it. He couldn't help but smile as he realized Lonetree had just thanked him for trying to save his life, even though he had failed miserably.

"I know you think you've got the market on crazy stories," Jack said. "But let me tell you what happened to me. Well, what I think happened anyway." He told Lonetree as much detail as he could remember from his near-death experience. He hadn't decided if the label was accurate, but he had to label it as something. A hallucination? A discharge of electrical impulses in his brain that created one final dream? Those rationalizations didn't feel right. Even considering them made him feel like he was betraying Melissa Gonzales again, belittling her act of forgiveness. He wouldn't do that to her. He had to believe that what he saw was real.

Lonetree listened to the story without asking questions. When Jack was done he said only, "She's your protective spirit. Your guardian angel if you like."

"But I still don't get it. I killed her. Why would she help me?"

"She told you, didn't she? Until she gave up her anger, she could not go into the light you saw. She had to stay in the shadow world until she could forgive you. Most religions talk about such a place. Somewhere between here and..."

"Heaven?"

"Maybe. Maybe it's the wrong word. Makes it sound like we can actually understand what it is. And just maybe we can't understand it or describe it with words at all." Lonetree shook his head like a dog shaking the water out of his coat. "Anyway, this is beyond me. All I know is that I hope your little guardian angel was right about one thing."

"What's that?"

"That we still have to find a way to beat the devil. You realize what the steps carved into the rock over there mean, right?"

Jack shone his light over to the steps, then back to Lonetree. "They used this place. It means this must connect to the main cave." He struggled to his feet. "We've got to get going."

"There's something I haven't told you yet. But now things are...well...different. I don't think you're going to like it."

Jack didn't like the sound of that.

"Look," Lonetree started, "I thought you were dead. Still, I was going to try and save your kid if I could. For whatever that's worth."

"Thanks. I appreciate that," Jack said.

"Save your thanks. See here's the thing. I told you how I rigged the cave with the C-4 charges, right?"

"Yeah?"

"Well, I thought you were dead. Hell, I thought I was dead at one point. The whole thing shook me up. If we hadn't gotten lucky, the bastards would have won."

"What are you trying to say?"

"I'm saying I decided I couldn't take any more chances." Lonetree checked his watch. "I started the timer. Less than forty minutes from now, there's going to be one hell of an explosion down here. So if we don't make this quick, you're going to die twice in one day."

SEVENTY-NINE

They made short work of the passage leading up from the river. Lonetree came to a halt and crouched to the ground, turning his helmet light off. Jack slid next to him and followed his lead by turning off his own light. The tunnel ahead of them glowed softly. They were getting close. Jack cupped his hand over his watch and pressed the light. Just the short passage from the river had already taken three minutes. Thirty-seven minutes until the explosion. He shook his head and whispered the status to Lonetree. They crab-walked forward, staying close to the walls until the tunnel opened to the main cave.

Lonetree nodded left. "We came in the first time over there. Looks like the river parallels this side of the cavern." He pointed to the lights on the right. "Our friends are already here."

Two halogen lamps set up on tripods bathed the area in stark white light. Although the lights were pointed the opposite direction from Jack and Lonetree, they still cast a faint circle of illumination across the rows of stone cages nearest the stone structure. Just as when Lonetree had first thrown the parachute flare into the open space of the cavern, Jack was shocked by the sheer enormity of the space. Even moving quickly, it would take them five minutes to reach the lights.

"I don't see any movement," Jack whispered.

"I thought I saw something when we first came in, but I'm not sure now."

"Either way, we've got to go. Let's do it."

"Right, follow me through the cages. There might be traps. Once we get close, hand signals only. I don't know what we'll find so we have to improvise. "Remember, if you have to shoot–"

"Head shot or multiple to the chest. Got it. Let's go."

Lonetree grabbed Jack by the arm and pulled him close. "We can do this." Before Jack could say anything, Lonetree was gone, a dark shadow picking his way through the maze of stone cages.

Jack followed quickly behind as a thousand skeleton sentinels silently marked their progress. He found himself wondering how many of the poor souls lying in these cages were the same creatures he'd seen in that dark in-between place where Melissa Gonzales had guided him. Had those who died here learned to forgive as Melissa had? Or would they stay in that dark place forever, caught up in their hatred and anger? Even with the adrenaline and the exertion of keeping up with Lonetree, Jack still felt a cold chill cover his skin. The skeletons all seemed to be watching him, as if they *expected* something.

As they closed in on their brightly lit objective, Jack searched for any sign of the men. They took care to block their movements by keeping a stone cage between them and the lights whenever possible. By approaching from directly behind the lamps, there was little chance of them being spotted by anyone within the circle.

But that was the problem. As they approached the lights, they couldn't see anyone around the stone structure. No voices. No movement. Nothing. It seemed as if they were alone in the cave. That was one contingency they hadn't thought out.

Lonetree crouched in the dark shadow of a cage and waved Jack to come in close to him. He broke his own rule against talking. "I don't get it," he whispered close enough to Jack's ear that he could feel hot breath on his skin. "I'm almost sure I saw movement under the lights when we first came in. Did you see it?"

Jack shook his head that he hadn't.

"OK, let's split up and meet here in five. Careful, maybe they heard something and they're looking for us." He removed his gun, pointed Jack to go right, and then headed left himself.

Jack slid the safety off his gun and took a deep breath. Keeping close to the stone cages, he ran to his right until he came to a break in the cages where a wide swath of light lay across his path. He dropped to the ground and spread out flat on his stomach. He leaned his head around the corner to look into the open space.

He had a clear view of the round structure – the Source. It was only sixty or seventy feet away from him. Seeing no one, he took the chance to stretch his head out farther to get a better look.

He froze. There were two men crouched on the ground on the opposite side of the stone structure from where he and Lonetree had stood a minute before. Jack was looking at their backs, but if either of the men turned around they would be staring right at him. He knew he should scramble backward and get out of sight, but he was fixated by what they men were doing.

They were hunched over, working hard on something lying on the ground between them. The man closest to him, the smaller of the two, was doing most of the work. His back was moving back and forth in a steady rhythm matching the forward and backward thrusting of his right elbow. Even from the distance, Jack could hear the man grunting from his exertion.

The man paused to drag the sleeve of his shirt across his face, like he was mopping sweat from his brow. He lifted a small object and handed it to the other man. This larger man then inserted the object into a small hole in the round structure. The object disappeared into the stone wall.

The smaller man decided to stretch before he resumed his task. As he stretched both arms into the air, Jack saw the instrument the man held in his hand.

A saw.

He wore yellow gloves. They were covered up to the forearms with blood.

It was the ritual, just like Max had described. The men in front of him were cutting up a victim and feeding it through the hole in the structure.

A cry escaped Jack's throat. Both men stood and looked in his direction, but Jack didn't care. It wasn't the blood on the man's gloves that had made him cry out. It was a flash of color on the ground. Yellow. No, not yellow. Blonde. Blonde hair.

Oh God. It's Sarah.

The men were cutting up his little girl with a saw.

Stuffing her body piece by piece through that little hole in the rock.

The world closed in around him. His peripheral vision blacked out, and he was looking through a tunnel. At the end of this tunnel stood the objects of his rage. Scott Moran and Jim Butcher, both frozen in place by this sudden intrusion from the outside world.

Without thinking, Jack crawled to his feet and ran screaming at the two men. He slowed enough to steady his gun. The first shot ricocheted off the rock structure behind Butcher. The second blew up a puff of dust ten feet in front of him.

Butcher stood dumbly in the line of fire, as if his brain couldn't quite process Jack's appearance. He stood with his mouth hanging open at the charging intruder.

Jack closed the distance fast. Nothing registered in his brain except his need to kill the men in front of him. The need to avenge his little girl's death.

His third shot hit its mark. The slug tore into Butcher's chest. The next one caught him in the throat and his neck erupted in a gurgle of blood.

Still Jack charged forward, shifting his fire to Moran. The smaller man had reacted faster than Butcher and was crawling on the rock floor away from the spray of bullets. Jack was merciless. He emptied his weapon into the man. Then he was on top of him, beating Moran's face with the gun while blood and bits of flesh sprayed over his chest and face.

Slowly, cautiously, sanity climbed back into Jack's mind. Exhausted, he gave in to it and slid off Scott Moran's disfigured body. He didn't want to look at what was left of Sarah, but he knew he had to. Maybe there was some way to restore dignity to her body. A few words of prayer before they were blown up together in this underground hell.

He dried the tears that clouded his vision and then turned to look at his poor, little girl.

A sob wrenched out from his body as he realized the impossible.

It wasn't her. The body was too large. It was a young woman. Maybe a teenager. The legs were gone, but the torso was there. And the face. Covered with a mop of blonde hair.

Jack grimaced as he looked over the girl's body. Dark sores covered most of the pale white skin. Gingerly, he reached out and pushed the hair off her face. Her eyes bulged out as if she were still capable of being shocked. A wet trickle of blood ran from her nose and covered her lips.

Lonetree slid into a crouching position beside him. "You okay?" His gun was drawn, and his eyes darted back and forth. He looked down at the bodies and then at Jack. "Who's the girl?"

Jack recognized her. The last time he had seen her was in a photo. She had been younger then, but not by more than a few years. In the photo, she had been standing next to her horse. Smiling. Happy to be alive.

"It's his daughter. The bastard killed his own daughter."

"C'mon," Lonetree said. "We have to get out of the light."

They both tensed at a sudden noise next to them. Like someone crawling over loose rocks. Lonetree started to move away, but Jack reached out and stopped him. The sound came again, closer this time. He turned in the direction of the noise. It took another movement before it registered where the sound was coming from.

Both of them stared toward the dark hole in the stone structure. Something was inside. And it was moving toward them.

EIGHTY

$\mathbf{H}$uckley pushed Lauren to the ground and blocked out the light as he stood over her. He pointed over to one of the horse stalls and grunted for her to move. When she hesitated, Huckley brought the heel of his boot down on her hip, followed by another kick into her rib cage. Pain flooded through her. A voice came from farther back in the barn. Janney. He was shouting at Huckley to take it easy.

She gasped for air. The last kick had knocked the breath from her. A dull pain spread from her side and radiated through her torso. A broken rib, she thought, maybe a couple of them.

The blows had caught her off guard, not just because of the pain but because of the suddenness of the violence. She'd always known she was in danger, especially since Huckley's instructions to the young deputy and the last ten minutes of his leering glances at her, but she held out hope that her deal with Dr. Mansfield would save her. She wondered if the doctor had changed his mind. The optimism she had felt only minutes earlier – that she at least had bought her daughter some more time – was gone, kicked out of her by Huckley's boot. Then again, Dr. Mansfield did say he couldn't look weak in front of the other men. She clung to the hope this was all part of the act.

She played the supplicant and crawled across the wood floor on her hands and knees, sliding on the thin layer of straw that covered the barn floor. The pungent odor of animal feces and machine oil filled her nostrils. She ignored the smell and searched the floor for a weapon. A screwdriver. A nail. Anything sharp. But there was nothing.

Huckley kicked the bottom of her foot to get her moving faster. Once in the stall, she turned and huddled against the wall as far from him as she could get. He grinned and swaggered closer. She noticed for the first time that his belt was unbuckled. As he walked, he slowly pulled at one end and slid the belt from his jeans. His tongue darted out from between his lips and flicked the air in a crude sexual gesture.

Huckley's pale face leered over her as if breathing in her fear. He threaded the belt back through the buckle and cinched it together. The resulting noose went over Lauren's head, and Huckley pulled until it was snug on her throat. He stretched the other end of the belt high up on the wall where a thick nail stuck out from the wood. Forcing the head of the nail through the belt hole, it created a taut hangman's noose that choked Lauren unless she stood up straight and motionless. Huckley pulled her hands behind her back and snapped handcuffs around her wrists. He stood back to inspect his work.

"Think you can handle this?" he said to the deputy.

Sorenson stepped into Lauren's field of vision. His eyes tracked over her body, looking everywhere except her eyes. His interests were elsewhere.

"Yeah, I can take care of this."

Dr. Mansfield walked by on the edge of her peripheral vision. She tried to turn to look in his direction, but the noose around her neck tightened at the movement. She heard his voice though. "Grab the girl and let's go."

Huckley patted the deputy on the back and gave Lauren a wink. "Too bad I can't sense your thoughts through all this white noise. The Source, you know. Bet it's a delicious mix of terror and hatred. Mmmmm...I can almost taste it."

She pressed her lips together. At least she could deny him the fun of seeing her react to his goading.

He walked over to Sarah, once again sedated after her earlier outburst, and hefted her off the floor. He carried her under his arm like she was a duffle bag, her arms hanging limply to the ground.

Lauren lunged toward her daughter only to have the belt noose tighten around her neck. She backed off, the belt cutting off her air supply. She wanted to scream at the three men as they boarded the elevator platform, but she could only stomp the floor in frustration. She twisted her hands against the handcuffs until she felt the warm slickness of blood cover them.

But nothing she did stopped the men taking her daughter. Huckley reached up to a control box, and the elevator sank into the shaft. She squinted through her tears to get one last look at her daughter. All she could see was her blonde hair hanging down in front of her face, her body pressed against Huckley's torso. As the elevator platform cleared the lip of the shaft, Lauren forced a scream from her constricted windpipe and pulled at her bindings again.

The belt cinched tighter on her throat. She felt the heat build in her face as the blood accumulated. Black shadows formed walls on all sides of her vision. The shadows grew darker and pushed toward the center of her sight.

She knew she was going to pass out, and if she did, the belt would strangle her. In a sudden moment of clarity, she realized she no longer cared. She didn't want to live. She couldn't explain why, but she believed somehow her daughter knew Jack was dead. Dr. Mansfield's promise now seemed empty, and she couldn't bear to imagine the things about to be done to her daughter. All it would take was to let her feet slip out from beneath her, and it would all be over. No more pain. No more terror. Just darkness.

She leaned forward into the tension of the belt. Her tunnel vision narrowed until only a blurry patch of light remained.

Then a free fall.

Thump. Her body hit the floor. The pain invaded her comfortable dark cocoon of semi-consciousness and filled it with the stark light from the barn's halogen lamps. The pressure around her neck disappeared, and she sucked down mouthfuls of air.

Her vision cleared with every breath. With her hands still cuffed, she sprawled awkwardly on the floor, trying to make sense of what had happened. In a rush of hope, she guessed that the belt had broken, or maybe the nail had come loose from the wall. It was her chance. But she had to get away before the deputy came back.

She rocked side-to-side to get the leverage to stand up, but as she did so, strong hands pushed down on the middle of her back. "Hold on," Sorenson said. "You're going to hurt yourself."

She kicked and twisted her body to get away, but the man was on top of her, holding her down. He was too strong. She couldn't move. She screamed. Over and over. She screamed from the despair of losing her family. She screamed at the animal pawing at her wrists and shouting at her. She screamed until tears flowed from her eyes like blood from a wound.

The few seconds of hope given her by Dr. Mansfield dissipated like a cruel dream. There was no escape. There was no way to help her little girl. She let her body go slack, exhausted from a fight she knew she couldn't win, resigned to the inevitable conclusion to her nightmare, so full of self-loathing for not protecting her daughter that she welcomed the humiliation about to be inflicted on her body. She stopped screaming and realized the man on top of her had been talking the entire time. She stopped struggling and finally listened to what he was saying, then burst into tears at the meaning of his words.

EIGHTY-ONE

Jack crawled over to the opening in the rock wall. The sound from inside the structure had changed. The crunching of rocks stopped. A soft rasping sigh took its place. Jack's first thought was that air was moving through the hole in the rock, as if the internal pressure were equalizing with the outside cave. But the sigh had an unnatural cadence, like the murmuring intonations of a dying man's last words.

That's what the sound was, it was language. There was a person locked inside the structure.

Checking quickly to make sure no one was coming, Jack whispered into the hole. "Hello. Can you hear me?"

"We need to get out of here. The others had to hear the gunshots," Lonetree said.

Jack ignored him. The rasping sound grew stronger. It seemed like the person inside moved closer to the hole.

"Can you understand me?" Jack said.

An eyeball appeared at the other end of the hole. The sight of it made Jack recoil. Even with the dim amount of reflected light from the halogens that entered the opening, Jack could see the eye was deformed. It was a bulging mass of exploded blood vessels and cataracts. The eyelids were gone, leaving a wide-eyed, unblinking stare.

Jack leaned forward, peering into the shadows of the hole. "What did they do to you?" he whispered.

A shrieking howl erupted from inside the structure. More animal than human.

Lonetree pulled Jack away from the wall, placing himself closest to the structure. "We have to go," he said.

An arm shot out from the hole and claws ripped deep into his skin. Lonetree cried out in pain and grabbed his shoulder. His gun flew from his hand and skittered across the rock floor. Acting on reflex, Lonetree jumped backward. By the time the creature's arm made its next pass, he was well out of reach. The arm continued to cut wildly through the air, seeking out more flesh to tear.

Jack stepped back, horrified at what he saw. There was no skin on the arm stretching out from the hole. Only exposed muscles, soft with decay, wrapped around yellow bones. Black talons extended from the fingers, clicking against each other in their frenzied search. Blood oozed from veins ripped open by the rough edges of the hole. There was no human prisoner inside the stone structure. There was a monster.

The first bullet hit the rock wall next to Jack's head. Sharp streaks of pain stung his face as rock shards ripped into his skin. Lonetree shoved him and he tumbled forward. He landed on the ground just as he heard the second shot burn the air next to his ear.

"Stay down," Lonetree hissed. He crawled forward on his stomach, using the uneven floor as cover. He retrieved his gun, spun around, and looked for a target. "You all right?" Lonetree whispered.

"Yeah, did you see where they were?"

"No. You?"

Jack shook his head and leaned his shoulder into the boulder they were using for protection. He thought the shots had come from beyond the lights in front of them, but he wasn't sure. For all he knew, they were surrounded, and guns were trained on his head as he sat there making a target of himself. They had to run, get out of the light. At least among the rows of stone cages they would have a chance.

"Jack, I know it's you," Janney called out. "Why don't you come on out before someone gets hurt?"

Lonetree tugged at his arm to get him to move. Jack positioned himself so he was ready to scramble from behind the rock, his breath coming in quick, ragged pants. He was about to surge forward when he heard a sound that sucked the air out from him and made him sag back behind the rock.

The scream came from the other side of the lights. Terror translated into a single, trembling high-pitched note. It coursed through the still air of the cave, echoes layering on top of echoes until the terrible sound came at him from all directions. The scream left no doubt that the source of the sound was in pain. But still Jack held his ground. He didn't run away, but neither did he run to help. He sat with his back against the rock, his body shaking, eyes clenched shut.

Janney's voice rang out over the screams. "You can make it stop. Just show yourself."

Lonetree grabbed his arm. "You can't do anything for her. The only way we stand a chance is to stay hidden."

Jack heard the words and knew they were true. He might even have been able to follow Lonetree if he had run to the safety of the black shadows only feet away from them. But then the sound changed. And with the change, Jack lost his grip on the instinct of self-preservation. He shook off Lonetree's efforts to hold him down, and he stood up from behind the rock. The bright lights made him squint. He threw his gun forward and stepped into the clearing even as Sarah continued to scream the word over and over, her voice so full of pleading that his heart ached.

"Daddy. Daddy."

Any other word and he might have made a run for it with Lonetree. Might have tried to fight it out. But not that word. That he couldn't take.

"I'm here, honey. Daddy's here," he shouted.

The scream stopped in an unnatural break – as if the cave floor had opened and swallowed her whole. The echoes reverberated for a few seconds more, but they too died down. The silence in the cave, broken only by the hum of the powerful lights, was almost as unnerving as the screams.

"Jesus, look at Jim and Scott," Janney said from behind the lights. "Look what they did to them. I think they're dead."

There was a disapproving grunt from farther to the right, closer to where Sarah's scream had come from. Janney must have understood the message because he shut up. Jack could almost feel Lonetree's eyes boring through him as they tried to pick out targets in the shadows. "Janney," Jack called out, "you know I wouldn't come down here without calling the police. The real police, I mean." Even Jack didn't think his shaking voice sounded believable. "Let Sarah go. She's only a baby, for God's sake."

"Tell Lonetree to get out here where I can see him," Janney yelled back.

Lonetree answered. "Fuck you. Come and get me."

"Jack, you better talk to him. If you need some encouragement, I can arrange it."

Janney didn't have to spell it out. Jack knew they would torture Sarah until he did whatever they told him. Once that started, Jack knew that he would shoot Lonetree himself if it would make them stop hurting her. What did it matter, anyway? His last glance at his wristwatch showed they had less than twenty-five minutes before the explosives detonated. There was no chance of escape. No way Lonetree could manage to fight the three men hiding in the shadows and still get out alive.

Sarah wailed in pain from a spot beyond the lights, just to his right. Her cry ramped up to a higher pitch as though someone were squeezing the sound from her. Jack's stomach tightened. He knew they wouldn't kill her. Not yet, anyway. But he couldn't stand to hear her in pain.

"Lonetree. Give yourself up. They're hurting her." He wanted to scream, *The cave is going to blow up soon, so give yourself up. Don't make my baby suffer more than she has to!* But even as he thought it, he realized that Lonetree didn't need to give up. No more than he needed to fight. He could run. Crawl away in the dark and escape through the tunnel they first came through. Moving fast, he could make it back to the surface just in time to be safely out of the way when the cave system started to collapse. Chances were, Lonetree had shouted at Janney to make them think he was staying and then turned and sprinted through the maze of cages on his way to the exit.

Sarah screamed again, her voice cracking from the intensity.

"Stop it. Leave the little girl alone."

Jack spun to his left to track the source of the voice. Lonetree walked out from a dark shadow only fifteen feet from where Jack stood. It seemed impossible that the big man had been able to move undetected from the spot where they had been pinned down, but there he was, walking with his hands extended over his head. His eyes moved over to Jack as if to say, *Are you happy now?* and then returned to the shadows where his enemies remained hidden, watching their adversary enter the light.

"Turn around," Janney called out. "Raise your shirt. Any weapons you have, I want on the ground right now."

Lonetree did as he was instructed. His face cast like a death mask, his eyes never leaving the spot where Sarah's screams had now been replaced with soft whimpering. Jack wanted to tell the man he appreciated the sacrifice he had just made. He wondered though if Lonetree really had given himself up for Sarah, or if it was that he wanted to look into the eyes of the devil he had hunted for so long. The Boss was on the other side of the halogen lights. Maybe he had decided it was worth his life to stand face-to-face with the man who had killed his brother and father.

"Cover me, Huckley," Janney said before sliding out from behind the rocks beyond the lamps. He walked carefully toward Lonetree, his gun trained on the big man's chest. The sheriff's face puckered from the stress of the moment, as if he were walking up on a sedated animal, not sure if the drugs had taken all the fight out of him yet. Jack also wondered if Lonetree was playing with them. He felt detached from the situation, just a spectator hoping something big was about to happen.

Janney patted Lonetree down, always watching his face for a sign he was about to attack. Finding nothing, he called out over his shoulder, "He's clean."

Huckley appeared first, looking like an animal that had maimed a bird and was now eager to have some fun with it. He clapped his hands together as if the sheer enjoyment of having

Lonetree unarmed in front of him was too much to contain. But Lonetree didn't look at him. His eyes were focused beyond the lights, waiting for the Boss to appear.

Sarah came running out from the shadows first. She screamed and sprinted to Jack with her arms out wide. Jack hadn't expected to see her free. He staggered a few steps toward her and sank to his knees to scoop her up in a bear hug. She jumped into his arms. He held her tight as her body heaved from crying. Jack rubbed her back and lied to his little girl over and over. "Everything's going to be all right. Don't worry. I'll take care of you."

"Hello, Jack. I can't say I expected to see you here."

Jack looked up, not ready to believe the voice he heard until his eyes confirmed the sight for him. Next to a stone pillar, his grey hair neatly combed back, stood Dr. Mansfield.

"You?" Lonetree said, giving a voice to what Jack was thinking. "You're the Boss?"

"That's right." Dr. Mansfield walked toward them, smiling at Sarah hugging her father.

"I don't get it," Jack said. "It's not possible."

Dr. Mansfield smiled. "You'd be surprised what's possible when it comes right down to it." He turned to Lonetree. "So now you know. This was what your brother died trying to find out. Even at the end, I don't think he ever guessed. Both of you might have come closer if you ever stopped to understand what I am trying to accomplish here. Your brother never appreciated what this was all about."

"Killing little kids? No, he knew exactly what you fuckers are all about," Lonetree said.

Dr. Mansfield shrugged. "Drug abusers, runaways, teenage prostitutes. These are society's throwaways. No one wants them. No one misses them when they disappear. I gave them something they would never have had whoring and drugging their way across the country. I gave their lives meaning. I gave their lives a purpose."

"You took their lives. For this...this thing locked in that stone cage."

"This all is for mankind's progress. Years from now, these children will be heralded for their role and honored for their sacrifice. They were part of a process that will change the world."

Jack squeezed Sarah tighter against him. "Why Sarah? Why are you doing this to her?"

Dr. Mansfield walked nearer, careful to keep his distance from Lonetree even though Huckley still had a gun aimed at his chest. "We have made so much progress, but there is a lot we don't understand about the Source. We have reason to believe this little girl, with her special abilities, can open a new world to us. To all of us."

"Don't talk about her like she's some kind of lab animal," Jack said, desperately trying to think of how to keep Dr. Mansfield talking. If his little girl had to die in this cave, he wanted to be able to hold her in his arms up until the last second. He willed Lonetree's explosives to go off sooner and end their nightmare.

Then Janney cried out and pointed toward the stone structure.

In slow, jerking movements, Scott Moran crawled toward the group, trailing a swath of blood behind him.

Scott Moran's shirt was soaked through with blood from the gunshots to his torso. The right side of his face was caved in across the jawline where Jack had beat him with the gun. Strips of skin hung off his skull from the deep lacerations. The left side of the face was untouched, and the eyeball on that side roved around manically, taking in the scene in front of it. The other eye was destroyed, ripped from its socket and mashed into the cheekbone. A groan came from deep in the man's throat as he leaned to the side and spewed a gush of blood and bits of black flesh.

"Jesus, what a mess," Janney said.

Scott Moran lurched in the direction of the voice, but he seemed paralyzed from the waist down. His wounds were healing, so slowly that it was only noticeable on the edges of the cuts. He grunted, low and wet, raising one arm toward Janney as if begging for help.

Dr. Mansfield walked over, took Janney's gun, placed the barrel against Scott Moran's forehead, and pulled the trigger. Jack held the back of Sarah's head so she wouldn't see the spray of blood and brain matter that dripped down the rock wall behind Scott Moran as he collapsed to the floor.

"He was healing. Why did you…" Janney's voice faded as Dr. Mansfield spun around and pointed the gun at the sheriff's head.

"He questioned my authority when the decision had to be made about his daughter." He cocked the gun. "Do you have a question too, Janney?"

"No, Boss. Of course not."

Jack watched in fascination as Dr. Mansfield pressed against Janney's head, bending the man to his will. He sneaked a look at his watch. Still seventeen minutes to go. It seemed like an eternity.

Dr. Mansfield lowered the gun. "All right, enough delays. Tie up these two. We need Mr. Lonetree to tell us where his information about us is hidden. Having Jack will make it easier to convince Dr. Tremont to assist me."

"I thought we were going to just tell her that her daughter was still alive," Huckley said. "Isn't that what you told her upstairs?"

"Lauren's here?" Jack cried out.

Dr. Mansfield ignored him. "That will only work for so long. Eventually she'll want proof. That's when Jack here will be useful. Did you have Janney's man do what I told you?"

"Of course. I assume you plan to kill him for the rape when we get topside. Make the Tremont woman think you're the good guy."

At the mention of the rape, Jack's mind went numb. The men's conversation grew distant, as if they were disappearing into a tunnel. His world coalesced to the space occupied by himself and his daughter. There was no way out – he knew that now. He was out of time. They would all die in the cave, and this madness would end. That, at least, was a consolation. But, with the men getting ready, it looked now as if Sarah might have to endure the cruel pain of the ritual before the explosives activated. Not only that, but he considered for the first time that the explosives might not detonate. Maybe there was a short in the charges. Maybe the cave could withstand whatever amount of C-4 Lonetree used. There was only one way for him to make sure his daughter didn't suffer. It was a terrible responsibility, but it struck him that it was the only thing he could do for the little girl he held in his arms. He just didn't know if he could bring himself to kill his own child.

All around him were stone cages filled with skeletons of parents that had to make the same horrific decision. The same angry, vengeful souls Melissa had shown him. Now Jack felt that every skull was turned in his direction and every black, empty socket stared at him, urging him to do his duty. He heard their voices.

Break her neck.

Bash her head on a rock.

You'll do it if you love her.

I did it.

I had to do it to all my children.

If you love her, you'll kill her.

And there was a murmuring undercurrent that ran through his head. It sounded like a swollen river, the kind that gurgles so that both vowels and consonants fill the air, almost words, like a foreign language that seems oddly familiar, but indecipherable. It was the sound of many voices, all saying the same sentence, overlapping so that words became unintelligible. But slowly, the more Jack focused, the more the voices synchronized until he could understand what the thousands of voices were saying.

You failed us, so you can suffer like us.

Sarah arched her back and pushed off her father's body with the palms of her hands. Jack let go enough so that she could look him in the face.

Jesus, did she read my mind? Does she know I plan to kill her?

Sarah nodded her head as if he had spoken the question out loud. He started to say something, but she held a finger to his lips. "Shhhh, Daddy. You don't have to do that. Melissa is here to help us. She brought the others. The ones who died here." She leaned in so her mouth was up against his ear. "Get ready to run, Daddy."

Before Jack could react, his daughter was ripped out of his arms by Nate Huckley. Jack cried out and lunged to grab onto her, but Janney's boot kicked him in the side, knocking the air out of him. He fell to the ground gasping for breath. When he looked up, he saw that Huckley had stopped in his tracks, Sarah hanging limp in his arms.

"Something's wrong," Huckley said. "I can feel it. I feel it in my bones."

"It's nothing," Dr. Mansfield said.

"It's a vibration."

"It's nothing, I said."

"How do you know?"

"You always say there's background vibration from the Source. All other extra-sensory ability is drowned out by it, that's what you always say."

"So?"

"So the vibration must be coming from the Source. It must sense what is about to happen."

"I don't know. All of a sudden I have a bad feeling about this," Huckley said. "The vibration is getting stronger. It's different somehow. Not from the Source."

"Come on, Huckley. You're the one who brought us to this point," Dr. Mansfield said. "This reaction must mean you were right. Think of what the Source promised us with this sacrifice. *Free from all limits.* Immortality could be minutes away for us. Immortality for the entire world. We have to find out."

Huckley squinted from pain. "Only part of the energy is coming from the Source."

He slid Sarah's limp body to the ground. Her flesh was as white as her clothes. Her lips were blue from cold. She panted in quick, short breaths.

"It's coming from her." Huckley closed his eyes, wincing. "The Source is drawing power from her. God, it's getting more intense. This isn't right. I can feel it in my head."

"What the hell is that?" Janney cried out, turning to the stone cage nearest him. There was a scratching sound like rats crawling over a pile of dry chicken bones.

"It's nothing. Just take the girl and…" Dr. Mansfield's voice trailed off as a howl came from high in the cave. The light didn't penetrate to the roof, so a layer of darkness hung over them, leaving the source of the howl to their imaginations.

"Just wind," Dr. Mansfield said. "Remember there's a storm outside."

Janney looked up. "Two centuries in the cave, and it's never made a sound like that. Not in any weather."

The scraping sounds in the cages increased. It wasn't just one of the cages – it was all of them.

Janney was near one of the halogen floor lamps. He reached up and swiveled the light so it faced out into the rows of cages around them.

Bones danced everywhere. It was like the floor of the cages had been transformed into the surface of a drum being beat at a furious tempo. There was no order to it. The bones remained a jumbled mess, rubbing and clacking against each other. Only the skulls had a specific orientation. A thousand dark eye sockets stared at the Source.

Huckley's howling was the only thing that tore Jack away from the sight of the skeletons. The man was on the floor next to Sarah, his hands pressed against his ears, screaming.

Jack took the opportunity and ran to his little girl. As he crossed between Lonetree and Dr. Mansfield, Lonetree surged toward the gun Jack had thrown on the floor when he surrendered.

The explosion caught them all off guard. It was too soon for the C-4 charges, but it didn't stop Jack from thinking it was all over. Chunks of rock flew past his head. The ground shook, and he fell forward to cover Sarah with his body. Debris fell on top of him, large enough to bruise but not to cause any real damage.

When he looked up, the area was bleached white by the halogens. The lights were ramping up in intensity as if a power surge was building in them. The lamp Janney had turned away from them exploded in a cloud of sparks. Then the second one blew, sending bits of glass and filament raining down.

Jack covered his face until it stopped, then took stock of his surroundings. It was a freeze frame, no more than one second to burn the image into his mind.

Huckley was still on the ground, his mouth open in a soundless scream.

Janney crouched down, his arms wrapped around his head. Lonetree lay on the ground, seemingly unconscious, large rocks surrounding him from the explosion. Dr. Mansfield had been farther to Jack's right, but now he was gone.

Out of his peripheral vision, Jack caught a movement to his left, from where the blast had come, the direction of the stone structure and the Source. Then he realized the explosion must have been the Source itself. He turned to see what the movement had been.

Just as he did, the last halogen flared into a brilliant supernova and exploded. The world turned black, the after-image of the burst of light hovering in front of Jack's face. From his left, a screech tore through the air, shredding it with an unearthly pitch. The sound turned into a howl. Then rocks chattered as something ran away. Silence settled back over the ancient cave, and Jack held his breath. He hadn't seen it clearly, but in the last instant before the light exploded, he was sure of one thing. A dark form had risen from the destroyed stone structure and was climbing out over the rocks. The creature they called the Source had escaped.

EIGHTY-TWO

Jack fumbled in his pocket for the glo-stick Lonetree had given him. He found it, snapped the middle, and shook it to activate the light. Sarah was conscious but disoriented. Looking her over quickly, Jack didn't see any obvious injuries.

"Mansfield got away," Lonetree said.

Jack jerked at the sound of his voice. He held up the glo-stick in the big man's direction. A thick flow of blood had matted the hair at his temple and coated one side of his face. In the green glow, he looked like an old painting of an Indian in war paint.

"You all right?" Lonetree asked.

"I should be asking you that."

Lonetree waved him off. "I'm fine."

"What the hell happened?"

"I have no idea," Lonetree said, moving toward him. "But we have less than eight minutes to get out of here. You want me to carry her?"

"No way. She's all mine."

Lonetree led the way. They ran as fast as they could over the challenging terrain, using only the glo-stick for illumination. A minute into their mad dash, Lonetree snapped a larger glo-stick, surrounding them with a ball of green florescence. It was risky, but they needed to move faster if they stood any chance. Sarah whimpered into Jack's shoulder and wrapped her legs around his midsection to hold on through the bouncy ride.

"How far to the exit?" Jack called out to Lonetree.

"I don't know. It can't be far." Lonetree turned back to answer, "There's a trail here. Should make it easier to—"

The gunshot came from behind them. The glo-stick shattered in Lonetree's hands, the fluorescent liquid exploding in a spray of light. Sarah screamed. Jack turned away, shielding her with his body.

A shadow flew from behind a stone cage and crashed into Lonetree's side. The shadow and Lonetree rolled to the ground, wrestling and grunting, both bodies covered now by splotches of fluorescent green liquid.

Jack held up his small glo-stick to illuminate the struggle in front of him. It was Janney. He had Lonetree pinned to the ground, straddling the big man with a knee on either side of his chest. Lonetree's hands gripped Janney's wrists, trying to push back the slow descent of a hunting knife toward his face.

"Run," Lonetree grunted. "Get her out of here."

Lonetree shifted his grip to the man's forearms. But Janney was forcing the blade down inch by inch toward Lonetree's eye, putting all of his weight behind the effort. Lonetree's arms started to shake. Janney seemed to notice, because he grinned and pushed harder, twisting side to side to weaken Lonetree's grip.

Jack pried Sarah off him and put her on the ground. He didn't have a weapon, so he ran at the struggling figures and lowered his shoulder.

The impact sent all three of them sprawling in a jangle of limbs. But Janney was quick to get back on his feet. Jack still clutched the glo-stick in his hand, making it easier for him to see. But it also made him an easy target. Janney charged toward him. As he did, Jack lunged at the man's legs.

He made contact right above the knees, wrapped his arms around, and drove forward with his legs. Janney tumbled over, hitting the ground hard.

A sharp cry of pain right next to him shifted Jack's focus away from Janney. Even in the faint light, he saw Lonetree slumped against the side of a stone cage. Jack saw the problem. Lonetree held Janney's knife by the handle, but with the blade pointed the wrong direction. It was buried six inches into Lonetree's side.

With a weak smile at Jack, Lonetree drew a deep breath, closed his eyes, and yanked the knife out. In the same motion, just before a scream of pain exploded from his mouth, Lonetree threw the knife toward Jack. It landed at his feet with a clang against the rock floor.

Jack grabbed the knife. But as he turned, Janney was on him, snarling, spittle foaming around his mouth. He grabbed Jack by the throat, his thick thumbs digging into Jack's windpipe. Jack plunged the knife into Janney's chest. The man's eyes bulged out from surprise and pain. Jack withdrew the knife and stabbed again. This time sinking it up to the hilt into Janney's abdomen. He forced the blade upward, twisting it back and forth to destroy as many organs as he could, hoping the blade tip could reach as far as the man's heart.

Janney released his grip around Jack's throat. A wet gurgle came up with a torrent of frothy blood that spilled out of his mouth and down his chin. He collapsed to his knees, grasping at the knife wounds. He raised his blood-soaked hands to his face and clenched them into fists. He looked to Jack, his face contorted with pain. He tried to say something, but it came out as a torrent of blood. Janney's eyes rolled, and he fell to the ground.

Jack ran to Lonetree.

"How bad are you hurt?"

Lonetree tried to stand. He cried out and grabbed at his side. His breath came in short, ragged bursts. He stood but remained bent over with one arm grabbing the stone cage next to him.

"How much time?" Lonetree wheezed.

Jack glanced at his watch. "Under six minutes."

Lonetree reached out and took hold of Jack's wrist. Jack thought he was going to recheck his watch, but instead the injured man drew him in close and whispered, "Take your girl. Follow this path. Elevator can't be far away." He pushed Jack's arm away. "Now. You have to go now."

Jack ran over to Sarah and put a hand on either shoulder. "Sarah, we're going to go home, all right, sweetie?"

Sarah nodded. She was scared, but she was staying in control. Jack could feel her whole body shaking, but she focused on what he was saying. He had no idea what had happened back at the Source, or what part Sarah had played – all he knew was that she was his little girl. She was scared but doing her best to listen to her dad. God, he was proud of her.

"I need your help." He handed her the glo-stick. "Hold this light and walk right beside me, okay?" He held her at arm's length to get a good look at her. "I love you, honey."

Despite the cold darkness around them. The blood and death. The silent skeletons that stared out at them from their stone cages. Despite it all, Sarah smiled. "I love you too, Daddy."

Jack hugged her, then turned and ran over to Lonetree.

"What are you doing?" Lonetree said.

"Come on. We're all getting out of here." He slid his shoulder under Lonetree's arm and shifted the big man's weight onto himself. Lonetree pushed off from the stone cage and hobbled forward, grunting with every step. Jack struggled under the man's weight, repeatedly losing his footing on the slick rocks beneath him. Sarah walked next to them, holding the glo-stick out in front of her as if it were a talisman against whatever lurked ahead of them.

"Faster. Faster," Jack urged Lonetree as they stumbled down the path.

"Leave me, damn it."

"No, you just move your ass. I thought you were a Marine or something."

Lonetree cocked his head to the side. With a gasp, he straightened himself a little and took more of his weight on his own legs. With this better distribution, they surged forward together. "Navy SEAL," Lonetree hissed between gasps for air. "Marines are pussies."

The trail turned and entered a tunnel carved into the cave wall. Jack noticed a glow of light ahead of them. "That has to be the elevator."

They pushed as fast as they could down the trail, around a bend, and finally into a brightly lit room. Halogen lamps glared like artificial suns. The mechanical hum of a generator filled the air. Against the far wall was a square metal platform with guardrails around the perimeter. The elevator. The way out.

Sarah screamed. Jack grabbed her and pushed her behind him.

In the middle of the room, shotgun hanging at his side, stood Nate Huckley. Beside him was Dr. Mansfield, his hair now wildly out of place, but otherwise looking calm and in control. The elevator was twenty feet behind them.

Dr. Mansfield called out to them. "I was starting to get worried. I thought maybe that idiot Janney had done something drastic. He always overreacts in a crisis."

Huckley pointed the shotgun at Sarah. "We don't want anything happening to you. Especially you, little girl. You're much too important to waste."

Jack and Lonetree exchanged glances. Jack had no idea how to get around this latest obstacle. He still had the knife he'd used on Janney, but it was no match for a shotgun.

Lonetree was gasping for air and clutching his side. And they had less than five minutes before the entire place came down around them in a massive explosion.

Jack's shoulders sagged as he faced reality. Despite everything they had done, they were all going to die.

EIGHTY-THREE

Lonetree collapsed to the floor, his body wracked by a coughing fit that produced a new flow of blood from his mouth. He rolled to his side, panting, wincing in obvious pain. Jack stayed with Sarah as Huckley walked closer to them.

"Looks like you're in a little pain there, Mr. Lonetree." He raised a gun. "Perhaps you'd like me to put you out of your misery?"

Lonetree managed to look up from the floor. He tried to say something, but the words came out in an unintelligible mumble.

"Don't be stupid, Huckley. We still need to know who he's told about us. And where his brother's notes are hidden," Dr. Mansfield said. "What the hell happened back there? What was that explosion?"

Huckley lowered the gun. "I don't know. If you didn't notice, I was the one on the ground in pain."

"You're not in pain now."

Huckley cocked his head to the side. "Not only that, but I can't sense the Source anymore."

"What do you mean?"

"Usually the Source is so loud that I'm totally overwhelmed. It's like white noise, a constant throbbing that fills my head. But now, nothing. I don't sense anything." Huckley stared at Dr. Mansfield. "You don't think..."

Dr. Mansfield turned pale. He looked at Jack. "What did you see? What was that explosion?"

Jack shrugged. "Nothing. I didn't see anything. There was an explosion. Then the lights went out."

"He's lying," Huckley said. "Without the background noise from the Source, I can sense what he's thinking." He closed his eyes. "He saw movement inside the cage. He thinks the Source escaped."

Jack stared at the wall behind the two men. He studied the smooth surfaces, the way the shadows filled the cracks of the rock. He tried to catalog the types of rock he knew. After Huckley had read his mind about what he saw back at the Source, he knew he had to keep his mind occupied. Anything to keep his brain active. Anything to keep from thinking about...

Huckley arched his back as if a current had passed through his body. His faced contorted savagely. He looked quickly at Lonetree. Then at Jack. "Explosives? How much? Where?"

"What are you talking about?" Dr. Mansfield demanded.

Huckley waved him away and concentrated. Jack tried to think of anything else, but it was impossible. He fought the urge to look down at his watch. The explosion had to still be at least four minutes away. Somehow he had to stall Huckley to keep him from escaping before the detonation.

Jack looked away. Still, no matter how hard he tried, the pure satisfaction of seeing Huckley caught in the trap seeped through the mental barricades. The look on his face betrayed his emotions.

"Where are the explosives?" Huckley screamed. "WHERE ARE THEY?"

Jack allowed himself to smile. He let the conversation with Lonetree about the fail proof feature of the charges to replay in his mind. He watched Huckley's face change expressions as the memory played in his inner eye, the last bit of color draining from Huckley's already pale complexion.

"This...this ...can't be." He looked back up the passageway toward the cave. "The Source will be destroyed."

"Tell me what is going on!" Dr. Mansfield shouted.

"The cave is rigged to blow. There are only a few minutes to go," Huckley said.

"Tell them to turn it off!" Dr. Mansfield screamed.

"They can't. It's on a failsafe." He turned and kicked Lonetree in the side where he was bleeding. "Goddamn Indians. I hate them. Always have."

"If the Source escaped in that explosion, maybe we can lure it out of the cave. Bring it up with us."

Huckley looked horrified. "Are you insane? How would we control it? There's no way. Here it was our slave, but up there?" He shook his head. "You don't get it, do you?"

"Get what?"

"*Without limits.* It was talking about itself the whole time. Somehow the girl gave it enough power to break free. It will want revenge against us. Both of us."

"We can't just leave it here," Dr. Mansfield shouted. "We can't let it be destroyed."

Both of the men turned as a low, coarse sound rose from Sarah's throat.

She reached for her neck as a violent cough convulsed her body. Her face turned red as if she were choking.

Jack kneeled beside her and rubbed her back, searching her face to understand what was wrong, but she pushed him away with surprising force. The sound coming from her changed pitch and tone as if she were an instrument being tuned.

Then her lips contorted, and strange and guttural round tones came from her, interspersed with clicks and grunts. They came fast, roiling and pulsating, uttered in a breathless rush, no more than a stage whisper.

Huckley and Mansfield stared at her, craning forward to hear the exotic, mesmerizing language pouring from her. She stood perfectly erect, her eyes fixed on Huckley.

Jack felt helpless. He thought he should shake her awake, hold her, do something. But he couldn't move. He kneeled on the ground. He recognized the language coming from his daughter's mouth. He had heard it earlier that night for the first time. It was barely distinguishable then too, coming in the same whispering intonation, coming from inside the stone structure in the cave. Whatever evil creature had been locked in that stone structure, it was somehow speaking through his daughter.

Jack jerked his head toward a sound to his right. It was Huckley. Dr. Mansfield stood next to him, confused, but Huckley was in a panic. Turning in a circle, his hands clutched to his ears to block out the sound. He gasped for air as if an invisible hand were crushing his throat. "Shut up! SHUT UP!"

But the language continued to pour out of Sarah. The color drained from her face. She swayed in place as she spoke ancient words. Her forehead and cheeks shone with sweat.

Huckley raised the shotgun at Sarah and marched toward her. He pressed the barrel against her forehead.

"No!" Jack screamed.

Sarah's mouth shut and the voice stopped. She looked up at Huckley. Her eyes were glazed and red as though she'd been crying. Her hands trembled, but her lips parted into a simple smile. "Someone wants to meet you," she said, jutting out her chin toward the passageway.

Both Huckley and Dr. Mansfield turned toward the mouth of the passage. A large shadow stood at the edge of the light, indistinguishable in the dark. Rasping, snorting sounds filled the air, as if the figure had held its breath until its introduction.

"Janney?" Dr. Mansfield called out, his voice cracking. "Is that you?"

The shadow shifted its weight from side to side as if the light on the passageway floor was a barrier it was reluctant to cross. Then with a lurching movement, it jumped forward into the lit cave, arching its back to reach its full height.

The Source. Jack saw the creature's arm, the same grotesque appendage that had attacked Lonetree. A twisted mass of bone and sinew, skinless, draining pus and dark blood. The other arm hung at an impossible angle, as though the bones had been shattered and allowed to grow back in a different form, not an arm at all, but a crooked, useless appendage that terminated in a curved black claw. A grey fungus covered most of the torso, and the skin that remained hung in ragged flaps over exposed bone. Ulcerous organs bulged through holes in the ribs and abdomen. Lesions oozed black pus. A jagged hole marked where the creature's genitals should have been, as if the area had been hacked out. The legs were exposed muscle punctuated by bone growths, improbable mutations that stabbed up through the muscle like pointed armor. The feet, like the hands, were gnarled claws, hideously thick with calcified joints.

The creature's face was human, but so ravaged that the similarity only made the likeness more grotesque. The head was more exposed skull than skin. Dark patches of broken and rotting bone appeared among strands of long wiry hair that hung down the creature's back. Teeth somehow remained attached to the jaw but were bent out at bizarre angles from crushed jaw bones. The nose was gone. Instead a festering sore filled the nasal cavity, eating through the face and consuming the right eye socket. The creature had only one eye that functioned, the blood red, cancerous mass that had stared down Jack earlier.

In a flash of mental image, Jack understood who the creature was. He saw the scenes carved into the side of the stone structure, but as real life, not as static stone figures. He saw the shaman arrive at the village, a handsome man dressed in long robes and adorned with feathers. Jack saw the sacrifice of the first women, the carnage of the wars, the atrocities that came after. He saw the shaman attacked by the men of the village, saw how they hacked at his body with knives and cudgels. Saw that the shaman was not killed.

Reduced to a twitching mass of pulp and gristle, the shaman was unable to die because of the energy he'd taken from his thousands of victims. That energy mercilessly forced him to live, caged in the dark confines of the stone structure, to suffer for over a thousand years. Adding to the insult, while the by-product of his feeding gave others the power of regeneration, it only gave him eternal life. Trapped in his destroyed body, the never-ending agony of his decaying body had transformed him into the visceral appearance of evil. He had become the devil.

Jack reached out for Sarah, but she held up her hand. "Don't worry, Daddy." Jack stared at his little girl. She looked not at him, but directly at the creature. "He's here to hurt them."

Huckley screamed with rage and terror. He turned and pointed the shotgun at the little girl tormenting him. Fire leapt from the muzzle as the gun fired. The impact lifted Sarah's small body off the floor and sent her flying through the air.

EIGHTY-FOUR

Jack screamed. He ran to Sarah. Blood already covered her white gown. He looked up and saw that Huckley and Dr. Mansfield were staring at the creature.

Jack seized the moment.

There was a piece of wood against the wall. He grabbed it and lunged forward, bringing the wood down as hard as he could on the back of Huckley's head. Huckley's knees buckled and he collapsed to the ground. Jack reined in his urge to keep attacking.

He turned toward Dr. Mansfield and saw the doctor walking toward the creature, his arms raised to show he was not a threat. Jack wanted to watch what would happen, but he needed to get his daughter out of there.

He threw the board down and ran back to Sarah, gathered her in his arms, and sprinted to the elevator.

It was an old-fashioned mining elevator, no more than an open platform with a waist-level bar surrounding the perimeter. He climbed onto the metal platform and looked up. Without a roof, he could see the cables extending up into the dark shaft above them. He saw a light at the end but couldn't gauge how far they had to go.

He looked back out across the floor of the tunnel. The creature hadn't moved, but Dr. Mansfield now stood directly in front of it. The creature's head was cocked to the side as if listening to what the doctor said. Then it gave its answer.

For such a large creature, the movement was surprisingly smooth. Its good arm was already stretched out to balance an awkward stance. Without warning, the creature swept the arm downward. The black talons of its claws, perhaps chiseled to perfect sharpness over the centuries for this exact purpose, sliced cleanly through Dr. Mansfield's neck muscles and vertebrae.

The doctor froze in place. A second later, his body slumped to the left, and his head fell to the right. The creature crouched over the body, stabbing it with the talons of its foot to be sure it was dead.

Jack pulled his attention away from the creature. He saw that Huckley was starting to move on the ground. Next to Huckley, Lonetree was conscious and looking his direction.

The second they made eye contact, Lonetree mouthed the word, "Go."

"Like hell," Jack said.

He propped Sarah against the low guardrail that surrounded the elevator platform. He ran across the floor, sliding on the ground to Lonetree's side. He shouted in his ear to get moving. Lonetree grunted as he churned his legs to propel himself forward. Jack pushed him along, glancing over his shoulder at the creature.

Once they started to move to the elevator, the shaman-creature screamed. The decayed throat created a high-pitched shriek. A sound no living thing could ever produce. The creature lowered itself until its good hand hit the ground and then charged forward in a bizarre three-legged movement.

"It's coming!" Jack shouted. "GO! GO! GO!"

Jack turned away from the fast approaching creature. He focused on the elevator. Only fifteen feet away. Now ten feet. Five.

The scream seemed to be right next to his ear. He swore he felt hot breath on his neck. But with a final push on Lonetree's back, they tumbled onto the elevator platform together. Jack climbed to his feet and searched for the control switch, surprised the creature wasn't already upon them.

"Up there," Lonetree groaned. "Up."

Jack saw it. A metal control box hanging from a chain against the back wall. He grabbed it and punched the green button. They didn't move. He tried the red button. Nothing. He pressed them together. Still they didn't work.

Oh shit. Huckley sabotaged the elevator.

"The release. Hit the release switch out there." Lonetree pointed to the control console out in the passageway.

Jack understood. He looked out into the passage. The creature had stopped its advance next to Huckley's body. They were already out of time, so Jack knew he had no other option. He sprinted out from the elevator and ran to the console. He expected to feel the slashing cut of the creature's claws at any second. The release was labeled. He flipped the switch and rushed back into the elevator. Lonetree had managed to pull himself up using the metal rails around the platform and held the control box in his hand. As soon as Jack's body cleared the threshold, he punched the buttons and the elevator started to rise.

Jack turned as new screams erupted behind them. These were not from the shaman creature. These were human. And they were pure horror. Peering out from the elevator, they watched what was happening in the passage.

Huckley was still sprawled out on his back but had regained full consciousness. At first Jack thought the creature stood in front of Huckley, but he realized he was wrong. The creature was *on* Huckley, each foot planted through one of Huckley's legs, the thick talons piercing through the muscles like iron spikes.

Huckley raised the shotgun, only to have his hand lopped off with one quick swipe. The creature reared back and screamed, overwhelming the pathetic whimpers that came from its prey. As the shaman lunged forward to tear into Huckley's stomach, the elevator rose into the rock shaft, blocking Jack's view.

They traveled upward, away from the grisly scene and toward the salvation hundreds of feet above them. Huckley's screams chased them up the vertical shaft. Whatever the creature was doing, one thing was certain, it was taking its time.

EIGHTY-FIVE

Jack sat on the floor on the elevator, rocking Sarah in his arms. As he rocked her, he tried to apply pressure to her wound to stop the bleeding. The blast had riddled her left shoulder and chest with shot. Blood was everywhere.

At least she was still breathing. He checked his watch. Less than a minute until the explosion. The elevator creaked up the shaft. He wasn't sure if they would make it.

Lonetree sat on the opposite side of the platform. Even under the dim light of the one bare bulb that hung suspended in the center of the cage, Jack could tell how pale he was. He clutched his side, and his breath came in painful bursts.

"Hell of a ride, huh?" Lonetree managed through clenched teeth.

Jack nodded up the shaft. "How long do you think to reach the top?"

"Maybe a minute, give or take." Lonetree said.

"Let's hope for some give. Otherwise we're shy about twenty seconds."

Lonetree nodded. Jack struggled to his feet, Sarah still in his arms. She moaned quietly as she was moved around. Lonetree craned his head back to look up above them. "I think we're going to make it."

As if in answer to his optimism, the platform slowed. A hollow sound came up the shaft from below them, like the thud of fireworks being shot off in the distance. Lonetree looked over to Jack. "Hold on."

No sooner were the words in the air then the platform was rocked by a violent earthquake. Jack curled his arms around Sarah, fending off the chunks of rock that crashed down from above them. The elevator gears whined as the cable holding the platform whipped back and forth like a downed power line. Still, the platform crawled upward, slower now, but gaining ground.

Another violent shock hit and threw the platform against the wall. Lonetree lost his grip on the rail, rolled across the floor, and slammed into the opposite side. One leg dropped off the edge and dangled in the air. The platform completed its arc and started back the other direction.

"Watch out!" Jack cried as the wall rushed toward them.

With a grunt, Lonetree hefted his leg back onto the platform just as the edge slammed into the rock wall. The maneuver left him face down, staring through the metal grid beneath their feet. Lonetree's body stiffened.

He lifted his head to shout something at Jack, but the noise from the earthquake was too loud. Lonetree stabbed his finger downward. Jack looked through the metal grate and saw the elevator shaft extend down beneath them. The light from below appeared to blink off and on. He thought maybe from a dust cloud gathering beneath them.

But soon he realized it was no dust cloud or an electrical short. The light blinked off and on as a shape passed back and forth in front of it. As his eyes adjusted, Jack saw the shaman-creature crawling up the shaft. And it was gaining on them.

"It's coming after us," Lonetree shouted.

"Sarah said it wouldn't hurt us. It was just after Huckley and Mansfield."

Lonetree looked back down at the creature climbing up toward them. "Something tells me that deal's off. The world down there is collapsing, and this is the way out." Lonetree reached out and pulled Jack close to him. "No matter what, we can't let that thing get out of here."

Jack lost Lonetree's voice in the rumbling of the earthquake around them. He looked up. The light above them was stronger now. They were almost to the surface. Ten seconds. They needed just ten more seconds.

But they didn't have it. The rock shaft started to disintegrate. The walls caved in at the lower levels first, mangling the safety cables that ran the length of the shaft. The platform stopped and danced wildly in mid-air, suspended over the carnage below. Lonetree shouted that the creature was still climbing up the walls. Jack watched in horror as fissures appeared in the wall next to him. In was only a matter of time before the walls caved in and buried them alive.

Then he saw it. A metal ladder attached to the rock wall. A service ladder. A way out.

He shouted to Lonetree and pointed. The crash of rocks below and the rumble from the shaking earth drowned out his voice. But Lonetree saw his gesture and waved for Jack to go first. Jack shook his head. "Can you carry Sarah?"

Lonetree nodded that he understood. Between the two of them, Jack was in better shape to slow the creature down.

Without hesitating, Lonetree hefted Sarah over his shoulder in a fireman's lift, teeth clenched against the pain in his side. He staggered across the platform, forced down to his knees every few steps by the spasms from the quakes. He gripped onto the ladder with his free hand and pulled himself up off the platform and started the climb. The rock wall continued to shake, but he moved one hand at a time, one foothold at a time.

Jack watched them climb up the shaft. They were so close. If only the ladder and the rock wall would hold for another minute. Even then, he wondered if they could stop Sarah's bleeding in time to save her life.

Jack pushed the doubts aside and focused on maintaining his balance on the platform. One thing at a time, he thought. Give Lonetree enough time to get Sarah out of the elevator shaft. Stop the shaman-creature. Get out of the shaft himself before he was crushed by a cave-in. Piece of cake. Still, just in case, he muttered a prayer as he waited for Lonetree to finish the climb up the ladder. And, even though they couldn't hear it, he told his wife and daughters he loved them.

EIGHTY-SIX

The creature was close enough that Jack could hear its high-pitched shriek above the roar of the earthquake. There was enough room on each side of the platform that the creature could easily get by. He considered using one of the large rocks on the platform as a weapon, but he couldn't defend the position. Better to get to higher ground and fight there. Lonetree had finally made it to the top, so Jack staggered toward the ladder, fighting to keep his balance as the platform continued to buck wildly.

The creature grabbed the bottom of the platform just as Jack jumped to the ladder, the right side buckling from the weight. Black talons bent the metal guardrails and dug into the rock wall of the shaft. It looked up to the light above, screamed, and pulled itself onto the platform.

Jack didn't waste time looking down. He climbed up the ladder as fast as he could. The rumbling earthquake turned into a series of quick jolts, and rocks pelted down on him from above. The metal ladder groaned as the metal bolts started to work loose from the rock.

Jack wondered why the creature hadn't caught up with him yet. Judging by how fast it had climbed up the shaft, the creature should have been able to reach him without a problem. He kept climbing, shocked with every step that he was still alive. He wondered if the ladder couldn't support the weight and the creature was stuck on the platform. Maybe it was distracted. He couldn't understand what was taking it so long to finish him off.

His speculation ended with a burst of hot air on the side of his face.

He froze.

Slowly, he turned to face the center of the shaft.

The creature hung suspended, legs grasping the elevator cable, its body outstretched toward him. Its face hovered less than a foot away, swaying as the cable moved. The creature's breath hit Jack's face in hot blasts of foul air. The creature leaned in, turning its head so that its one eye matched up with its prey, its clawed hand clicking its talons in a slow rhythm.

For a moment, Jack and the creature stared each other down. The blood pounding in Jack's ears blocked out all sound. The world moved in silent, slow motion. He knew what he had to do. His muscles flexed. He shifted his weight for the jump off the ladder and onto the creature. It was the only option left. The only way he could stop the creature was to throw himself at it and try to drag it down into the shaft as the walls collapsed.

The creature's mouth opened in a scream. It drew its arm back over its head. Talons flexed into a claw. Jack cried out and started to push off from the ladder, ready to meet his opponent in mid-air.

A shadow flew down from above him. Close enough that he felt it more than saw it. His reflexes kept him on the ladder, a move that saved his life.

The rock struck the creature in the back. It spun to the side, but was struck by another rock as the lip of the shaft crumbled above them.

The creature stretched out desperately for the rock wall as the elevator cable went slack. It dug its talons into the wall.

The elevator's surface machinery toppled over the edge of the shaft and came crashing down. The creature looked up and screamed, trying to block the mass of twisted metal with an upraised arm. The metal wreckage scraped the creature off the wall. Together, they fell down into the dark shaft, the twist and grind of metal mixed with the unearthly screams of the shaman-creature until the noise was lost in the roar of the earthquake.

Jack watched in astonishment, his breath coming in ragged gasps. The machinery had come within inches of him, but he was unharmed. A sharp whine of metal bending brought him back to his senses. The ladder was coming out of the wall.

He pulled himself up the rungs, ignoring the small rocks that bounced off his shoulders and arms. The ladder bent backward as he climbed, the bolts pulling out from the rock. He was so near the top. Only a few feet to go. He was so close. All he needed was a few more seconds. The ladder tore away in a grind of metal. He wasn't going to make it.

A hand shot out from above him. Jack cried out and reached for it just as the ladder came completely off the wall and fell into the shaft. The strong hand gripped onto his wrist and held him dangling. A face appeared above. It shocked him enough that he almost lost his grip. Deputy Sorenson.

"Come on," Deputy Sorenson said. "Give me your other hand."

Jack let the deputy pull him from the shaft into a brightly lit room. They were inside a barn. Dust and straw danced in the light, shaken from the rafters by the earthquakes. Timbers creaked ominously as the whole barn swayed from the tremors.

"You okay?" Sorenson said with a nod to the elevator shaft. "I saw that thing down there. Son-of-a-bitch."

Jack looked around the room, confused by the deputy's appearance but too worried about his little girl to ask questions. He saw Lauren crouched over Sarah, compressing the shotgun wound with a cloth.

She looked up. "Jack, thank God you're okay."

"How is she?" Jack shouted.

Lauren shook her head, her eyes red from crying. "I can't tell yet. She's lost a lot of blood."

Jack turned back to Sorenson, who was tending to Lonetree's wound. Lonetree grinned. "Jack, meet Nick Sorenson. Navy SEAL."

Sorenson matched the grin and stretched out his hand to shake Jack's. "Ex-Navy SEAL. Retired to help out a friend." He looked over at Lauren and said, "Your wife is a fighter. She gave me a couple of bruises before I could explain that I was one of the good guys."

Jack shook the man's hand, took a deep breath, and released it slowly. The adrenaline of the last hour was catching up with him. His mind was too tired to do anything but accept what his eyes told him. Sorenson was working for Lonetree. Lauren would take care of Sarah's injuries. The earthquakes had stopped after he'd been dragged from the elevator shaft. It was as if the earth had spit them out and was then content to settle down. In the quiet of the barn, it finally felt as if they had made it. They were safe.

Sarah lay on the floor, pale from blood loss. Her mother had pulled back the gown to inspect the child's wound. Jack crawled over to them, staying an arm's length away to give Lauren the room she needed.

She looked up at Jack, the strain showing in her eyes. "It's bad. She's lost too much blood. Without a hospital, she's going to die."

As she spoke, the ground jolted. The barn swayed and the wood timbers groaned. The edges of the elevator shaft caved in, sending a torrent of dust into the barn. The earth shook violently. Jack used his body to shield Lauren and Sarah from the debris raining down from the rafters.

"The cave system is still collapsing," Lonetree shouted. "We have to get out of here."

EIGHTY-SEVEN

Jack grabbed Sarah and pushed Lauren toward the barn door. Lonetree struggled to get up with Sorenson's help, holding his side and spitting blood. Sections of the barn collapsed around them. Another tremor shook the barn, and a rafter crashed down behind them. Timbers began to snap.

They darted out of the barn door just as a sharp earthquake hit. There was a loud crack and then a slow groan. Jack looked over his shoulder. A full moon hung above the roofline of the barn. His eyes hadn't adjusted after the bright light inside the barn, but he could see enough to know they were in trouble. The entire side of the barn was falling over in one piece. And it was headed right for them.

"Go! Go! It's coming down."

They scrambled away as the barn wall gathered momentum. The shadow of the wall chased them across the ground. Lauren screamed as Jack covered her with his body.

The wall slammed into the ground behind them. They huddled together while dirt and splinters of wood flew through the air. As the debris fell around them, they coughed from the dust cloud that engulfed them.

"Are you okay?" Jack asked.

Lauren coughed. "Yeah, I'm fine. How about–"

"We're here," Sorenson said, appearing behind them covered with dust. He shouldered most of Lonetree's weight as they staggered forward. Sorenson's face was covered with deep cuts. He blinked away the blood from his eyes.

"We're right over the cave here," Lonetree said. "These tremors are small compared to what they'll be when the main cave goes."

Jack understood. When the main cave below them collapsed, they would be in the center of a giant sinkhole. The seismic force of such a collapse would be incredible.

"The Land Rover is mine," Sorenson said. He pointed to a cluster of cars by Huckley's house. "Key's in the ignition."

The group ran toward the Rover. Sorenson and Lonetree lagged behind. Jack carried Sarah. Once they reached the beat up vehicle, Jack transferred Sarah to Lauren's lap in the back seat. He climbed into the driver's seat and turned the engine over. It roared to life just as Sorenson opened the rear gate. He piled Lonetree into the back and jumped in next to him, then shouted that they were clear.

Jack jammed on the gas.

The tires churned through the gravel, found traction, and the car lurched forward. He fumbled to find the lights, almost careening off the dirt road as he did. Once he got the lights on, he almost wished he hadn't found them.

Fissures were opening in the road in front of them. The cave system was collapsing layer after layer in a massive chain reaction. He bounced over the first ruptures in the ground, thankful for the ruggedness of the Land Rover. The next fissures were deeper and wider. The tires slammed into the gaps with the force of hitting speed bumps at fifty miles an hour.

Jack pushed the truck faster and tried to steer away from the largest gaps opening before them.

Lonetree cried out from the back.

Jack chanced a quick look in his side mirror. Huckley's house had sunk into the earth up to the roofline. The subterranean underworld was being destroyed, and soon a giant sinkhole on the surface would be its only testament. Jack just hoped they wouldn't be in it.

"Faster. Faster." Sorenson shouted.

The ground behind them was falling away, disappearing into blackness. The edge of a crumbling fissure followed them as if a dark shadow was chasing them out of the valley.

Jack twisted to look at Sarah in the back seat. Lauren was holding onto her, whispering to comfort her. He turned back and squinted into the night. The tremors had kicked up dust, and the headlights turned the particles into a thick fog. Then the dust cloud cleared and revealed a massive fissure opening in front of them.

With no time to stop or turn, Jack floored the accelerator. They hit a natural ridge right before the ten foot wide chasm and the Land Rover launched into the air. They hit the other side hard on the back right tire. The Land Rover tilted to the right, but the metal beast corrected itself and landed back on all four tires. The tread dug into the ground, and they sped down the road, the fissures falling away behind them.

"Lauren? How is she?" Jack cried out.

"God, Jack. I'm losing her. Just get us to the hospital. Just get us there."

Jack nodded and gripped the wheel, listening to Lauren whisper words of encouragement into their daughter's ear. He pushed the car as fast as he could and still keep control on the dirt road. They turned onto the main road, the asphalt like smooth air after the turbulence they'd been through. He jammed the accelerator to the floor and headed for Midland Hospital. Regardless of what they had endured in the last few hours, and the impossible odds they had overcome, it would be all for nothing if Sarah didn't survive.

EIGHTY-EIGHT

Jack leaned forward and put both hands flat against the shower wall. He lowered his head until the hot jet of water hit the base of his neck. Reaching up, he kneaded the thick knots bunched across his shoulders. He cranked the heat up higher and braced himself for the scalding water. Steam filled the shower. He breathed in deep and savored the hot, moist air.

After fifteen minutes, he forced himself to get out of the shower and towel off. A quick look in the mirror showed the last five days had done little to heal the bruises that covered his body. He dragged a comb through his hair and plodded into the bedroom.

Lauren had laid a suit for him on the bed. Charcoal grey with a black silk tie. Appropriate. He sat next to it with the damp towel wrapped around his waist. The house was silent. Lauren must be outside, he thought. Or sitting in the living room with a cup of coffee, staring out of the window. She spent hours doing that. Even at night when there was nothing to see.

He didn't want to put the suit on. Everything had finally started to fade, and today promised only to make it real again. But Lauren had extracted his promise that he would go. So he grabbed the suit pants and got dressed.

When he walked down the stairs, Lauren was in her chair, coffee cup in hand. Buddy was on the floor next to her, helping to keep vigil with his master, somehow in tune that something was wrong. His thick tail pounded against the wood floor when he saw Jack. Lauren looked up.

"You look nice," she said. She was dressed in a grey dress, her hair pulled back conservatively.

"Thanks," Jack said.

He waited at the base of the stairs. The last few days had been strange for them. Neither of them knew what to say, how to comfort each other. Lauren had approached him when they had a few moments alone and apologized for not believing him at first.

He told her not to worry, that he understood, that there was nothing to forgive. Still, things were different between them. He wondered if it would get better over time, if somehow they would learn to deal with it. To get past it.

"Are you ready for this?" he asked.

Lauren stood up and crossed over to her husband. She leaned forward, snuggled into his chest, and pulled his arms up around her. He held her tight and brushed her hair with his fingers. They stood there for a full minute, rocking softly. It would get better, Jack thought. They would get through this together and remake their lives. He leaned down and kissed her forehead.

"Ready?" he asked, fully aware that the meaning of the question had changed.

"Yes, I am," she said.

EIGHTY-NINE

Half of Prescott City turned out for the funeral. Every pew of the Presbyterian church was filled, and massive floral arrangements drenched the altar in color. The pastor consoled his congregation and lamented the thoughtlessness of life taken so prematurely. Heads nodded in agreement. Discrete hands wiped away tears.

After a song that Jack barely heard, the pastor invited him to speak. He had been told he would speak first, but he was still caught off guard, lost far away in his own thoughts. Lauren nudged him with her elbow to get his attention, and he rose to walk to the podium next to the altar.

The church members rustled paper programs nervously as he made his way to the microphone. Men adjusted their legs. Women dug into their purses. But once Jack took his position, the church settled in a still hush.

Jack looked out over the congregation and gripped the podium with both hands. He turned to look at the coffin positioned in the center of the altar. Bouquets of blood-red roses covered the lid and spilled out in every direction.

He cleared his throat. Just as he feared, being here made everything rush back to him. Bits of memory flashed in his mind. The accident with Huckley. The visitation at his house. His first time in the cave. The creature locked in the stone structure, now buried forever. Seeing his little girl shot. Holding her bleeding body in his arms.

Nervous coughs from the church brought him back. He looked down to Lauren who sat holding Becky's hand. She smiled bravely and nodded for him to go on. Lauren the brave. Lauren the strong. She was still there for him.

Beside her, still to Jack's disbelief and wonder, sat his little Sarah, smiling so sweetly that tears jumped to his eyes. Nothing had prepared them for her miraculous recovery from the gunshot wound. Lauren still found herself trying to explain the rapid healing to colleagues, but Jack found himself wrestling with other questions.

If Sarah's interaction with the Source had given her the ability to self-heal, how else had the experience changed her? How would those changes manifest?

But these were questions for another time. He turned his attention to the full church waiting for him to speak.

"Thank you for coming today." He paused and looked at the woman next to his wife. Kristi Dahl sat with her youngest daughter on her lap and her oldest hanging on her arm. Jack nodded toward them. "Thank you, Kristi, for asking me to say something about Max. He was a good friend. A loving husband and a father who would give anything for his two little girls." Jack fought back the emotion in his voice and eulogized his friend.

Afterward, sitting in the pew for the rest of the service, he realized that he alone fully knew what Max had been and what he had given out of love for his children. He wondered if Max's last selfless act somehow made up for so many sins he'd committed in that dark cave. Jack looked up at the cross hanging in front of the church and believed for the first time in his life that someone else would be judging Max. Maybe there was someone like Melissa Gonzales who would be there ready to help him. Max didn't deserve it, Jack knew that. But then again, neither had he.

Jack closed his eyes and prayed that Melissa Gonzales had finished her journey and was at peace. He said the same for his friend, Max Dahl.

NINETY

The sun settled behind the far hills and turned the cemetery into rows of long shadows. Jack, Lauren, and Becky stood together as the pallbearers lowered the coffin into the ground. During the short ceremony, Jack caught sight of Joseph Lonetree watching the proceedings from a distance. Once people headed back to their cars, he whispered to Lauren that he would catch up. Lonetree waited as Jack made his way up the small hill toward him.

"Thought you weren't coming," Jack said.

"Came to say goodbye. Knew you'd be here," Lonetree said.

Jack studied the big man's face. Unreadable as always. "So where are you going?"

"Not sure. Maybe take up my father's work," Lonetree said.

Jack smiled. "Dig around in caves looking for bogeymen?"

"Pretty much. Why? Want to come along?"

Jack held up his hands in protest. "I'll leave that to you and your buddy Sorenson." They shared an easy laugh together.

Lonetree nodded toward the cars. "How's your wife handling it?"

"It's been hard on her. She's a scientist, and what we went through doesn't fit into any of her medical categories.

She's already created a hundred different explanations for things."

Lonetree shrugged. "If it helps her."

"We'll work it out," Jack said, realizing that he truly believed they would.

Lonetree nodded toward where Sarah and Max's daughter Jesse ran around on the grass lawn.

"And how about Sarah?" Lonetree asked.

Jack smiled. "She's doing great. Almost like nothing happened." He looked down at the ground. "You think she's going to be all right?"

"Huckley and that creature knew there was something special about her. I'm guessing you're in for an interesting time. Same with Max's daughter with the heart problem. He said he transferred the energy to her. Who knows what that will do."

They stood quietly and watched the little girls running down to the cars. Night was coming on, and the cold breeze rattled the few dry leaves still on the trees. Jack broke the silence. "Listen, we're going to go get something to eat. Why don't you come along?"

"Are you trying to bond with me, Jack?"

Jack laughed. "No, it's just that I feel safer if I know where you are. Don't like you slinking around in the shadows."

Lonetree pursed his lips and looked down. "I don't know."

"Come on. You saved her life, for God's sake. You might as well get a hug."

Lonetree finally nodded. Jack smiled and jabbed him in the stomach. Lonetree doubled over. "Hey, watch the stitches, bruiser."

"Gee, and I thought SEALs were tough," Jack said.

They walked down the hill together, slowed by their injuries and bruises, but sped along by the chance to put the past behind them.

At the car, Lauren opened the door for Lonetree and gave him a smile as he climbed into the back seat with the kids. She closed the door behind him as Jack walked by. She reached out, stopped him, and pulled him into a hug. Jack held her tight.

"Let's get started," she said.

"You bet."

He leaned in and kissed her on the lips.

Suddenly there was a loud knocking on the car window beside them. They looked over and saw Becky and Sarah making funny faces at them.

Jack and Lauren both laughed.

Lauren climbed into the car. As Jack walked around to the driver's side, he couldn't help but take one more look at Max's newly dug grave. The, mix of emotions swelled up in him once again. Max was a monster who killed others so he might live, but in the end this consuming selfishness proved no match for a father's love for his child. Ironically, Jack found that final act of giving had brought Max closer to immortality than anything the Source could have given him.

Max had realized it too late, after nearly destroying that which he loved the most. Jack resolved he would not make the same mistake.

"Rest in peace, Max."

Jack got into the car, fired up the engine, and wound his way through the cemetery.

Inside the car, Lonetree felt Sarah suddenly shudder next to him. He looked over at her and saw a plume of breath come from her as if she were sitting in a freezing room. She looked out sharply over her shoulder at the rear window and Lonetree followed her line of sight.

There, on the hill above the gravesite, a solitary figure dressed in a black trench coat watched the car leave.

Lonetree watched the man in black until the car dropped down the hill and the man disappeared from view. He looked over at Sarah who stared up at him. He reached out and took her tiny hand in his.

She smiled and leaned her head against his shoulder.

"How long are you planning on staying in the area, Joe?" Lauren asked from the front seat.

Lonetree looked down at Sarah leaning against him.

"I think I'll stay around for a while. See if I still have any friends living here."

Jack caught the edge in Lonetree's voice. As he slowed the car to a stop at an intersection, Jack made eye contact with him in the rearview mirror

"Do you think that's a possibility?" Jack asked.

Lonetree turned away, saying nothing.

Jack sat with the car idling at the stop sign. The seconds stretched out, but still the car remained motionless. Finally, Lauren reached out and took hold of his hand.

"We're together," she said. "Whatever happens, we can deal with it."

Jack smiled and squeezed her hand. With another long look in the rearview mirror, Jack pulled out onto the highway and took his family home.

Author's Note

Thank you for reading Night Chill. I hope you enjoyed the journey into the dark side of human behavior and inclination. While the supernatural elements of this story came from my over-caffeinated imagination, the abduction of children by deranged individuals is a real and terrifying issue.

Fortunately, the world is also filled with good people willing to fight to protect the innocent. A special thank you to the law enforcement officials who tirelessly search for America's missing children and for the good work done at the National Center For Missing And Exploited Children. To see how you can make a difference in this important issue, please visit www.missingkids.com

Thank you.
Jeff Gunhus

About the Author

Jeff Gunhus is the author of the Middle Grade/YA series The Templar Chronicles. The first book, *Jack Templar Monster Hunter*, was written in an effort to get his reluctant reader eleven-year old son excited about reading. It worked and a new series was born. His book *Reaching Your Reluctant Reader* has helped hundreds of parents create avid readers. *Night Chill* is his first novel for adults. As a father of five, he and his wife Nicole spend most of their time chasing kids and taking advantage of living in the great state of Maryland. In rare moments of quiet, he can be found in the back of the City Dock Cafe in Annapolis working on his next novel.

This book is part of the independent publisher movement and your support is greatly appreciated. If you enjoyed this book, please help by sharing with your friends and writing a review. I truly appreciate you taking this journey with me. Thank you!

Jeff Gunhus

www.JeffGunhus.com

CPSIA information can be obtained at www.ICGtesting.com
Printed in the USA
LVOW04s2352150615

442542LV00040B/3363/P